THE WHITE CITY

SIMON MORDEN

...ed in Great Britain by CPI Group (UK) Ltd, Croydon CR0...

This edition first published in Great Britain in 2017
by Gollancz

First published in Great Britain in 2016
by Gollancz
An imprint of the Orion Publishing Group Ltd
Carmelite House, 50 Victoria Embankment,
London EC4Y 0DZ

An Hachette UK Company

1 3 5 7 9 10 8 6 4 2

A CIP catalogue record for this book
is available from the British Library

ISBN 978 1 473 21149 0

Typeset by Deltatype Ltd, Birkenhead, Merseyside

Print[ed] [...] Ltd, Croydon, C[...]] 4YY

1

The moon was overhead, and Mary was on her back, staring up at its vast ivory seas.

'Do you think,' she said idly, 'do you think I could fly there?'

'No.' Dalip, lying nearby, sounded definite, but she wasn't so sure. She could see the shadows cast by the lunar mountains shift as they passed overhead, and if she reached up, she thought she might touch them.

She raised her hand, extending her fingers, stretching out. But all she felt was cool air, not the dry granularity of another world. She traced the curves of the craters, the lines of the rilles, and wondered.

'Why not?' She let her arm fall back and rested her wrist across her forehead.

'The atmosphere's only, what, eighty kilometres thick, and for almost nine-tenths of that it's too thin to sustain life. The moon's further away from Down than that. A lot further.'

'Sure?'

'Positive. Our moon is four hundred thousand kilometres away.'

'Okay.' She batted away a tiny flying thing that seemed intent on hovering between her nose and her top lip. 'But what if it's not like that here? What if, you know, magic?'

1

'This moon doesn't have an atmosphere. If it did, it'd have weather, and we'd be able to see clouds. The shadows are too sharp, too. Light scatters in air – that's why the sky's blue – and there's no evidence for that. So, yes. Magic. But you can't fly to the moon. Not even here.'

His voice grew increasingly exasperated, and she tutted. The silence between them dragged out.

'I ...' said Dalip finally. She heard him turn on his side to face her. 'I'm worried.'

There was a lot to be worried about. They had control of the biggest cache of maps that Down had ever seen – at least according to Crows, but he was an inveterate bullshitter – and that level of wealth was going to draw the wrong kind of attention. And in Down, almost all attention seemed to be the wrong kind.

She twisted her head to see Dalip. She was on one side of the rough wooden trunk containing the maps, and he was the other. Though it wasn't big, the size of a large suitcase, the trunk obscured him from shoulders to knees. She touched the planks to remind her of the riches and danger inside.

'So what are you worried about?' she asked. 'Apart from thieves, assassins, monsters, the weather, Crows, the portals, the journey and this city we're supposed to be heading for? Tell me if I've left something out.'

'Tides,' said Dalip.

'Fuck off.'

'No, I'm serious. A moon that huge should create tides higher than mountains, and that's without thinking about the earthquakes it should be causing. It doesn't make sense.'

'I can turn into a giant fucking eagle-thing, and you're saying the tide doesn't do what it should?'

The pale light from above cast deep shadows on Dalip's face. One eye was bright and glittering; the other, dark and hidden.

'Down has to follow rules, even if they're different to what we're used to.'

2

'Does it?'

'Yes. And we know most of them are similar, because if they weren't, we wouldn't even be able to exist here. Gravity—'

'Gravity?'

'— is an intrinsic property of mass. We don't feel any heavier or lighter, so it must be about the same here, and yet the moon doesn't behave like it is.'

He was lecturing her, so she took her revenge and shook her fist at the sky. 'Fuck you, moon,' she called.

He rolled back and drew his lips into a thin line. She'd offended him again, something she didn't mean to do yet managed almost as often as he pissed her off by parading his education. To her, his quest for order amongst the chaos – a chaos as woven through Down as a silver thread through a banknote – seemed pointless. As far as she could tell, Down did as it pleased: it gave and took away, capricious as a gang leader. Sometimes it was generous, sometimes it was searingly violent, but it was never predictable.

'I'm sorry,' she said, 'that Down doesn't do what you want it to do. It doesn't do some of the things that I want it to. But unlike you, I don't expect it to.'

He groaned, 'I know. It's … I want it to be logical. And there are patterns. The thing with the portals, the lines of power, the villages and castles, the instruments Bell used – they had to be measuring something, or she wouldn't have had so many of them. Down orbits its sun, and the moon goes round Down predictably. There are rules—'

'Even to magic?'

'Even that. If we can understand them, then we can start to predict events, and then maybe control them.'

'But what if it isn't like that? Bell was batshit crazy. I've got scars on my back to prove that.'

'Then,' he said, 'this box of maps is worthless, and we may as well cut them up for toilet paper.'

He had a point. Everyone, but especially Crows and Bell, whose opinions about this were the only ones that really counted, thought like Dalip: given enough information, an answer would fall out and give them control of the portals. That was pretty much what being a geomancer was all about. Mary had her doubts, though. Down was more like the kids' homes she'd been brought up in than the schools that had tried to educate her. Lots of rules; almost all of them broken, almost all of the time.

Mary put her hand in front of her face again and looked at the moon through the bars of her fingers. One side of them was silvered. The side closest to her were black shadow. She concentrated on that darkness and dragged it like ribbons through the air, five ragged lines whose edges trembled in time with her fingertips.

She stared at what she'd done, at what she could do. It was simple enough now she knew how. Crows had showed her, and she'd practised. And yet, when the others – Dalip, Elena, Luiza, Mama – had tried, none of them could emulate her. It was a gift to her, and her alone. As far as she knew, science didn't work like that. It didn't prefer one person over another.

So if there were patterns, they were fucking weird. Easier perhaps to believe that she was Down's favourite: unlike poor, mad Stanislav, who had been blessed in an entirely different way. She could still see the eyes and the teeth in her dreams. So many eyes, so many teeth.

She blinked the image away, or at least tried to, because it seemed to be burned on her retinas like a bright light.

'I remember toilet paper,' she said to distract herself. 'I remember the first fag of the day, and leaning out the window to blow the smoke away. I remember the traffic on the street below, and the people on the pavement. I miss the toilet paper.'

'Oh, come on. You were made for Down,' said Dalip, and he sat up, leaf litter clinging to the back of his orange work overalls. He pushed himself up using the box until he was kneeling, hands

Praise for Simon Morden:

'Once again Simon Morden takes the fantasy genre and moulds it wonderfully ... What makes *Down Station* so great is the immaculate pacing and the way character shapes fate for each of the well-drawn main characters'   *The Sun*

'It's the character's experiences that make this a fresh take on the "cut off from civilisation" subgenre ... we're drawn in by their responses to this world'   *SFX*

'There are horrors that surprise as well as moments of wonder. The story is patient, and every sequence is both a physical battle and philosophical teaching that merge with well-placed hooks'
                                                                      Sci-Fi Now

'Amazingly original mindblowing ideas that completely rewrote and reconfigured a familiar London into something much more sinister and post-apocalyptic'   *The Digital Fix*

Also by Simon Morden from Gollancz:

Down Station

on the lid. 'But I don't know about the rest of us.'

The moon, still vast and close, passed with uncanny silence. In her mind, it rumbled and growled past like a huge truck. The trees, the ground, the air itself, should be shaking.

'I don't know why I don't miss those things. Okay, it was all a bit shit, and I was in a fuck-ton of trouble, but I was getting it together. I even had a job, for fuck's sake, a crappy cleaning job, but I wasn't going to do that for ever. I didn't ask for London to burn down, and I didn't ask to come here. But now we're here ...'

'... we have to decide what we're going to do.' Dalip leaned heavily on the trunk, making it creak, and when he got up, he did so carefully, stiffly.

Mary had given him those injuries, nearly killing him in order to save him from smearing himself against the iron-hard surface of a lake. She still felt guilty. She watched him stretch, and squeeze a finger between his scalp and the band of cloth he wore instead of his turban. He scratched and sagged, and she looked up at him, looking down at her. Her red dress, long to her ankles, bare to her shoulders, was less vibrant than when she'd first worn it to go Stanislav-hunting, but it was still more than serviceable. She'd put on the mantle of the Red Queen. Maybe one day she'd actually be that person: she'd sit on a throne, and let all the responsibility that title brought settle on her proud head.

The presumably airless moon had drifted in the direction of her feet, affording her an oblique look at the ring of mountains surrounding one crater. The sunward slopes were bright, those in the shade utterly dark. Beyond it, the sky was blank, like a wall of night. No stars, no other planets, nothing. Down, its moon and its sun, was all there was.

'What do you think happened?' she asked. 'To London.'

'There's a thing called a firestorm.' Dalip shrugged and sat down on the trunk. 'Learnt about it in history. If enough stuff

5

burns – and we're talking about a city-sized amount of stuff – all the hot air rising causes a hurricane-force wind to suck in fresh air from all around. It feeds the fire with fresh oxygen, and it gets hotter and hotter until there's nothing left to burn. We made it happen in the Second World War, dropping incendiaries on German cities. Killed tens of thousands of people. Not soldiers, either. Just civilians, hiding in their cellars from the bombing, roasted alive by the heat. Like we almost were.'

'Fucking hell,' she said.

But they'd escaped. They'd opened the door to the street, caught a fleeting glimpse of an inferno, then been in Down in all its baffling majesty.

'Nuclear bombs can do the same sort of thing. It doesn't take a thousand bombers any more. Only one. But' – and he clenched his teeth, showing them white in the darkness – 'you're right. That's not what happened. We would have felt the bomb go off; it would have been like an earthquake. Unmistakable.'

'There were bangs and other noises first. Like thunder, in the distance sometimes, then closer. I thought it was actually thunder. Then I went underground, and I couldn't hear it any more.'

'And an hour, an hour and a half later, the whole of London was burning down.' Dalip stood again and raised himself up on tiptoe. 'If it wasn't a bomb, then I don't know. London just caught fire, everywhere, all at once. If we made it out, then maybe other people did, if there are other portals attached to our time. They'd all be starting off at different points on Down, and they'd all be as clueless as us. And assuming we stay alive, we might bump into them one day.'

'That'd be weird.'

'No weirder than meeting a whole bunch of people from the sixties, or the thirties. When did Crows say he crossed over?'

'Thirty … six? They cut him. Badly. If he hadn't found Down, they would have killed him.'

'That doesn't make him a decent man. Or rather, it didn't. Let's face it, none of us deserved to be saved. None of us are wiser, smarter, stronger or prettier than all those we watched die. Whatever criteria Down uses, how worthy we are doesn't come into it.'

She climbed to her feet and brushed her skirts free of leaf litter. 'So what if it was just luck? I didn't want to die, and I still don't. I wanted to live, which is what I can do now. Don't tell me you don't feel the same?'

Dalip looked at the ground, then at the trees around the edge of the small clearing they'd co-opted for their camp.

'It's not just the lack of tides that scares me,' he finally said. 'I'm not very … I just … Look, I have to face up to the fact that I'm comfortable being told what to do. I know where I am with that. I'm safe.'

'You were nails taking on Stanislav. Fucking nails, man. You threw us off a mountain to finish him off.'

'And where did that get me?'

'Here. Alive. What the fuck are you complaining about?'

'My own choices nearly killed me. When I sleep, I dream I'm falling. Sometimes I don't wake up in time. Sometimes, you don't catch me, and you know what? It hurts. I hit that water so hard, it's bits of me that sink.'

She regarded his shadow. 'Why didn't you say before?'

'Because you're so obviously enjoying yourself, there didn't seem any point in, you know. Raining on your parade.'

'I thought we were mates. Proper friends who told each other stuff.'

'I'm,' he said quietly, 'I'm not supposed to be weak. I'm supposed to be a lion. It's even my name. One of our gaolers called me "Little lion man", but not in a good way. He knew. He knew I was weak.'

'So what happened to him?' she asked Dalip.

'Stanislav killed him. Stabbed him a dozen times in the guts.'

He shrugged again, and she didn't know what to say. She was used to the empty posturing of street kids, posing for shaky-cam videos while brandishing kitchen knives and ball-bearing catapults, where weakness was the one thing you didn't dare show, let alone tell anyone else. It didn't matter whether they were cowards, or too stupid to run when it all went down: it was the act, and that was the one thing that Dalip's tightly controlled world had never taught him.

If she wasn't careful – if he wasn't careful – Down would eat him alive. It might have already started, and she couldn't tell.

The others were on the opposite side of the fire; four still shapes, curled in various configurations on ground that, no matter how soft it started off, always ended up like concrete.

'That bloke's gone, and you're still here. And you know what? That's what counts. You found it when you needed it, and when you need it again, you can always find it again. I don't know what you think a man is, but I've put up with kids pretending that they're all grown up, all big men, and they can fuck right off. You don't want that any more than I do. We all know what you did, and none of us think you're weak. Fucking hell, look at you. You were this stringy thing, and now you've got all the muscles and stuff.'

He acknowledged his subtle transformation with a shrug. 'My grandfather—'

'Fought the Japanese when he was still a kid, you told me, like a dozen times. And what a pain in the arse he was to live with.'

For a moment, Dalip's expression darkened and deepened, and he held himself tense and still. Then he let it go, and looked up at the receding moon. 'You sound like my mum.'

'Maybe you should have listened to her.'

'I did. I do. I … I'm hanging on to the few certainties I have left.'

Mary walked the few steps to him, and landed a slow, deliberate punch on his shoulder. 'We need you, not your grandfather.

The war veteran we had turned into a soup of eyes and teeth, and I don't want you going the same way.'

He nodded, but she could see that he was scared of that, too.

'You're not, are you?' she asked. If he was, there'd be very little she could do, except ask him to leave. Stanislav had hidden his transformation so well that by the time it had taken him completely, he'd been almost impossible to kill. Almost.

'No, that's not happening,' said Dalip. 'At least, not that I know of. Keep an eye, or three, on me.'

'That's not a good joke.'

He shrugged, and the glimmer of his smile shone in the moonlight. 'I was never any good at telling them. Always the serious kid in the corner. I thought I might lighten up a bit.'

'All work and no play, right?'

He shrugged again. 'Something like that. I'm not actually dull, just … people tell me what to do, and I do it. It's a habit.'

'No one's going to tell you what to do here. Not now you're free of Bell and her Wolfman.'

'There'll be others. Once they find out what's in the box, it'll be everybody.' Dalip looked at the ground, then at her. 'If we pull this off, we'll be the luckiest people ever.'

'What if that's it? We don't have to be the smartest or the strongest. Just the luckiest. What, if out of all of London, we were the luckiest?'

'Then,' he said, 'everything we ever knew, everyone we ever knew, is ash. My family, Mama's babies: they're all gone, and it doesn't matter what we learn or if we can open the portals: there's nothing to go back to. Perhaps it'd be better to hope we're not lucky at all.'

Mary had forgotten that her escape was his captivity. She burned, and started to walk away.

'It's all a bit academic, though, isn't it?' he said at her retreating form. 'We don't know, we won't until we try to find out. And I'd rather know than not.'

'I'm sorry,' she said. She was, too.

'I'll wake Mama and Luiza. It's time.' His bare feet brushed through the grass of the clearing, leaving her with the crate of maps.

She knelt next to it and undogged the hasps that held it closed. She creaked the lid open, just a little way, so she could glimpse the jumble of paper inside. There was so much of it, and they'd barely looked through any of the sheets, let alone tried to work out how, and if, they might fit together.

She lowered the lid again. Crows seemed to be fast asleep, but a single black bird perched on the tree above him, staring down at her, its eyes bright with reflected fire. Mary scowled at it and, with a flutter of dark wings, it was gone.

2

The sea stretched out ahead of them. A couple of green-topped islands sat some miles offshore, indistinct with haze, and the distance precluded seeing any further out. However far it actually was, it was going to be a long way.

'The choice we face is to either go around or go across,' said Crows, looking down at Dalip from the higher branch of the tree where they'd climbed. 'But boats are rare on Down, and good sailors rarer. So we may not have a choice at all.'

Dalip, on the branch below, could see nothing of the other side of the bay. He was assured it was there, but it couldn't be proved. It looked, as with all horizons, like the edge of the world.

'But if you've been to the White City once, you've gone this way before,' he said. 'What did you find then?'

'That the sea has its own dangers. The same boat can be used for fishing or piracy, and sometimes they are used for both. Catching fish is little different from catching men.' Crows stared back out across the stretch of rolling green forest they had yet to navigate. 'You must consider the merits of walking.'

'Can't you magic up a boat?'

'No,' he said. 'That is not how it works. And even if it was, you would not trust one made by me.'

'There's always Mary.'

'You may ask her yourself. She will give you the same answer.'

'So what did you do? You didn't walk to the White City, did you?'

'I swam,' said Crows. 'I walked into the sea and changed.'

'You wouldn't be able to carry us, or the trunk. Mary couldn't either.' Dalip reached up to brace his hand to steady himself against Crows' branch. He'd wanted to see for himself, but now that he had, it added very little to Crows' initial report. And the only reason Crows was up there was because Dalip was: he had his flock of black birds to do his seeing for him.

If they couldn't find a boat large enough for them and the trunk, and someone with the skill and the inclination to take them across, that would be that. They'd have to trudge along the shoreline, dodging inland when they reached estuaries – he, Mama, Luiza and Elena at least – and who knew how long that would take?

Or how much time they had.

'There's no sign of any smoke,' Dalip said.

'Some do not light daytime fires, for fear of attracting rogues.'

'It doesn't make it easy for us to find them, though.'

'That is the point. We are the rogues they fear.'

Dalip looked up sharply. 'They've no reason—'

'This is Down, not London. They have every reason to fear us, just as we have every reason to fear them.'

'If we act decently towards them ...'

Crows was limber and lithe. He lowered himself down level with Dalip and looked him in the eye. 'We might have hundreds of miles and weeks of travel on land, across hills and valleys. Who knows what lies between us and the White City, and what we might encounter. Another Bell, another Stanislav? I wish it was otherwise, but your honour will not shorten the journey by a single step.'

'Well, what alternatives are there?'

'We take the first suitable boat we find. It is simpler, and we are many. They will be few.'

Dalip pulled himself closer to Crows. He was aware of his own scent, of freshly dug earth and sharp sweat. Crows always seemed sweeter, somehow: clean and slightly spiced.

'I don't know how long it takes to build a boat, but it has to be months, if not the better part of a year. We can't steal someone's boat. That's …' and he tried and failed to think of a word other than just plain wrong.

'Our need is great, my friend.' Crows touched Dalip on the shoulder, barely holding on to the trunk with his other hand. A few weeks ago, Dalip would have felt physically ill just watching the man capering high in a tree, let alone climbing up himself.

Let alone throwing himself off a cliff.

'I know what we need, but that's no excuse.'

'Oh, I know it is no excuse. But it is expedient. What if Mama cannot walk all the way to the White City? We would, at some point, be faced with another choice: whether to leave her and carry on without her, or all stop and make the best of it, wherever we might be. Perhaps she would be agreeable to that, because we are very accidental travelling companions, and there is no reason we have to stay together.'

'We can't leave Mama behind.'

'Then,' said Crows, 'we must consider matters plainly. This is all I suggest: if we are fortunate enough to find a boat then a long journey, full of uncertainty, might be avoided.'

His logic was impeccable, up to the point where theft was involved. 'Crows. We can't—'

'If it was put to a vote, which way would it fall? Mama with her sore feet, and Luiza – there is something of the night about her. Quiet Elena might not be swayed, but Mary is no stranger to a little light-fingeredness.'

Dalip glanced down. Though it wasn't far to the ground, the others were out of earshot. It was just him and Crows.

'This is a test of character,' he said. 'Just because we can do something, doesn't mean we should.'

'I am not suggesting it for mere devilry.' Crows pressed his lean fingers against his own chest. 'Our situation is such that it outweighs the obligations of decency.'

'That's very convenient. It's only a short step from there to putting me in the pit to fight animals.' Dalip felt his blood start to rise. 'I won't start down that road because I know where it ends. Honour actually means something to some of us.'

Crows swung back, and pursed his lips. 'I will leave you to explain your decision to the others. But consider this, Dalip Singh: your honour did not kill your friend Stanislav. Your cunning did.'

He slipped down the tree trunk, sure with his handholds even where his feet were left dangling. He landed lightly on the leaf litter, his black cloak momentarily rising about him like wings, then he was looking up at Dalip, his high cheeks and broad smile nothing but an invitation to trust.

Dalip looked away, out over the land, over the ocean. There was nothing but the natural landscape. No sails cracking in the wind, no white foam breaking around a wooden hull, no tell-tale finger of grey smoke. He traced the line around the bay as far as he could see. It was, granted, a very long way, and he'd have to walk every single step of it, and then further into the unknown.

Crows was right: Down was dangerous and unpredictable. But it was also wide and glorious and empty, and it was people like Crows that made it difficult. That, and the occasional storms that seemed to demand a sacrifice as they passed by. Was that going to make being here nothing but a series of seemingly reasonable compromises until he became as wicked as Bell or as sly as Crows?

He growled at his own equivocation. He knew what he should – and more importantly, shouldn't – do, no matter the personal consequences. While the decisions would have to be made by all of them, it was up to him how strongly he objected to the choices made.

There was nothing to stop him from walking away, but then he'd be on his own. He always imagined, living vicariously through books, that he could survive in a situation like this. The reality was, he didn't know. He guessed he could probably cope, at least for a while, with the vagaries of Down: it was the way Down altered people, mentally and spiritually, not physically, that caused the biggest problems.

And if he thought like that, then other people rescued by Down would too. So again, Crows was right, and he felt grubby acknowledging that. But if there was nothing stopping him from becoming the worst of himself, then there was nothing stopping him from being the best of himself either.

'Dalip? Are you coming down?'

He blinked, and there was Luiza, orange overalls half-lowered and tied around her waist by the arms, staring up at him.

'Just a second.'

He took another long look at the coastline. There was nothing; nothing to indicate that they weren't the first to ever pass that way, even though Crows assured them that the way to the White City was well trod.

That gave him the inkling of an idea, and before he reached the bottom of the tree, it was fully formed.

'How far?' Luiza asked him.

'A couple of hours before we hit the coast. After that, who knows?' Dalip was already looking about him differently, searching for signs that other feet, naked and shod, had passed their way. 'Crows says there might be a boat, but that we might have to steal it. He says he can't make one.'

'Crows is full of shit, yes?'

'Yes, but he nearly always tells the truth, even while he's betraying you.'

15

They walked back towards the trunk, where Mama was sitting on its flat wooden lid.

'If there is a boat to steal, well. We can do that. There are six of us, and we have two – whatever you want to call them – with us.' Luiza pulled at her ponytail. 'What will that gain us? Can any of us sail? Or do we put a collar on Crows so he can pull us?'

'I don't know. I've done some sailing. But when I say some, I mean a week in a little dinghy on a reservoir. I could probably not drown us in a light breeze. Anything more than that?' He shrugged.

'There is another problem. Would you trust Crows on water?' she asked.

'I don't trust Crows on land.'

'Here,' and she stamped her foot against the soft ground, 'he is a man who can do magic and send birds to look for him. We are barely his equals. Out there, at sea, he is a master and we are nothing. I will not get in a boat with him, or near him.'

'He wouldn't risk the maps.'

'He could pick us out of a boat, one by one. He would eat us before we could throw the trunk over the side. Mama knows this. Even my silly cousin knows this. You know this, too.' She stepped back and regarded Dalip from his bare brown feet to his covered hair. 'Only Mary thinks she can tame him.'

'I can't do anything about that.'

Luiza sniffed. 'If she leaves us for him, they will take the maps. There will be nothing we can do to stop them.'

'She's not going to leave us.'

'She will, if he makes her choose.'

'She won't.' Dalip turned away. 'She's better than that.'

'Who's better than that?' asked Mama, raising her head from her chest.

'Mary,' he said.

'That child is headstrong and wayward. But she has a good heart.' Mama stretched her legs out in front of her, and twisted her ankles until the bones clicked. 'Is it time to move on already?'

'Dalip says the sea is not far.'

'Not far? And where's this White City? Can you see it yet?'

'It's further, Mama. Further than I can see.'

She frowned at the news: more than that, because she turned her face away and ran a fingertip firmly down the side of her nose, drying it with a wipe of her thumb before anyone could see the single tear that had leaked out.

This. This was the complicating factor: Mama hated walking. How much simpler to find a boat and try to sail across the wide bay. If they took precautions, if they made sure Crows couldn't just get rid of the inconvenience of them and seize the maps? Then what? Did that make stealing a boat more palatable?

Mama would say that it wouldn't, even as she imagined herself being carried over the waves.

'What else could you see, Dalip?'

'Just … Down. More Down. There's a couple of islands out in the bay, but there's nothing really. We're quite low here, this close to the sea. Mary will scout ahead and tell us what's on our route.'

'No sign of anyone?'

'No. I want to get the maps out when we reach the coast, see if we can work out where the villages and castles are going to be.'

She nodded, and slowly, wearily, stood up.

'This is taking too long,' she said. 'I should be back, taking care of my babies. We've been gone for weeks.'

'We don't know,' he started, but Luiza tossed her head back with a grunt of frustration.

'London has gone, Mama. The door was destroyed. It does not matter if it was two minutes or two months ago.'

'I will not believe that. My babies are waiting for me to come back, and don't you dare say otherwise.'

They squared up to each other, Luiza pale and pinched, Mama flushed and folded-arms angry. Dalip pressed his hand to

17

his forehead. He'd never been a peacemaker; normally he hid when family members turned, always temporarily, on each other.

'It's academic anyway,' he said. 'We don't know what's happening in London, and we don't know how fast time is moving here, relative to home.'

'What are you saying?' Mama was suddenly reminded of his presence.

He chose his words carefully. 'When we get back,' he said, avoiding the word 'if', 'it might be that five minutes has passed, and no one will know we've been gone.' He stared at Luiza, daring her to undo his good work.

She opened her mouth, then closed it again, pursing her lips.

Mama snorted. 'You wishing it won't make it so.' But she bent down to pick up her boots and stalked off into the trees.

'She is lying to herself,' said Luiza, 'and you are encouraging her.'

'What else am I supposed to say? That her babies are dead, and long burned to piles of unrecognisable ash?'

'It is not kind to pretend there is hope,' she hissed.

He took a deep breath. 'I'm not pretending. Sometimes I think you're right, that London has gone, and everyone in it. Sometimes I think she's right. But we're not going to know until we can check for ourselves. Until then, speculation is useless, and it only causes trouble. I . . . It's even more complicated than that. I don't think we have to worry about how long we spend here.'

'Because?'

'Down is a time machine.'

Luiza's face froze.

'Should I explain?'

She nodded.

'If we can get the portals to open from this side, and assuming it still exists, we can go back to London, yes?'

She nodded again.

'What if we didn't go back to twenty twelve? What if we used the door that Bell found? We'd be in nineteen sixty-whatever. Or the one that Crows used, from the thirties? If we can find – or make – a door that's last week, last month, last year, however long it takes, then it doesn't matter how long we're here. We could go back before we'd even left.'

Luiza worked her jaw, slowly becoming more animated.

'And you think this would work?'

'I have no idea. But there's no reason why not. If the portals let people from different times come here to the same time, then they might let us back to whenever we want.'

'Into the past? That is crazy. That is dangerous,' said Luiza. 'What if we make a mistake? Do you know what might happen?' She grabbed hold of his overalls at the shoulders and shook him. 'What if this has already happened? What if this is why we are here?'

'Yes: yes, of course.' He tried to free himself, but she maintained her strong grip. 'We could also go into the future.'

'This is what the geomancers lust for,' she said. She let go, pressing her hands against him and pushing him gently away. 'Control. Not just of Down, but of London too.'

'All of the Londons.' Dalip blinked. 'We're going to have to think very carefully about this.'

The sky flickered. A great bird-shape blinked over the clearing. Both of them glanced up, and when they looked back at each other, the tension had broken and was dribbling away.

'Hungry?' she asked. She put a hand in the outsized pockets of her overalls and proffered several glossy brown hazelnuts.

Dalip took one, and then two when urged. Each was as big as his thumb up to the first joint, big enough to bite in half and show the white flesh inside. He wasn't hungry as such, because Down seemed to yield just enough, just when it was required.

Then he pressed his hand to his forehead again. 'How could I have missed that?'

'What?'

He chewed and swallowed, and still had to chase pieces of hazelnut around his mouth with his tongue.

'Down. It never fails to surprise.'

3

Mary flew in over the beach, over the heads of the others, checking one last time that they were alone and nothing was going to sneak up on them. There was no sign of anyone, just their own filling footprints in the soft white sands of the dunes.

She turned back, feathered her wings, and touched down just below the still-wet strand line. The seagulls, scarce and scared, wheeled around to mob her – but she changed and left them without a target, just a young woman in a red dress, toes flexing and digging into the cold, gritty sand beneath her. She walked up the beach, stopping to collect a long length of driftwood in each hand to add to the already-smouldering fire.

'Does anyone know what a coffee plant looks like?' She cast the wood across the burning pile, and sat down with a thump. 'I suddenly miss it.'

'I thought ...?' said Dalip, sitting cross-legged to her left. He stopped, and inspected the soles of his feet.

'I just fancied a cup, okay?' She knew what she'd said, that night in the dark of Bell's broken castle, how she didn't want drink or cigarettes any more. And she didn't, but her habits had a tendency to creep up on her when she wasn't looking and mug her with need. 'Anyone?'

'The coffee of my homeland was the finest in the world,' said Crows. 'Rich and flavoursome, dark and strong. Once roasted to perfection over an open fire, the beans would be worth more than gold.' He stared into the heart of the fire. 'If there is coffee, then it lies far to the south. It is too cold here.'

'I guess that goes for tea, too.' Mama tutted. 'I do like a nice cup of tea.'

'We do not even have cups,' said Luiza, 'and Dalip has more important things to say.'

'Do you?' Mary felt aggrieved. He should be telling her his ideas first. Luiza had Elena.

'I don't know,' he said, and carried on picking debris from the deep, leathery creases in his feet. 'It's a bit of a long shot.'

Mary glanced again at Luiza. 'You going to share it with the rest of us, or ...?'

Dalip got up and dragged the map trunk across the sand until it took his place in the circle.

'It seems – Crows tells me, at least – that magic has its limits, and we can't just wish ourselves across the bay. Magic, however, also has its rules: the most important one being that power, for the want of a better word, leaks out of portals. If you draw a line between portals, the power flows down that line, and if you stop on one, a house grows. Where the lines between pairs of portals cross, you get a castle. If you've a big enough map, you can predict where all these things are: portals, castles, villages. With me so far?'

Mary knew that maps were like bank notes, and what was in the trunk made them rich. She'd never been rich before, but now she was, she had nothing to spend it on. She fingered the tattered hem of her dress and waited for him to continue.

Dalip continued. 'Okay. Now, given that all the portals from all the past Londons—'

'And future ones too,' said Luiza.

'Wait.' Mary held up her hand. 'What?'

'We're from Crows' future. We're from Bell's future. We have to assume that there are people here from our future too.' Dalip laid his hands on the lid of the trunk, fingers splayed wide. 'All of the Londons connect to now. So, even though the numbers coming are low for each portal, the overall count has to be the sum of all the portals, and therefore not insignificant.'

It took Mary a moment to work out what he was saying. 'So where are all these people, then?'

'The attrition rate's high. We've lost Grace, and Stanislav. If seven of us hadn't came through at once, we'd have been carved up and spat out by Bell. However safe Down is, people make it dangerous. Despite that, we can and will survive here. So where did everyone else go?'

'Wherever they wanted?'

'And where do they want to go?'

Mary stared at Dalip, and he stared back.

'The White City,' said Crows. 'At some point, everyone goes to the White City.'

'Is that actually true?'

Dalip shrugged. 'Let's say it is. Everyone goes, or tries to go, to the White City while they're here. They learn that there aren't any answers there and they go away disappointed. Maybe some people go more than once, just to make sure. Whichever it is, if you have enough people going to one place, across a natural landscape like this, where there are routes that are easier to walk than others, what are you going to get?'

'Fuck, I don't know.'

'Roads,' said Mama. 'He's talking about roads.'

'More well-trodden paths, but yes. Roads.'

'We've been walking for weeks, Dalip,' said Mama. 'There are no roads hereabouts.'

'No. Which means something else, for us, here, specifically.'

'Does it? Lord, but I'm tired.'

Mary stole a look at Crows. He'd never mentioned roads. She wondered why not.

'We know that if you stop on a line, you get a house. We also know that houses are no use under the sea. So I'm willing to bet that at the point where a line crosses the coast, you don't get a house.'

'You get a boat?'

Dalip nodded, and Mama's weariness suddenly left her.

'Where then?'

'We have absolutely no idea. But,' and he tapped the trunk, 'we might be able to work it out.'

'What are we waiting for? Get them out and we can start putting them together.' She lumbered to her feet and worked her way around the circle.

'There is a problem,' said Luiza. She pointed at Crows. 'Him.'

Crows pressed his hand against his chest. 'Me?'

'Yes. Water is where you are strongest, and we are weakest. I do not believe you when you say you will guide us to the White City. You say that to make us think we need you. But I say we can find our own way, with the maps.'

Luiza fixed Crows with a glare that would have sent most recipients scurrying, but he sat there with a subtle smile on his face.

'This is true. Water is my element, where I can manifest my most obvious power. And yes, with the maps, you ought to be able to find the White City on your own.' He rubbed his palms together, sand trickling out like rain, and said nothing else.

Mary wanted to trust Crows. She didn't, but she wanted to. She'd known a lot of people like that. She was probably one herself.

'We've already agreed,' she said. 'Crows comes with us, and he gets the maps once we've copied them.'

'He gets a free ride,' said Luiza.

'He helps protect us from Down.'

24

'And who will protect us from him?'

'Oh you two, hush.' Mama glowered at them. Elena was looking into her lap, and Dalip was pressing his fingers into his temples, trying to massage the stress away. 'How much time will crossing the sea save us?'

Crows was quick with the answer. 'Many months of travel and hundreds of miles walking.'

'That's settled, then. If Down can magic us up a boat, that's what we'll do.'

Mary looked around the circle. 'Dalip?'

'Out on the open sea, in a boat none of us is familiar with, let alone able to steer, with a massive sea serpent for company? If we get into difficulty, and we probably will, Crows could be the only one who could save us. Or he could dispose of us as he saw fit, and keep the maps. Which is what he was doing when he left us to face Bell.' He sighed and let his head fall forward. 'On the other hand, it's a very long way across the bay, if that's where the White City really is.'

Crows had never mentioned boats, or the sea, when he'd promised to behave himself. Mary's eyes narrowed as she pulled at a spiral of hair. 'You only said it was a long way. You didn't tell us what we had to do to get there.'

'I can do nothing about the distance, Mary.' Crows looked up at Mama, standing right behind him, over him almost. 'And it is your choice how you cover it. If you wish to walk, I will walk with you. If you wish to sail, then I will sail with you. I have some modest experience that might help.'

He settled himself into the sand, leaning forward to rest his forearms on his long, folded legs.

'So?' said Mary. 'We don't even know if this boat thing will work.'

Mama flicked her fingers at Dalip. 'Get the maps out. Let's see.'

Dalip waited for a moment, and when no objections came, he

undid the clasps on the lid. 'We'll need to find some stones to weigh the maps down, hold them in place.'

Luiza looked mutinous, but she nudged Elena with her foot, and they went off together down the beach.

'She doesn't like you,' said Mary.

'Sometimes even I do not like myself,' said Crows.

Mary took the first map from Dalip – the one that she'd drawn herself, and the one they were going to use to orientate all the other maps. She'd made those scratches, marked in the coast, the river, the island with its closed portal.

'Are these going to be, you know ...'

'Accurate?' said Dalip. He lifted another grubby piece of parchment out into the light of day and squinted at it. 'No. They might even be deliberately misleading. We have no way of knowing. But it's all we have.'

'It's a jigsaw,' said Mama. 'And I'm good at them. Why don't we look for the edges first?'

'Good lady, Down has no edges.' Crows was bowed over the open trunk, seemingly inhaling the aroma rising from it.

'It has a coastline, though, and that's what we need to look for.'

There'd been jigsaws in the homes Mary had grown up in, and out of sheer boredom, she'd joined in completing them. But they'd always had the picture on the box to go by. It had always seemed like a massive cheat to her: where was the challenge in mere recreation?

This, though: they didn't even know if they had enough, let alone all, of the pieces to reveal a clear picture.

'Okay, let's do it.'

The four of them sifted through the trunk, looking for maps that showed, or conceivably could show, the coastline. It didn't matter where on the map it might be, because very few of them had north marked, and they were all different scales. It was a jumble of inaccuracies and wishful thinking.

After a while, Mama raised her eyes. 'This isn't working.'

'It has to,' said Dalip. 'We're just not doing it right.'

'Well, now. If you've any suggestions, don't keep them to yourself.'

He pursed his lips and scratched under his hair cover.

'Crows,' said Mary, 'how's this supposed to fit together? We've got all these maps, and some of them have to join on to each other. It's like we've got too many. How would a geomancer make sense of all this?'

Luiza and Elena returned, pockets full of stones, which they turned out on to the sand.

'Where are we?' Luiza asked.

'Lost,' said Mama, frowning. 'We could be anywhere on any of these.'

'That is not true. We might be on none of them.'

Mary wound a curl of hair up and down again. 'No, hang on. Crows. You've been this way before, right?'

'Yes, of course.'

'How did you get to the White City?'

'I swam.'

'Of course you did. So where's the map that shows where you swam from? Where's the map that shows your route from your portal, to the sea?'

Crows was silent for a moment, then held out his hands for the sorted pile of maps. He leafed through them one by one until he grunted.

'This one, I think.'

'You think?'

'It was a very long time ago, Mary. Would you recognise your own hand from even five years ago?' He passed her a long strip of paper, marked with tiny, indistinct scratches along its length.

'You know what, Crows? This is crap.'

'I was young when I made the journey, and older when I made the map. This is what I could remember, imperfectly.' He shrugged theatrically. 'If I had known how important it was, I would have paid more attention.'

She handed the strip to Dalip, who knelt on the soft sand and laid the map in front of him, weighing it down against the breeze with a stone.

'Put it the right way,' said Mama.

'It … doesn't matter?' he said, looking up at her stern face.

'Just like a man.'

Dalip lifted the stone, turned the fragment until the coast part of it pointed towards the coast. Then he took Mary's map when proffered and placed it below, again orientated to fit with the landscape. He squinted at it and saw that Bell's castle was a fixed point on both.

'Okay.' He dabbed his finger at the Down Street portal, and traced it up the river, through where they'd found the abandoned houses, to Bell's castle. 'Another portal has to lie on this line, to the north.'

'And another so it makes a line with Crows' castle,' said Mary. 'But if you draw a line from the nineteen thirties' portal, does that go through Crows' or Bell's?'

'It could go through both. You said yourself that some of this is crap.'

Mary looked up and down the coast. The beach sloped towards the sea, and all she could see of the land were the lines of marching dunes. But if she stood at the top – or if she took off and gained height, because she was an idiot and still not used to thinking like that when she was in human form – she'd be able to see the distinctive twin mountain peaks.

'The line should cross the coast just up from here.' She pointed around the bay. 'Or even here. Actually here.'

Her eyes narrowed at Crows.

The man seemed unperturbed. 'Without the maps, without your insight, we would never have guessed.'

'Says you.'

Dalip held out his hands for the collection of maps that Crows still held. He gave them up with only the merest hint of reluctance.

Mary watched as the boy slowly leafed through them one by one. He was looking at them with his eyes almost closed.

'Are you all right?'

'Just,' he said, and then nothing more as he continued his search. He looked down at two maps already positioned, then back at the one in his hands. 'It's not here.'

'What isn't?'

'If Crows made this one, then he made another one, from where he made landfall to the White City. But we don't have it. Or if we do, I don't recognise it.'

Luiza went to the trunk and seized the larger pile of discards and gave half to Elena. 'We can check through all these, or you can tell us the truth.'

Mary clenched her jaw and felt her temper begin to rise. Visions of the Red Queen started to blot out rational thought and she had to turn away, stamping her way down to the wash of the waves. When she was ankle-deep and the biting water tugged this way and that at her, she let out a noise that started as a moan and ended up a shriek.

When she stopped, and was resting herself, leaning forward, hands on her knees, she heard someone else wade up behind her.

'He's never been to the White City, has he? Not even close.' Her throat was raw, and her voice hoarse. 'We don't even know if it fucking exists. He could have heard someone say it, and he believed it. Or thought that we'd believe it.'

'It could be a myth, like Shangri-La or R'Lyeh.' Dalip had waded next to her, staring out to sea. 'I don't know if anything he's ever told us can be trusted.'

'Of course it fucking can't. But he does tell the truth. Sometimes. Mostly. Fucking chancer.'

She kicked at the water, and found the effect unsatisfying. She wanted it to be Crows' head. Or his balls.

'We still have the maps.'

'They might be lying too. We've no way of telling.' She subsided. 'Is this better than being burned to death?'

'On balance?' He wiped spray off his face with his lean fingers. 'Yes.'

4

Dalip made the most of the light, going through the maps one by one, discussing them with Mama, finding it more effective to talk about the features that each showed, than to simply stare blankly at the lines and scratches and then put them to one side. The few words written on them were mostly in English, but sometimes not: the French, Italian, German or perhaps Dutch or Danish he could pronounce even if he couldn't understand it. There were others in alphabets that weren't Latin, and one beautiful and enigmatic sheet that was not so much drawn as painted, calligraphic characters of either Chinese or Japanese adorning the side. No Punjabi: he could be Down's first Sikh.

Sitting there, on the beach, with pieces of paper riffling about them in the late afternoon breeze as it swept on shore, they made a small but significant discovery.

'We're right, aren't we?'

Mama flexed her bare toes in the sand. 'Well, it looks that way to me. I don't know what it means, but let's say we are.'

'It might mean that we can put the maps together more easily, now we know what to look for. It might mean that it's impossible, because none of them overlap.'

'Whether we can do it at all depends on finding somewhere to do it.' Mama regarded her surroundings. 'We can't do this here, taking everything apart and putting it back together again every day, worried about the wind and weather. Pack it away, Dalip. Pack it all away, while I go and soak my poor feet.'

She rolled upright and walked wearily down to the sea's edge, while Dalip started to tidy the maps away, blowing them free of sand and placing them back in the trunk.

'Done?'

Mary dropped more driftwood on the pile next to the fire.

'Every single map shows a portal,' said Dalip. 'As far as we can tell, none of them show two.'

'Is that …?'

'Significant?' He put the only two maps they had convincingly put together on top, then heaved the lid closed. 'Yes. It has to be, but I don't know how.'

'Oh.'

'Where's Crows hiding?'

She turned around slowly, trying to locate him. 'He said he'd fuck off until we decided what to do with him.'

'He may never come back,' said Dalip. He refixed the hasps and pushed the locking pegs into place. 'Are you ready for that?'

'What do you mean?'

He didn't honestly know; his comment had just popped out. 'You seem to like him. Despite—'

'Everything?'

'Yes.'

'Fuck. I don't know. You'd think there'd be something about safety in numbers, running with a gang, that'd mean he'd not try to shaft us at every available opportunity. He's on his own otherwise.' She raised her gaze to the sky. 'Maybe we should cut him free, if that's what suits him best.'

'He'll always come back for these.' Dalip thumped the lid of the trunk. 'If we let him.'

'We can't …'

'We can't stop him unless we either kill him or cripple him.'

'And you're going to do that? You?'

'Of course not.' Dalip twisted away. He had a knife, a kitchen knife that was his kirpan, bound to him with a strip of cloth around his waist, under his overalls. He'd probably be no match for Crows' magic in open combat, but a stealthy first cut to the back of one of his legs would bring him down without killing him.

Of course, stabbing someone with a dirty blade was a double death sentence on Down. If infection didn't get him, the weirdness of the landscape would.

He was too squeamish. Stanislav had been right all along.

Could he do it? He knew how to. If getting rid of Crows was the only way to protect himself and his friends, was that enough of a moral imperative for him to act pre-emptively?

'Would you let me?' he asked.

'What? Crows? I ... We're just kids, Dalip. How the fuck did we end up like this?'

Dalip watched Mama standing in the sea, her trouser legs neatly turned up to her knees as the waves broke around her generous calves.

'We ran,' he said. 'We did what we needed to survive. And we kept doing it. You got away from the Wolfman, we broke out of the pit, we fought Bell, we fought Stanislav. We chased Crows, we captured the maps.'

'Do you ever wonder what happened to Grace?'

'Maybe she escaped. Maybe she died. Whichever, we've seen no sign of her since, and we wouldn't know where to start looking.' His shoulders shifted, stretching back against his natural tendency to stoop. 'But, yes. Every day. I try and picture how I'd be coping on my own, against all this.'

'Down gives,' said Mary.

'And half the time the gifts could kill you.'

He had another thought, a terrible, world-changing thought, and the only way to see if he was right was to look.

He opened the trunk again in slow, deliberate moves, lifting the lid and lowering it on the hinge side, then lifting out each map in turn until he was sure he was right.

And when he was, he tilted his head back and yelled. 'Crows? Crows? Get back here and tell me how you did it.'

He hadn't gone far. Barely had the cry died away that a familiar thin black shadow crested a dune and started to lope down towards the beach.

When he arrived, they were all assembled.

'Every single one of them, right? Every single map was made by some poor sod emerging from a portal.'

'That is correct,' said Crows. His gaze darted from one to another, as he tried to judge their mood.

'And almost each and every journey ended at a castle.'

Crows didn't speak, just nodded.

'Tell me why. Tell us all why.'

The breeze ruffled Crows' cloak of night for a moment. 'Because the geomancers do not permit people to travel further. New arrivals have information that would be valuable to others, so they are either kept as slaves, or are, well … There are exceptions. But that relies on knowing to evade the geomancers and their slavers from the very first moment of arrival in Down. Most are so affected by the circumstances of their escape from London that they do not escape a second time.'

'You did. You even stole Bell's maps.'

'It is unusual to find two castles little more than a day apart. I had previously enquired of the maps before I left her and, by taking them with me, ensured that she would not be able to find me.'

'You rescued Mary from the Wolfman.'

'It was my duty to do so. It was not my duty to tell her, or you, everything. Or anything.' He spread his fingers wide. 'Trust is hard to come by. Betrayal is everywhere. I do not trust you. You do not trust me.'

Dalip worried at his sparse beard. 'What happened when you first stepped out of your portal?'

'Most geomancers keep a careful watch over the portal closest to their castle. I arrived at an opportune moment, when the guards were distracted. To my mind, they did not look like the kind of people to show me mercy. I hid, almost in plain sight, and waited for nightfall. I bled into the ground from the cuts that still scar me, and I did not move. When their eyes were blinded by their night fire, I crept away, and while I was still close by, the portal opened again. I saw what happened, and was glad I trusted my instincts.'

'Crows, just how many free people are there?'

'A few. A very few. Listen: Down is not exactly paradise but, inshallah, it will not kill you.' He ticked his tongue behind his teeth. 'How this iniquitous rule of slavers and enslaved started, I do not know. But it strangles any chance of a righteous life here.'

'You were taken eventually, though?'

'By the Wolfman, and I was brought before Bell. I made myself useful. Then I made myself necessary. In the end, I made myself indispensable. All the while, I learnt my magic, and I scoured the maps for somewhere to go where I could escape my captors. Being a prisoner is not in my nature, though many become accustomed to it if they believe there is no alternative.'

Mary balled her fists. 'Why the fuck didn't you tell me any of this?'

'Trust, Mary. I took advantage of you, yes. I sheltered you and fed you and taught you as well. I did not hold you against your will, neither did I require any service from you. I asked nothing of you but your map. You were free to go, even to your death. As exchanges go, ours was quite equal.'

She turned away and, after taking some half-dozen steps, wheeled back round. 'You cold-hearted bastard.'

He bowed. 'I can hardly deny it. But I am better than many, if not better than most.'

Mama huffed. 'That doesn't speak highly of you now, does it? Poor Mary, deceiving her so.'

'She has survived my minor cruelties and has flourished.' He glanced over to Mary. 'Why did you not stay at the castle? It was yours. You had the land between there and the portal. The Wolfman would have served you as he served Bell.'

'It burned down,' said Luiza.

'Castles grow again,' countered Crows. 'You would have been secure, and not have to wander the face of Down like this—'

'Looking for somewhere that does not exist,' she screamed in his face, 'this White City is just a lie.'

Elena pulled at her cousin's sleeve, and Luiza shook her off. 'Everything you say is a lie.'

And with that, she launched herself at Crows, tumbling him to the sand and knocking Dalip aside, then pinning Crows' spindly limbs with her own lean arms and smashing her forehead down into his face.

Crows twisted his head aside at the last moment, so that she connected with his cheek instead.

Dalip, on his back himself, struggled to his knees, and Mama, with all her maternal strength, picked Luiza off Crows as if she were no more than a piece of underground litter.

'You calm down. This is dangerous. Dangerous for all of us.' She carried Luiza a distance away before setting her down again.

'Dangerous for him.' She pressed her hand to her head, but made no effort to have another go at Crows.

'No. Dangerous for you, especially. Down looks into your soul, and sees who you really are. Am I right, Crows?'

'Truly, madam, you speak the truth.' He checked that no one else was going to assault him, and got to his feet. He extended a hand to Dalip who, after a brief hesitation, accepted.

'What does that mean? For us?' he asked.

'The good lady is wise. She knows we all have secrets from

36

each other, even ourselves. But we cannot hide our true nature from Down.'

Dalip looked at the others, one by one. He knew them, in part, in the same way he'd known Stanislav. He realised what a mistake he'd made there, and wondered what mistakes he was making now.

'Down is what? Alive somehow? Watching us?'

'No,' said Crows. He crouched down and scooped up a handful of beach, holding it in his fist. As he straightened back up, grains dribbled out between his fingers. 'Down dreams of us. We sparkle in its mind like the sand.'

Dalip traced the trickle of powder as it fell and become one with the beach again.

'Are we dead? Are we actually dead?'

'Is this your fear?' Crows' eyes grew large. 'That you did not escape? That you burned with your colleagues?'

There was a lump in Dalip's throat, and he swallowed against it. He was all too aware that he was the centre of attention, and he didn't like it one bit.

'It,' he said, summoning up the courage to name his terror, 'just makes more sense than any other explanation.'

'And yet you fight.' Crows opened his fist and held his palm flat. 'Here, look.' He took a pinch of sand and proffered it.

Dalip held out his own hand and Crows rubbed the sand free of his fingertips.

'This is you, and Mary, and Mama, and Luiza, and Elena. This is me and Bell and the Wolfman. This is all of us. Down cannot tell us apart. It does not favour the faithful and punish the wicked. It gives each of us what we want.' He shrugged. 'Imperfectly but generously. You know, Dalip Singh, that you are not dead. You know you experience pain and fear and joy. You know you are alive because you know death and you are not it. You know it here.' Crows pressed his sandy hand against Dalip's chest.

'What if we don't get what we want?'

'Then you are mistaken about what it is you really want. Down sees through the lies you tell yourself, the masks you wear, the roles you play. Which is why your friend Mary is a glorious falcon, Bell a dragon, and I am—'

'A snake.'

Crows shrugged again. 'Mama is not wrong. Your angry friend Luiza needs to watch herself. And you need to watch her too, and help her understand that her anger is as likely to be rewarded as your courage.'

Mary absently brushed the sandy handprint from Dalip's front. 'But Dalip can't …'

'You do not tell the gift-giver what gifts to give,' said Crows. 'But if you follow me, you will see.'

He slipped out from the group encircling him, past a still furious Luiza, who he bowed low to – honestly or sarcastically, who could tell? – and walked back up the beach to the dunes.

'He could just tell us,' said Mama.

'Perhaps he doesn't think we'll believe him.' Dalip watched him shrink into the distance. 'He'd be right about that.'

'Come on,' said Mary. 'What else are we going to do?'

Dalip found himself next to Elena.

'My cousin,' she said, her voice so quiet that Dalip had to lean in, 'is he saying she will change? Into a, a …'

'Monster?'

Elena nodded, mute again.

'I think he's saying we're all going to change, over time. But I'm sure nothing bad will happen to Luiza. It's just that Crows makes us all angry, trying to pin him down, only to find out that when he says one thing, he means something else.'

'She does get angry. She gets angry with me sometimes.'

'It'll be fine,' said Dalip, with no confidence that it would be. 'We just have to work out what's going on, and then it'll be …'

'Fine,' she echoed.

They climbed up the face of the dune, following the collapsed footprints left by Crows, coming and going. As they crested the dune, they saw Crows below them, standing next to a post jutting out of the sand.

'Come,' he said. 'Come and see.'

They slithered down, all except Luiza who stayed at the top.

Dalip patted the wooden post. It was curved like a tusk, weathered with salt and worn by the sand.

'What is this?'

'Dig at its base.'

Frowning, Dalip got down on his knees. He could tell that someone – presumably Crows – had already pushed the sand aside, and covered it up again. He dug his fingers into the cool dry sand and scooped it away, following the bend of the wood.

It flattened and ran into the lee of the dune. Dalip scraped and shovelled along its length, a task made difficult by the sand from above falling back into the hollow he was making.

There was something buried there. Protrusions at right angles to the main beam, jutting out each side in pairs. First one, then another, and after that it got too difficult to excavate any more.

He sat back on his haunches, and wiped his hands on his shins.

'Well?' asked Mary.

'It's a going to be a boat,' said Dalip. 'Not today, not tomorrow, but in a couple of days, it's going to be a boat.'

5

There was nothing they could do to speed up the boat-building. Down worked away, quietly, secretly. Mary saw Dalip creep back to the site and watch for a long time, just to try and catch something being added. He left, frustrated, and yet the next morning when she'd gone for a look, it was half ready.

It had a hull, and the first signs of a deck. From being buried deep in the sand, it was starting to float up through the dunes in which it was being born. When it was – what? Finished? Ripe? – it would pop to the surface like a rubber duck in the bath. They'd just have to drag it to the water's edge and push it out to sea.

Crows had been a stoker, below decks on a steamship, shovelling coal into the belly of a red-hot furnace. He'd said he had experience: believing that included little sailing boats was an assumption too far. Dalip was the only one with any relevant knowledge at all, and he didn't know how a Down-grown ship was going to differ from a modern fibreglass dinghy. He'd confessed that he might end up killing them all.

And that was without the risk of having Crows in the same boat.

It was going to have to carry six of them, for as long as it took to cross the bay. The White City, if it was more than an artefact of Down's collective imagination, may not be there after all. But at least they wouldn't have to have walk all the way, and if Dalip's idea of using the portals as a time machine was actually possible, it wouldn't matter too much how long they spent looking for it.

She patted the boat and went back down to the beach, where Dalip and Mama were sifting through the maps again, this time looking for any mention of this mythical city made of white stone. She crouched between them and watched for a while.

'Any luck?' she asked.

'It's difficult to tell. There's this one.' He passed her a dog-eared scrap little bigger than a Post-it note. 'It doesn't seem to have a portal on it, but whatever this is was still important enough to draw.'

'There's no writing on it.' She looked at the front, with its faded fine lines, then at the back, which had a completely different pattern on it. 'And they used both sides.'

'There are old books in the British Library where people have written an entirely different text sideways across an existing one. Paper's going to be really rare, so yes, every last scrap gets used. Lots of these have two, three, even four maps on them.' Dalip rubbed his eyes and screwed up his face. 'I'm going blind staring at these things.'

'Do you think the White City exists?' she asked.

Mama stretched out her sore legs and wriggled her toes against the sand. Her blisters were already starting to heal. 'Crows hasn't outright denied it,' she said. 'If this is a map of it, then I guess it might.'

'It has to,' said Dalip.

'And why is that?' asked Mary.

'Because we want it to.'

'I thought,' she said, 'it was supposed to be the one place that didn't rely on Down's magic. So wishing it real isn't going to make it happen.'

'I've been thinking about that. Do you know what the blind spot is?' Dalip half-turned towards her in a shuffle.

'I ... maybe.' Mary didn't. She knew what *a* blind spot was, but not *the* blind spot.

'It's the bit at the back of your eye where the optic nerve collects all the signals together and sends them to the brain. It's the only area where there aren't any light-collecting cells. Normally, you never notice, but there's this trick you can do with a dot and a cross drawn on a piece of paper. Stare at the dot and move the paper closer or further away, and at a certain point, the cross will simply disappear.'

'So ...?'

'If you want to hide from Down, you want somewhere that doesn't have villages, castles, portals, or anything worth fighting over. Down's blind spot. The White City.'

'You're just making shit up now, aren't you?' Mary peered deep into the map fragment for a hidden meaning.

'It's all I've got. Sorry.'

Mama looked down at her feet. 'Crows was running to somewhere, girl. He might not know where, or even if, but he was moving with purpose. And that man, he does nothing without intending to profit from it. May as well call where he was heading the White City and have done with it.'

'You see, that makes much more sense.'

Mary handed the map back to Dalip and stood up. Out to sea, a serpent's head rose above the swell and turned their way. She waved before she realised what she was doing, and Mama rolled her eyes.

'He'll do you no good, girl,' she said. 'He'll take everything, and leave you with nothing.'

Dropping her hand by her side and feeling both foolish and angry, Mary had a ready response on the tip of her tongue. Then she glanced at Dalip, who was almost cringing in anticipation.

'You know what, Mama? Kind of worked that out for myself.

The idea of having Bell's seconds is just a little bit ... you know, sad.' She swished her skirts and turned away, still feeling the tingling in her fingers and the tip of her nose that she always experienced just before she was going to blow.

But it was better this way. More grown-up. She didn't have to bite every single time, even though Mama's advice was unasked for and, for fuck's sake, all she'd done was wave. She clenched her fists and kept on walking, down the beach and towards the strand line. Tomorrow morning, they'd be heaving the boat down to the shore – all this bickering would be done with because they'd be on the move.

'Wait,' called Dalip, trotting up behind her, his feet sinking into the soft dry sand and causing him to have an awkward, almost stumbling gait.

'You got something to say too?'

'Me? No. What I know about relationships could be written on a stamp.'

She laughed despite her mood.

'What is it, then?'

'I wanted to,' and he stopped, his lips twisting and no words coming out. 'It's complicated.'

'Fuck, Dalip. Sometimes you need to just say it.'

'Okay.' He took a deep breath. 'If it comes to it, save the maps, not us.'

'What?'

'At least that way, one of us might survive. If you can't carry the box, because it's the wrong shape and too heavy, how many maps do you think you can hold in your claws?' He waited for an answer, but she was too stunned to say yes or no. 'We might get five minutes from shore, when I do something stupid and turn the boat over. If those maps get wet, they're ruined for ever. So even if it's just an accident, and we can get right way up again, we've lost the point of the journey. So you have to get as many maps as possible to safety, whatever happens to us.'

'You want me to watch you drown?'

'No. But who are you going to save? Me? Mama? Luiza or Elena? And while you're doing that, you're not saving the maps.' He looked surprised at his own words. 'We've all talked about it, and we're agreed.'

'Without asking me.'

'Or letting Crows know.' He held up his hand to forestall argument. 'We have to consider that he'll try and take the maps, just like we have to consider storms, shipwreck and me screwing up.'

'Okay. Okay.' She felt even considering the matter was a defeat. They might have decided she would be the last woman standing, but she didn't have to go along with that when the time came. She could say yes with her mouth, and no with her heart. It wasn't like she didn't lie every five minutes back in London. 'I'll try. Carrying you was hard, but at least you were the right shape. Prey-shaped. What if we ditch the box, maybe rig up some sort of sling I can grab?'

'It's not that we won't try and save ourselves. None of us want to die, and who knows? Crows might do the saving for us, flip the boat back over and dump each of us on board. It still means that you have to go for the maps first, because while you have them, we're worth saving.'

That was a good reason, and she felt happier. 'I said okay.' Crows wasn't going to renege on his deal, the deal they forced out of him, with promises of destitution and mutilation being his only alternatives. Was he?

She watched Crows play in the breaking waves, threading his sinuous black-scaled body through the walls of water as they rose and rushed inland. She knew what a gold-plated bastard he was, and yet … She chewed at her lip. Sooner or later, he was going to betray them. They all knew it, even – especially – him. All the kindnesses, the advice, the food: none of that would matter. Not to him, not to her.

At that moment, there was one person she really wanted to talk to, and that was Bell.

'I thought that conversation was going to be much more awkward,' said Dalip, and she tuned back in. Apparently he'd been saying some other stuff, but if it had been important, she'd missed it and she wasn't going to ask him what it had been.

'You're fine,' she said absently. The wind carried the smallest grains of sand across the beach, blurring it. She felt it tug at her skirt, and wished it was pulling at her feathers. She watched Crows for a few moments more, then deliberately turned her back on him.

'We need more firewood,' said Dalip, 'and we used most of the nearby stuff last night.'

'What happens when we run out?' she said, more thinking aloud than an actual question. 'We've got nothing.'

'It's not that bad. We've got enough to be getting on with.'

'That's not it, though, is it? We're living like, I don't know, cavemen or something. No wonder everyone ends up in a castle.'

'Those brass instruments of Bell's mean that there's somewhere here that makes them. It's another reason to believe that the White City is real place. Those things have to come from somewhere.'

'But what if they don't? What if there are paper trees and metal bushes and cotton mines, or stuff pops up out of the ground like the castles do? What if the White City doesn't exist and we're all just Down's bitches?'

'We'll find out soon enough,' he said. 'Our one advantage is you. You can fly up and search a huge area quickly.'

'I could do that now!'

'You'd be gone for days, and we'd be alone with Crows.' He sighed. 'We wouldn't stand a chance.'

Her enthusiasm deflated like a slashed tyre.

'Don't think I hadn't thought of that,' said Dalip. 'You're the only thing keeping us and the maps together.'

He knew it too, then, that Crows would ultimately turn on them. And, like her, he lacked the balls to get rid of him first.

'The boat'll be ready to go in the morning,' she said, for the want of anything better. 'How far do you think those islands are? When I'm flying, they look like I'd be gone for hours.'

Dalip shielded his eyes from the sky-glare and stared at the distant smudges of land. 'It's impossible to say. I can't make out any features, except there's a mountain on one of them. Could be five miles, ten miles. Twenty miles.'

'Further than that.'

'It is what it is. If Down is ... flatter. Bigger.' He shook his head. 'Every time I look up, I get a little bit more of an idea of just how vast this place is. Nowhere on Earth is this empty. Nowhere. It's easy to forget.'

She gave him a sceptical look, and he shrugged.

'Okay, not that easy. But it's possible. This looks like places I know, places I've been to.'

'Lucky you.' She thought again about Greece, about the video advert she'd seen just before the fire, about the blue water and white sand and the tanned, toned girl in a bikini. Maybe one day.

'And then, of course, a sea serpent comes into view and ruins the illusion.' He spread his arms wide as Crows' sleek, serpentine head emerged from the depths. 'I'm on a beach in a different universe, I'm dressed like a Guantanamo convict and my best friend can turn into a falcon.'

'It could be worse,' she said.

'It was worse.' Then, in an effort to brighten the mood, Dalip said, 'We still need to find more firewood, or we'll be cold and hungry tonight.'

'Where's Luiza?' She didn't need to ask where Elena was, because either by choice or habit, they were almost always together.

'I think they went inland.'

'To ...'

'Look for food, I suppose.'

She glanced over to where Mama sat, next to the map box.

'How long have they been gone?'

'Most of the morning. I think Luiza, at least, wanted some time away from Crows.' He turned to face the line of dunes backing the beach. 'Do you want to check up on them without looking like you're doing it?'

'Better than picking up driftwood and hauling it halfway across Down.' She was still self-conscious enough about changing in front of him to want to find somewhere private. She'd done it before, but not while he was in any state to notice that there was a moment – blink and he'd miss it brief – when what she was wearing disappeared but the physical transformation had yet to begin.

Crows always changed underwater, so she hadn't known, and quite why she cared she couldn't say: except that Dalip would be embarrassed, and she didn't want that. Well, perhaps a little. But not enough to cause more problems between them.

'I'll go,' she flicked her hand in the direction of the dunes, 'and take a look.'

She picked up her skirts and set off, climbing up one soft-faced dune and down the other side, sand falling into her footprints behind her. She was alone. Her toes transformed into talons and her skin ripped and flowed. With one, two, three lazy wing-beats she was aloft, heading away from the sea and rising over the crowns of the scrubby, salt-stunted trees towards the forest proper.

Her pin-sharp eyesight started to scan for the giveaway flash of orange through the shroud of green. She wheeled and soared, tracking a line parallel to the coast, then further and further inland. After a while with no sighting at all, she flew down until she was almost skimming the uppermost twigs, the wake of her passing stirring the leaves and causing them to whisper.

And then – did she hear that? It sounded like a cry, cut off, brief and uncertain. Maybe her ears weren't as good as her eyes. She'd have to find a clearing, and check on foot. She circled again, finding a place nearby where a fallen trunk was rotting into exuberant life and a ring of saplings fought towards the light for dominance. It wasn't ideal, and the springy trees whipped her as she landed, but she was back on the ground, rubbing her sore, bare arms and gazing into the shadowed undergrowth of the forest.

She cupped her hands around her mouth. 'Luiza! Elena!'

There was no response. Not even bird calls.

Which struck her as odd, as there was always noise – tweets and trills and caws – along with the flashes of colour that marked the startled warning behaviour of the birds as they trooped by underneath. It was more than that, though. It was almost perfectly quiet.

She shivered. This wasn't normal behaviour for Down. Down was generously alive: something was always on the move.

She dropped her arms, then raised them again, bringing the forest floor with her: twigs, leaves, fragments of bark and browned petals. Little beetle things wriggled their legs frantically as they were suddenly denied the ground.

There, almost behind her, just beyond the edge of the clearing: a grey-green smudge the same colour as the dappled shadow. She clenched her fists and threw the hovering debris in one thick stream at her target. The outline of a man appeared, raising his arm against the spray of dirt and turning away so most of it struck his back and shoulders.

The deluge petered out, and the last few sticks rattled back to the ground. Her effort had left her momentarily breathless, and she didn't have the energy straight away for another attack. In the calm, the camouflaged figure straightened up and grew more visible.

As did his wolves, which materialised out of nothing and after a moment's straining on their iron-linked chains, were free to bound towards her across the clearing. Their shaggy heads were low, their powerful legs pumped, speed not magic blurring their oncoming shapes.

'Fuck,' said Mary.

6

Mama was telling Dalip how smart her nephew was – one of her nephews, at least – when he noticed the first crow on the map box. That it fixed them with one beady eye was nothing out of the ordinary. Both of them were used to having one or other of Crows' birds nearby.

It cawed and ruffled its feathers, and Mama looked around for something to throw at it. It didn't matter that they weren't discussing anything important. She just didn't want Crows eavesdropping on every last thing they said.

'Shoo,' she said, flapping her fingers at it. 'Go on, get.'

Then there were two, hopping and flapping.

'This isn't a joke, Crows.' She levered herself to her feet and batted at the birds with her hand. They easily avoided the swipe, rising and settling as it passed. When they landed again, there were three.

Dalip stared at the crows just as another of them folded itself out of nothing and started to hop from foot to foot. He pushed himself upright and scanned the horizon. Crows himself wasn't in sight – didn't seem to be in sight – but there was clearly something wrong.

Mama's cry made him turn around. A good dozen glossy black

birds burst up from the lid of the box and into the sky. They cawed and called, their wingbeats clattering as they scattered.

'Stay with the maps, Mama.' He took a few steps towards the dunes. 'Don't let anyone near them. Especially not Crows.'

He started to run, across the soft dry beach and then up the unstable seaward face of the first dune. He'd almost broached the top when instinct made him duck.

Mary, flying hard and fast, flashed inches over his head. Loose sand, stirred in her wake, left him blind and spluttering. He spat and blinked, and tried to dust his face free. By the time he could see again, they were almost on him.

There was no finesse in the man's first attack. He was out of breath already, red in the face and unsteady. He lunged with his heavy-bladed machete when he should have swung it, and all Dalip had to do was sway to one side to avoid the blow.

He reached out, pushed the man's outstretched arm away and down, trapping it against the sand, and followed through with his open palm against the side of the man's head. He went down, with Dalip on top of him.

He tried to free himself, while Dalip kept his weapon-hand pinned. He arched his body and kicked his legs, and scrabbled his fingers towards Dalip's face.

Dalip punched him in the throat, and ended the argument. He now had a machete, weighty and long, which he took a second to scoop up before running back towards Mama. She was one side of the map crate, waving her small knife at the green-grey-garbed man on the other side. He was circling at the same speed she was, but he was just toying with her: he could have stepped over the trunk and batted her weapon aside without risk. Mary, back in human form, was running towards her, a writhing mass of seaweed lifted from the strand line building behind her.

'Mama,' she called. 'Duck.'

She didn't have a clear shot until Dalip had almost reached him. He skidded to one side to avoid being caught in the brown, slimy mass that smothered the other man.

'Get the maps,' he said. 'Down the beach, go.'

Mama pocketed her knife and gripped one of the rope handles. She started off, backwards, dragging the box with her. Mary caught up with her, took the other handle and together they ran towards the sea.

The knocked-over man started to rise. The tendrils of seaweed slid slippery on to the sand, and he shook the last of it off. He was leaning on his knife-hand, and Dalip would never have a better moment.

All he had to do was raise his machete and bring it down hard on the man's wet hair or sandy shoulders. He looked at the length of metal extending from his hand, clutched at the cord-bound handle, felt the weight drag his arm down. He hesitated, half-raised the blade, then lowered it again. He made a decision, stepped back, and let him stand.

The man wiped the last of the slime from his rough face and narrowed his eyes at Dalip.

'Won't save you,' he said. 'I'll beat you like I did last time, and I don't have to stop, either.'

Recognition flared. In the woods, by the river, where the Wolfman caught up with them all, this man had helped kick and punch Dalip insensible.

'Where is he?' asked Dalip. He set his feet apart, bent his knees, lifted the machete ready to either parry or strike.

'He's coming, boy. He's coming.' His own blade was shorter, but pointed and double-edged. He made a swipe at Dalip's forearm, and steel rang against steel. He tried it again, and Dalip moved fast and countered with ease.

For Dalip, there was a gratifying moment of re-evaluation from his opponent, who tried to get past Dalip's guard again, once, twice, and each time his blade was knocked aside. Dalip watched him closely, looking out for weaknesses or strengths just as Stanislav had taught him.

'You can still leave,' said Dalip. 'Go. Run.'

That seemed to infuriate the man, who lunged wildly at him, grunting with effort.

Without having to even think, Dalip turned away and kept turning, using his momentum to swing his machete down and through the man's unguarded wrist. The blade was blunt. It didn't slice cleanly, but all the same, bones cracked and blood sprayed. The man staggered and fell, folding in on himself and shrieking.

It was the noise, rather than the injury, which turned Dalip's stomach. He checked his position, and sprinted across the beach to Mary and Mama. The map box sat between them.

'Are you hurt?' Mary asked.

'No. No, I'm not.' He was surprised. Neither of his attackers had so much as touched him. 'Where's Crows? Where are Luiza and Elena?'

'I don't know. I mean, there are crows, but no Crows. I couldn't find the other two.' She sounded desperate. 'Crows! Crows! Fuck it!'

'What did I tell you, girl?' said Mama.

'All right. But if the Wolfman gets the maps, Crows doesn't. He'll be here somewhere.'

'The Wolfman? These are his men?' Mama looked at her stubby knife. 'God preserve us and send his saints to protect us. We are in so much trouble.'

Dalip was more immediately concerned about where the two men were going. The one who'd attacked him first was making his way unsteadily back up the dune. The other, finally realising that he wasn't going to die immediately, was stumbling between being on his feet and crawling on his knees. His injured arm was pressed hard against his curled body.

'How many of them were there?'

'Four, five. Maybe six. They're almost impossible to see in the forest until they move.' Mary scanned the horizon for Crows again. 'Where the fuck is he?'

A head bobbed into view, lean and lupine, and a wolf stood on the crest of the dune. Dalip nudged Mary and pointed. A second wolf joined it, and behind, walking almost casually, came the Wolfman. Behind him, struggling, was Luiza, pinned in the grip of one of the Wolfman's followers.

'Well, shit,' said Mary.

'What are we going to do?' Mama dry-swallowed.

'We're going to do whatever it takes to save our friends,' said Dalip.

Elena was pushed roughly over the edge of the dune by another man. She ran the first few steps to steady herself, then began the slow walk towards the shore.

'The maps in exchange for Luiza?' said Mary.

'Looks that way.' Dalip also started to look around for Crows. 'Do they even know he's here? If they didn't hear you shouting for him, then … he might be planning something.'

'But we don't know what that's going to be, do we?'

'We're too far away to do anything to them.' Dalip looked for confirmation from Mary, and she gave a tight, terse nod. 'Then, as much as I hate the idea, we'll have to hope Crows has something up his sleeve.'

Elena closed the last of the distance between them with an apologetic run.

'I am sorry. So sorry.' She dropped to the ground, and Mama helped her on to the crate. 'They were everywhere, like before. We could not stop them.'

'Hush, girl, and tell us what they said.'

'They want everything.'

'The maps, right?' said Mary.

'No. That is what they want us to believe. That we will give them the maps, and they will give us my cousin. But I heard them say that once they have the maps, they will take all of us too, to kill or keep.' Elena took several trembling breaths. 'The only thing they care about is the maps, not keeping their word. I wish we had never taken them.'

'Avarice, that's what it is, girl. Avarice and greed.' Mama rested her hand on her shoulder. 'We've got ourselves a whole passel of trouble here.'

'Can we fight them off?' asked Mary.

Dalip clenched his jaw. 'There are three of them left worth worrying about. And two wolves. If they didn't have Luiza, then yes. They know us too well, though. We're not going to try anything with her captive.'

'What,' said Mary, 'what if we threaten to throw the maps into the sea?'

Mama baulked: 'Those maps are our way out of here.'

'They're useless at the moment,' said Dalip. 'We can't even exchange them for Luiza, because as soon as we do …' He frowned. 'Hold on. If we give them the maps, they give us Luiza: we can then just take the maps straight back. They can't fight Mary, and us, at the same time.'

'What are we missing?' Mary straightened up and looked around. 'There has to be something.'

'This exchange, Elena. How's it supposed to be done?'

She shuddered and managed to control herself for long enough to say: 'Take the maps to the middle. Luiza walks to us, they collect the maps.'

'And they think we'll trust them to do that?'

'They will kill her if we do not do as they say.'

Already, there were signs of impatience on the crest of the dune. Shouts drifted across the beach, words blown into incoherence by the wind and the distance, but the gesturing with knives close to Luiza's stretched-out neck were clear enough.

'We're going to have to do something soon,' said Mary. 'They won't wait for ever.'

'They won't kill Luiza. Not while we have control over the maps.' Dalip squared his shoulders, and started towards the Wolfman.

'What? Wait. Dalip, where are you going?'

'I'm going to reason with them. If – if it comes down to it, are we prepared to throw the maps into the sea?'

'No,' said Mama.

'Yes,' said Elena. 'If it will save Luiza.'

'I don't know!' Mary grimaced. 'I've never been rich before. I don't know how it feels to just give it all up.'

Dalip kept walking until he was at the base of the dune. The Wolfman's wolves strained on their chain leashes, baring their teeth at him, but the Wolfman himself laughed.

'Well met, Dalip Singh. As you can see, your friend is un-harmed, and lively.'

The man holding Luiza had one hand tight in her hair, drag-ging her down to a hunched half-squat. His other held a long, thin knife that hovered against her kidney.

'Let her go,' said Dalip, 'and face me like a man.'

'Though you didn't lack courage when we first met, I could have broken you like a twig. Now, I'm not so sure. So why don't you stay down there, and do what we told your little friend to do. Give us the maps, and we can go our separate ways.'

'I don't believe you,' said Dalip. 'I don't think you'll stop at the maps, because once we have Luiza back, there'll be nothing stopping us coming after you.'

'Good luck with finding us, lion man.'

'We found Crows. We can find you. And you know that. So stop lying and tell me what you really want.'

The Wolfman jerked at his wolves' chains to stop them growling. 'Gloves off, is that it? Cards on the table? Bit of plain speaking needed? It's like this: we'll take the maps, and anything else we fancy. If we leave you with anything, you can be grateful for our mercy.' He laughed again. Mercy was a joke for people like him.

'Bell wouldn't have accepted that,' said Dalip. 'Certainly not what you're intending.'

'She had odd ideas about what you can do to slaves. I don't share them.'

'I noticed.'

'So what's it to be, lion man? Do we get to stick a blade in your gypsy friend, or do you give us the maps?'

'You can't use the maps for anything but starting fires. You're too stupid, too scared to work out what they mean.'

Crows, rope over his shoulder, pulling the almost-finished boat behind him, crested the dune. 'I, however, am neither.'

Despite the size and weight of the hull, and Crows' stick-thin limbs, the boat seemed to move easily enough. The keel balanced on the dune's apex before the bow tipped towards the sea.

'You. You're behind this?'

'I know, I know. I am betraying everyone yet again, and for what? A few lines on a few sheets of paper or skin. Walk with me, Dalip, while I try both an explanation and an apology.' He adjusted his grip and leaned against the drag of the rope. 'Luiza will be perfectly safe. Isn't that right, Daniel?'

'Just as long as there's no shenanigans, Master Crows.'

'No shenanigans indeed. No more than have already been conceived and put into motion, at least.'

Dalip stared at Crows' back, then had to move aside for the passage of the boat.

'Luiza. Just . . .' He shouted his frustration and ran to catch up.

'You will ask me what am I doing?' said Crows.

'I was going to put it more strongly than that.'

'It is very straightforward. I do not want you to make copies of the maps. I do not want to share them with you at all. So I want to take them from you and go to the White City by myself. Daniel seeks someone new to serve, now that you have driven Bell away. I have offered my services as his lord, and he has graciously accepted. So there you have it. When we are safely away, we will drop Luiza off, perhaps on one of the islands out in the bay. In time, a new boat will grow, and you can go and pick her up. That is, in the circumstances, the best I can offer.'

'The best? The best?'

'My preference is that you all live, Dalip. I do not wish you dead, any of you.'

Dalip raised the machete, and Crows carried on hauling.

'If you attack me, Luiza will die. I do not think you want that weight on your soul.' He glanced around. 'If you do not lower your weapon, there may be a tragic mistake. Please understand, you have been tricked into giving up what you do not need in exchange for what you most dearly want. Accept it for what it is.'

'How can I accept this?' But his arm hung by his side again. 'This is an outrage.'

'You are right. Of course you are. You have no choice, though. You are a better man now than I will ever be. You will not risk the life of your friend, and I would, though it shames me greatly to do so, let alone say it.' He sighed. 'This would be quicker if you helped me.'

'No. Pull it yourself.'

'As you prefer,' said Crows.

The keel cut a lengthening line through the sand, while the distance to both the map box and the sea was diminishing with every step. Dalip thought so furiously that sweat started to bead on his forehead. He could think of nothing, though, no way out of the trap Crows had so carefully constructed.

And if the others imagined that Crows had, in his own fashion, managed to pluck a victory for them all from the salty air, then they were going to be disappointed.

'There is one ray of sunlight in the darkness, of course. When you give me the maps, I will take Daniel and his men along. They will never bother you again. Is that not fair? And if I discover the secret of the portals, then surely that will benefit all? Yes: you can go to whichever time you wish. Come and find me, and collect your favour.' He nodded to himself. 'You see? I am actually helping you, even though you refuse to help me.'

Dalip was in agony. He knew – knew in his heart – that the maps needed to be saved, not just in exchange for Luiza, but for their own sake. The answer to Down was hidden somewhere in their ink-scratched surfaces. Yet to capitulate so thoroughly? Defeat was as bitter as bile.

As they came down to the strand line, where Mary and Mama and Elena stood, hopefully, expectantly, he could barely bring himself to speak.

'Give him the maps.'

7

Mary watched it all unfold: the sudden appearance of Crows, his dragging the boat – their boat – down the beach, his conversation with Dalip and the boy's animated response, and at one point she thought that Dalip was going to attack Crows. She held her breath, but was confused by the slump of Dalip's shoulders. This didn't look like they were winning.

Mama strained to see. 'What is it? Why does Dalip look so angry?'

'I don't know. I can't tell.'

'It is Crows,' said Elena. 'He has done something, made a deal without us.'

'He wouldn't do that,' said Mary, and reconsidered very quickly when Mama and Elena both stared at her like she was mad. 'Okay. Let's not lose our shit before we find out what's happened.'

Crows hesitated as he walked – slowly, he was dragging a boat – up to them. He almost looked Mary in the eye, but turned his head away at the last moment and kept going to the water's edge.

'Crows? Crows, what the fuck have you done?'

Dalip chewed at his lip and rubbed his fist over his chin. He seemed close to tears.

'Give him the maps.'

'What?'

'You heard me. He's ... I should just kill him, I—'

Elena dragged his arm down. 'No. Luiza.'

'And that is the only reason he's still got his head on his shoulders.'

They watched as Crows dragged the boat to the line where the waves broke and ran up the beach. The boat itself looked perfectly seaworthy, sturdy and with enough room for all of them. Except, Mary realised, that was no longer her, Dalip and the others.

'The Wolfman?'

'Apparently so. Crows has hired him like some henchman.'

'But why?'

'It's the maps. He doesn't want to share.' Dalip barely controlled himself. 'Isn't that right, Crows?'

'The longer this goes on, the more likely it is that someone will have an accident. Please, Elena, put the box of maps in the boat.'

She didn't. She spat on the sand instead.

'Your cousin is still captive. She is in grave danger.'

'You are a bastard, Crows,' she said.

'Very well, I will do it myself.' He left the boat, with the waves washing up around and under it, and came back up the beach. 'If you could all step back two or three paces. I am afraid I do not trust you.'

'Well, that's rich,' said Mama, and put her hands on her hips.

Dalip waved them all back. 'Let's just get this over and done with. There's no point in arguing. They've got Luiza, and they'll kill her if we don't do as Crows says.'

They were a sullen group, standing away from the crate as Crows took hold of both handles and staggered with it to the side of the boat. He lifted it up as high as he could, then pinned it there with his scrawny chest while he adjusted his grip. He pushed it up to the gunwales, and it teetered for a moment before falling inside, thumping its way down to the deck.

'They will let her go now?' asked Elena. The Wolfman and his crew started towards their vessel, Luiza still with them, held captive by her long hair.

'If they did, then maybe Mary could follow them, maybe even sink them. They're going to take her with them and kick her out on one of the islands.'

'That is not right. We have done everything he asked. She should be free.'

'I'm sorry. There's nothing I can do.' With that, Dalip walked away and stared at the beach rather than witness Luiza being put into the boat and it sailing away with her.

'Mary, you must think of something.' Elena's fingers closed tight on Mary's bare shoulders and shook her. 'You cannot allow this.'

'What am I supposed to do?' Her voice was high and tight. 'I don't know what I'm supposed to do.'

'Something. Anything!'

Mama folded her thick arms around Elena's body and gently eased her away. 'We'll get her back. We'll get her back and it'll be fine. No point in getting angry with anyone but Crows – we've been played, and that's all there is to it.'

Mary whirled around. Crows. She started towards him but he held up his finger.

'They are warned, Mary. They know what you are capable of.' He waited until she reached a fist-clenching stop, then reached up and pulled himself up into the boat. He disappeared for a moment as he swung over the side, then his head reappeared.

'I can't believe you're doing this,' she said.

'You know me well enough to know I was always going to.' The sea seemed to slap the hull hard, and it lifted a little. When it fell back down, it was deeper in the wash. 'Let me tell you one last story before I go.'

'I don't want to hear it, Crows. Shut the fuck up.'

'Ah well. Perhaps another time then.' The next large wave sucked the boat out further.

'There won't be another time. When I see you next, I …'

'What? You will kill me? I have done you no harm, Mary. I have saved you three times now. Once from Daniel, once from Bell, and now from the maps. They would have only brought you misery: best to let them go without regret.'

'They were our maps. We were going to use them to go home.'

'They were Bell's maps. Then my maps. Then your maps. They were other people's maps before they were Bell's, and now they are mine again.' The boat rocked, and Crows held on to the side. It was properly afloat now, and there was clear water between it and the beach.

'Crows?' Mary looked behind her. The Wolfman and his men were barely halfway towards them. 'Crows? What are you doing?'

'It is a shame you did not want to hear my story,' he called. 'It would have explained much.'

She walked into the sea up to her knees, but she knew the beach shelved away steeply after that. If she went much further, she'd have to swim.

'Crows,' she called. 'What about the Wolfman?'

'Please extend to him my deep sorrow at having to break our contract so early on. Such is the ever-changing nature of life.'

The boat was moving further away, and though his voice carried clearly, Crows was dwindling into the distance.

'Crows. You have to stay.'

'I regret that I am done on this shore. Farewell, Mary.'

'What about Luiza?'

'They will release her. They have no reason not to.' With that, Crows' head dropped from view.

Dazed, she reached out her arms and shouted: 'Come back. Crows. Come back.'

She lost her footing, and the next wave bore her up and back towards the beach. She floundered to her feet, dripping wet, to see the Wolfman running past Dalip, towards her – no, towards the shrinking shape of the boat.

'Hey!' He splashed into the sea, raising a wave of his own. 'Hey! Crows! We had a deal!'

Without sail or oars, the stern moved steadily away. White water started to break around it as it bobbed through the region where the waves started to rise, towards the open sea. The Wolfman pushed out further, his wolfskin cloak becoming more bedraggled with each step.

'Crows!'

His wolves remained on the beach, running backwards and forwards, heads rising to yelp and yip. Their chain leashes rattled.

'He's not coming back,' said Mary, to herself and the Wolfman. 'He's leaving without us.'

The Wolfman found the drop-off, and went from thigh-deep to neck-deep in a matter of moments. He gasped and splashed.

'Crows!'

She turned her frustration on him. 'Don't you get it, you fucking idiot? He played you just like he played us. He's got everything he wanted, and we've got nothing.'

The Wolfman found his feet and waded quickly back to dry land. His jaw was set and he was breathing hard. Further away, the man holding Luiza had come to a halt, uncertain what to do. The other man with him was, in turn, shouting back to the two more distant figures at the top of the dune.

Mary took a second to register the situation: everyone was angry, afraid, and upset. She'd seen this before: yes, it was a beach, but it was also very street. As much as she wanted to set off after Crows – and she could, she realised – it would mean leaving this incendiary mix to combust all on its own.

She started for the shore herself, lifting her sodden skirts clear of the water. She stared meaningfully at Dalip, who had stopped looking at the wolves for long enough to realise what was going on.

His hand flexed around the handle of the machete, and she deliberately, subtly, shook her head. She pointed at Elena and Mama, and began to innocently make her way towards them.

The Wolfman bent over, hands on his knees, gasping. His wolves trotted around him, high-stepping out of the surf, alternately gazing out to sea and then looking up at their master. He straightened up, wiped his nose with his sleeve, and tilted his head back.

His scream of rage and abandonment went on for so long that Mary thought that it sounded more wolf than man. The wolves crumbled to dust, their chains lasting for a moment longer before they too flowed into the sand.

Mary and Dalip stood shoulder to shoulder, making a wall of their bodies to protect Mama and Elena. They were both tensed and ready.

The Wolfman didn't even look in their direction. He strode out, walking quickly for a few steps, then broke into a loping run, back up the beach, towards his men.

'What's he doing?' asked Dalip.

'Fuck knows.' They were suddenly alone. 'We need to get everyone together, and, and …'

'And what?'

'Get after Crows.' She looked over her shoulder. The boat was only a black speck now, bobbing up and down with the waves. She looked back, and felt Dalip stiffen. The Wolfman was still running. His long knife was in his hand and he was heading straight for the man holding on to Luiza. 'No. He can't.'

Dalip put his head down and sprinted, and she began to do the same, before realising that neither of them was going to make it in time. She had to hope that it wasn't as bad as it looked, that nothing was going to happen, that he was just running off his fury.

The Wolfman seemed to punch Luiza in the stomach so hard

that she folded almost in two around his fist. The man holding her couldn't untangle his fingers from her hair fast enough to just let her drop to the ground; instead, she hung there, hands trying to fend off her attacker, pushing ineffectually at his face and chest.

The Wolfman stepped back, and she flopped on the sand, at first to her knees, then toppling hard on to her side. Her head hit the ground, and didn't move.

Dalip ran a few more steps, and stopped. Mary walked slowly forward until she was almost, but not quite, within arm's length of the Wolfman.

The man held up his bloodied hand. He was soaked to the elbow.

'Why did you do that?' she asked him.

'Revenge,' he said.

'But—'

'Revenge on Down. Revenge on you and him and everything.' He shook his fist at her. 'Do what you will. I'm done with this place.'

'You stabbed her.'

Dalip knelt down and his hand hovered over Luiza, uncertain as to what to do next. He brushed her hair from her cheek. Her eyes were wide open and unblinking. He looked up at Mary. 'I … she's …'

Elena tumbled down next to her cousin, and threw her arms around her. She gathered her up, and the way that Luiza's head lolled, her mouth opening slightly, left no doubt. There was no breath left in her, no heartbeat, no light.

Mary already knew. It wasn't like she was a stranger to it.

'You didn't need to do … that. You just didn't.'

'You're wrong. So very wrong, you little black whore. I did need to do it. I'm going to keep on doing it from now on. Kill and kill and kill until there's no one left on Down. And there's no Bell or Crows to stop me.'

Dalip stood up and scrubbed a tear away with the back of his hand. 'I'll stop you.'

The Wolfman laughed in his face and lunged at him with his bloody knife. Dalip parried, once, twice, then launched his own counter-attack, stepping surely over the uneven, shifting surface as he swung and swung at the Wolfman's weapon hand.

Mary could end this, quickly and simply. Conjure up a storm of sand and thrust it down the Wolfman's nose and throat, choke him and let him die, clawing at his heaving chest. But Dalip seemed intent on finishing it himself. His face was expressionless, save for the slight furrowing of his brows, and his body moved in a ballet of blows and blocks that defied his opponent's crude violence.

The Wolfman retreated before him, grunting with effort. His long knife was narrow and wholly unsuitable protection against the cleaving machete. Yet neither could he get anywhere near Dalip: every feint, every stab, was either knocked aside with finger-numbing force or avoided with a lithe twist of his body.

'Help. Help me,' he said to his colleague. His knife snapped halfway up the blade, the pointed end spinning away.

The man saw Mary's slow shake of her head and started to back away.

Dalip brought the heavy edge down, cut through the meat and tendons on the back of the Wolfman's hand. The rest of the knife dropped to the ground, and the Wolfman reeled.

Now he was alone, deserted by everyone he'd counted on. He snarled one last time and went for the knife hilt, sticking up out of the sand. And Dalip cracked his skull like a coconut. Death was instantaneous, but it still took a few moments for his fur-clad body to stop moving. The beach began to darken around him.

The machete was still wedged tight. Dalip put his bare foot on the Wolfman's unprotesting neck and worked it free.

'That,' he said, 'was no more than justice.'

Mary brought her hands up to her face and dragged her fingers down from her forehead to her chin. 'Do we let the others go?'

They watched their heels running back up the beach towards the dunes.

'We could spend days hunting them down. It's not worth it. Without him, they're scattered. And we need to stay here, to get the next boat.'

She swallowed hard. 'I'm sorry.'

'It's not your fault.'

Looking out to sea, Crows was nowhere to be seen, though he had to be somewhere in the swell between the shore and the horizon.

'I'm going after him,' she said.

'We're all going after him.'

'No. Now.' And with that, she changed, no longer caring about what Dalip might or might not see. She called once, a piercing, high-pitched shriek, and then she was off, streaking over the beach, passing over the upturned faces of Mama and Dalip, over Elena's bowed head and Luiza's sightless eyes. She worked her wings to gain both speed and height, and then headed determinedly out over the breaking waves.

She had no idea what she was going to do or say when she found him.

8

He left the comforting to Mama. He didn't know what he could say that would alleviate Elena's grief, so he said nothing. That felt wrong, too, and he knew that he couldn't hide from that for ever. In fact, the longer he left it, the worse it would be. But he couldn't do it now. He took himself aside and stared at Mary's tail feathers until they merged with the clouded sky.

He would need to dig a grave. Two graves. Not next to each other. He had nothing to dig with but his hands, so he thought somewhere in the dunes would be best. Make them too deep, and the sides would collapse, burying him as well. What he'd end up with would be two shallow scrapes which, in time, would do nothing to deter scavengers. Perhaps the animals wouldn't put in an appearance until after another boat had grown and the four of them were off the beach for good.

Four left. Grace gone God only knew where, Stanislav obliterated by lightning, Luiza pointlessly killed by the Wolfman. Who he, in turn, had killed.

Stanislav – his death had been an act of mercy, and even though Dalip had baited the trap, Down itself had pulled the trigger. The Wolfman – Daniel, he had a name after all – was a different matter. When they'd fought, it had seemed so straightforward. It

69

was only after he'd won that Dalip started to gather his doubts about him. Had killing him been necessary?

His grandfather would have said yes. But this was the man who'd lied about his age and run away to war. He'd been fierce and proud and fearless, even in old age when Dalip had known him best. In the end, he'd been barely able to stand, but he'd still shake his fist at the television and shout obscure Punjabi curses at besuited politicians. He'd do the same to Dalip's mother, but only after she'd left the room.

Protecting others was one of the reasons Sikhs carried a kirpan. And he'd failed to save the person he needed to. But there were all the unknown others the Wolfman would have gone on to kill, but now wouldn't. Perhaps that was a good enough reason. There were no authorities for either of them to answer to. Yes, he was judge, jury and executioner all rolled into one, but the Wolfman was guilty, condemned by his own hand and words.

The gurus said it was right to draw the sword when all other means had failed. This is what they'd meant, even if he'd never quite understood that before.

He deliberately looked back at the scene off to his left. Elena keening over her cousin, head buried in Mama's substantial chest and her frame rising and falling with her sobs, Luiza's body now discarded on the sand like the driftwood they collected, and the Wolfman lying a little way off, spread-eagled and still.

This was all Crows' doing. His fault – he'd planned it, set it in motion, and had simply shrugged his bony shoulders at the havoc he'd left in his long-vanished wake. For certain, he was more charming, more superficially decent, than the Wolfman. But underneath, he was far more dangerous, more lethal than even Bell, and she'd been cold, callous and cruel, entirely devoid of empathy and utterly self-centred.

Crows was, without doubt, the worst person he'd ever come across. He'd destroyed everything they'd salvaged from the wreckage of Bell's castle. And for that, he would face the only kind of justice that could be delivered on Down. Dalip doubted whether Mary would do what was necessary: she liked Crows, and she was conflicted. So for the sake of everyone here, and yet to come, it would be Dalip Singh who rid this world of him.

Trying to untangle his decision from his own burning sense of betrayal and his terrible need for revenge was futile. If that was all there was, then he might have given himself a stern talking-to. But no, his cause was right, and the crime enormous. There was the evidence: two dead bodies, one of a friend, the other an enemy, and Crows' baleful influence shrouded both.

There was nothing left to see on the horizon. Mary would come back when she'd said what she needed to say, done what she needed to do. Part of him wanted her to sink Crows' boat and destroy the maps. But if they were the key to unlock Down, then keeping the collection intact was more important than Crows' temporary wealth. It would also make it sweeter to take them back, afterwards.

He got up, machete in hand, and slogged up the dune to take the view from the top. There was no one in sight, even though he knew there were at least three men relatively close by. Down had a habit of just swallowing people up in its landscape: they could be miles away, or just over the next ridge.

'I'll be just over here,' he called to Mama. 'Shout if … you know. If.'

Mama nodded. She turned herself to try and shield Elena from the bodies, to lead her away, but it didn't work. She patted Elena on the back and let her cry.

It left Dalip wishing for all the alternatives. If Down was a time machine, then maybe, just maybe, there was a way around this.

He slid down the face of the dune, then walked along the slack to where the boat had been birthed. There was a hollow in the sand, and a track, broken by wide, collapsing footprints, where the keel had been dragged out towards the sea.

There would be fewer of them on the beach, waiting for the next boat to fruit. It might be smaller, and it might take more time to grow. Assuming it did. If nothing happened, they'd have to leave.

He climbed the next dune inland and took stock again. Below him was a long marshy area, green with thin weeds and scummy algae. He was half-minded to toss the Wolfman's remains in there, despite his faith tradition of cremation. The Wolfman didn't deserve the correct observances. All the same, Dalip knew he was going to do his best anyway. No one was going to applaud him for the choices he made. They might even criticise him for them. It didn't matter. He was the one who was responsible for what he did, and he wanted to be able to live with his decisions.

He descended to almost the bottom, and turned to face the slope. He cut through the tough grasses and their long, fibrous roots, sawing with the machete blade until he could pull back a mat of vegetation. Underneath was grey-brown sandy soil, some of which spilled out of the hole, but as he dug further, it kept its shape and the sides didn't slump into the void. He cut and pulled and dug and scooped, until he had a trench six foot long and a couple of feet wide, big enough to shove a body into, without much ceremony, and cover over again. If he went much further into the dune face, the ground would slip, and as well as working hard for no result, he'd be in danger of getting caught in a major slide.

So he stopped, thought it good enough, and went to collect the Wolfman.

He walked back to the beach, wondering how to do it. If someone died in Southall, the family gathered and the undertakers were called. Prayers were recited, the Guru Granth Sahib read, the body burned in the local crematorium and the ashes scattered into the Thames.

Death was, in reality, messy. There was the head wound, the hand wound, and the post-mortem bowel movement, none of which he wanted to get close to. He circled the Wolfman, lips pursed, and made an abortive grab for the wolfskin cloak. He pulled, realised it would simply come off in his hands, and let go again.

Mama frowned at him, and dipped her head towards the Wolfman's feet.

'Come with me, sweetheart,' she said to Elena. 'Dalip's going to see to things here.'

Dalip waited for them to reach a respectable distance before reaching down and grasping the Wolfman's ankles.

How much did a soul weigh? In the Wolfman's case, it must have been a lot, because his mortal remains seemed incongruously light. Dalip dragged him away, face down, arms trailing, then at the top of the first dune sent him rolling down the landward slope to the bottom. The body tumbled and flopped, coming to an awkward rest on its back.

He stood over the Wolfman, staring at the way the sand clung to his grey skin and infested his glazed open eyes. Where had the animating spirit gone? Had it merged with the Godhead, as he hoped he would one day? Had it already been recycled as some base creature with no thought or consciousness? The tattered remains of the Wolfman were just that: discarded clothes, an empty husk, worn and used. There was nothing there to be mourned. He took hold of the ankles again and dragged the corpse up the next rise, before easing it down next to the freshly prepared grave.

It turned out that the Wolfman had been shorter than Dalip, which surprised him as he'd loomed very much larger. His feet, however, looked roughly the same size. He remembered a conversation with Mary, weeks ago, just after they'd arrived in Down. His own boots had been ruined by the fire, and she'd suggested taking someone else's – after they'd died, of course.

And here they were, a dead man's boots. Dalip stared at them for a while, before unlacing them and slipping them off. They were worn, and their construction was workmanlike. The laces were thongs, the sole thick tanned leather, the uppers soft and supple. He knocked them out, and tried them on. His own feet were hard with calluses, but it felt good to wear them.

It got Dalip to wondering if the boots were the only thing the Wolfman could offer him. He'd already started down that road. It would seem foolish not to take it to its logical end, even if it meant rummaging through a dead man's pockets – distasteful, perhaps, but in a world where manufactured goods were at a premium, necessary.

He put his doubts aside, and started to peel back the layers of clothing.

There were a lot of them, accreted like paint on an old door. Some of them were almost dust, a few spidered threads suggesting the outline of a garment. Some were more substantial, and a few had items of note in them: coins of various ages, dull brown wheels of copper and blackened silver, impressed with the unreadable faces of kings and sometimes queens; jewellery – a chain, a bracelet, again tarnished to inglorious trinkets, a gold ring worn so thin its edges were sharp; a tooth, an actual tooth, roots and everything, with half its mass made of yellow metal.

Dalip guessed they were trophies of a sort, things taken from the Wolfman's unwilling, unwitting victims as tokens of his prowess at lying, cheating and killing.

Then there was a white oval that sat in the hollow of his hand like a small egg. He frowned at its incongruous natural shape and its obviously artificial origin. Its surface was rough with a thousand tiny scratches, and there was an obvious finger-shaped dimple on the fat end so that it would sit up when placed on a table.

It wasn't made of stone, more a hard plastic that was warm to the touch. He tapped it with a fingernail, and it sounded hollow. There was no obvious way in, no continuous line describing its circumference, no screw holes or cover to open.

There was no way of asking after previous owners, either, which gave Dalip a moment of wry, black humour.

'Take your secrets with you, Wolfman,' he said to the corpse. 'We'll work it out without you.'

He pocketed the items and arranged the body the best he could on its ledge. He took a double handful of dirt and cast it up. It settled in clumps, and he went back for another and another, scooping and flinging, until the human shape became softened and obscured. He hesitated for a moment when the last of the Wolfman's face was about to be swallowed by the rising soil, then came to some sort of accommodation with what he was doing – burying a man that he'd killed – before finishing the job by relaying the square mats of scrubby plants he'd cut out.

He pressed them down, wiped his hands on his thighs, and acknowledged that he hadn't done a bad job, considering that it was his first attempt.

But if burying someone who hated him and wanted to kill him had been hard, how much more difficult would it be for a friend, who he'd shared meals and journeys and captivity and escape with?

As he tramped back to the beach, his new-old boots unfamiliar on his feet, he thought again about cremation. The sheer amount of wood they'd need pretty much ruled it out for Luiza: the one he'd witnessed in India had had a bier of densely stacked cut logs almost as tall as he was, that extended out both lengthways and widthways beyond the body laid neatly on top. Anything less wouldn't be sufficient to make ashes – and the memory of the thick black smoke spiralling away into the sky had stayed with him for weeks. He didn't think that Elena was ready for that.

Then there was also the matter of a ceremony. Luiza was a Christian of some sort, while he most certainly wasn't. Mama was, but he didn't know what type. And he didn't know how seriously Luiza had taken her religion. Not that she was necessarily going to care, because her soul had returned to the cycle of rebirth that included all of humanity. Or there was Heaven and Hell, neither of which he believed in.

He'd leave it to Mama. That seemed safest.

Dalip climbed back up the shoreward-most dune and stared out to sea. There was no sign of either Mary or Crows' boat. He checked the sun, and was surprised to see it had slid around to the south-west. Hours had passed. He scanned the horizon again, from side to side, but there was nothing.

He ignored the ice-water feeling in his stomach, and slipped down the face of the dune to where Luiza was lying. Mama was with Elena down on the strand line, Mama's arm over Elena's shoulder, and looking determinedly away from the land.

He really didn't want to have to do this, and yet there was no one else.

Was this what defined adulthood, then? Doing what was necessary? His own father was so mild and inoffensive, intent on passing through life with barely making a ripple, he couldn't imagine the man doing what he was doing now. His grandfather – yes, he knew that he had, in those numerous jungle engagements conducted at almost point-blank range, where the enemy dead were hurriedly hidden in shallow scrapes in the ground.

He slid his hands under Luiza's armpits and straightened his back. She was stiffening, and her head wasn't sure whether to fall forward, or roll back. Her skin was cold and inelastic, but her hair still fluttered with the breeze. He could see where the blond strands faded into dark roots.

She wore no jewellery but a little gold stud in each earlobe. No rings, no necklace, nothing to pass to Elena with his condolences. He still didn't know how he was going to offer those.

He dragged her to the top of the dune, down the other side, and stopped where the boat had been born. Here? Further along? Would burying her near where the boat had grown cause problems with the fruiting of another one?

What would Down think of the intrusion? Would it notice?

Would it mind one way or the other? And if he was already having thoughts about Down being alive, and having a personality, why not go all the way and behave like it was true? Because it made as much sense as anything else – more sense than treating this world the same as he had his old one.

If he was sad, how could he communicate that to Down? By burying someone he had cared about on one of its lines of power.

He excavated the hollow made by the boat, enlarging it downwards and into the dune. The sand was slippery and soft, the grains trickling down to fill the hole almost as quickly as he dug. But slowly, the sides began to keep their shape, and it was more or less noon by the time he'd done what he thought others would consider enough.

He lifted Luiza into the hole, arranged her with her arms folded across her stomach, closed her eyes with tentative brushes of his fingers. She looked, if not at peace, at least at a slightly perturbed rest. Her hands partially covered the rent in her overalls and the ugly dark stain. Flowers and reeds from the waterlogged slack over the next dune would hide the rest.

He went to collect a posy, checking over his shoulder as he climbed, expecting to see Mary swoop in at every moment. She'd been gone now for hours: five, maybe six. He didn't know if Crows could hide the boat like he could hide himself. Maybe he could, and that was what was delaying her. Instead of searching for the single boat in an open sea, she'd be searching for an ephemeral wake amongst the wind-blown waves.

How long could she stay aloft, looking? Even when they'd been searching for him before, she'd taken rests. At sea, there were no convenient perches, so where was she? Either she'd found him, or she hadn't. Either way, she should be back with them by now.

He stood on top of the dune and looked for her. What if she'd lost her bearings, ended up on a different part of the coast and was struggling to find them? They'd relied on Crows and Mary for both fire and food. They'd burned driftwood and eaten fish while waiting for the boat to grow. He was already tired, hungry and thirsty, and tonight, he'd be cold.

What if she didn't come back? She'd gone alone, impulsive and angry, to challenge Crows. He could have killed her. Incapacitated her enough to bring her down. She'd be left miles from dry land. She couldn't swim well. She'd drown.

He swallowed hard. Such thoughts were unworthy of both him and her. She knew how much was at stake. She wouldn't take stupid risks.

He started to pray for her return in order to stave off his growing despair.

9

She was taking the biggest risk of her life. She could forget about the petty thieving, the breaking and entering, the clambering over unsafe roofs, the uninhibited experimental drug taking, the excessive drinking and the dangerous sex. Convincing Crows that he'd persuaded her – slowly, reluctantly, and harbouring the gravest doubts – to join him rather than starting a fight that would risk the precious maps? That had been the easy part. He used all his sugared words. She didn't trust him, told him so to his face, and they'd reached a stalemate, him down the back end of the boat, her at the front, with what felt like only a few feet of boards between them.

The thing was, Crows was easy to believe: he said everything right even while doing everything wrong. It wasn't a surprise that he'd so infuriated someone that they'd tried to carve their name on his belly. He was a liar and a cheat of the worst kind, and that had been back in London. Down had made him truly, epically, devilish. She'd be surprised if he could lie straight in bed.

And, like the Devil, he was charming, self-assured, and so very believable.

Mary thought she might have left it too long. She had weakened, rallied, and softened again. Had she judged it right, folding at the very last moment, agreeing to his impassioned pleas about greatness and mastering Down? Did he now doubt her conversion, and was secretly planning to do away with her?

Was he planning to do that anyway?

No less than she was. But the maps were safe: she had her eye on them, even if she couldn't claim ownership yet. And Dalip – he'd find a way, wouldn't he? All roads led to the White City, wherever the fuck it was, and he'd only have to wait a few days for another boat to grow: he'd be able to sail it, with Elena and Mama, and catch up with them eventually. They'd overpower Crows, seize the maps, and everything would be right again. Apart from Luiza, of course. Nothing would bring her back.

Crows had cried real tears when she'd told him what the Wolfman had done. He said he couldn't have foreseen it, that it was the Wolfman's unreasoning hate, not his betrayal, that had led to Luiza's murder. But just because he was sorry didn't mean he lost any of the responsibility.

It was the maps. Everything came down to the maps. If they were at the bottom of the sea, everything would be so much simpler. Without them, though, what chance was there of ever reuniting Mama with her babies, or Dalip with his family? Elena could make her own choice, though Mary suspected she'd leave Down in a heartbeat. So rather than destroy them, she was kneeling at the prow, staring ahead, while her friends slipped slowly further astern.

She still didn't know what she was going to do.

It was easier to look forward than back, in every sense. Behind her was her past, but also Crows, hands folded lightly in his lap. The boat was moving on its own, sliding on the downslope of the ever-present wave that followed them. She had to learn how to do that – Crows would need to rest, and she didn't want to be reliant on him. If he wanted to becalm her, he could. She might be able to fly, but not with the maps. Well, maybe with the maps, if they weren't in a heavy, awkward wooden crate, and she had hands rather than claws.

She thought back to the idea of a bag, a big duffel bag with a drawstring top. That would work.

If she had enough cloth, a length of thin rope, and something sharp, she could make one for herself. Then wait for Crows to be distracted long enough to decant all the maps, transform and fly off with them.

He, naturally, wasn't going to let the maps out of his sight. He wasn't stupid. There might be a chance later, though – much later, when he'd grown used to her presence and thought her no threat.

The boat moved on, its bow cutting through the water with rhythmic splashes as the oncoming waves slapped up against the boards. Apart from the island coming up on their left, the view was otherwise empty. What she thought had been the whole of the island was only a headland, hiding more behind it. The wedge-shaped mountain rose from one side – around it were lower, flatter lands which angled gently into the sea.

It was no good. At some point, she had to talk to Crows about something normal. It may as well be now.

'You been there?' For a sea serpent, the distance between the island and the mainland wasn't far.

Crows, distracted, let their driving wave fall away for a moment. The boat, no longer moving forward, rocked with unfamiliar motion, and she put her hands on the rails to steady herself.

'The island?'

'Yes, the island.'

'No. There is nothing there.'

'Oh,' she said. Of course he knew it was empty, despite never having set foot on it. 'So why can I see smoke?'

Until she'd said it, she'd been convinced she was imagining it. It was no more than a smudge, a slight thickening of the already blue haze that distance lent the scene.

'It is no concern of ours.'

'It is if it's the White City.'

She saw his expression flicker from serene to annoyed and back. Perhaps he'd been playing a triple bluff, and had known exactly where the White City was all along. He'd used his first lie to get them to the coast, his second to leave them and make a deal with the Wolfman, and now couldn't reveal his third. He'd have to pretend that it might be, or give himself away.

'It is not likely to be there, on that island.'

'Why not?' she asked innocently. 'It's as likely as anywhere else. If you point us that way, when we're close enough I can fly over it and see.'

She could see with her own eyes, because trusting what Crows said about anything was pointless. He might be right, but trusting that could be the end of her.

He faltered for the briefest instant before regaining his smile. 'You might be right. And while we are here, it cannot hurt for you to explore.'

There was a lever sticking out into the boat from the stern. She hadn't paid it much attention before, but Crows pushed it horizontally away from him and the front of the boat started to turn. The island turned too, until it was more central.

'It will not take us too far out of our way.' He shrugged. 'We will not even have to stop.'

He was right: she could take off from the boat, fly over the island, and land again, confident of finding him.

The coast slowly resolved out of the haze. Wide beaches, tall headlands, but not many trees – rolling green grass covered most of what she could see. It all looked like a picture postcard, with the rising mountain peak behind waving a flag of cloud into the blue sky. But as they closed, and Crows turned the rudder again to run them parallel to the coast, she could make out shapes planted on the beaches, where a boat might want to land.

'What,' she asked, 'are those?'

Crows strained forward, shielding his eyes from the sun. 'I cannot tell. But neither can I go closer. There is a reef between us and the shore, and the tide is beginning to run.'

Mary scanned the surface of the water, and there was a line of white waves standing off from the coast, but she didn't know what that meant. If Crows had been this way before, he would know anyway, without interpreting the sea state.

She stood up, trying to keep her balance against the movement of the boat underneath her. She really couldn't see, but she felt she ought. The motion of the sea made it harder than it should be, and there was nothing for it but to transform and take a better look.

'You're not going to go anywhere, are you?'

'Even if I was, where could I hide from you? Your eyes are the keenest in all of Down, and your swift flight would overtake me in minutes.'

He was right, and she left it at that. He couldn't escape her, and she couldn't leave him. She crouched down, steadied herself for a moment, aware that launching herself up and over the sea without the expectation of belly-flopping into the churning sea was just ridiculous. And yet, when she straightened her legs and stretched her arms out wide, it was only her wingtips that caught the tops of the waves.

She flapped hard, gained height, and circled the boat. She could see it small against the sea, and Crows' upturned face looking back at her. She noted the landmarks – the long finger of land stretching out, the tall cliffs with their bases white with foam, the long sandy beach, and the mountain rising tall towards the back of the island – and flew down.

So this wasn't a good sign. Anywhere in the world, a cross with a bleached white skull hanging on top of the upright meant only one thing, and that was a heartfelt 'fuck off now'. She turned and piloted a course parallel to the beach, where she found two more crosses with two more skulls. None of them looked particularly new, though that they were all still standing made her think someone was making sure the posts kept upright and the skulls were grinning.

She banked inland, passing over the grasslands, not seeing anyone, but that ragged pillar of dark smoke told her that people were living there. The ground rose and fell, with more rising than falling as she came closer to the mountain. The grasses waved at her, uncut, ungrazed, green with new growth and purple with flowers.

The smoke was three ridges away, then two, then it was the next. She rose higher and saw its source – a dirty black scar like a bomb crater – before she recognised anything else. There were little clusters of wooden buildings arranged in four lines like streets, radiating from a central stone pavement that pressed itself up against the steep side of the valley. Most were falling apart, like the ones she'd seen in the forest on the way to Bell's castle. She knew, then, that they were Down-made, fading through lack of inhabitants.

Yet there were people in that little village. She could see two of them swinging a bundle on to the fitful fire, which was placed at the end of one of the rows of houses. As she flew through the smoke, she smelled burning wood and burning flesh.

Something she'd smelled before, in the dark tunnels under London. She focused on the fire, and saw that the pathetic smouldering rags contained a pale corpse.

She couldn't make sense of it. If the fire was for burning the dead, and the fire was always burning – the only wood she'd seen was in the houses – then where did all the dead come from? The island seemed beautiful – idyllic even, like a holiday brochure, with its wide beaches and soft hills – but it had this stain at its heart.

As she dropped lower, she was spotted. One of the men, little more than rags himself, pointed up at her, and the pair of them watched open-mouthed as she passed overhead. They moved to keep her in sight, even as she spiralled downwards, looking for a place to land.

The obvious place was on the circular stone pavement, which she now realised had been built into the side of the hill. The escarpment was walled with more stone, and in that wall was a door, leading underground. She was intrigued and, with a final series of flaps, settled on top of the wall, on the grassy bank that extended upwards.

The two men appeared at a run between two of the dilapidated buildings, and she could see now just how gaunt and grizzled they were. Their clothes were grey and ragged, much like their sanity. They stopped on the opposite side of the pavement to her and the first man dipped down to pick up a loose stone the size of his fist.

'Throw it, Nathaniel. Drive it away.'

The stone, when it came, landed well short. The man called Nathaniel simply didn't have the strength, let alone the accuracy, to hit her. It clattered across the pavement, and Mary looked down at it as it spun and clacked against the base of the wall.

He seized another while his companion uncertainly raised his arms and tried to shoo her. 'Go! Fly, beast, fly!'

She was, in bird form, more than twice their size, and it didn't seem credible that they would try and take her on, but here they were, two men dressed like tramps, trying to scare her away when for all they knew she was planning to have them for lunch. The second stone struck the wall just below her clawed feet, and she decided she'd had enough rock-throwing and nowhere near enough explanation. She changed, and they stared at her for a moment.

Then they ran, back the way they'd come, as fast as they could, disappearing behind the line of houses.

She shrugged and walked along the top of the wall as it curved down to meet the ground, and jumped when the distance was narrow enough. She looked around: everything seemed on the verge of collapsing, like she'd walked on to the scene of some end-of-days catastrophe.

The door in the wall didn't look like it could be locked. It was old and wooden and warped, but she could see nothing between the cracks in the boards. There was no handle or knob on her side, and even though there was a place where she could squeeze her fingers between the door and its frame, it wouldn't flex, let alone open.

She frowned, then became aware of being watched.

The two men were back. Nathaniel, the stone-thrower, had armed himself with a club. His colleague was empty-handed but for some rope.

'Why don't you hold it right there,' she said, 'because I'm not into the whole hit on the head and tied up thing.'

The rope-carrier licked his thin lips and the pair of them edged forward a step, each one daring the other to go first.

'I can either fly away or knock your sorry arses into next week. Your call.'

The stone, hidden in Nathaniel's other hand, flew straight for her face, where it stopped an inch from her nose, turning slowly. She reached up, plucked it out of the air, and dropped it next to her.

'You're not getting this, are you?'

They looked ready to run again. The rope-carrier touched his free hand to his chest, four times in quick succession, making the pattern of a cross. 'God protect us. A witch.'

Mary had been called a lot of things in the past, and given she could turn into a falcon and light fires with a snap of her fingers, she let this one slide.

'We can talk, or we can call each other names. You're not exactly Brad Pitt yourself.' When they didn't respond, and just quivered with fear and uncertainty, she decided that she'd nothing to lose going with a direct approach. 'I'm looking for the White City. Do you know where that is?'

'We know of no such place: ask your demon familiar instead. Now, back to Hell, witch, and take the plague with you.' Nathaniel raised his club higher and gripped it harder.

'Whoa. Hang on.' She thought about burning bodies and rundown houses, the crosses and skulls. 'Plague. You're shitting me, right?'

'Your tongue is as coarse as your manners, you heathen blackamoor. Perhaps I should send you to Hell myself.' He took another step, and Mary took one back.

'What's the other side of that door?' she asked, pointing behind her.

'London, for all the good it does us,' said the rope man. 'We are marooned here, and still the pestilence follows us through.'

'Do not furnish her with answers! She will use them for devilry.'

'Aye, that she might, but the sin will be hers, not mine.' The man dropped his rope, recognising the exercise as futile. 'You have a name, witch?'

'Mary,' said Mary.

'A Christian name?' He wiped at his pale, sweaty face. 'Beelzebub goes by many disguises.'

'Whoever that is. You're serious about this plague, though?' There was something half-remembered tickling the back of her mind. 'What year is it through there?'

'The year of our Lord, sixteen sixty-five.'

'Fuck. The Black Death.'

'It is a judgement for our iniquities,' said Nathaniel. 'If we turn back to God, then we will be saved. As it is, we serve him here. When we are not consorting with witches, that is. We try to live lives of penitence and mercy, for as long as it pleases Him to spare us.'

She took another step back, and she felt cold, inside and out. 'You have the plague.'

'Aye,' said the rope man. 'Brother Nathaniel is miraculously recovered and seems to enjoy God's ongoing protection. I confess that I do not. So we burn the bodies of those who come through that door to die on these lonely shores, just as I will be burned in turn. 'Tis a good cause, to keep these lands free from the disease, since we cannot do that for our own.'

'They come through that door?'

'A dozen a day, more this past fortnight.' He turned away and coughed long and hard. When he turned back, his sleeve was speckled with fresh bright blood, and his breathing was laboured. 'Witch though you surely are, you had better be gone on those wings of yours, or else stay with us for ever. These houses are nearly full, but there'll be plenty of room soon enough.'

She knew almost nothing about the Black Death, except that it killed thousands, was spread by rats, and it ended when London caught fire.

'You've gone nowhere else but this island?'

'Some try,' said Nathaniel. He lowered his club and tapped it in his empty hand. 'I persuade them to stay if I must. Most can be reasoned with, being honest Englishmen and women, though truth be told, there is no escape.'

She could tell him about the boats, how they grew up out of the sand. There was a portal here, and the lines of power connecting it with other doors to London would cut the coast in several places. Perhaps even the beach where she first spotted the skulls and crosses.

'I think you're very brave,' she said. 'It gets better. It really does.'

'Cold comfort from you,' said Nathaniel. 'John will take his place in the houses, and I will conscript some other damned soul to help me dispose of the dead. If that is better, then I do not know what is worse.'

'I'm sorry. I'll go.'

'Aye, go,' he said. 'Go before the door opens, and we have to be about our dread business.'

She definitely wasn't going to tell them about the boats. They'd quarantined themselves for a good reason, and she wasn't going to put temptation in their way. So she nodded and trotted back to the wall, climbing up on it and running along the top of it.

John called after her. 'Before you go, tell us if you can: where is this place? Are we in some cloister of England, or are these the foothills of Heaven?'

'Neither. It's just … Down,' she said, and she raised her hand in farewell.

10

Mama dumped herself next to Dalip on the crest of the dune and splayed her legs out in front of her. She took a while to get comfortable, wriggling the sand into shape with little movements of her hips and shoulders. Then she sighed.

'You know that girl's not coming back, don't you?'

Dalip chewed at his lower lip and, rather than answer, he reached between his knees for a handful of sand and let it slowly dribble away.

Mama nudged him in the ribs to get his attention. 'She's been gone all day. Either Crows did for her or, the other thing happened, as we all feared.'

There was nothing to see that he hadn't seen for himself every time he looked up. The beach, the bay, the sea, the distant island: that was it. Once in a while, a bird would drift into view and his heart would leap, but they were only ever regular seagulls and they broke his hope a little more each time. Now, the sun was going down and he was in pieces. Today's achievements had been to dig two graves, lose Luiza, lose Mary, lose the maps, lose the boat and lose Crows. They'd gained a handful of loose change and a plastic egg.

All in all, not a fair exchange.

'Perhaps she can't find her way back,' he said.

'We're like pimples on a face, Dalip. We're in plain view for all to see – we're the orangiest things in the whole of Down. No one is going to miss us here, least of all Mary.' She waggled her toes. 'We're the only ones left, so we have to decide what to do now.'

'We have to stay here, in case she comes to find us.' He remembered a similar argument, not so long ago, even though it felt like a lifetime had passed. He'd been on the other side then, persuading the others to move on and away from the portal, while Mama had been all for staying put. He made a face. 'I know how it sounds.'

'We can't stay, can we? We all understand why. There's nothing left for us here.' She gestured at the empty beach. 'We have no wood, no way to light it, no food, no way to catch it, and we can't hang around here for another boat because we can't go chasing after them when we have no idea where they went. We've got to get on with living as best we can.'

'What does Elena want?'

'That girl doesn't know what she wants at the moment. But the sure thing is, if we stay here she'll do nothing but weep over Luiza's grave, and I don't trust Down to leave her alone in her grief. Once this place has its hooks in you, it doesn't let go.' She leaned in, butting her biceps against his. 'Us three have to stick together, because this place is as cruel as it is beautiful.'

She knew she was right, and so did he. He'd had all those thoughts himself. 'We can't go anywhere now. It's going to be night soon.'

'We can go under the trees. It'll be warmer out of the wind.'

'But that'll mean ...' He clicked his tongue. She knew what it meant, which is why she suggested it. Get Elena away from her cousin, stop him staring out to sea. 'Okay. We'd better move while we still have some light.'

Mama hauled herself to her feet, using Dalip's shoulder as a brace. She held out her hand.

'Come on, Dalip. We can't give up now.'

That stung him. He wasn't giving up, least of all on Mary. She hadn't deserted them. Not when they were Bell's prisoners, and not now. So why would he give up on her? She wasn't dead, either. Not her.

He wanted to say something to that effect to Mama, but all that came out was a growl. He took her hand instead, and she pulled him up. He looked one last time towards the far horizon, and there was still nothing. How was all this possible, when the sun had risen on such promise? He deliberately turned his back and blotted out the view by descending the far side of the dune.

'We're,' he started. He still hadn't found the right words to say to Elena, and these weren't right either. 'We're going into the forest. We might not be able to light a fire, but I can build a shelter, or at least a windbreak.' He had a machete, so he wasn't promising anything he couldn't deliver.

Elena looked up from the heap of sand that covered Luiza's body. She'd placed flowers on top, and the plastic egg against the side of the dune at the head end. Those were the only things she had to lay there. Sikhs didn't mark graves – shouldn't even have graves – but this wasn't his relative or his religion and he didn't say anything.

Mama went around behind her and gently lifted her up, guiding her with an arm around her, whispering in her ear as she went. It was going to be okay, she said, when the truth was the worst had already happened, and it might never be okay ever again.

At least the forest was still there, and they camped in a little hollow in its scrubby fringes. Dalip found that the machete was incredibly useful: he could cut saplings, split them ready for weaving, sharpen stakes with the edge and hammer them in with the flat side, and chop undergrowth to cover the frame.

It was past twilight by the time he'd finished, and he was utterly exhausted. It was little more than a low semicircular trellis, with a rough roof lain across it, but it would have to do. Mama rolled in, and encouraged Elena to follow. By unspoken agreement, Dalip would sleep just inside the entrance. Best, perhaps, if any of the Wolfman's men were still hanging around, but that didn't seem likely. Tomorrow they too would be gone, in a direction yet to be decided.

He got down on the ground himself and stretched out. It was hard, and uncomfortable, but he'd forgotten what it was like to sleep on a bed, and was so tired at the end of every day that it didn't really matter any more. He lay there, not moving but for his chest and his eyelids, listening to the noises of the night. Mama and Elena were making little mutters as they turned and shuffled, and the softening wind made the shelter creak and scratch. Further out was the static hiss of fluttering leaves, and beyond that was the profound, deep silence of Down that threatened to drown out everything else.

The sky outside darkened to impenetrable black, and even the insects seemed to quieten. His thoughts started to become discordant as he began to drift off, amongst scattered moments of clarity that he would remember later.

Mary would be waiting for them when they woke up, sitting on the beach, wondering where they'd got to.

He could try to make fire: he had soft steel and hard stone to spark together, and plenty of time to practise catching bone-dry tinder alight.

The coins and jewellery would have value as refined metal and cut stones. Keeping them was more than a sentimental connection to home.

He didn't want to be responsible for Elena and Mama, but just because he didn't want to be, didn't mean he wasn't.

With his hand still curled around the machete's grip, he slowly fell asleep.

And just as slowly, he woke up.

Yesterday, the moon had risen some time after midnight, and

had still been in the sky in the morning before being chased away by the sun. Tonight, he could see the vague glimmer of silver through the woven walls of the shelter, and knew there were still several hours of darkness. That wasn't what had woken him.

There was a pressure, a weight against him, down his right-hand slide, pinning his arm and the machete against the sandy soil of the shelter floor. In his befuddled state, he couldn't work them free, and it was only when he pulled hard and Elena grunted against his chest that he realised she was almost lying on top of him, arm across him, leg hooked over his, her head in the hollow of his shoulder.

And he had an erection.

At least he managed to stop himself from panicking. He wasn't responsible for what happened in his sleep, and neither was she. If he could extricate himself without waking her then no one but him would ever know.

He took a couple of deep breaths to steady himself, and slid his leg out from under hers. She made no sign of stirring, and he took encouragement from that. Inch by inch, he eased himself away, and even managed to lift her head so that it rested on his arm rather than his shoulder. He reached under her for the machete, and carefully pulled it free.

Only his arm remained trapped, and there seemed no way of moving it without disturbing her. The situation was so foreign to his experience that he was desperate enough to try something he'd seen in a film once.

He bent over until his mouth was near her ear. 'Elena, roll over,' he whispered.

She murmured her assent and turned to face the other way, as Dalip slid his arm clear.

It had worked, and he was surprised, but now he had to creep away quietly and find somewhere he could wait his erection out. He tried to rationalise his shame away as he slowly stepped through the deep shadow, but however he tried, he was just embarrassed. His own body betrayed him – his cheeks burned with the still-warm memory of her pressed against him – and left him vulnerable to improper feelings of lust. There hadn't been time to build two shelters, but the thought hadn't even occurred to him, and it should have.

He was a grown man, not a boy, and sharing sleeping space with women wasn't going to help him keep pure. Especially Elena. He didn't know if he found her attractive. He didn't even know if he should be thinking about it, with Luiza not even cold in the ground.

He crouched down and remembered to breathe. It really wasn't his fault. They were all vulnerable, none of them thinking straight, and nothing untoward had happened. He was doing the right thing now, and that was what was important. He wasn't some beast who couldn't control himself: he was fulfilling his vows and keeping the faith.

There were two lights.

The moon was behind him, halfway up the dome of night, a quarter full and appearing as bone-white horns behind the haze of high cloud. Then there was a lesser glow, coming from the beach.

At first, he thought it might be a fire, and that the remains of the Wolfman's crew had come to the beach. Or Mary. But the light was constant and more blue than red, illuminating the cold mist that was collecting over the dunes. When he stood to check properly, he realised that it was roughly in the direction of both graves.

There was a chance that investigating was exactly the wrong thing to do. No one ever said Down was safe, and this might be one of the bad things that it might inflict on the unwary. On the other hand, if he didn't hurry, he might miss whatever it was. Down, even when it unleashed storms that required a sacrifice to dissipate them, seemed to have the knack of choosing the right victim.

He picked his way through the brush until he reached the dunes. Climbing the first one confirmed his suspicions, that the light was centred on Luiza and the boat-womb. The air above it shone with a luminous fog that must be visible for miles. It was a beacon – if Mary was up there, then she would see it. If not, then, well … whoever else was abroad would look up and wonder.

Dalip walked down to the slack, then up the other side. This was the dip in which he'd interred the Wolfman. No night-time light show for him, weighed down with a load of damp, dirty sand, just decay and corruption. The fog thickened, and glowed brighter.

He didn't quite know what he was going to find, but it was unexpected in that it wasn't something from Down at all. As he slipped down the dune, he could see the source of the light was the small plastic egg that Elena had placed as a grave marker.

He picked it up, and he could see his bones through the redness of his fingers, though he could barely look at all. It was bright enough to bring tears to his eyes, even though the egg itself was cool to the touch.

Was it technology from some future London, or was it magic? Would he be able to tell the difference? He hadn't been able to work out what the thing was before, but a portable light was a portable light and therefore had a high utility.

As he stood there, contemplating the marvel he held, he heard the unmistakable sound of a heavy chain, the metallic rattle of links as they passed over some solid object. For a moment, he thought of the Wolfman, but he was dead and gone and this noise was different anyway: slower and more reverential.

He put the egg back in its hollow and went to look out to sea.

There was a boat – no, a ship – off shore. In the moonlight, he saw its long, low shape and single mast, and the way both prow and sternposts arced towards the sky. It was big, too, judging from the small rowing boat that had been lowered over the side and was slowly splashing its way towards the gently sloping beach.

Now here was a dilemma worthy of the name. Other people had, without fail, brought nothing but trouble. Dalip should simply hide from them, wake the others and skip further into the forest. If these sailors had been drawn by the light, they could take it – if that meant them leaving him, Mama and Elena alone.

And yet, hadn't he just been thinking about the gifts that Down gave? Here, unbidden, was a ship that might take all of them to the White City, and it looked fast. Perhaps they might even beat Crows there.

If he was a good man on Down, then there had to be others, eventually. If it all went sour, then he could escape and go with his first plan. He took his courage in both hands, and his machete in one, and walked down to meet them.

There were three people in the rowing boat. The two rowers had their backs to him, but a man sat in the stern and spotted Dalip's silhouette on the shoreline.

'Hello!' he called brightly. 'Friend or foe?'

'That depends,' Dalip shouted back. 'Who are you?'

'Pirates,' came the reply, 'but the good kind.'

'I know enough about pirates to think you're lying.'

'Very well. I'm lying about being a pirate. But we do have a pirate ship.' The man got up from the stern and crabbed his way towards the bow, stepping over and between the rowers. 'If I throw you a line, will you take it?'

'Go on, then,' said Dalip, and a wet rope uncoiled through the air and smacked down at his feet. He scooped it up and wrapped it through his fists, pulling the line taut. The boat bobbed as the rowers lifted their oars clear of the water, and he walked backwards, pulling the boat through the last of the surf until the keel grounded hard against the sand.

The pirate captain jumped to the beach and scanned the rest of the shore cautiously.

'No one else? Just you?'

Dalip didn't know how to answer without knowing the man's intentions. He said nothing, just rested his hand on the handle of his machete.

'Can't be too careful, old man. Calling ourselves pirates usually scares away the baser sort of cove, but there's always one or two tricky blighters who spring something unexpected.'

The man nodded to his crew, and they stowed the oars.

'Yonder is the *Ship of Fools*,' said the man, 'and I am Captain Simeon. We saw your beacon light at sunset, and determined we'd see what great wonder or great peril caused such illumination.'

'Dalip Singh,' said Dalip. 'I'll take you to it if you like.'

'Gods,' said Simeon and leaned forward. 'A Sikh chappie. What a stroke of luck: Pater was ten years in the Punjab and had nothing but respect for your people. Came back riddled with malaria and a fondness for curry, mind. Forever going on about how bland our food was – drove Cook to despair.' He turned to his crew. 'Come on, then, men. Look lively.'

The two sailors clambered out of the boat and heaved it a little further up the beach. Both were shorter than Dalip, but considerably wider. They looked more than capable of being pirates.

'Right then, Singh. Lead on.'

Dalip started towards the dunes, and Simeon fell into step beside him.

'Why do you call it the *Ship of Fools*?'

'Well, it was called that long before I ever set eyes on it, long before I became captain, so I can't take credit for it. But everyone on board is a fool, so the name is most peculiarly apt.'

'I don't …'

'Fools for ever stepping through that door, Singh. For accepting this fate rather than the one God ordained for us. Cowards and fools, every man jack of us. Still, we make the best of it, right, Dawson?'

The square outline of Dawson gave a grunt that could have been yes.

'There was a fire. A big fire.'

'And you were at your wits' end, trapped like a rat, and opened a door. Was that it?'

'Pretty much. You?'

Simeon laughed. 'Oh, nothing so dramatic. My gambling debts had caught up with me, I'm afraid, and I was hiding in a broom cupboard under the stairs. The, shall we call them gentlemen, I owed money to – several hundred pounds at the time – were searching my lodgings upstairs. And when I say search, I do mean they were very thorough. I could hear my worldly goods breaking through the stout planks, and then heard their feet above my head. Some urchin, damn his eyes, on the promise of a shiny sixpence or two to keep mum and direct the dastards back on to the street, gave me up and gained a shilling for his troubles. Nothing for it, I thought. They could drag me out and do whatever they wanted to my mortal frame, or I could show them a clean pair of heels.'

'And you saw Down.'

'Indeed I did. I couldn't work it out at first, then like the impulsive idiot that I was, thought I'd chance it. Many adventures later, here I am. Not the same man, either.' Simeon paused long enough to twist his mouth into a sour smile. 'But everyone here changes, eventually.'

They were at the top of the dune, and Dalip pointed to the brightest part of the luminous fog.

'I buried one of my friends yesterday. I took the light from the man who killed her.'

Dawson slid down the slope and retrieved the egg, and held it up for Simeon to see.

Simeon rubbed his pointed chin for a moment. 'Just one question, old chap. Why did you let it shine?'

'We left it here to mark the grave, not knowing it was a light. But when I woke up, and found it like that, I ... what was the worst that could happen? We're pretty much beaten. We've nothing left but hope.'

'You do realise that one of those damned geomancers could be along in a minute to stitch you up like a kipper and drag you away to their lair?'

'We've already done that. Didn't fancy it much, so we escaped. Are you,' asked Dalip, trying to stop himself from pleading, 'taking on crew?'

'Who are the we?'

'There's three of us left. Everyone else is either dead or missing.'

'We have berths. It's an uncertain life, being a pirate, but I've found it's safer on the briny than land, and we're a merry band – Dawson notwithstanding. The rules are few, but we have to work together to protect our freedom. Jeopardise the ship and you're over the side, which is somewhat unfortunate if there's no land around. If you agree to follow my orders and learn to be useful, we'll take you aboard. What do you say?'

'I'll put it to the others.' Dalip thought for a moment, then dug through his pockets. 'I don't know if this means anything but I can pay our way.'

He held out two fistfuls of coins and let them fall into Simeon's cupped hands.

'Hah. I told you. Sikhs: good, honest men.' He tipped the treasure into his three-cornered hat. 'Go and fetch your fellows. We'll wait for you by the boat. Dawson: hide that light.'

11

'You are very quiet, Mary.'

She'd made shit up, about finding everyone dead and there being a slow, smouldering fire on which they all burned. It was close enough to the truth that she didn't have to tell him about the portal, because knowledge of the portal was power. If there wasn't a map of it in the crate, she'd draw it herself when she could. For now, she'd have to remember the shape of the land and the directions of the lines of houses.

What she said she'd found was excuse enough not to talk. The truth was, she didn't know how easy plague was to catch. She hadn't seen any rats, and the men hadn't got anywhere near her – but she'd touched the stone Nathaniel had thrown at her. That, surely, wasn't enough?

And if it was, she'd be making damn certain she gave it to Crows before she died.

How long? A day? Two? She should have asked. Or she shouldn't have hung around long enough to ask. All she had instead was uncertainty.

So, yes. She was quiet. Checking herself for fever, or a cough, or feeling sick. She felt fine, though. Tense, nervous, sad, but not ill.

'Just leave me alone.'

'Very well. I will, I believe, catch myself some breakfast.'

He hadn't taught her how to power the boat – not refused as such, more simply neglected to pass on the information – so when he collapsed the standing wave that pushed it forward, the wave travelled ahead of them and washed into the swell. The boat began to slow, and to bob.

Crows moved from the stern seat from where he controlled the rudder, to perch on the side. The boat tilted, and the waves lapped at the rail. Crows lifted his feet and pitched backwards into the green, churning sea. The splash he made was lost almost immediately. The boat righted itself and, just like that, he was gone below the surface. Moments later, a loop of scales rose from the surface, the water cascading from the edges of their overlapping edges, and a head, sleek and snake-like, leaned over Mary from a great height.

Mary stared into the glassy black eyes, determined not to look the least bit concerned. He could, easily enough, eat her. But she wouldn't go quietly: he could fit a small brown girl in his maw, but not a giant falcon. He risked the maps, if nothing else, and he didn't dare.

'Go, if you're going. It's not like we're moving while you're pissing around in the water.'

The head turned away and scanned the horizon. Looking for land, or the best place to fish? Who knew? The waves closed over the crown of Crows' black head and he was gone.

She waited a minute – actually counted out the seconds, one elephant, two elephant – then searched the boat from stem to stern.

Down had provided a locker at the pointed bow, and it was almost big enough for her to climb completely inside. She found coils of rope, heavy parcels of thick white cloth, and odd-shaped pieces of wood as long and thick as her forearm, square at one end, rounded at the other. There were paddles, too, short and broad.

A sail, then, and something for when the wind didn't blow. Dalip hadn't expected to move the boat by magic, and if there was a sail, there had to be a mast – she knew that much. When she turned around and looked properly beneath her feet for the first time, she saw the long tapered pole lying in the bottom, next to the beam of the keel. In the centre was a wooden bung, which she heaved out, and there was the hollow to receive the mast.

She couldn't lift it upright on her own. There were other lengths of wood too, but she'd exhausted her knowledge. There'd be no sailing away for her, and even if she could, she couldn't outrun Crows in serpent form. If she got the better of him in a fight, tied him tight with the rope so he couldn't change, then she was still stuck. Unless she was able to recreate the wave which chased them across the bay, that was.

Too many ifs. Her head was starting to hurt. What she could do, was what she'd already thought of: make a bag from sail cloth and carry the maps aloft, out of Crows' reach. She'd never been one for needlework, but she was willing to give it a go and, somehow, she was going to have to do it right under Crows' nose and not have him suspect anything. It was a plan, but she needed tools. A knife, at least.

She traced an uneven path, past the crate, to the back of the boat, and found two more cupboards, closed with little brass catches.

If there were sails, there might be a way to repair them. And there was: a series of thick, hooked needles as long as her finger, thread that was as stiff as wire, spring-gripped shears, curved knives with bone handles, squares of spare cloth.

At the very back of the cupboards, which shared one space between the two doors, was something like a small biscuit tin. She had to duck under the rudder arm in order to reach it, and she almost dropped it when she finally got her fingers to it, it was so surprisingly heavy.

She checked the four quarters of the sea for sight of Crows.

He wasn't there, so she sat down with the tin in her lap and wrestled it open.

It was a clock. No, not a clock, because it only had one long hand and there were no hours marked out. Well, it could be a clock, a Down clock that worked by its own rules. She lifted it up to listen to it and check for ticking, and as she did so, the hand pivoted about its middle, and the whole glass face rocked.

She put it back down and poked the dial, which not only moved under her touch, but turned every which way. The hand swung back and forth across the markings on the dial.

This was treasure. Not just the boat and the sails, but the needle and thread and this ... thing. And it had all been grown out of Down's land. She looked at it through half-closed eyes and it reminded her of Bell's brass instruments. Had Down given them to Bell, just as it had given her this?

A compass. There was only one direction marked, west, but if she gave it some thought, north and south should be easy enough to work out.

If she only knew how, she could now sail the oceans of Down, and navigate at the same time. Her breath came in quick, shallow pants. In the right hands – not hers, obviously – this was almost as good as a map, and she had it. She couldn't remember Crows showing any interest in the contents of the lockers. For him, the boat was simply a means of transporting the maps across the bay without getting them wet.

First things first. She checked again for Crows, and saw him in the middle distance, loops of his body rising and falling in the water. She had time, then.

The compass: lid on, and moved to 'her' end of the boat. Then she heaved up a corner of sailcloth and tucked it securely underneath. She went back for some of the spare cloth, the needles, the shears and one of the knives, and stowed it as far from the door as she could reach. It seemed dry enough in there, despite the sea being just the other side of the planks.

Then she dragged it all back out. That wouldn't work – she didn't need to hide the sail-making equipment, but to have a reason to have it out, on show.

She'd been cold last night. She'd make herself a cape: a big, all-encompassing cloak that she could turn, with a few tugs and folds, into a giant carrying bag. What could Crows do about that? He would gaze at her, and she at him, and she'd go back to her stitching.

There was only one problem with her plan. She didn't know how to sew. For sure, they'd tried to teach her but, as with so many other skills she'd been shown by well-meaning teachers, she'd abandoned the lesson because she didn't want to learn something so mundane. She could get her clothes from market stalls, or nick them from department stores, so why learn to hem and stitch and shape?

If they'd presented the task with a warning that her life depended on being able to make a buttonhole, she might have approached it – and her whole life – differently. As it was, she'd have to guess as she went along.

She took one of the squares – a piece big enough to cover a restaurant table – and cut it in two, then into four, so she had something to practise on. The needles were too fat to slip between the weft of the cloth, even when she wedged one against the side of the boat and tried to ram the cloth over it. She went back to the stern lockers and searched. She found one of the needles wasn't a needle, but a metal spike which would punch a hole clean through with a grunt of effort. The hole was big enough to squeeze one of the needles through, and the hooked end could work the cord-like thread after it.

She realised that whatever she was going to make, be it simple or complicated, it was going to take a fuck-load of time and energy. She almost gave up before she started, looking for an easier solution. Or she could just not do it, because she always avoided doing anything difficult.

Mary scowled at the cloth, the needle, the cord, and picked up the hole-maker. It was sharp enough in its own right to qualify as a weapon. Useful. Crows had better not come too close.

It was only when the boat tilted rather than rocked that she looked up from her work. Two brown hands were clinging to the side rail, the nails pinked with effort. An elbow hoisted itself up, and Crows' head appeared, then his foot hooked over. He tumbled, soaked, into the bottom of the boat, and lay there for a moment, before turning over to look at her and what she was doing.

'You took your own sweet time,' she snapped. She glanced up, then concentrated on getting the tension in her thread right. Too loose was no good, but too tight made the cloth bunch.

'What are you doing?'

'I'm doing something that's not quite as boring as staring out to sea, while waiting for you.'

'All that was here? The cloth, the needles?'

'Came with the boat.' She held up the piece she was working on, and gave the two halves an experimental tug. The seam stretched. It looked pretty amateur – she wasn't even sure she'd used a recognised stitch, and from Crows' expression, she hadn't – but at least it held.

'Is that so?' He raised himself up, and concentrated on driving the moisture from his clothes. Mist rose around him, as if he was steaming. A neat trick, and another she'd have to learn. He was joined at the rudder by a pair of crows, who rattled their beaks and clattered their wings before rising into the sky. 'We may have drifted,' he said. 'I must see where we are, before setting a new course.'

'It's almost like you know where you're going.' She didn't look up this time. 'Do you?'

'Whether I do or not remains to be seen,' he replied, not admitting one way or another.

She snorted. 'What is it with blokes and directions? Always too fucking proud to admit you're lost.'

'We are in Down,' said Crows. 'For some, that is lost, and for some, that is found.'

She searched the horizon for any sight of land, but saw none. It was water as far as she could see. She had never been this alone before in her life: her experience had always been the noise and chaos of a children's home, when there was always someone around. It was wealth and privilege that bought privacy, locked doors and high walls.

She started to laugh, and Crows looked at her as if she was deranged, which only made her laugh harder, until she was all but incapable of speech. She was rich, not in any way she could understand, but she was here to stay. Down was everything she'd ever wanted. It wasn't heaven, it was more like hell, but it made her feel alive.

'It is good to laugh,' said Crows, still not sure what to make of it, or her. 'After the … unfortunate incident on the beach, I thought your heart would always be sad.'

Mary panted for a while, and managed to sit upright again. 'Oh, you'll pay for that, one way or another, one day. And just so you know, when that moment comes, you're on your own.'

'Your friends have to catch me first.' A wave rose slowly from the deep and rolled towards the stern, at the same time a trough formed ahead of the bow. The boat pitched forward, and the sensation of movement, if not the visible signs of it, began.

'Don't write them off too fast.' She rearranged the sewing in her lap. 'They're full of surprises.'

Crows considered it. 'One old women, one scared girl, and your Dalip Singh, who is brave but naïve and simply too trusting to survive here. You should not pin your hopes on seeing them again.'

'Ever?'

'Down is vast, and ever is a long time. But Bell is not the only geomancer, and hers not the only castle. It would be a kindness if they were taken by someone else; at least, they would not then starve.'

'I'm not saying you're wrong. Just … you know. Stuff like that has a habit of coming back and biting you on the arse.' She punctuated her words with stabs of the hole-maker through the sail cloth.

'I will watch my arse carefully.' Crows folded his hands into his lap. 'You are right. Miracles do sometimes happen, and so may Dalip Singh.'

She made more holes, then started to thread them together. She would find a way to open the portals, get her friends home, and … then what? Would the chaos brought about by the geomancers end because she'd finally cracked the problem? Or would she have to fight them all, either one by one or in groups? Because she was up for that. The Red Queen's army would sweep across Down, opening every last dungeon and freeing every last captive.

'You are smiling,' said Crows.

'Am I? Just concentrating.' She needed the maps first, before any of that could happen. How long was this journey supposed to take? Probably not long enough, but if she was walking – or flying – she wouldn't be able to sew at the same time. Better get on with it. Stop daydreaming and stitch like it was all that mattered in this world.

Mama could do this sort of shit, she bet. Luiza and Elena too, maybe. Dalip – did Sikh boys get taught needlecraft? She thought probably not. So there was at least something she could do better than him. She pulled and sewed and tightened, frowning at the stiffness of the cloth and the springiness of the thread.

Yet when she tied a knot in the end of the line, and snipped off the excess with the shears, she was – if not happy – satisfied with the result. The two pieces of sailcloth didn't part when she pulled at them, and when she let go, they sprang back along the join. There were still things like drawstrings to consider, that would change a wearable cloak into a functional sack. There'd be no point in stealing the maps and then dropping them, one by one, into the ocean as the wind took them.

She had no idea about patterns or how to cut cloth in order to give it shape. There was no way around that problem: she'd just have to manage with as much guile and tenacity as she could muster. One thing was certain, and that was: she was learning. Her second attempt was far better than her first.

Crows was watching her closely, his eyes half-closed. She held up her handiwork for his inspection, and he pursed his lips and looked to one side.

This will be your undoing, she thought. Not magic, not power, not weapons, not cheating or lying, neither great plans nor sudden surprises, but this: your cynicism. I know what that's like, but I'm better than that now.

'You are smiling again.'

'Just, you know. Finding something I'm not bad at, after years of thinking I'm shit at everything.'

'Your stitching is workmanlike,' he said.

'What's wrong with stitching like a workman?'

He fanned his fingers wide. 'I could show you how to do better,' he said. 'Sailors have always had to mend their own clothes, even after the age of sail.'

This was better than her plan. Crows would show her how to stitch the bag she'd use to steal the maps.

'You're on. Can you do that at the same time as you move the boat?'

Whether he said yes or no, she had her answer ready.

'It would be,' he considered, 'difficult.'

'We're in no hurry, right?' Mary gathered up her practice pieces, the thread, the needles and the wickedly sharp spike. 'And I need something to do while you steer.'

She waddled towards the stern and dumped herself on the other side of the rudder.

'Now?' He seemed disconcerted by her eagerness to learn.

'Now,' she said firmly.

She'd backed him into a corner, and he had no graceful way out. He shrugged. 'It is a strange request, but, very well.'

He took the first of her attempts, snipped through the securing knot, and unthreaded in an instant what had taken so long to create. He selected a needle from the assortment, then arranged the work over his knees.

'Like this,' he said.

12

Once Dalip, Elena, and Mama had been manhandled aboard, the anchor was dragged up from the sea bed and the sail lowered.

Quickly, quietly, the ship headed out to sea, and the dark line of the shore slipped away.

The crew – difficult to count in the dark – numbered some two dozen. They seemed to know their duties, because they neither blundered nor swore at each other as they pulled on lines and lowered big boxes through hatches in the main deck.

Simeon warned them to keep out of the way, but nothing else. A few words with the steersman at the rudder, and he was off through the crew towards the prow, checking everything as he went.

The three of them huddled together, nervous. But, after a while, the activity slowed: some of the crew were assigned to take the watch, while the rest either broke into small groups to rest and talk, or individually to curl up on the broad deck and sleep.

Dalip listened to the creaks of the ropes and the soft flutter of loose canvas, and settled back against the bulwarks.

'Who are these people?' Mama hissed. 'And where are we going?'

'We're going wherever they're going. That's okay, isn't it? For a while, at least?'

Mama harrumphed, and put a thick arm around Elena, who sat between them, shivering. 'It may be the best offer we have, but I don't have to like it. If these men are pirates—'

'They just call themselves that—'

'And if I called myself a crack-head baby-killer, what'd that make you think about me, even if I wasn't one?'

She had a point, even if Dalip wasn't quite willing to concede it. 'We've sunk so low that an offer from a bunch of pirates is the best offer we have. We may end up chained to the galleys and rowing ourselves to death, or made to walk the plank, or whatever, but no one here seems to be a slave, and there aren't many places to hide them either.'

'Trusting folk hasn't exactly worked for us so far. They come to us with open hands and the minute we let our guard down, they close them into fists to beat us with.'

'I'm sorry,' he said. 'I've run out of ideas. And the time to argue was before we got into the boat.'

Mama would have usually folded her arms at that point, but one was still holding Elena tight. 'You never used to sass me.'

'This is the best I could do.' He looked up at the moon, now almost overhead, the mast drawing a line between sea and sky. 'We just have to hope that it's enough.'

'The boat is okay,' whispered Elena, so quietly that Dalip had to lean in to hear. 'It cannot be as bad as the beach.'

Perhaps it could. They might be about to find out. Simeon was now making his way back to the stern, his three-cornered hat marking him out from the others.

He pulled up one of the chests that was still on deck and sat astride it, his knees almost touching the boards.

'It's all shipshape and Bristol fashion. Tomorrow, we'll show you the ropes – because there's one thing this tub doesn't go short of, it's rope – and you'll see how it all works. Rules are very simple here on the good *Ship of Fools*: captain's law. If you disagree with that, now or at any point, you get put ashore at the next available opportunity.' He drummed the top of the chest with the flats of his hands. 'But we're all survivors here. There are no passengers on board, but there are no slavemasters either. Muck in, and you'll do perfectly well.'

Mama disengaged herself from Elena and moved forward. 'They're good words, Mr Simeon, fine words even, but we haven't seen much kindness from strangers hereabouts. What makes you so different?'

'All we want to do is live free. We don't want magic, we don't want castles, we don't want to own anyone or anything, save the skins we stand up in. We've escaped the madness of the land to cope with the more straightforward vagaries of a life on the ocean. We'll protect that way of life if we have to, damn the geomancers to Hell and back, but for the greater part, they leave us alone so long as we have nothing they want.'

'And us? What if they want us?' Dalip spoke into the silence.

'Hasn't happened yet, old man. To them, we're all pretty much interchangeable as planks or bricks, and there are lower-hanging fruit than taking on a band of bloodthirsty pirates.' Simeon slapped his knee, as if to prove his piratical credentials. 'We're also sailing away billyo from our last port of call. It's what we do: in fast, out quicker. Throw the pursuers off the scent and show them a clean pair of briny heels. Whatever happened back there, you're safe now.'

He changed, just like that, from pantomime caricature to someone possibly worthy of trust.

'Thank you,' said Elena.

'You are very welcome, madam. It's not often we get to save damsels in distress. Women, well: Eve's race is somewhat under-represented here.' He raised himself up on to the gently swaying deck and doffed his tricorn hat. 'Dawson will bring you your mess shortly. With that, goodnight. May we all live till morning.'

Mama waited until Simeon had stepped away before she reached over and tapped Dalip's knee. 'And just how is this supposed to get us home?'

The boat wasn't so long that a raised voice wouldn't be missed at the other end. 'Mama, keep it down.'

'I am not spending the rest of my days on this glorified rowing boat.'

'Where would you like to spend them?'

'Home. In London.'

He'd found them, after a day of chaos and grief and against all expectations, a place of respite: somewhere they might just be able to make sense of everything, at their own pace, in the company of people who weren't trying to either kill them or worse.

'I don't know what you want from me. We lost the chance to go home when Crows took the maps and Mary didn't come back. Something might come up that changes everything. Maybe we find Mary again, I don't know. For now, there's nothing I can do except learn how to steer a ship, raise the sails and row.'

'So we're not going to look for Crows?'

'This is not a taxi,' he growled. 'It isn't going where we want it to go, and it's not ours to command.'

Elena put one hand on Mama's shoulder, and one on Dalip's – which made him shiver. But rather than a light touch, she clawed her fingers and dug her nails in until neither could ignore her.

'We played at being geomancers. That is why we are here, and why Luiza is lost to us. If we want to keep playing, we will all die. Either we have to become like Crows, like Bell, like Mary and all the other monsters, and do it for real, or we stop playing, stop pretending that we are like them, and try to live our lives as we wish.'

The mention of Mary in the same breath as Crows and Bell surprised Dalip, but the pressure on his shoulder relaxed slightly, and he decided now wasn't the right time. Eventually, he nodded. 'She's right. I'm not ruthless enough,' he said, 'and neither are you, Mama.'

'I just want to go home,' she murmured. 'If only there was a way ...'

'It's what we all want.' Dawson appeared out the shadows. 'But it ain't happening.'

He set three bowls on the sea-chest that Simeon had used for a seat. Each was full of a variety of things that none of them could make out yet, so they didn't know whether to be pleased or disappointed. He slipped a waterskin off his shoulder and handed it to Dalip, who only worked out what it was by its weight. Then he left them without another word.

Dalip sighed. 'Mama, I wish I was better at this. I'll talk to Simeon in the morning, but I can't insist that the entire crew risks their necks to follow or fight with Crows. Whatever happens isn't up to me.'

He doled out the bowls, which contained dried fruits, nuts, and some kind of hard cracker that had to be gnawed on to soften. But it was food, and not unsatisfying, and they hadn't had to scavenge for it themselves. Working the waterskin required a certain amount of practice, but after dumping a good cupful straight into his face, Dalip managed to drink from it, and passed it round.

By the time they were done everyone, except the sailors needed to keep the ship on an even keel, was asleep. It was the small hours of the morning: the moon was racing ahead of them to the west, already touching the horizon and revealing a far distant and unknown landscape of ragged mountains that would have otherwise been invisible.

There were no stars to steer by, yet the helmsman seemed to be happy with full sail and a lookout. They had to know where they were: every sea had its hidden reefs and shoals, and every voyage held the risk of shipwreck. Either there was a secret, or he was missing something obvious. The land was in darkness – no lighthouses, no lanterns to mark even where it was. Perhaps it was simply familiarity from plying the same coast for years. Still, to navigate like that was a prodigious feat.

And with such thoughts playing in his head, Dalip fell asleep exactly where he lay.

His dreams were strange and he remembered nothing except this: that he was lost and alone and scared, and a great wooden ship swooped down out of the sky to rescue him. Everything else evaporated in the morning light, and he found he was wedged up against the bulwark of a Viking longboat, authentic in every detail, right down to the unfurled striped sail.

Puffy white clouds floated high above him, and the sun was coming up behind him, turning the sea a violent orange. The ropes strained and creaked, and the waves broke rhythmically against the steep sides.

Not a dream, then. But what kind of rescue?

He levered himself up and picked his way through the still crew to the prow.

'When do you sleep?'

Simeon didn't take his eye from the telescope, nor did he unwrap his arm from the dragon-headed prow.

'When I must. A captain is always on duty: his the command, his the responsibility.' He scanned the horizon and, finally satisfied, looked back at Dalip. 'The safety of my ship and my crew are paramount.'

'I'm sorry. I didn't mean to—'

Simeon used his lopsided smile. 'No offence meant and none taken. We are but minnows in the stream, and none will pay us more interest than the pike or the kingfisher. So, Singh: what say you? Will you join us, or is the pirate's life not for you?'

'Before I answer, I need to tell you something.'

'Oh, oh?' Simeon swung around and contracted the telescope against his thigh. 'A confession? You are secretly a prince of the Punjab, the girl a countess, and the lady is the Queen of Sheba?'

'It's not like that.' Dalip hesitated, before adding: 'It's about how we got here, and how you found us.'

'A story,' said Simeon. 'Will it be an honest one, or packed with fictions?'

'I'll make it as accurate as I can.'

'Good. Your captain deserves honesty.'

'We had a box,' said Dalip. 'A sea-chest like yours. Full of maps. Possibly all the maps. It's impossible to tell, because we only had them for a short while, and we were only able to go through a few of them, before …'

'Let me guess: before you lost them again.'

'Elena's cousin was killed. And, possibly, Mary. At least, she didn't come back.'

Simeon tipped his hat into his hand and tucked it under his arm. He dragged his fingers through his greasy hair. 'And who is this fell adversary of yours, that betrayed you and murdered your friends?'

'He goes by the name of Crows.'

Simeon said nothing, but his eyelid twitched.

Dalip bowed his head, but he shouldn't have been surprised. Even here, Crows was known and hated. 'I'm sorry for wasting your time, Captain. I'll go and find someone to teach me their job.' He started to retreat, but there were words thrown at his back.

'D'you know where Crows is now?'

'He's out here somewhere, heading for the White City. If it exists. If he knows how to find it.'

Simeon beckoned him closer again. 'What's his plan?'

'He stole our boat, and our maps, and left us for dead. He didn't share his plans, I …' Dalip shook his head. 'I think he wants to sell them, or use them to buy influence, or something. I don't know how it works.'

'And what was your plan, Singh?'

'We were going to put the maps together. They were all

fragments: mostly of one portal and one castle. But there were, I don't know, hints, that we could join them up and finally reveal the shape of where the portals are across Down. Even then, we don't know how to open any of them and make them go in reverse. It was a hope, that somehow the answers would fall out of a completed map. That was it. That was what we were going to do.' He shrugged. 'Out loud, like that: it sounds pathetic. You get caught up in the madness of it. No wonder the geomancers are all so ...'

'Unhinged?' offered Simeon, and Dalip nodded.

'It's cost us too much already. We need to give it up.'

'But part of you wishes that this dastard Crows pays through the nose for his murder and rapine?'

Clenching his fists, Dalip said: 'I'd kill him if I could.'

'Oh, there's quite a queue ahead of you.' Simeon fiddled with the brim of his hat before setting it back on his head. 'So he's heading for the White City – yes, he knows where it is, have no fear on that score – and with a king's ransom of maps? Well, now. That is interesting.'

'He can turn into a giant sea snake. He'd sink the *Fool* and kill everyone on board if he thought you were going to try to take the maps. I'm not asking that of you: in fact, I'm begging you to forget the whole idea and I'm regretting I ever mentioned it.'

'He can do that now, can he? A bit different from when we were lowly mates together, back in the day. He had no ambitions then, save survival – same as the rest of us poor dogs.' The captain put his foot up on the side and stared out to the north-west. 'Have no fear, Singh, old chap. It's perfectly right and proper that you've told me all this. Lots to think about.'

'I'll go and do something useful,' said Dalip.

'Yes, it's good to keep busy.' Simeon seemed overly distracted by something in the far blue distance. 'The Devil makes work, eh?'

Dalip wasn't quite sure what that meant, but he took it as a dismissal. Many of the sleeping crew were now stirring, but even so the deck seemed too large, and too empty. There weren't enough of them to make it look full. It could easily have held twice their number.

And yet, if everything he knew about Down was true, these few were the only truly free people. Everyone else, all the refugees from disasters and dilemmas, were either held in thrall by the geomancers, living secretly and desperately, or dead.

It was pitiful. Down was a way out, a fresh start, and it had been corrupted by the very people it had saved. Rather than living lives of duty and honour, enough had chosen the way of selfishness, greed and violence to poison the land for all. The sea only remained pure because it had no portals.

If that was the way it had to be, then he would accept it. The maps were lost, Grace was lost, Stanislav dead, Luiza dead, Mary gone. He'd accepted life as a pit fighter. Why not a sailor? He was young and strong and, apparently, brave. Neither was he afraid of hard work.

Two men were starting to unfurl the gathered sail. Dalip took a position behind them and gathered a length of the loose rope in his hands. His fingers, already calloused, gripped the damp fibres, and waited for instruction.

13

Crows controlled the boat's speed and course, and guarded the trick of creating a standing wave closely. Mary had seen him do it often enough to think she could probably crack it on her own without accidentally summoning some nameless creature from the deep, given some practice, but he never left her alone for long or ranged far enough for her to do so in secret. She had her sewing to keep her occupied during his fishing trips, and she was learning patience. She was certainly learning how to ignore the hollow feeling in her stomach and the increasing thirst that was drying her throat to a croak.

'How much further?'

It could be a way of forcing her off the boat and away from the maps. He could simply circle the same patch of empty ocean until she was compelled to take to the air to search for water and food. Could she find him after that? She didn't know how far away the nearest land was – or rather she did, and it was infested with plague. She'd have to find somewhere on the mainland, or another island in the bay which had fresh water, and then hunt for something raw and bloody and substantial.

'A way,' he said.

Fine. That was how he was going to play it. He underestimated her resolve to stick to him like glue.

'Then next time, bring me some fucking fish, okay?'

'A simple enough request, but we have no fire to cook them. I do not think—'

'Look, what's that stuff the Japanese eat? It's fish, right? And it's not cooked. So it's either that, or land the fucking boat somewhere.'

He spread his hands wide, fanning his fingers. She'd come to realise that the gesture meant he was giving in. 'Perhaps by the end of the day.'

'Or earlier? Can you manage that?'

'Perhaps.'

'Good.' She'd called his bluff. If he thought that she'd suffer in silence, or plead with him, then he was wrong. She bent over her work again, and pretended not to notice that the sun slid over the stern of the boat and over to her left. He'd changed course. He knew where they were going.

Facing away from the bow meant all she saw when she glanced up was Crows and, behind him, the horizon. When she next happened to glance over her shoulder, and all she saw was cliffs, she couldn't help but stand and back away.

The rock was hard and grey and jointed. Heavy, worn blocks littered the wave-swept shelf that had formed at its base. She looked up and up, and the cliff did nothing but loom back at her. The swell rose up to the shelf, spilled white foam across it, then sucked down by her height and more. It looked lethal.

'Is this it?' she asked.

'No,' he said. The bow eased around and aimed for the next headland. 'But it is not far now.'

She should have heard the booming of the waves against the shore – it was all she could hear now – and it both angered and worried her that she'd let herself get so distracted. If she was going to beat Crows, she needed to be sharper than that.

The bow crested the promontory, and she had her first sight of the bay beyond. It was deep, and the cliffs high like battlements. A cobble beach ran for part of its length, and on it lay the bones of boats like rotting whales, their timbers gone and only the ribs remaining. Hollow, gaunt and bleached by the salt sea.

And there were so many, of every size, from child-like rowing boats, fit only for a trip around a duck pond, to broken-back ocean-going ships, whose curved timbers reached up like praying arms to the sky.

'Everyone comes to the White City,' said Crows. 'Sooner or later.'

All of those boats, sailed or rowed into the bay, abandoned and left to be dismembered by time and tide. It was ... real? The White City was actually real?

The boat slowed, began to bob with the waves, then started to drift towards the sheer cliff.

'Crows? Not so close.'

He tutted, and kicked the ship's mast and tackle aside to reveal broad-bladed paddles. He passed one to her, and took the other himself. He took a position on the rear left, and indicated she needed to hang over the front right.

Her strokes were fast and ineffective to start with, and the rock shelf was just off the side, near enough that she could almost use the paddle to push against it.

'From here, we must do this for ourselves. Long, slow and steady,' Crows directed. He leaned over and in, and the bow inched over. She reached down and tried it. Her arms pulled and her muscles burned.

The boat seemed to hang in space, not moving away, held by some invisible force. She pulled again and, gradually, they broke free.

It was cold, and still, and it grew colder and more still the deeper into the bay they drove. The sound of the moving water echoed off the rock and made her want to whisper. There were ghosts here, and she didn't want to disturb them.

'How long has this been going on?'

'For as long as there has been time here.' Crows pointed towards an almost-empty spot between wrecks. 'From the founding of Down to its end, this bay, this beach: this is the way to the White City.'

She looked down through the reflecting surface of the water to the sea bed. It was littered with the disarticulated remains of many more vessels, planks and masks and keels, encrusted with weed and shells.

'Stroke hard,' said Crows. They were heading straight for the gap on the beach, and he clearly intended to strand the boat as far up as possible.

The hull scraped, and she caught hold of the side, bent her legs and braced. The whole boat roared and rattled. Then it tipped, spilling her against the side, and her thread and needles on top of her. The box of maps slid slowly against the same side, and she put out a hand to steady it, making certain that it wasn't going to pitch over and out into the surf.

Crows walked over it, over her, and jumped the short distance to the cobbles. He straightened himself up and placed his hands in the hollow of his back, staring at the back wall of the bay.

Mary looked up from amongst the debris and followed the direction of his gaze. There was a notch at the base of the cliff, little more than a dark smudge. She stared harder, and finally saw it. Obscured by the shadow was the start of a staircase, barely more than steps crudely cut into the rock.

'Up there?'

He nodded.

'Fucking hell. They don't make it easy, do they?'

'No. Not easy at all.'

She gathered up her strewn sewing, and everything else she thought she might need from the forward locker. She hid the compass in the folds of a spare square of canvas, and piled it all next to her. Righting the map box, she unclasped it.

Crows watched her as she carefully placed the cloth and tools on top of the maps, and just as carefully closed the lid again.

'Why are we adding to our load?' he asked.

'Because I want to.'

'You may change your mind.' He stepped closer and reached into the boat for the nearest of the rope handles.

She pushed the box up and along the top rail, so that Crows could drag it out above the surf line. She jumped over the side after him, and clattered wearily up the beach. Her dress was the only splash of colour in the graveyard of ships.

Looking back at their boat, she asked: 'What's going to happen to it now?'

'It falls apart. It has outlived its purpose. Houses without people, castles without kings, boats without crew. They all decay.'

Mary picked up the other handle, and made they their awkward way to the base of the cliff.

'But these haven't rotted, have they? They're not being sucked back into the ground, they're being broken up. What is it that's different here?'

'There is no magic.'

'Down's blind spot.' She remembered what Dalip had said, though it felt like years ago. 'But I thought that was just something Dalip made up.'

'Yes. Dalip Singh, for all his protestations, understands Down better than most. So, from now on, we cannot rely on our other abilities: just on our wits and our luck.' He pursed his lips. 'We do not travel to the White City because it is safe. We travel because it is necessary. I thought you understood that.'

They were at the bottom of the steps, and Mary was able to comprehend their full terror in one sweeping look. They were carved, one tread at a time, into a fold in the cliff face. The narrow crevasse was angled only slightly away from the vertical, and in places seemed to be little more than a ladder with no-where to cling.

'You have got to be fucking kidding me.' The height didn't scare her, rather it was the utter ridiculousness of it. 'Someone made that?'

'Most likely many someones.'

'I can't climb that.'

'We have to. Together. You cannot fly to the top – and I cannot support the weight of the box on my own. Not all the way up.'

'Is this it? Can't we sail around the coast until we find an easier way? Because this is fucking nuts.'

She couldn't see the top, even though she knew it was there.

'If we want to get to the White City from here, we must use this stairway.'

She was dizzy, and on the verge of agreeing with him, when she realised she wasn't in any fit state to do what he wanted.

'No,' she said. She turned her back on him and sat down on the cobbles. She could hear his weight shift on the stones behind her as he considered his options. Perhaps he really couldn't climb with the box. Perhaps it was a trap – another one – for her. It was probably both. 'I didn't come all this way to be shafted by you now.'

'I understand,' he said. He wasn't going to let it stop him, of course. He was Crows, and it was his nature.

She could sulk all day if she had to, and the silence thickened about them.

'How are we to do this, then?' he finally asked.

'Find me something to eat and something to drink, and then, if I feel strong enough, I'll help you.'

'But there is nothing here, Mary.'

'You should have thought of that before bringing me to the one place on Down where I could find myself a thousand feet up without wings. Or is that what you wanted? Rather than having to push me off the cliff yourself, you get to watch me fall off it instead? Well, fuck you.'

She reached down for a fragment of bleached wood and held it up in front of her. She snapped her fingers at it, and nothing happened. She tried again, because just once was never going to be enough. The wood was dry and brittle, and should have caught alight easily, but it wasn't happening.

'What we want is at the top,' he said.

'Then go and get it for me. I'll wait here and look after the box.'

'This is not unfolding how I imagined it would.'

'What? You with the maps at the top of the cliff, and me at the bottom, broken as these boats?' She threw the wood away and hugged her knees. 'I'm not stupid, Crows.'

'I had better begin, then.'

'Yes. You'll be back sooner that way.'

She listened carefully. He didn't move for a while, and it was just the sound of his breathing. Then the cobbles creaked and clacked as he went to the bottom of the first step. The slight grunts he made as he climbed faded, and after a while, she looked surreptitiously over her shoulder.

Crows was perhaps a quarter of the way up. It looked for all the world like he was just hanging in the air, the steps indistinguishable from the rock face they were carved from.

He took another step, and rose a little further. He seemed to have no interest in looking down: as a child of high-rise blocks of flats, vertigo wasn't a problem Mary suffered from. Coming down again was going to be hard on Crows if he did.

She moved the short distance to the map box, and sat down next to it, waited another moment or two, then nonchalantly undid the clasps. Her sewing was nestled in the top, and she retrieved all the pieces and laid them out on her lap.

Did she have time for this? Possibly. Was this the plan? No. Was this the only chance she was going to get? Yes, yes it was. Even though she couldn't turn into a falcon and fly away with the maps, she could still bag them up and climb the cliff herself. While Crows was doing whatever he thought necessary to persuade her up, she'd be already halfway to the White City.

As for which direction to head – it was a city. How hard could it be to find? And once there, she could lose herself in its streets and he'd never find her.

All she had to do was sew up the two halves of the cloak, deliberately left unfinished, and with a few deft tugs, the seams would tighten and become a functional, if not pretty, kit bag. The holes were already punched, and she was sure she could whip through this in a few minutes.

She checked on Crows' progress. A third of the way up. She could do this, if she concentrated.

She kept making mistakes, and having to go back on herself. She blinked and scrubbed at her face, and the thread she was using swam in and out of focus.

She deliberately poked herself in the leg with the hole-maker, hoping that the pain would sharpen her senses, and it did, for a little while. Her sweaty, trembling hands couldn't grip the needle properly, and she almost fainted – or fell asleep: she couldn't tell which.

Crows was almost invisible, his black cloak merging with the shadows. Magic or no, he was still very difficult to spot.

She kept on, and when she was finally finished, she put it all aside and staggered down to the sea.

The cold was biting, sharp like teeth on her arms as she plunged them in. She knew what she was going to do next would hurt, and she was right. Her head and neck submerged, and the effect was like a slap. She was awake, and gasping, almost howling her breaths. She still had to climb.

People had been subjected to worse than being a bit hungry, a bit thirsty. There was a refugee kid in the same hostel as her, who'd walked across half a continent with his clothes hanging off him. If he could do that, she could do this.

She looked up, and couldn't see Crows.

She picked her way to the open box, and the maps stirring in the soft breeze. She looked at them, and having dried her hands on the back of her dress, she pressed down on them, compressing their volume and making it much more likely that she could carry them all off.

She laid out her sail-canvas cloak on the ground, and started shortening the seams, pulling the thick thread a little at a time along its outer length, gradually bunching the cloth up until she had a deep pocket.

Slowly, it changed. She needed a way to fix it to her – some of the sail lines from the boat would be just right – but it was as good as it was going to get. She took the first handful of maps, and laid them gently at the bottom, then went back for more. The box gradually emptied as the bag filled.

The compass went in on top, and she couldn't help unwrapping it for a look before tucking it away again.

The needle swung lazily around, and settled to point resolutely inland. If that was meant to be a sign, then she'd take it as one.

She worked the thread tighter, and gathered the loose material in her fist. She lifted it up to test it. It turned out that a pile of loose papers weighed a fair amount, but much less than the crate they lived in.

Now to cover her tracks. It took her three goes to get the chest far enough up against the side of the hull for her to get underneath it and finally topple it back inside. If that was difficult, she now had to put her shoulder to the prow of the boat. At first, it wouldn't move, not even a little. She knew, frustratingly, that Dalip would have had the answer, but she was too tired to try and think like him, and all she could do was swallow down the rising bile, redouble her efforts and push all the harder.

The keel rasped, and the cobbles rattled.

She put both her hands against the wet planks, and like a miniature Atlas, tried to lift the world. The boat slid back down towards the sea with a jerk, and then stopped. A wave came in and raised the stern slightly, then it retreated. Mary slumped against hull, gasping. Another wave, another slight rise and fall of the boat.

One last go. She waited, and watched, and pressed her back to the underside of the curved bow, and waited some more. Then the instant she felt the wood shift, she dug her feet in and heaved against them. She fell backwards, and tumbled into the surf, but the boat was back in the water. It bobbed and bucked, and with each cycle of wave peak and trough, it floated a little further away.

She dragged herself back to shore, and watched for a few seconds more. The boat was now side on to the beach, and drifting towards the rocks.

She didn't know if it would work, but if she, the maps, and the boat had all disappeared by the time Crows got back, then of course he'd go and look for her.

She wouldn't be here to be found, though.

Mary wrapped a cut line of rope around her waist, once, twice, and fastened it. The ends went through punched holes in the sail cloth, and tied tight.

She was ready. She had no idea what waited for her at the top of the cliff, but it had to be better than whatever Crows had planned for her. All she had to do now was to put one foot up on the first stone step and begin.

14

The prow of the *Ship of Fools* nosed into the cove. Dalip, taking his cue from the other rowers, shipped his oar and held it upright. He looked behind him to see where they were heading.

From the open sea, the island had looked little more than a hummock of green. Closer up, it was surrounded by wall-like cliffs. Simeon unerringly guided the ship towards them and a gap in the palisade appeared. He ordered the sail to be furled, and the oars broken out.

Dalip rowed, like Elena and Mama rowed, inexpertly. But by watching and learning, he could keep stroke, and not crab his oar. By the time the opening narrowed to barely twice the width of the hull, he'd mostly got the hang of it.

They raised their oars to allow the grey walls to slip by. The cliffs softened, and then sloping land met the sea at an arc of white sand. It was a hidden anchorage, safe from storms, and somewhere to rest: a pirate hideout, even.

The oars went back into the square-cut holes in the bulwark, and they rowed cleanly and crisply towards the beach. The keel grounded – Dalip felt the gentle lift under his feet – and that was all there was to it.

The oars were stowed away again, and the sea-chests. The

deck was cleared, and even the mast demounted. It didn't take long, and when it was done, the crew either jumped over the side or lowered themselves down into the thigh-deep water.

Mama wasn't so keen.

'Where are we, and why are we doing this?'

'This is shore leave, good lady,' said Simeon. He batted his hat against his leg, and scrubbed some of the remaining salt off with his sleeve. 'There are no portals here, and there is nothing else of worth to a geomancer either. As long as we are discreet, we may come and go as we please.'

Mama went to the side and looked down. 'Have you a ladder?'

'We have rope.'

'Well, you'd better get me some of that, or I'm going to be here all day.'

Elena went first, and helped support Mama's weight as she was lowered down. They waded ashore, and Dalip watched as the other crew wended their way inland.

'Where are they going?'

'There's a hollow, where fresh water collects. There are huts too, and fire pits. And before you ask, no.' Simeon looked sour. 'We can't settle here. One or two, perhaps, but there are no native trees here, and nowhere that'd grow houses or boats. The people who stayed would be marooned. That, Singh, is our problem in a nutshell. Everywhere we might rest our weary heads is so frightfully dangerous that we daren't so much as close our eyes.'

'You've got several of these secret anchorages, dotted about the coast?'

'And in time, you'll learn how to find them too. We use them for rest, mainly. This is no pleasure cruise, but a hard life, marked out in leagues and fathoms. I wasn't always captain of the *Ship*, and I won't be captain for ever. Someone else will pick up this hat one day, pop it on their noggin, and there'll be a new captain to guide this motley crew.'

Dalip had wondered about that, and saw his chance to ask.

'So how do you do it? You don't have a compass, or a clock, or a sextant even.'

'Well, how do mariners in your age find safe passage to port?'

'I don't think you'd believe me even if I told you.' But perhaps he was underestimating the man. 'It's a box, and it tells you where you are to within a few metres. Or feet. It talks to … artificial moons that circle the Earth far beyond the atmosphere. That's how.'

'There are,' and Simeon smiled wistfully, 'older ways that serve just as well. One is to simply know the coast, and recognise where you are. There's the sun and the moon to help with the cardinal directions, and if you don't stray too much off your patch, then you don't stay lost for long.'

'And if there's a storm?'

'You beach the boat if you can, run before it if you can't.' He slapped the ship's timbers. 'The tub's good and seaworthy, and floats like a cork. It'll take more than a storm to sink her.'

The one storm Dalip had lived through had been a vicious, living thing, intent on taking a life. He didn't want to face another any time soon, but the thought of being at sea while it raged was …

Simeon saw his sceptical face. 'Oh, it's batten down the hatches and all hands on deck, splice the mainbrace and tighten the lines. But we've done it before, and we'll do it again. Blow wind, and crack your cheeks!'

'*King Lear*,' said Dalip. 'Act three. Scene two. Did it for an exam.'

'Did you not do it for the love of it?'

'There wasn't really the time for that, I'm afraid. My loss, I expect.'

'Come on, man. We're here jawing, while the company makes merry without us. Over the side and to shore.' Simeon launched his hat like a three-cornered frisbee on to the beach, and vaulted the side. He splashed down and waded ashore.

Dalip, like Mama before him, frowned at the distance, but eschewed the rope and lowered himself down, arms, elbows, fingertips, then let go. He was wet up to his knees, that was all. The water was cool, and the sand soft.

Simeon shook his hat out and settled it back on, and they walked the path trodden through the grass inland.

'I've been thinking,' said the captain, 'about what you said.'

'You should forget about it.'

'There's plunder to be had, and what sort of pirates would we be without a treasure chest to chase?' He snapped off a spiky length of grass and chewed its fat, moisture-laden end. 'I'm tempted.'

'It's just a bunch of maps. How long have the geomancers been trying to open a portal back to London?'

'For ever. Since the first Adam stepped foot in Down. Here's the rub, though: they've singularly failed because they fight each other rather than share their precious knowledge. This is our chance to steal a march on every man Jack of them, and put those damnable maps to work. Take them somewhere out of their reach and study them at our leisure.'

'And as soon as word gets out, every geomancer in the land will be breathing down our necks.'

'We won't be on land.'

'Some of them seem to be able to fly.'

'They won't find us, Singh. Do you know of any geomancer who'd willingly share the location of every single map in Down?' He snorted. 'They'd kill each other first. And if we're quick, they'll never even know.'

'We'd have to fight Crows.'

'We have to kill Crows,' corrected Simeon. 'But you're forgetting one thing: the White City is the one place where magic doesn't work. A gang of bloodthirsty pirates can overpower him as easily as they could you or me – easier, I'd say, because the dastard isn't used to honest violence.'

'He doesn't like fighting. He does anything to avoid it.'

'Then we have him. No mercy, a bit of cold steel, and his treacherous ways are over.'

'You make it sound simple,' said Dalip.

'It's a good deal less complicated than bearding the King of Spain.'

Below them was the hollow Simeon had mentioned, where rainwater collected and crude circles of stone were spaced around it.

'What will they think?' Dalip nodded down at the crew. 'Will they follow you?'

'I can put it to them. The question they'll put to me will be "is it worth it?" What do you say, Singh? Will any good come from taking the maps, or will we be engaging in such folly that we'll be truly worthy of our ship's name?'

'I can't answer that,' said Dalip, 'but the geomancers think so.'

'Say I was a gambling man. Say I was willing to stake everything on this. Tell me what would happen if they were wrong.'

Dalip puffed out his cheeks. 'If they're wrong, proving them wrong will mean, at the very least, they won't be able to hold the idea of going home over people's heads. On the other hand, if they're right, we can offer a trip back to London to everyone who wants one.'

'Those sounds like odds I can live with.'

'But are they odds you'll die for? And ask other people to die for? Look, I don't know anything about the White City, where it is, how dangerous it is, who lives there, who runs it, or anything. I'm guessing you know a little more than me, but that doesn't mean much.'

Simeon wasn't to be dissuaded. 'I know how to find the White City, though I've spent half a lifetime avoiding it. In fact, I've spent so long running away, I've forgotten what it's like to have a mission, a purpose in life. And by George, my dander's right up. Maps or nothing. Death or glory.'

'Tell me again how you got into debt?'

'Pish. That was entirely different. I'm older and wiser now, and a damn sight more careful. I'm a captain by election, not some greenhorn lieutenant straight off Eton's playing fields.'

'And were you?'

'Yes. As a matter of fact, I was.'

'And Mary thought I was posh.'

The men glanced at each other, both with one raised eyebrow.

'Are you sure about this?' asked Dalip.

'I'll treat the others, see what they say. But you have to appear to be of firmer mind than you are if this caper is to be put in motion: if I call on you, you'll have to have your powder primed and ready to discharge. How's your flint? How's your steel? How's your resolve? Ready to bring Crows to book, or will you neglect natural justice?'

Dalip held his hands up in surrender. 'I'll do it, I'll do it. Against my better judgement, but okay.'

'Good man.' Simeon slapped him on the back, making Dalip stumble forward. 'We'll do it tonight, when the fires are lit and their bellies are full.'

They walked down into the hollow, and while Simeon made his way around the crew, Dalip found Mama and Elena by the side of the pool. Mama had her feet in the cool, clear water.

'We have to drink that,' said Dalip, sitting down beside her.

Mama pointed to the swimmers over on the other side, and wriggled her toes. 'My feet aren't so much the issue. So what were you and Mr Simeon talking about?'

Dalip looked around to see who was near. 'Not now.'

'No?'

'No. You'll know what's happening, when it happens. But let's change the subject.' He took a deep breath and leaned forward. 'Elena, are you all right?'

She was the other side of Mama, knees up, arms tight across them, her head on her hands. She nodded. He thought that was the only thing he was going to get out of her, but she turned her face towards them.

'Luiza was always the strong one. She pushed harder, argued more. She pulled me behind her, sometimes where I did not want to go. Our village was poor: we had hard lives, but we had family and friends. She wanted more than that. She wanted money and clothes and good times, and she would do what she needed to do to get them. In London, we were still poor and we still had hard lives, but we only had each other. She wanted to stay, so we stayed. Things, they got better, slowly. Our English, too.' She wiped away a tear that was tickling across the bridge of her nose. 'She is gone, and now I must make my own way in the world. I have to become strong, like her. This is what I choose.'

'Don't you worry yourself,' said Mama. 'We'll take care of you. Right, Dalip?'

He thought about them hunting down Crows: nothing but an open boat against a sea serpent.

'Right?' repeated Mama.

'We'll do our best,' he said, and felt like an utter bastard when Elena sniffed and smiled back.

Perhaps there'd be a way of them avoiding being on board when the time came – they could simply ask to be left on the island, because while Simeon said that it wouldn't support all, it could be home for few people, for a short time. Or he could just put them ashore on the mainland, away from any portal, for the duration, and come back for them once all the dangerous adventure was over.

He excused himself and went to help raise the roofs of the huts, and dig out the firepits. Once it was dark, the fires would be lit using bunkered wood, and fresh food cooked, and the mere idea of it made his shipmates excited. Even Dawson, who cracked a chip-toothed grin as he and Dalip wrestled with one of the hut centre poles.

'Hot meat and grog,' he offered. 'It's a good day.'

By grog, Dalip assumed he meant some sort of home-brew spirit, because rum, and the sugar cane to make it with were conspicuous by their absence. And even the thought that a hot meal and getting drunk was the best Dawson had to look forward to was depressing, because if they didn't go after Crows, that was all any of them had to look forward to. A life of sailing the same seas with a full watch, going ashore to grab supplies from a hostile shoreline, and only occasionally making safe harbour – and the only release would be death. They were free, but what were they doing with their freedom? There was nowhere to put down roots, and build up a society worth living in.

'I know this will be a stupid question, Dawson, but where are the children?'

'What d'you mean?'

'One person's told me that their mother and father met here on Down, and had him, and Down was all he knew. But he was a liar. I've not seen a single child. Not here on board, not in the castle where I was – there were men and women, but no children.' Dalip grimaced. 'I know how babies are made, so ...'

'Well,' said Dawson. He wiped the sweat from his forehead and scratched behind his ear. He kicked at the floor and slapped the centre pole hard enough to make it shiver. 'There just ain't any.'

'Don't people still,' and he started to colour up, 'do it?'

'They do, when they can.'

'But no one gets pregnant?'

'Well, the men don't for sure.' He looked bemused by the question. 'But neither do the lassies.'

Dawson picked up one of the roof spars and rested it in the slot, and Dalip lifted its opposite number into place.

'Doesn't that strike you as odd?'

'I suppose, but that's not the oddest thing about Down, is it?'

He was right. Of course he was right. It wasn't.

'Thanks, Dawson.'

Dawson shrugged. To him, it meant nothing, but to Dalip it was another piece of information, to be reconciled with everything else, something he had to fit into the architecture of Down, along with the portals, the lines and nodes of power, the magic and the beasts. If the maps were a jigsaw, Down's mysteries were too.

What would happen, assuming it was possible, if he put them all together to make a Grand Unified Theory of Down. If the geomancers were right, they were so very wrong at the same time. The maps were only part of it – though a small, vital part – and in themselves meant little. Like fighting over a single cog when the rest of the mechanism was scattered.

Dawson was waiting for him to put the next roof beam up, patiently, almost bovine in his acceptance of his building partner's faraway look. Dalip hefted it and dropped it into place.

So this was his destiny. Oh, he'd still kill Crows if he could. But this: had it ever occurred to anyone else to try and stitch all the seamless elements into a whole cloth? Of course it had, and he knew they'd all failed, because success would have meant absolute power for someone. What had they done wrong, and what was he going to get right?

When Simeon made his pitch tonight, he was going to be able to speak in its favour, with all the passion he could muster. The maps weren't the key: they were going to show the pattern of the lock. The key would follow. He didn't know what form it would take, or how he would make it, but he felt, for the first time, confident that it could be done.

He lifted the next spar into position, and they were finished. It was time to move on to the next one. Others would cover the roof with cloth, and then the sun would set, the fires be lit, and the grog broken out. There was a purpose to it now, and Dalip couldn't wait.

15

First a finger, then a hand, then a head, and Mary could finally see the land beyond the top of the cliff. She reached out for the last flat stone, slapped her palm down on it, and heaved herself up. She didn't have much strength left, but the sight of the short, scrubby bushes that dotted the inland slope gave her just enough encouragement to tip her body over the final ledge and crawl forward until her feet were no longer dangling over the precipice.

She lay there for a moment, feeling almost floaty, before rolling over on her back and reaching between her legs for the length of rope that ran taut over the edge. Her arms were so weak, they were trembling, but the longer she allowed herself, the higher the risk of Crows coming back.

She hooked the rope, pulled carefully until the sack appeared just above the top step, then inched across so she could lean over and lift it clear. It was stupid, really. She never used to be cautious, but then again she'd never had to expend so much effort to do anything. It was always easy come, easy go: now that a single mistake could spell the end of everything, she was meticulous.

The canvas bag creaked as she hugged it. That was half the hard thing done. Now for the other part: get to the White City without Crows spotting her. Firstly, she needed to move away from the staircase, and quickly. The scrub would help hide her, but it'd also hide Crows' approach, and he needed no encouragement to sneak.

She scrambled off, sometimes on two feet, sometimes on all fours, until she'd put some distance between herself and the coast. The booming sound of the sea lessened, and the cold north wind rattled the gnarled branches around her. She crept under a bush, where the soil was bare and dusty and the black wood knitted a shelter of twigs and leaves over her head. She was exhausted, and she had to keep going. She knew that. She wasn't safe.

She was woken, just as it was getting dark, by a cry of loss and anger.

She sat up with a start, caught her hair in the thorny branches above, and quickly ducked down again. She calmed her breathing: Crows hadn't found her, but he'd discovered her, and the maps', absence from the cobble beach.

That meant she still had time to make her escape, get to the city before him, even though she'd been careless in falling asleep and was now going to have to make her way at night. She crawled out from under the bush and stood up in the twilight, trying to orientate herself. The sun was setting, and was almost gone, just a red line on the horizon with pink clouds above it. Apart from that, she couldn't see anything – no lights, no smoke, no walls. All she knew was she had to head inland.

She slung the bag over her shoulder, blinked in the gathering gloom, and set off, the sea at her back.

It was impossible to steer a straight course, because trees didn't grow like that. The scrub of the cliff-top gave way to a light, open woodland as the land descended, and the canopy began to obscure the sky. Robbed of sight lines and cues in an unknown landscape, she slowed, and then stopped. She was already lost.

'Fuck,' she breathed. Crows knew the way, didn't he? Didn't he? He could already be at the top of the cliff again and striding out while she was blundering from tree to tree and swearing at the night. Holing up somewhere and waiting until morning, or waiting to take advantage of the late moonrise, seemed to be her only options.

She slumped down against a tree trunk and realised just how tired her legs were. Then she hauled herself up again. No. She wasn't going to do that. She was the Red Queen and she wasn't giving in.

The ground was sloping away, but there was no guarantee that if she followed the gradient, she'd end up where she needed to be. If the moon wasn't going to be up for another four or five hours, then it was going to get properly dark. Neither she nor Crows could use magic to light their ways: she couldn't fly, and he couldn't send his crows up. They were suddenly mortal, the pair of them. He had more experience of Down, but was much more cautious. He'd wait for the moon.

She could use that time, if she dared, to beat him.

The maps weren't going to be of any use: they only showed portals, and there were none here. It wasn't as if she was going to sort through them anyway, not now.

Then she remembered. She loosened the fastenings on the neck of the bag, and delved for the compass.

She could only assume that it was tiredness, hunger and thirst that meant she hadn't thought of it earlier, but it was obvious really, even if she'd never used one before. Once she'd wrestled the lid off, she held it up to the last glimmer of light. Behind the glass, the dial turned slowly, and the one thing she did know – that the sun set in the west – was confounded by the direction the compass showed. West wasn't over there, deeper into the forest, but pointing along the coastline.

She tapped the tin and turned it, but it was resolute, and wrong.

'Well, fuck you too.' It didn't work. Or she couldn't work it. But compasses were supposed to point north whoever was holding them, even ones where north wasn't marked and only west was. Unless the W was north, in the mind of Down. It had given her the compass: of course it worked, because what kind of shitty gift would it be otherwise?

She took a sightline down the dial, shouldered the maps and started walking. There was so little light to see by, though. She wished she'd started so much sooner. The trees closed over her, and killed even the ephemeral skyglow.

Anywhere else, she would have snapped her fingers, lit a dead branch or something. Here, so close to the White City, that wasn't going to happen. She felt for the lid of the compass, to put it back in the bag, when she realised that she could still see the dial. A pair of tiny green dots, invisible by day, marked the cardinal point. Why not? How else was a navigator going to steer during the dark hours, without stars or other reference points?

It was still painfully slow going. She walked, compass in one hand, close to her body, the other outstretched in front of her, feeling for the trees. She'd had to tie the maps to her like a tail so they wouldn't drag on the ground.

Everything was black, but those two little flecks of light. They swam before her eyes, and it was a struggle to keep them still. At first she headed downhill, then it levelled off into a series of small rises and falls, alternating boggy ground and dry leaf litter. She could see nothing, going only by the sounds her feet made and the textures they encountered. She could walk off a cliff and only realise as she was falling, so she strained every other sense, even the difference in the echoes and the change in pressure around her.

There were flying things. Little buzzy insects and, chasing them, the high-pitched squeak of bats. They were distracting, and she couldn't afford to be distracted.

She pressed on, and there was a new noise, the low, slow sound of a river.

Water. But she resisted the urge to run towards it. If she fell in, she could drown. Even if it wasn't that deep, she'd ruin the maps and get the compass wet – it should probably still work after that, but she could drop it and lose it as she floundered and splashed.

If she had gone tentatively before, she ended up on her hands and knees now. The river grew louder as her fingers crept forward, her legs shuffling along after. Then, suddenly, nothing. She could smell the water, though, just below her, and hear it gurgle as it rolled along the bank.

Mary put the compass behind her, where she could see the dial but not run the risk of knocking it flying, and reached down. The cold against her fingertips was surprising, shocking even. She jerked her hand back, but when she licked the moisture still clinging to her skin, she went back for more, cupping her palm and drinking until she was slaked.

Her belly was full to sloshing as she knelt up. She gasped and wiped her mouth, and saw another light.

It was tiny, and impossible to tell how far away it was – just a chip of yellow in the utter blackness that surrounded her. She groped for the compass and held it out. The dots swung around and settled. They pointed at the light which, as far as she could tell, was on the far side of the river.

So close, so much still to go wrong.

The slot of sky above the river showed no detail. Moonrise was still at least an hour or two away. She didn't feel she could afford to wait – Crows didn't have to worry about crossing like she did. She wasn't a good enough swimmer to hold the maps over her if it got too deep. Either she found some shallow stretch she could ford, or she'd have to wait. Crows could be miles behind her, or very near. Or ahead of her, waiting. She couldn't control that, only her own progress. She was going to have to try and reach that light, no matter what.

She collected the compass, adjusted the map bag and turned left. One step, listen. Another step, listen, and compare it with what she'd just heard.

And it did change, gaining a note of hollowness that grew, then faded. She retraced her steps, slowly, so very slowly. Her fingers felt something rough, when they should have touched only air. She dug her nails into its slightly yielding surface. Wood. Cut wood. She sniffed at it. It wasn't new, but neither did it smell of decay. Beyond that, there was another ... what? Plank? Half-log?

Was it a pier sticking out over the bank which would end abruptly mid-stream, or might it be a bridge? She didn't dare hope. She crept out, aware of the water all around her, feeling for the sawn edges to either side of her. No hand rails, no parapet, no margin for error. Her heart banged in her chest, and she could barely breathe. She swallowed hard, and reached out for the next rough section.

The water swirled beneath her, and the boards creaked. She didn't even know how far she'd gone, or how far she had left to go. If she got disorientated, she'd just have to stop and wait. But the little fleck of light beckoned her on, and she crawled closer.

Nothing. She patted around, and there was nothing. She lay down on her front and stretched out. Her hand waved uselessly, not connecting with anything. She reached down, and even that met with nothing. It was as if the universe ended and beyond it was empty.

'Fuck. Fuck fuck fuck.'

It made no sense. There was no reason for this structure to be here – it had to be man-made – if it just ended in the middle of, or even further across, the river. If it was a bridge, it could have been washed away. If it was a jetty, then what?

She felt for the corners. One was sharp, one had a post. She shuffled closer to it, and something brushed her hand. She held her breath, and felt it graze the back of her wrist again. Swinging. The next time it came past, she caught it. It was a rope, thin, a knot on the end. And as she explored it, there came a metallic clang from over her head.

She almost fell in. She gripped the edge of the platform so

fiercely that it cut into her hand. It was a bell, that was all. The maps were still tied to her, the compass just to one side. Everything was fine. Nothing was lost.

If she rang the bell, who would she be calling? Yet she was stuck, and there was nothing she could do but ring it. It would be loud, it would attract attention, and not just from the person she was trying to raise.

She found the rope again, and steeled herself for the noise.

When the bell stopped sounding, and she could hear again, she noticed there were two lights ahead of her in the darkness: the original, and another that was bobbing on an irregular path towards her. The light shone on the ground, and on bushes and trees, and on a pair of feet. Then on another wooden jetty, and a flat barge which was little more than a raft. The light was then suspended on a pole, and the bargee, cast in deep shadow, fished a rope out of the water and began to pull on it, hand over hand.

As the light got closer, she could see around her, and how short a distance she'd actually crawled along the pier on her side. She could have taken four of her usual steps and arrived at the bell-post. She felt embarrassed, and determined that she wasn't going to show it.

No one came out of the forest behind her while she waited for the raft to cross.

It bumped into the jetty, making it shiver. She looked down at an old man in a hat.

'Come on, then.'

'Is it safe?' she asked.

'It's all there is.' He held up his hand to her. 'Sit on the edge and jump down. I haven't lost anyone yet.'

She could see the reflection of the water sloshing between the raft's lashed-together logs.

'Seriously? I don't mind getting wet, but I've … stuff here that does.'

'Then hold it up. I can just leave you here, if that's what you want.'

'I don't.' She closed the compass up and squeezed it back through the opening of the bag, then swung her legs over the side of the jetty. His fingers were damp and strong, and he pulled her easily off the edge.

The raft swayed. A wave of water crossed it, up to her ankles, before disappearing back through the gaps. Her toes curled, trying to grip the wet wood. He steadied her as she splayed her legs and lifted the maps high.

'Most people don't come with baggage,' he said. He let go of her, and she teetered as he ducked down for the now-submerged rope.

'I'm not most people.'

He started to pull on the rope, and the end of the pier disappeared, drifting away in the night. This wasn't how she'd imagined it, but it would do. The man's hand-over-hand rhythm was purposeful and calm and reassuring. Even though she couldn't see the far bank, she knew it was there.

'Has anyone else crossed tonight?'

'If they have, it's their business and not yours.' He coughed. 'I don't mean it to sound that way, but that's how it is. I'm not telling anyone about you, either.'

'That's ... thanks.'

'All part of the service. First time?'

'Yes.' It was cold, out on the water, with the river rising and falling through the raft. 'This is the way to the White City, right? Only I don't even know if it actually exists.'

'Not only is it on the way, you've arrived. There's a little further to go, but you're as here as anywhere. Brace yourself.'

The other jetty loomed, and he stopped pulling, allowing the raft to drift gently up to the black-stained piles. It touched, almost kissing, and he tied them on with a loop of rope. The deck of the jetty was at waist-height, but if she moved to the edge, the raft would tip.

'How do I get off this thing?'

'If you clamber up, I'll stand across here and balance things out.'

The surface was inconstant, and she wasn't certain, but she had to trust his word and his skill. She made little steps forward until she could get her hands on the solid platform, then launched herself up in one quick jump. She lay half-on, half-off, the map bag dangling below her from her waist, and she scrabbled to drag it to safety.

'Not the best I've seen. Not the worst, either.'

While she gathered her wits and her skirts, the man lifted the lantern pole clear and simply climbed up. She looked at his dripping feet and water-darkened turn-ups.

'It won't sink. It might tip and turn, but it won't sink.' He tapped the staging with the pole. 'Come with me, and I'll set you up.'

She looked back across the river one last time. There was nothing to see – all that existed was the bubble around the lantern – but nothing to hear either. No tell-tale splashes, nor the tolling of the bell again. Wherever Crows was, he wasn't right there.

She got to her feet, picked up the bag, and followed the man up a narrow dirt path towards the chip of yellow light she'd seen before. A badly fitting door on a ramshackle hut was open just enough to let the inside out. She'd spotted it, not because it was bright, but because everything else was so dark.

The man kicked his way through the door, blew out the lantern he was carrying and leaned it up against the wall. Mary hesitated on the threshold, staring in at the piles of clutter and heaps of rags and stacks of boxes.

'No one cares. I certainly don't. Close the door, and find somewhere to sit.'

She pushed the door shut behind her. She assumed the one chair in the room was his, so she drew up a box and perched on it. He grumbled and muttered, and eventually sat opposite her.

'First things first. You don't have to tell me your name, or anything about you. Where you're from, what time you're from, how you got here and what's happened since. I know nothing, and I don't need to know anything either.'

She nodded mutely.

'Take this.' He opened a chest on the floor by his side, and fetched out one of the little cloth bags inside. Each one was different: hers seemed to be made from an old handkerchief, complete with an embroidered monogram ES.

She opened the top and looked inside, then tipped some of the contents into her hand. Discs, thin and sharp, like coins but blank. 'What are these?'

'Those are your honour. Spend them wisely.'

'My ... honour?'

'Your honour,' he said firmly. 'Don't think of it like money. It's not money. It can be used as money, but it's so much more.'

'So I can buy stuff with it. What else?'

'You'll find out,' he said. He closed the chest and folded his hands into his lap.

'Oh come on. You've got to give me more than that.' She narrowed her eyes, picked a couple of the coins off the pile in her palm and proffered them. 'What are these really for?'

He snorted a laugh and waved her honour back. 'Think of it as your reputation, your influence. It's how you get answers to the questions you have.'

'Okay. What happens when I run out?'

'Of honour? Well, you become dishonoured. You have to leave.'

'And I can't come back and get more?'

'What do you think?' He leaned back in his chair and waited.

'No?' she offered.

'You catch on quick, girl. Now, are you armed?'

She'd left the hole-maker back in the bay. She'd meant to bring it with her, but had been too exhausted to remember. Her shoulders sagged, but it didn't matter, since he would have taken it from her anyway. 'No.'

The man levered himself out of the chair, shuffled across the floor and pulled back a blanket from a pile. On the next one down was arrayed a hotchpotch armoury. His hand hovered as he made his selection. 'Fifteenth-century misericord. You don't want anything too heavy – I'm not saying this is a woman's weapon, but I think it's a good fit for you.'

He passed it to her, hilt first.

It had a narrow, triangular blade, a short cross-guard, and a grip almost as long as the blade. The pommel was engraved with a flower.

'I don't understand. Why do I need this?'

'Because you haven't got one.' He threw the blanket back over the rest and took to his chair again. 'You can't count on others to protect your honour, only you.'

She hefted the dagger and tapped her finger on the tip. 'So you hand out knives to those who don't have them.'

'I don't make the rules. I just try and help those who need help. I am right that this is your first time, yes? Some say it is when it isn't.'

'I haven't been here long enough to come twice.' Her gaze roamed across the hut's walls and floor. 'Is there anything else I need to know?'

'Nothing you won't find out for yourself in time. Most come for answers. Most leave disappointed. Some don't leave at all, for one reason or another.'

'If it's "welcome to the White City, here's your sword", I can guess what one of those reasons is.' One part of the hut had a stone floor – not that she could see much of that under the clutter. A fire smoked listlessly there, drawing up into a crude chimney that led outside. Above the fireplace was a rack, and on that rack was a rifle.

To see something of such modernity was almost a shock, as if she'd forgotten that such things had ever existed. It wasn't even a new rifle: it looked like a museum piece, or something she'd see in an old film. But it was talisman of power and violence.

'What about that?' She pointed with the dagger.

'What about it?' he countered.

'It's a fucking gun.'

'My gun. It's a reminder to everyone who passes this way that you do so at my sufferance. The knife I gave you was for your protection. The gun is for mine. But,' he said, 'I can't recall ever taking it down, except once.'

'What happened?'

'It ended badly.' He sucked his teeth and tutted.

'Tell me there's food in the White City,' she said.

'There's food, and drink, and much more. Much, much more.' He was threatening her with abundance.

She threaded the dagger into a loop at her waist. 'Thanks for the lift, and the knife, and,' she held up the bag with her honours in, 'these. I'll probably see you on the way out.'

Mary was almost out of the door when he called after her.

'Good luck.'

16

'The wind's not favourable, but we'll tack across it.' Simeon stood at the top of the beach and pronounced the day's weather with a handful of dried grass seeds. Below lay the *Ship of Fools*, stranded in the shallow water like a great dark whale. 'And when we can't sail, we'll row.'

The fresh water barrels were rolled down to the sea, and the cooked food stored for later: the hardtack would last for ever, the stew only a day. Dalip wondered about scurvy, and how long that would take to set in. None of the crew seemed affected – perhaps all the ones that were had died, or perhaps Down's fish were rich in vitamin C. And if there was plenty of anything, it was cold, dried fish.

Simeon was like a lot of boys he'd met at school. Not the sons of labour, but the sons of wealth: they weren't necessarily bad, they weren't all stupid, they weren't all heartless or useless or any of the other lesses. But they were overconfident. They believed, simply and completely, that the world was there for them, and they could reach out and take it.

There were maps. Simeon would take them. In his mind, it was already done.

Dalip wasn't so sure. There was no safety net if anything went wrong, no getting out the chequebook to make a problem go away. He hoped to temper Simeon's exuberance with some caution.

They had to load the ship first, and set it ready for the voyage. There was the raising of the heavy barrels up in nets, storing the food so that it wouldn't become contaminated by sea-water, hauling on the ropes so that the mast was fixed in place, the readying the oars. Nothing, of itself, difficult, but all time-consuming and everybody had to lend a hand. Finally, they had to heave the boat off the sand and into deeper draught.

Dalip joined some of the bigger men in the water. They looked at him and his youth with scepticism, but although they couldn't see the strong muscles under his shapeless boilersuit, they didn't suggest that he shouldn't be there, or was taking the place of a more able sailor. He put his shoulder to the hull with the best of them, and with a timed count, they pushed.

The ship slid gracefully back into the bay, and the oars lowered to stop it from floating out of reach of those not on board. Dalip splashed and half-swam to the lowered nets with the others, and strong arms hauled him in when he reached the gunwales.

The rowers backed the stern away from the shore, turned it about its axis, and headed for the open sea through the narrow opening in the cliffs. There was enough wind from the right quarter to lower the sail, though the sea-chests and oars remained on deck. The rowers stood down and the sailing crew kept trim.

Mama, holding the small of her back like it was a porcelain teacup, sat down next to him.

'How did you do it?' she asked.

'Do what?'

'Persuade Mr Simeon to go after Crows.'

'He persuaded himself. It's his own idea – that we can rid Down of the geomancers once and for all. Truth be told, I tried to talk him out of it.'

She started. 'Why would you do that?'

'Because it's really dangerous and we could die. Not just us, but everyone on this boat. If we met Crows in open water, as a sea serpent, it could end very quickly and very badly for all of us.'

'But he's going to be in the White City. There won't be any changing into snakes there. You said so.'

'Mama, since when has anything Crows said changed what he actually does? I don't know where he's going. For all I know, he went back to his castle, now we've seen Bell off.'

'Maybe we should go there, then.'

'And this is the problem. We can't go haring off around Down, looking for Crows when Crows doesn't want to be found. The only place we stand any chance of finding him, or Mary, is the White City. If he's not there, we'll just go back to pirating,' he said, as if pirating had been his life so far.

Mama hunched her shoulders. 'That's not going to get us home.'

'I know what I said last night, but it's a whole tower of guess-work balanced on an awful lot of ifs. But if we lose people, and we can't put the maps together, then, well: those left alive will have every right to be seriously pissed with us.'

'And their captain.'

Dalip checked the deck for Simeon's position. He was wrapped around the prow again, telescope to his eye.

'This ship's whole purpose is to keep the decent people away from the bad ones. Now, that contract is broken. Simeon is taking the ship, and everyone on it, into the unknown. I can't predict how this is going to turn out, and for all his fine words, neither can he.' He pulled a face. 'I just wonder if a better captain would have made a different decision.'

'He made the decision I want,' said Mama.

'We're all going to have to live with it, come what may.' Behind them, the island was diminishing, and their destination was still over the horizon. 'Seriously, how does he navigate? He's not taken a bearing since we left the bay. He's not got a clock or a compass. He's just pointing us in what he hopes is the right direction and leaving the rest to chance.'

'Well, however he's doing it, no one looks scared.'

The steersman at the rudder certainly seemed content with the course laid in by his captain. The sail ahead of him was bowed and full of wind, and the ropes strained to transmit all that raw power to the rest of the boat. The rest of the crew who weren't tending the wooden blocks and pulleys were delving in their sea-chests for swords and knives and whetstones.

The atmosphere on deck was more akin to a carnival than a sombre troopship. Practice fights spontaneously broke out, some of which made Dalip genuinely fear for the safety of the participants. If they arrived at the White City bandaged and furious with each other, or worse, so incapacitated that their already depleted numbers reduced further, then their plans would come to nothing.

And Simeon seemed content to ignore the high spirits and the threat, so fixed was he on the far distant horizon. He might have looked back once to acknowledge something was going on, but returned to his telescope almost immediately.

'Where's Elena?' asked Dalip.

'She wasn't with me last night,' said Mama, 'I thought she might be ...'

'What?'

'With you.' She raised her hands. 'What you youngsters get up to is none of my business.'

Dalip blinked, distracted for a moment from the swordplay going on around them. 'She's—' At least five, nearly ten years older than him, not a Sikh, and recently bereaved. 'She wasn't with me.'

Last night he'd eaten and listened to the stories told around the fire, but when the grog started making its way around the circle, he'd excused himself and hidden away from the forced, loud jollity that resulted. He'd slept alone, which wasn't necessarily what others had done, judging from some of the sounds that had crossed the moonlit air.

Mama was right: it wasn't her business, and it was certainly none of his. But he hadn't had a chance to work out his feelings about Elena before any chance was closed down.

She was there, near the bow, with a group of sailors. She was holding what looked like a cavalry-pattern sabre, and the man behind her – tall, lithe, tanned – was guiding her movements, stepping her forward, moving her backwards, turning and feinting for her. Compared with the chaos on the rest of the deck, it seemed an island of calm and choreographed purposefulness, and strangely intimate for such a public place.

She was safe, he told himself: that was what was important.

Mama followed the direction of his gaze and narrowed her eyes. 'Looks like she doesn't need us any more.'

'That's not really fair,' he said. 'We're part of the crew now. She can spend time with whoever she wants.'

'Be that as it may,' said Mama, 'I hope that girl knows what she's doing.'

'Probably no more than we do.' Dalip put any feelings he might have had back in their box, and shut the lid. They'd escaped fire and dungeon with each other, that was all. He couldn't read anything more into their time together.

And while he wasn't watching, someone got cut. A man reeled backwards, almost tripping over Mama's feet, his sword arm staining red on the biceps. His opponent, a short, bald greybeard lunged again with rapier, only to see his blow miss its mark as he was dragged back by an arm around his neck.

Mama reared away, barging into Dalip, who lost his balance. The hurt man roared and raised his hatchet, intent on plunging it into something. He didn't seem to care what: he started forward, and Dalip, sprawled on the deck, could only watch.

The steersman caught the man's arm, right where the rapier's thin blade had punched through, and squeezed hard. The hatchet bounced away, and the fight was suddenly over. Simeon stood between them, arms outstretched, staring first at one man, then the other, until they both decided that carrying on wasn't in their best interests.

As to whose fault it was, there was no way of telling. The captain seemed content not to cross-examine any of the witnesses. Blame wasn't apportioned, and guilt or innocence stayed unestablished and, gradually, the deck quietened down again.

There'd been a couple of other mishaps, which were treated with salt water and rough stitches, and the blood scrubbed off the deck with rags. Everyone else treated the incident as one of those things, like spilling a drink or dropping a plate at a party: a strange, cavalier attitude to Dalip.

He understood how it was easy to be reckless with your own well-being because he'd been a teenage boy and that was what it was like – climbing things, falling from things, taking things, doing things – but mock fights with real knives? These people were adults, and their sudden wildness scared him. There could easily have been a death, accidental for sure, but he suddenly had no doubt that the body would have been pitched over the side, and the perpetrator given extra duties for the duration – and then it would have been forgotten. And these were supposed to be the sensible ones, the good people, who'd escaped from the clutches of the geomancers and decided to live free.

The ship readied to come about. Ropes were loosened, and the sail flapped and billowed, snapping in the wind until the rudder forced a change in direction. The sailcloth filled again, and the ropes tightened. For all their disregard, they were a decent crew. Or perhaps because of it. How long could you stay at sea, dodging beasts, without craving the danger that came between bouts of extreme boredom? Raiding the land was as exciting as it got: hunting animals, picking fruit and nuts, gathering firewood, drawing water.

Dalip realised he hadn't understood a single thing about

the ship or its fools. They weren't cowards, running away from danger. They were like vermin, ruthlessly exploiting the one gap they could find in a screwed-up ecosystem. If that meant they had learnt to run sometimes, then it also meant they had learnt to swarm ashore and strip a coast clean.

Opportunistic: that was the word. And with the maps, Simeon sensed the biggest, juiciest opportunity of all. No wonder the crew had chewed the idea over, then swallowed it wholesale. This was something they excelled in.

Perhaps they could pull this off after all.

'Whose is this sea-chest?' he asked Mama.

'No one's come for it.' She looked around and settled her sights on the steersman. 'What do we do about this?'

'Fight over it if you want,' he said, not taking his eyes off Simeon at the far end of the ship. 'Or share what's inside.'

'So what happened to the previous owner?'

The steersman did his best to shrug while holding the tiller. 'He got left behind. That could mean anything: dead, taken, deserted.'

'And no one went to find out?'

'Never do.' It was a statement and a warning, rolled into one. Either muster on the beach at the time of departure, or don't, but there'll be no waiting around.

Dalip and Mama contemplated the idea for a moment before moving to sit on the deck with the open chest in front of them. It looked like it had been sorted through already, and what was left was mostly threadbare rags. A couple of shirts, holed woollen stockings, a pair of long shorts which had gone at the seams, and something flat, wrapped up in waxy cloth.

'This is slim pickings,' said Mama.

'It's a pirate ship. What did you expect? A casket full of doub-loons?'

Mama held up the stockings to the light. They would have functioned better as fishing nets. 'Do people not make anything here?'

'Grog. The biscuits we break our teeth on. There may have been looms at Bell's castle, but I never saw any.' He pulled a face and stared into the distance. 'Do you remember when Mary needed something to wear, and there were all those boxes of clothes?'

'Sure.'

'Every single thing in them had been worn by someone coming to Down. Every single one of those women were dead by the time Mary picked that red dress out.'

Mama inspected the stockings again, and folded them back into the sea-chest. 'Well, isn't that depressing.'

'At least we've worked out where everyone is.' Dalip picked up the wax-clothed bundle, and noticed that there was a corroded pen and a small, squat glass bottle nestling with it. 'They're all captured or dead, and we're the survivors.'

'We've been here a month, Dalip. Maybe two. We've survived so far, but I don't think that makes us survivors.' Mama sucked her cheeks in. 'I want to go home. More than ever.'

He unwrapped the little bundle. Inside was a little hardback book with black leather-covered boards and raggedly cut pages. Although it looked old, it smelled new, and when he cracked it open, the paper was still white and crisp.

The writing was in a small, neat hand, the script flowing and steady.

'I can't read it,' said Dalip, and showed it to Mama.

'So what language is it?'

'I'm going to guess at Latin, or ...' He squinted at the page. 'Hang on. That's English.'

'That's no English I've ever seen.'

'They made me do Chaucer at school. Middle English. Medieval.' Sucking at his teeth, he tried a few words, running his finger beneath the letters as he stuttered his way through. 'Wol – will I turn to London again.' He leafed to the start. 'This is someone's diary, I think.'

'Then perhaps you shouldn't be reading it.'

'The owner will be past caring by now.' He moved to the last entry, but didn't try and decipher its meaning. 'This stuff always gave me a headache. It's like trying to read Punjabi.'

'Can't you?'

He shook his head. 'A bit. Everything was in English, and I was ... lazy. I can speak it better, though that's not saying much. I know some prayers, some of the Guru Granth Sahib. I couldn't hold a conversation in Punjabi, though. My grandfather would have hated that thought.'

'He would have been very proud of his grandson.'

'Maybe. He would have still told me off for not learning the language of our ancestors. But he would have blamed his son for not teaching me properly. And my mother.' He lapsed into silence, turning the book over in his hands.

'We'll make it back,' said Mama.

'The man who wrote this didn't. If we want to go home, we have to make it happen. No one's going to open a door and offer it to us.' He placed the book back in its wrapper, and returned it to the chest. Then he took out his machete and tested its edge with his thumb.

'We're going to fight, then?'

'We're pirates,' he said. 'It's what we do.'

It wasn't what she expected. Even though she realised it was never going to be the city of her imagination, with palaces carved from marble, crowded streets teeming with busy people, the noise of markets and the call of traders, while kings and queens were carried aloft in curtained chairs borne by muscled, silent servants, it still should have been grand. The White City was man's only mark on Down, the only place where buildings had both a history and a future.

After leaving the ferryman's shack, she'd picked her way up the stony path and into a steep-sided ravine. The river ran below her between rock walls, and the path grew perilously narrow. Then it widened, and the valley with it.

The path became a road, and bowed down to run at the same level as the river. The cliffs to her right poured cones of broken taluses at their feet, and produced a series of slopes that led to the valley floor. Ahead, the valley closed up again as tightly as it was behind her. Here, then, in front of her.

This was no city. It was a collection of high stone walls – compounds – and in each, a few unimpressive buildings, sometimes set away from the walls, sometimes incorporating them in their structure. One or two seemed to have taken over the whole of their compounds, hollowing out in the middle to leave court-yards. There were no trees, and the only vegetation was down on the lowest slopes by the river.

Even at night, the place seemed thin and mean and dusty. There were lights at some of the windows, but behind their walls they were cold and aloof, not warm and welcoming. The sound of water thrummed off the stone, an unsettling bass hum that hurt her teeth and made her empty guts ache.

The buildings and the walls were cut from white stone. That, at least, was as advertised. Nothing else was. It looked a cross between a desert village and a town from the Wild West.

She had no idea where she was supposed to go next, or where she was supposed to stay. She had unimaginable wealth in her hands, yet it was only hers if she could hold on to it. Crows would be here by morning, so she had to be ready.

She walked slowly past the terraced fields that lay between the road and the river, towards the compounds, which clustered as if thrown down at the bottom of the widest part of the valley. Every single door was closed and barred and silent. If they knew she was coming, then this was a strange kind of welcome.

She knew cities. She was the street kid, wise to every scam and every opportunity. This? This was the Kensington and Chelsea end, private houses with private security, and blank-faced embassies with brass plaques by the doors. Without a doubt, she was being watched, both coming in and going out again, back up the road to the opening into the valley.

She hoped it would be different in the morning, but for now, everything was shut tight and locked down, and she was so, so weary, her bones ached. It was only when she'd gone back as far as the beginning of the narrow ravine that she spotted several blank cubes set into the rock debris. At first sight, they'd looked like random blocks of fallen stone, but with a second look, they were too regular and sharp for that. The stones she picked a path across were also sharp. Her lack of shoes was telling here in a way it wasn't when it was sand or leaf litter, and the soles of her feet, though hard, felt every corner of the scree. She swore almost every step, and decided that she wouldn't mind paying for a decent pair of boots.

She'd trudged her way up to the nearest. It was made of the same pale stone as the bigger buildings, broken pieces laid like little bricks in courses to make walls, larger and longer chunks to form the frame of a door.

The door had had a big iron key in a rough keyhole, and when she'd pushed on the wooden planks, the door had creaked open. Inside, it was dry, and she found that she could take the key out and lock it from the inside. There was no one else present, and she'd felt all the way around the floor and the ceiling to check before hunching up in a corner and falling instantly asleep.

In the morning, when the sun was higher in the sky than she'd wanted, she unlocked the door again and looked down over the White City.

It … She couldn't hide her disappointment from herself any longer. There was perhaps one building that was worthy of the name city – a single circular building with a domed roof, all dressed in the ubiquitous pale stone that was almost but not quite white. The rest were obscured in a haze of blue woodsmoke that hung in the steep-sided valley like smog. The river rumbled along its narrow channel, looking dark and mutinous, and the cultivated terraces next to it were green and brown. Other than that, everything was the colour of old bone: the cliffs, the scree slopes, the walls and buildings. Her red dress was the only splash of colour.

She stood at the doorway for a long while, memorising the lie of the land. All the compounds sat adjacent to the single road, a road that seemed to peter out at the far end. Most squatted above the track, and only a few below, wherever the ground seemed flat enough for building. Her shelter was one of a dozen, balanced on the edge of the loose rock and built into the gradient. Each had a door, and each had a lock.

She tried a few, then all of them. None were occupied, none contained anything useful. Indeed, they contained nothing at all, just a dark square space not even tall enough to stand up in.

A waterfall came off the cliffs above her, mostly turning into spray as it fell, and coalescing again in a hollow forced into the rock at its base. It seemed as good as any place to start. She retrieved her bag of honours, slid her dagger into the loop at her waist, and locked the maps inside the shelter. The key went in with the sharp metal coins.

The water blattered down on her from the waterfall, each drop like a shot and cold enough to make her squeal. At the centre of the hollow made by its falling was a pool, its surface jumping with splashes, and it appeared to drain away through the broken rock without overflowing at the margins. Before she reached the edge, she was drenched and pummelled. In the pool itself, the water seethed, as much air as there was liquid. It was numbing and exhilarating, and she dragged herself away out of range feeling washed and tumbled all at once.

The sunlight sat hidden by the cliff behind her. By the time it came to mid-afternoon, it would briefly illuminate the slope she sat on. Shortly after, it would be obscured by the other cliff. Consequently, it was always going to be cold, and she needed to remember that. There was a reason for the fires.

As she sat, shivering and drying out, she spotted her first people. They were coming down a staircase that stretched from the top of the opposite cliff to the bottom, much like the one that brought her up from the sea, though not quite as precipitous. Each carried a load of wood on their bent backs. As they came to the river, she lost sight of them. Perhaps there was a bridge there, or it was shallow enough to wade across.

It was easy enough, in the narrow ravine, to forget that Down extended in every direction, for ever. Just as easy to forget that

Crows would be here soon, if he hadn't already made the short journey from the ferry to the city.

She walked down the scree, past a few more of the stone shelters, to the road.

Mary faced the last of the compounds. The wall stretched two storeys above her, pierced on the top floor with small slit-like windows. There was a gate, too, tall and wooden and firmly shut. She frowned at it, and went to the next one. It was just as silent and forbidding as the first.

What was she supposed to do? Knock at a random door and see where that took her? There seemed nothing to choose between them.

She squared her shoulders, raised her fist.

'No.'

She turned, and there was a man standing a little way off. He was as pale and dusty as the stone.

'No?'

He shook his head. 'No.'

'Why not?'

He walked away, back towards what she'd taken to be just another shelter but was, on second look, more substantial and certainly more lived-in.

She raised her knuckles again, and hesitated. She had twenty honours. Was it worth spending one to find out why she shouldn't? It might be a scam, a way of tricking the newcomers out of their honour and sending them back on the road again, poorer and none the wiser. She might be new to the White City, but she wasn't new to the street, and she could work her own scams.

So she followed him back to his house. He was sitting on a stool next to his front door – if there'd been any sun, he'd have been sunning himself. As it was, he was just sitting outside. He glanced at her as she approached, then went back to his expression of disinterest.

'Well?' she said.

'Well what?' said the man.

Mary looked down the road. She could count a grand total of three other people. Two passed each other on opposite sides of the road, almost in opposite gutters. The other was brushing a front step in a desultory manner. She wasn't going to be disturbed, then. She held up a coin, flicked it into the air and caught it again.

'What's so bad that I shouldn't even knock?'

He snorted, but couldn't even raise a half-smile.

'Okay.' She put the coin back into her honour bag and started to walk away.

He was up in an instant, reaching out for her, when he found himself with the point of a sharp blade against his wrist.

'I'll fucking cut you, and I know where to make it bad.'

He slowly withdrew. 'Sorry. I didn't mean to startle you.'

'Touch me and I'll do you. Right?'

He wasn't scared of her. She could see no trace of it in his pale eyes. But all the same, he sat back down, and put his hands ostentatiously on his knees.

'No harm done,' he said.

'You want to take my honour? Do you?'

'Only what you're prepared to give me.'

She sheathed her dagger again. 'I bet you say that to all the girls.'

He half-grunted a laugh. A release of tension. Then he looked at her properly, and she at him.

'Not that door. Not any of the doors up here. That's not where you start, if you get my meaning.'

'So where should I start?'

He chewed his lip for a moment, but her purse remained annoyingly closed.

'I could have killed you,' she said. 'That has to be worth something.'

'Down by the river. The one on its own. That's where you should have gone. You'll know it when you see it.'

'Thanks. I ... look: I'm not like that – or maybe I am, but I'm trying not to be like that. Is this your house, your shop, whatever?'

He settled back further, leaning against the wall behind him, which was as white as his hair. 'I'm here when I'm needed.'

'You'll get your honour, at some point. I just need to work out the system before I start handing it out for every little favour and I'm left with nothing.'

'You'd better go. Remember which door you need to be at.'

She nodded, still uncertain what horrible fate she'd avoided. The road bent towards the west cliff, but the detail was obscured by the compounds to either side. Seeing around them was impossible, looking over them showed only towering rock. There were a few more people out, half a dozen and no more, all as individuals heading somewhere with hurried purposefulness. They stared at her when they thought she wasn't looking at them. As soon as she locked eyes with them, they looked away. No one spoke, either to each other or her. Not even an acknowledgement, a raising of the hand, a tipping of the hat. Mary walked down the middle of the scuffed road itself: everyone gave her a wide berth. At first she thought it might be her, but those who could conceivably be fellow townspeople tended to avoid each other, even to the point of crossing the road.

Only once was there anything resembling a side-street. She peered up it, to see a fraction of the dome-roofed building staring back down at her. That it was different made her want to explore it, which was probably reason enough to leave it alone. She had a destination: better she stuck to it than get distracted.

She worked her way down the road, past yet more anonymous compounds, paying full attention to all the details, until she reached the right-angled turn. Between her and the river, all the way to the narrow entrance of the ravine, were the terraced fields. Above the road, buildings.

And at the point of the turn, a track that ran down the slope to the river itself, where there were stepping stones, and on the other side, the steep stairs she'd seen the wood-carriers descend. There was one building, all on its own, next to the water's edge. Like the rest of the White City, it was a block made out of smaller blocks, and as welcoming as a gun emplacement, but she assumed that was her destination.

A few of the fields were under cultivation: there were backs bent over neat rows of green leaves, and feet in the thin soil. But the majority were wild, and the terraces were breaking down, spilling stones and earth downhill into the river and away.

She eyed the decay. It was reminiscent of Crows' castle, before she'd moved in, even if everything here had to be maintained by hand, not by magic. Things were falling apart, and for the same reason: not enough people to keep it running.

The track ended. The stepping stones across the river were tall pillars, thinner than she expected. To cross would require both confidence and skill to avoid pitching into the running river below. She looked across and up to where Down started again, at the top of the cliff. It would be easy to grab the maps and scale the cliff, but everyone seemed so sure that the answers were here. Now that she'd seen it for herself, she wasn't so convinced.

But she was still going to have to chance it. She turned her gaze down to the building next to her. No windows in the ground floor again. It struck her that there had to be something to be afraid of, to design it like that.

There was only one door – she checked by walking all the way around the outside – so she reached up and rapped hard on it with her knuckles. If this was the wrong decision, she was going to look a right idiot.

She waited, long enough to think she was going to have to knock again. Doors which presented a blank face to her made her feel like she was in a cell, even when she was outside. It was worrying, and made her wonder if what lay on the other side was better – safer – than where she stood. She'd spent half her life looking over her shoulder.

Just as she was going to pound again, she heard noises from inside. She stepped back, and the door swung open towards her.

'What?' said the woman who wore a face that simultaneously startled and intrigued Mary.

'What do you mean, what?'

'Why are you here?'

'Fucked if I know. Some bloke back there told me that the door I was going to knock on was going to get me killed or something, and that I should try this one instead.' Mary shrugged. 'Was he telling me the truth? Is this somewhere I should be?'

The woman folded her arms in a way that reminded her of Mama. 'What have you got?'

'Depends what you're offering. That's how it works, right? I have to decide how much I think it's worth, then we argue about it, then shake on a deal.' She was guessing, but she'd done this on market stalls and street corners for years. All she was doing was letting the other woman know she wasn't about to be taken for a ride.

The woman leaned around the door, and saw that Mary was alone. 'You'd better come inside,' she said. Her voice was no less distrustful than before. 'We'll talk.'

'I'd rather eat, then talk.'

'We'll see.' She stood aside, and Mary slipped into the cool darkness beyond.

18

The coast became a line in the distance, and still Simeon fixed all his attention on it. Dalip couldn't bear it any longer, and worked his way along the deck until he stood at the prow.

'I'm sorry, but how? I know you told me, but I just don't believe you.'

Simeon unplugged his eye from the telescope. 'Can't you just trust your captain?'

'You said there was no magic on board.'

'Nor is there. Filthy stuff.' He held out the telescope to Dalip. 'See for yourself.'

Dalip took the instrument and examined it. It seemed a perfectly normal ship's telescope, not that he'd ever handled one before. 'Where did this come from?'

'That's lost in the mists of time. It was handed to me by the last captain. I'll pass it on when the time comes. Along with the hat.' Simeon went to take it back, but Dalip needed one last favour.

'Do you mind if I look through it?'

'Will you keep quiet about what you see?' Simeon asked, whispering.

Dalip nodded, and Simeon opened his hands to indicate the wide sea and sky were his.

At first, he could see nothing, but that was because he couldn't make his sight lines work. Then, when he'd got flashes of waves and wood, he couldn't hold it still long enough to focus on anything.

He braced himself against the side of the ship, and trained the telescope on the coast. The black line moved out of sight upwards, then downwards. He compensated for the movement of the boat, and finally got it under some sort of control.

He could make out some of the taller headlands, which presumably Simeon knew and could use to navigate the inshore waters. It still didn't explain how he steered a straight course when there was no land in sight. It was just a regular telescope, a lens at either end of a collapsible tube.

He lowered it and inspected it again. He didn't want to give it back, either, because he knew he was missing something. But he had no excuse not to, and he reluctantly gave it up.

'What did you see?'

'Down.'

'Nothing else?'

Dalip pursed his lips and shook his head.

'It's all in the eye of the beholder, Singh.' He gave the end of the telescope a little twist. 'Why don't you try again?'

He was suspicious now. What had Simeon done? He braced himself again, and raised the telescope up. A wash of colour startled him, and when he looked again, he could see that the colours, brighter than any rainbow, were arranged in broad stripes across the sky. He turned, and he moved from red through to blue. He turned back, and the colours cycled the other way.

'Polarising filters. You've got polarising filters on this.'

Simeon took the telescope away and leaned in. 'I don't know how it works. All I know is that I can lay a course even on the cloudiest day, at twilight, and sometimes at night when the moon is full. Midday is difficult, but not impossible.'

'Whoever made that …'

'Knew what they were doing? Yes, by Jove. Without it we'd be reduced to following the coast all the time, and part of the beauty of being on the ship is being able to head out beyond the horizon and lie low for a while.' He hooked his arm over the prow. 'I could teach you. What d'you say?'

'Yes?'

'When we can, then. First, I have to find the right bay and the right beach. Which isn't, I hasten to add, the damnable Bay of Bones. Horrid place. Some say it's cursed. Some also say it's the only way to get to the White City, but they are most definitely wrong.'

Simeon tweaked the telescope again and concentrated on the dark line ahead. Then without taking his eye off the coast, raised his hand and made a couple of gestures to the steersman.

'Ready to come about,' came the call.

'Slightly to the west, but not bad, all things considered.' Simeon's mouth twitched into a satisfied smirk. 'Get yourself ready, Singh. We're going ashore.'

The bow turned to the east, and the boat heeled over as the sail ran almost parallel to the deck. The wind was against them, and they tacked hard left and right to slowly close on the palisade-like cliffs.

Ropes didn't pull themselves, and it was hard work. But not as hard as rowing, which they had to do to stop them from going backwards, or into the rocks. They hauled themselves into the headwind, hunched over as if it would make a difference to their speed. As it was, they crawled along: individual features moved by glacially, causing the crew to mutter and curse. Some even said they should head to the Bay of Bones and be done with it.

Dalip exchanged glances with Mama across the width of the deck, and the steersman apparently thought the same.

'Row, you dogs. You know the Bay of Bones isn't for the likes of us.' He spat over the side to emphasise his point.

They hauled and groaned, and finally made way around the

headland. The wall of rock seemed just as impenetrable, and the wind redoubled its efforts. Dalip dug in, but it was clear that some of the other rowers were flagging, Mama included.

'I'm not built for this,' she said, voice quavering.

'Ten more strokes,' shouted the steersmen. 'Ten is all. Come on.'

At the back of the boat, Dalip couldn't see why, but as he ground out those last few strokes, the first hint of lower land and a shelving beach showed themselves. The boat leaned to port, and suddenly they were in clear water.

'Ship oars. Raise the sail.'

Uncertain if he had the strength to stand, Dalip dragged his oar back in and rested for a moment, elbows on his thighs and his head almost at his knees.

'We need sail! 'Ware the rocks!'

The rope party lurched into action, already exhausted, and managed to get half the sail unfurled. On Dalip's side of the boat, a line had seized in the block, and half a sail clearly wasn't going to be enough.

It was three steps away. Then two, as he barged through the middle of the men. He held the line taut and brought his machete down on the braided cord. It twanged away, and the rest of the sail fell into place. The severed line snaked and cracked, and someone else caught it.

Dalip's guts had knotted from the effort, and at that moment, he neither knew nor cared whether they were going to avoid the submerged rocks on the port side. The boat rocked and pitched, then surged away as the steersman leaned hard into his tiller.

Mama caught him and dragged him into the clear aisle between the sea-chests.

'We're fine, we're fine,' she said. 'You did good.'

Dalip swallowed hard against the acid fire in his throat and tried to breathe. 'As long,' he gasped, 'as long as they don't make me splice that rope back up again.'

'I'm sure they have someone who can do that.' She patted his arm and sat him up so he could see that they'd steered away from the rocks and were heading smoothly towards the back of the bay and the shingle beach there.

Rather than landing the ship, Simeon ordered the anchor dropped and the mast unstepped. They sat offshore while they recovered – water and food were passed around, and some measure of good humour mixed with relief was restored to the crew. Dalip took some time to look at the bay surrounding them: a river ran into it, a shingle beach gave way to a salt marsh, and further inland, a forest. The land rose up and became a hard-edged plateau some miles distant.

'So the White City is over there?'

'This river runs through it. It's not an easy journey, nor is it short, but it's more certain than others.' Simeon stowed the telescope in his sea-chest. 'Down's magic still holds sway out this far, so be on your guard.'

Then Simeon reached past the telescope and started to assemble what Dalip thought was going to be a crude firearm. Certainly the first piece was a stock with a trigger, but the next wasn't a barrel, but a guide, and the third a steel crosspiece.

'A crossbow.'

'An arbalest.' He lifted up the winding mechanism and screwed it into place with his thumbs. 'There are things out there you don't want to have at with a sword.'

'I know.'

'Oh-oh? That story's one for the fireside, I'll wager.' He hooked a bag of crossbow bolts at his waist and attached a strap on to the iron rings front and back on the arbalest. 'Break out the boat. Volunteers for guard duty, see Dawson.'

He adjusted his hat firmly on his head, and Dalip went to find Mama.

'Stay or go?' he asked her.

'You have to go,' she said. 'That is, you wouldn't be happy if you stayed. Me, I'm not so sure, what with all that walking, and the clambering down to the rowing boat. That's not what I enjoy.'

'You have to see the White City. Just once.'

'Dalip, I'm not cut out for adventures. For sure, I'll stand up for myself if trouble comes my way, but I'm not going looking for it. I've found somewhere safe to stay for the while, and if I'm a fool for not leaving it, no better place than a *Ship of Fools* to be.' She saw Dalip's disappointment. 'I'm not young, not like you. You need to do these things, to see what you're made of, to prove to yourself that you're a man and not a boy. I know what I'm made of, and some bloodthirsty pirate is not it.'

She was right. Right for her, anyway. She went to find Dawson, and Dalip joined the queue for the boat trip ashore.

It inevitably took a long time, at four passengers a journey, to decant the raiding party to dry land. Some of the crew drifted away from the beach and into the forest – there seemed to be no reason not to follow them, so Dalip did the same.

It was similar to the landscape they'd first washed up in. Virgin forest, patterned in light and dark, with clearings of saplings centred around one or more rotting trunks of the fallen. The birds swooped and flitted between the branches, and it was cool and still under the canopy. After the constant movement of the ship's deck, it was strangely static.

Which might have been why it took him a while to realise that the ground was oddly stepped. Though the ubiquitous trees cared little about where they sprouted, the land itself was divided up into platforms, with their edges softened with age.

He couldn't be the first person to notice, surely? Others who'd passed this way would have seen what he was seeing, and commented on it to someone. He dropped to his knees and parted the undergrowth with his machete, cutting the roots and digging through the leaf litter until he came to something hard. Then he laid his weapon aside and used his hands to scrape what he'd found clear of debris.

It was a pavement of regular stone blocks. Most were cracked, some were missing, but there was enough left to show how the whole would have looked. He brushed his palms against his legs and picked up the machete again, holding it loosely by his side. He took in everything that he could, imagining the pavement extending from where he knelt to the next step. Beyond that, and to each side, to another pavement.

There'd been a city here once. Not a castle, or a collection of wooden huts: a city, with everything that the name entailed. A city which had fallen, and had been clawed back into the ground by Down, except that it was so vast that it still wasn't completely consumed. The memory of it remained, buried under the rotting leaves and broken by the soaring trees.

In the distance, a horn sounded long and low. He was being summoned back to the beach, and yet he knew it was more important to investigate the ruins and find a reason for the city's demise. When he'd uncovered those few paving stones, they were glazed white – and where would do that except at the site of the original White City?

The horn sounded again. He had to go. He kept looking back as he walked towards the sea. There should be towers, not trees. And if this was the White City, then where were they going?

When they formed up on the shingle bank, they numbered thirty or so. Ten had stayed aboard. It wasn't many, considering the *Ship of Fools* would comfortably hold twice their current number. He wondered how few they could get away with and still crew the boat safely. If things went badly for Simeon during the next few hours and days, he might have to hang his hat up permanently.

When they were ready, there were no stirring words, just a look into each man's or woman's eyes, and their captain turning his back on the sea and setting off along the bank of the river.

'Dalip?'

He stopped daydreaming and found himself walking next to Elena.

'You are well?'

'I ... yes, fine,' he said. 'I just have a bad feeling about this.'

'You think we will find Mary?'

He'd got used to the idea that he wouldn't. Now he had to contend with the idea that he might, and what he was going to do about that.

'I don't know.'

'What if she is with Crows?' She rested her hand on the pommel of her sabre. 'What will you do?'

'I don't know that either. We'll talk, I suppose.'

'I am sorry, Dalip. I have had much time to think, and I have decided: whatever Mary has done for us in the past, she is also responsible for Luiza. If she is still alive, then we have no choice but to take our revenge on her, too.'

'Crows is guilty. That's obvious. Anything else is up in the air.' He looked down at her, small and scared and determined. 'We have to give her a chance to speak for herself, if she's there. Which I can't see, myself. She went after Crows, and she never came back. If she could have, she would have.'

'You will not kill her, even if she deserves it?' He thought it was a question, but eventually realised it was a statement. And she was right: there was very little he could do about how he felt. 'It won't come to that.'

'The Wolfman is dead. Crows is next. Sebastian will kill Mary if I do not.' She nodded in the direction of the man who'd been giving her sword-fighting lessons.

'Perhaps you ...'

He wasn't in charge of her. He never had been. She got to make her own choices, and it appeared that one of those was to persuade another man to fight Mary.

'I should what?' she asked him.

'She's my friend. She needs to have the chance to explain

what happened. I'll protect her, if that's what's necessary.'

'You will fight me?'

'Will I fight you?' He chewed at his lip. He'd left this conversation far too late. If he'd said something sooner, then he might have been able to deflect her from her chosen path. As it was, they were now on a collision course. 'I'm so very sorry about Luiza. If Mary was involved in it – and I don't see how she could be – then okay: I'll stand aside. But if she's innocent, it's my duty to help her.'

Of course she wasn't going to fight him. But Sebastian might, if he thought the risk worth the reward. It all depended on Elena. And she'd changed, he suddenly realised. Changed from how she'd been before, and on her way to becoming ... what?

She was silent for a while, just walking next to Dalip, as she had done many times before. Then she shook her head and moved away, over to the other side of the group.

He didn't want to have to fight everyone, but it looked increasingly likely that he was going to have to. The prospect didn't fill him with joy, and he wondered what he could do to turn his fortune around. In the absence of Mama, he could talk to Simeon, see what he said.

They were at the forest, and they instinctively turned from a loose bunch to a ragged line. The shadows by the waterside still couldn't disguise the worn-thin structures further in. The riverbanks were thick with loose white stones, and the riverbed too, where they turned green with weed. Dalip could see it, and apparently no one else could.

There were answers here, and he knew he was missing them.

19

Mary was led along a corridor lined with doors, and across an open courtyard in the middle of the building. The pale stone walls that bounded the square had large windows – openings, at least – that overlooked her, but she couldn't see anyone else. Then she was back inside, and ushered into a dark room with vague shadows of furniture.

'Sit,' she was told. The woman opened a pair of shutters, and the weak light revealed a long table and a large, but empty, fireplace.

Mary perched on the very end of a low bench and waited. The room was cold, with a hint of damp lingering in the air. There were hooks hanging from the rafters, though whatever used to hang from them had gone. Stone sinks and scrubbed wooden counters seemed to suggest kitchens, but there was no food being cooked today.

The woman sat opposite her, subjecting her to a gaze so forensic that she felt her tongue start to loosen. She bit back on the impulse to talk, and deliberately folded her arms.

'What are you doing here, girl?'

'Wish the fuck I knew.' Mary chewed at her lip in lieu of anything more substantial. 'This is the White City, right? I mean, if it's not, I'm wasting your time and mine.'

'This is what they call the White City, yes.'

'It's a bit of a shit-hole.' She shrugged. 'Just saying.'

'It's not as it once was. But it's sufficient. Now, why don't you tell me why you're here?' The woman's voice wasn't impassive; she was far more interested in receiving than giving answers.

'This is where people with questions come. And I've got a fuckload of questions.'

That earned her a look of scorn. 'That's just lazy. What questions do you think can be answered here, rather than anywhere else?'

'How about why the fuck am I in Down, and not dead in a fire back in London?'

'Anything else?'

'A million things. The moon – I mean, what the fuck's that all about? Then there's the castles, the villages, and how they tie in with the portals? The magic, the beasts, the things that don't make any sense; like storms that want to kill you? Where the fuck are all the stars? Geomancers and their stupid map obsession, time travel, this place with its no-magic black hole, and the big one: where the fuck is everybody?' Mary leaned her elbows on the table. 'If we could make a start with those, I can probably think of a few more as we go.'

The other woman wore the monologue with blank-faced disdain.

'You didn't ask how to get home.'

'Did you expect me to?'

'Everyone else does.'

'I'm not everyone else.' She was pleased with that, and now the woman's expression softened slightly.

'What do you want from me, girl?'

Mary took the opportunity to ask the most pressing thing on her mind: 'Who do I have to kill round here to get some food? You?'

The woman looked pointedly around the room. 'You'll find me singularly indigestible.'

'I didn't mean that. Though, do they do that here?'

'Not … not here.' She equivocated. 'What happens in the rest of Down isn't my concern.'

'Oh, well that makes it so much better.' Mary put her full purse on the table in front of her, and opened it up. Fortunately, the iron key had worked its way down, and stayed hidden. 'So how much is this going to cost me? And what exactly's on offer here? If it's not answers or food, or both, I'm going somewhere else.'

'There is nowhere else. It's here or the road.'

'There are plenty of other doors to try.'

'You can try them all, but none of the others will open to you. You want to talk to someone, you have to talk to me.'

Mary dipped her hand into her honours and skimmed some off the top. She let them fall back into the pile, one at a time. 'If that's the case, why do I have these?'

'Tradition.'

'I think you're lying. I think if I walk out of here and ask around, I can get a better deal.'

'You want food?'

'I want food.'

'Wait here.' The woman stood up and went to the door.

Mary stayed precisely where she was just long enough for the woman's footsteps to echo away, then sprung from her seat to explore the room.

It didn't take her long: what little there was was on view. There was no clutter, no debris, nothing of normal life, just the dust of age. There should have been something, though, in a corner or under a shelf. But the room had been picked clean long before she'd got there. She eyed the ceiling hooks suspiciously and went to the window, to peer out across the courtyard.

Nothing else stirred. She could hear the river's deep rumble, and that was all. Which was why, when she turned her head and saw another man leaning out of the next room along, doing the same as her, she gave an involuntary squeak.

He stared at her without blinking, his wide, dark-ringed eyes full of desperation and regret.

'What?' she said, recovering. 'Seriously, what? You're giving me the fear.'

'You're not one of them,' he finally managed.

'One of them?'

'A Lord or Lady,' said the man, scraping his long, thinning hair up over the top of his head.

'Are you saying I've got no manners?'

'The rulers of the White City, I mean. You must have seen them.'

'I've not met any kings or queens, if that's what you mean.'

The man leaned forward, gripping the window frame. 'You should get yourself away,' he said to Mary. 'Refuse to give them anything. This place. This whole place. It's nothing but a trap.'

'But I'm here for answers!'

'That's what they want you to think.' He was leaning so far out of the window he was almost falling into the courtyard. 'They put this rumour about that they can answer all your questions, and maybe they can, but what they do is take everything that you know and give you back nowt. A little bit here, a little bit there, but it doesn't make anything clearer.' He nervously glanced behind him, then at Mary. 'We come from all over Down, fight our way here, die on our way here, and for what? I had a friend. A good pal. He ... changed. Couldn't help him. I'm left wondering when it'll be my turn.'

They stared at each other in silence for a moment.

'Go,' he urged. 'While you still can.'

Then he was jerked away, dragged back in to his room by unseen hands. She spun around and found that she was being watched from the doorway. The woman, now carrying a steaming bowl, narrowed her eyes.

'What did I tell you?'

Her tone was perilously close to that of a school teacher, but Mary was sufficiently alarmed not to rise to the obvious bait. 'To wait here. And I did. Who was that? And what did he mean, this place is a trap?'

'Don't concern yourself about him. He ran out of honour, and has to leave. That's all.' She put the bowl on the table, and shoved it in Mary's direction. The smell was slight, but it triggered all of Mary's hunger.

What it was exactly was difficult to identify – some sort of stew. But as she was having to focus on not dribbling, she realised she didn't care. Even with the man's warning ringing in her ears, she was drawn towards the bowl, and the crudely carved spoon protruding from the brown mess.

A few minutes later, she glanced up. The woman was watching her with amused detachment.

'What? I'm fucking starving.'

She scraped the edge of the spoon across the grain of the wood and thought about picking it up to lick it clean. She just about stopped herself. She pushed the bowl away, and hoped there'd be an offer of seconds, but there was none forthcoming.

The woman started to circle the table, and Mary kept a wary eye on her, her hand resting on the dagger.

'Why don't we start with your name?'

'Why don't we start with yours?'

'You've nothing to bargain with, girl.'

'So what are these for?' Mary threw a handful of honour on to the table, where they rattled and rolled. 'I came for answers, not questions.'

'You're just another squib. Come back when you know something.'

'I'm not going anywhere. I've done things you wouldn't even believe, that I couldn't imagine anyone doing, let alone me. Now I'm finally here, in what's supposed to be Down's only city.'

She pushed her seat back and brandished her dagger. 'I've had enough. If you know what the fuck's going on, you're going to tell me.'

'If we gave you the dagger,' she said, 'what makes you think it can be used against me?'

'You bleed the same as me.'

She didn't confirm or deny that, just continued circling and moving out of Mary's immediate range. 'Can you use magic?' she asked.

Mary wondered what Dalip would say. 'Why don't you tell me what magic is and where it comes from, and I'll tell you if I can use it.'

Another question was poised on the woman's lips, but she instead sat down opposite Mary. 'We've started off on the wrong foot,' she said. 'I know you've come here looking for answers. We're looking for answers too. Think of it as pooling our information. We stay here, and we record what travellers tell us about what's happening in Down. We try and make sense of this world, so we can help those who come to us.'

'That man next door: did you help him? Or did you do a number on him, slap him around a bit, work him over for what he knows? Because he didn't look very helped.'

'Some people expect us to have all the answers, and are disappointed when we don't.' She gave a theatrical shrug. 'Coming to Down doesn't appear to require any sort of test of intelligence or wisdom.'

'Well, you got here,' said Mary, and saw that she'd momentarily got to the woman. But rather than annoyance, there was blank-faced confusion that flicked on, then off. Something was definitely going on, and she didn't know what. One last try, then. 'That bloke: the one I talked to, the one who was telling me to run. I want to see him again.'

'And what good would that do? He doesn't have any answers.'

'Neither do you, it seems. For all this "let's hold hands and share everything" patter, you're not giving anything away, are you? He was right. This is … fake.'

'Sit down, girl.'

'Fuck you.'

'You know this isn't how it's supposed to work, don't you? You're supposed to come here, and tell us your stories of where you came from, and what you've seen, and then we send you back out, just as ignorant as when you arrived, to get more information for us. Sometimes you even come back, you're that pliable. That gullible.'

The door was the other side of the table, and the woman between it and Mary. But there was always the window at her back, and Mary was no stranger to using one as an exit.

'For those who see through the charade, it's a little different. We make you tell us. We make you tell us everything.' The woman reached up and peeled her face away, dragging it off like it was a scab. The skull underneath was moist and running with a pink fluid. She gasped like she was coming up for air as her exposed white bone started to dry.

'Fuck.'

It wasn't a skull. It was a mask. White, porcelain, oddly beautiful; anorexic-model beautiful, with immobile features, huge dark eyes, and cheekbones like knife-blades. She pulled her hand down across her forehead, her nose, her chin, and flicked the last of the slime on to the floor. Her pale, matt features were almost, but not quite, human. Then she pulled her hair off her egg-like head and held it nonchalantly in her hand.

Mary grabbed her bag of honours, and was up and over the windowsill before anyone could stop her. Now, if only she could remember the way out.

No, she was good at this: she knew which door to run for, how to barge through it without stopping, how to scan the corridor ahead for obstacles and threats. She was already at the outer door by the time the first figure blocked out the light at the other end.

'There's no need for this,' called the woman. 'You won't get away.'

'The fuck I won't,' said Mary to herself. Her heart was banging its way out of her chest, just like the old days when she was dodging the foot traffic on Oxford Street, uniforms a distant second. It took her a moment to wrestle with the unfamiliar door mechanism, and she was outside, looking around and panting.

Except she still wasn't alone.

Coming down the dirt road was a loose knot of people. Two wore long, floor-length electric-blue robes, with white masks peering out from under their hoods. Two were just men, grey and dirty-looking. And one was Crows.

It was the colour that startled her most. Where did they get the material from? She'd seen nothing like it so far in all of Down: they were like parakeets in the park, in amongst the browns and greys and blacks of the other birds. The fact that Crows was with them dragged her mind back to the moment.

He looked no different from when she'd last seen him, climbing up the cliff. The same serious smile, the same self-deprecating manner.

'What have you done?' she snapped at him. 'You didn't tell them, did you? Say you didn't tell them.'

There was movement behind her, and she swung around, backing into the road, standing between the two groups. The woman stepped out just beyond the threshold, and two more men were behind her. At least, she assumed it was the woman from the clothing. The white mask she showed was identical to those the two in blue wore.

Mary was confused. And scared. And angry.

Crows edged forward, not wishing to leave his … friends? Allies? Shit. This was why he'd wanted to bring the maps to the White City.

'They are not yours, Mary. It is time to give them up.'

'They're not here, and I'll never tell you where they are.'

'They know they're in the valley, Mary. They know. The ferryman is one of them, and he saw you with a sack of what could only be the maps.'

'What do you get, Crows? What do you get in return?'

'Down.' He looked almost embarrassed as he said it. 'I get Down. These good people: they will rule here. And I will rule the rest.'

'Is that what they told you? You think that's what they'll do?'

'Once the maps are assembled, and the shape of Down finally revealed, yes. They are not that interested in us. They care nothing for us. Once I have served their purposes, then I will claim my reward.'

'You want the maps, Crows?' She levelled her dagger over the distance between them, pointed directly at his heart. 'Why don't you come and take them?'

'That is not how we do things, Mary. Come. Be reasonable.'

'Reasonable? Reasonable? You killed Luiza. I'll give you fucking reasonable.' She lunged at him, and he retreated rapidly.

'Daniel has paid for his sins.' Crows held his hands up. 'I work only for the greater good.'

'No.' She whirled around to address the woman. 'If you don't stop him, then whatever game you have here is finished. He'll screw you over just like he screwed me.'

The woman inclined her head. The blue-robed figures did likewise. As if they were listening to another voice. They were deciding her fate, and she couldn't even hear what was being said.

They were, however, busy for the moment.

She glanced to one side: the river, and its precarious stepping stones. Up the valley side and away. She guessed that if she ran, empty-handed, they'd not follow her. On the other side, the road led back towards her locked shelter, and the maps. If she was quick – quicker than the Lords and Ladies and their servants – she could grab them. Then she just had to get past the ferryman and back out into the land of magic.

And he had a rifle.

No one was ever going to accuse her of making things easy for herself.

20

As they moved inland, the trees grew sparse and stunted: less a majestic cathedral and more an abandoned waste ground. The river cut more deeply, embedding itself between high-sided banks, until it flowed fast and deep.

The land seemed to funnel itself towards a point in the distance, where slabs of rock reared up out of the valley floor and the river emerged from the high plateau above through a slit. They'd been walking towards it all morning, and they were close now.

Then, rather than the constant slow rise, there was a dip, just before the river-cut. At the bottom of that bowl of land, there were two jetties facing each other across a point where the water was briefly wide and slack. On the far side, Dalip could see a little square raft of split logs tethered to the pier, and beyond that a tiny shack with the thinnest of banners of blue smoke waving above it.

They were getting somewhere. Simeon did indeed know the way.

The river between the piers wasn't so deep as to prove a particular problem, and the raft looked more of a courtesy than a necessity. At the end of their jetty was a bell on a post. Their captain had already decided that a dozen trips by raft to ferry his raiding party across would go against the spirit of their endeavours. He motioned for them to stay quiet, and enter the river in groups of five.

Because he was the captain, he was in the first group; and because Dalip was worried about Mary, he was too.

The water was cold and heavy. He could touch the bottom almost all the way across, his feet churning up the soft silt, the colour of the water downstream becoming milky. They emerged again just below the other jetty, using its uprights to assist their climb up the bank.

They crouched in the scrub, waiting for the others to cross. Simeon shook the water from his arbalest, and wound the string back using the cranks. The metal arms creaked slightly as they bowed, and the trigger mechanism clicked as it engaged.

Slowly and steadily, the other groups pulled themselves up and took up positions hidden behind bushes or clumps of wiry grass.

The inhabitant of the hut showed no sign of having spotted his unannounced visitors, and it became clear that Simeon wouldn't make their presence known if he could avoid it. He crept forward to have clear sight – and clear aim – of the closed door, and indicated that each group should go on towards the sharp river-made scar in the wall of rock ahead.

None of them used the track which ran by the side of the shack, instead creeping through the undergrowth. If anyone had looked they would have been seen, especially Dalip in his orange overalls. They were, however, quiet. No one heard them, and the sounds of their passing were easily camouflaged by the low rumble of the river and the bright hiss of the wind in the leaves.

Simeon was the last to leave, his cocked arbalest ready to shoot as he skirted the structure. No one came out to investigate. They passed undiscovered.

The next obstacle was the narrow path that ran by the river as it pierced the rock wall. The straight-sided slice taken out of the plateau echoed with the sound of white water below, and the wind whipped through, blustering and making it feel far more dangerous than it really was: the path was flat and dry, and the long, snaking line of pirates only had to concentrate on where they were putting their feet to come out the other side.

The valley widened out into a long scar that followed the course of the river, and after the dim gorge, the acres of bare, pale rock were almost blindingly bright. Dalip moved up further to allow those behind him entrance. He crunched up the scree, shielding his eyes from the glare with one hand.

He blinked as the scene slowly resolved. There was a crowd of people a little way off, in amongst a series of what looked like half-buried cubes. Beyond them were more substantial buildings, and there were fields and a waterfall and other features, but his gaze was drawn hypnotically back towards the people.

There were at least two distinct types. One formed an outer perimeter, their pale faces at variance with the block-colour gaudiness of their robes. They seemed to be standing and silently watching as the grey-and-brown workers attempted to dismantle one of the cubes, shouting and swearing as they darted in and out to grab pieces of stone.

The stone, inexplicably, was fighting back, judging from the number of men clutching their bloodied hands.

Dalip drew close to Simeon, who was having equal difficulty understanding what was happening.

'Are they mad? Are they taken with drink or poppy juice?'

'I have absolutely no idea.'

The rest of the pirates filled the slopes, each gazing with wonder at the bizarre sight and the mean collection of buildings.

'Is this supposed to be …?' asked Dalip, He knew that the real White City was the overgrown ruins down by the sea. This place was a shadow of it, barely a conscious aping of the fallen grandeur.

'Yes.' Simeon knocked his hat further down over his eyes. 'Not much to look at, is it?'

'No. But if this is where Crows came, this is where we're supposed to be.' Dalip felt his fist instinctively tighten about his machete's grip, because there was Crows, standing amongst the robed figures, his tattered black cloak all but a shadow.

He searched for Elena in the faces around him, wondering what she'd do, now that she wasn't alone and unarmed, but instead had an army at her back.

He didn't have to wonder. She was already running forward, sabre outstretched.

'Crows! Crows, we have come for you!'

'So much for keeping a tight ship,' said Simeon. Rather than be left behind, he started after her, catching her up and then pulling ahead.

Dalip felt his legs move, despite his better judgement, or because of it, he couldn't tell. But he was advancing too, and with him Dawson, the steersman, Sebastian, and everyone else: a loose, uncoordinated wave, washing towards the strange robed figures, their flighty, dancing servants, and Crows.

They were spotted, although it wasn't as if they were trying to hide any longer. Crows saw several faces he knew and had never expected to see again. He was the first to back away, but certainly not the last. All of them began to withdraw, those wearing robes first, their men afterwards, moving away from the stone cube they'd been so intent on dismantling. They headed down the slope towards the road and the buildings.

Elena picked up her pace. So did they.

Then it became a chase, and rapidly a rout, as the pirates raised their weapons and roared and whooped and ululated. They ran them down the street, and those in robes with their immobile white faces peeled off, heading to one door or another, thinning the pack down by twos and threes.

Dalip caught up with Elena, hooked his hand around her arm

and pulled her back. She tried to shake him off, but he refused to let go.

'Crows,' she said.

'We're too spread out. Simeon, tell her.'

'Chased the dastards indoors, but unless we go house to house, dragging them out by their scruffs, there's no further advantage in our current position. Singh – you and Dawson gather the troops up at the defile, seal this place up tight like a cork in a bottle. I'll hold the fort here until an orderly retreat – unlike our advance – can be achieved.'

Simeon sounded the horn, and the chasing pack slowed and milled about, staring up at the high, blank walls and tiny, out-of-reach slitted windows.

'Come on, you sea-dogs. Rally and regroup. If the cowards won't stand and fight, we'll have to stir them in their lairs.'

Elena growled, and directed her frustration at Dalip.

'We could have caught him.'

'We were nowhere near catching him. And we know he's here, that's the important thing.'

'This cannot wait!' She backed away from him. 'He must pay.'

'He will. Just not this very second.'

'If he escapes—'

'We'll have to make sure he doesn't. But there's no magic here: he can't use his crows or cover himself in darkness or anything like that.'

'You know,' she said, 'that his lying heart is the most dangerous thing about him. He needs no magic for that.'

'Elena, we've cornered him and he's not getting away. Let's do what Simeon says, and you'll have all the help you need to catch Crows.'

Dawson, holding the horn, sounded it again and started the general retreat towards the scattered cube structures. Dalip obeyed, and when she realised that everyone else was following, so did Elena, stamping her feet, cursing loudly and swiping at the air with her sabre. Dalip stayed away, and so did the others. Even Sebastian walked behind her, out of range.

They gathered amongst the stone cubes, which weren't solid, but hollow, with heavy slabs making the roofs, and lockable doors built into the downslope faces. Which was interesting, considering that the robed people and their minions had been trying to pick one apart.

Dalip tried to find which one it was. Up close, they all looked the same, and it was only by carefully comparing where he'd been standing earlier with what he could see now that he found it, further uphill and at the end of a row.

The ground around it was no different – the cliff wall spalled shards like shattered bricks, so none of the buildings had used dressed stone. Just that where the edges of the other structures were straight, this one was ragged. Dalip circled it at a respectful distance, and wondered what it contained.

The door, when he tried it, was locked fast. But such was the dry-stone construction that he thought he might be able to peer through the cracks to see inside. The instant he put his hand on the wall, he felt a sharp sting. He jerked away, and clenched his fist tight. A bright drop of blood squeezed out.

When he thought he could, he unrolled his fingers and inspected the wound. Something had punched a hole in the palm of his hand, and it was bleeding. The steersman saw him and went to inspect the structure himself. Dalip waved him back.

'Careful.' He held up his hand as proof of the danger.

'What's inside?'

'Something sharp.' Dalip clenched his fist again. 'They seemed very keen on getting it out.'

'I'll tell the cap'n.'

Simeon came over and inspected the problem.

'If it was important to them, it's important to us. Get it open.' He frowned at door. 'Have you tried knocking?'

'Do you think it'd help?' asked Dalip.

'If it's some fell beast inside, no, and we can safely leave it where it is. If it's a captive of theirs, then the poor soul can be released into our care. The enemy of my enemy is my friend, and all that.'

He strode forward and, avoiding any of the open stonework, rapped his knuckles on the thick wooden door.

'Ahoy in there. Are you man, or monster?'

'Fuck off.'

Dalip's eyes went wide. 'Mary?'

'You can fuck off too.'

'You know her? You're full of surprises, Singh. Winkle the good lady out, if you please.'

Dalip approached, still nursing his hand. 'Mary? It's Dalip. You can come out now.'

There was silence. Then: 'Dalip? Are you sure?'

'As sure as I can be.'

'Tell me something only Dalip would know.'

'I …'

'Well, go on, man,' urged Simeon.

'Boots. You wanted me to take someone's boots, but only if they were dead.'

'Did you?'

He looked down at the Wolfman's boots. 'Yes. Yes I did.'

The lock turned with a heavy click, and the door creaked open a sliver.

'Come where I can see you.'

He stepped to one side, and he could see Mary's dark eye flicker in the darkness. She looked him up and down, and after a moment, emerged blinking into the light. She had a slim dagger in her hand.

'Did I do that to you?' she asked.

'This?' He held up his hand. 'Yes.'

'Sorry.' She shook her head. 'What the fuck are you even doing here?'

'I could ask you the same thing, but with less swearing. You went after Crows. You didn't come back.' He felt himself grow short of breath. 'We thought you were dead.'

'I had to stay with the maps,' she said. 'I couldn't come back without them.'

Simeon stepped between them. 'As touching as this unexpected reunion might be, I hear the call of treasure. Madam, does Crows still have the maps?'

'Who the fuck is this clown?'

'This is the pirate captain who took us on board, looked after us, sailed us across the sea and just chased those robed weirdos away.' Dalip went to wipe the sweat away from his face with his hand, and winced as he inadvertently smeared himself with blood. 'What happened to you?'

'The maps?' repeated Simeon. 'We have an aversion to the land, and wish to be about our business. That business being, stealing the maps, spitting Crows like a spatchcocked hen, thumbing my nose at the Lords of the White City, and valiantly running away.'

'You want the maps?'

'Indeed. No greater prize exists in all of Down. Again, I ask you: does Crows still have them?' The captain fixed her with a hard stare.

'If you want Crows, then you'll have to dig him out. He's somewhere down there.' She pointed over the top of the scree slope at the compounds. 'These places are built like castles. You'll have your work cut out for you.'

'Indeed we will. We are, however, dread pirates, and shirking is not in our vocabulary.' He bowed low, sweeping his hat off for the grand gesture. 'Your appearance is most timely, and we are, as ever, pleased to serve the cause of freedom in this captive land. Dawson? Rally the troops. We have work to do.'

The horn brought the raiding party to order, and they moved as a mass, heading across the rocky slope towards the road. Mary called out to Elena as she passed by, but the blank stare that met her shout confused her.

'I thought ... what's with her? Isn't she, you know, glad I'm not dead?'

'It's complicated. She thinks you conspired with Crows to steal the maps from us, and get Luiza killed.'

'But I didn't.'

'She's not really worried about the truth. Promise me you'll stay away from her until we can sort this out. She's grieving, and Down knows it.' Dalip looked at his palm, which had almost stopped bleeding, and was beginning to really hurt. 'I should go with them. I'm part of the crew now.'

'Where's Mama?'

'Back at the boat. She's not exactly a fighter.'

'And you are?'

'For the right cause.'

She looked behind her at the stone shelter, then back again at Dalip. 'I've got the maps here, in this shelter.'

'You've what?'

'Shut up. Not so loud. I went through some seriously fucked-up shit to get them, and I'm not going to hand them to Captain whatever-his-face-is, am I?'

'God give me strength,' he groaned. 'I've got to tell them.'

She grabbed hold of his arm. 'You do not. We need to get these maps out of here, back into Down proper, and work out what the fuck is going on. The ones wearing the long dresses – I don't think they're even human.'

Dalip pointed his machete at the backs of the ship's crew disappearing over the rise. 'They saved us – me, Mama, Elena – after you vanished. I – we – owe them.'

'You might, but I don't. Listen to me. Crows told us a whole load of bullshit: if there are any answers here, we'll never find them. He brought the maps to the White City to give them to the Lords and Ladies, and in return, he thinks he's going to rule

Down. We need to find out how that happens, and we're not going to if I hand everything over to your captain. Come with me, now, while they're busy looking for Crows.'

Now he was breathless for an entirely different reason. 'Is this worth people dying for? Because that's what's going to happen.' He shook his head. 'No. It's not worth it.'

He tore himself free and ran after Simeon, the loose rock slipping and sliding beneath his feet.

21

As Mary watched him go, she remembered what Dalip had said, what seemed like an eternity ago. Whoever controlled the portals, controlled not just Down, but all of the Londons over all time. That was what Crows really wanted. And if the maps really did allow that, then whoever caught her first would win. Who would she rather see in control: a bunch of faceless monsters that Crows seemed happy to deal with, or a shipload of pirates that now inexplicably included Dalip, Mama and Elena?

There was really only one person she trusted, and that was always and only ever going to be herself. And even then, she wasn't so sure.

Perhaps she could have gone after Dalip. She could have tried to bring him down and stop him, but he wasn't the timid, skinny little thing he'd been before. She wanted him to come with her, and the maps, but it looked like that wasn't going to happen.

'Fuck,' she said, and retrieved the bag, holding it by its gathered neck. She stood at the entrance to the shelter and looked hurriedly around. Where could she go?

There were two ways out of the valley. Behind her, through the gorge, and ahead of her, across the river. The stepping stones and the path up the cliff were totally exposed. And the way through the narrow gorge was blocked, not just by the ferryman at the other end, but by a couple of lairy-looking pirates on guard at this.

There was nowhere in the valley she could hide, was there? All of the compounds were out: apparently that was where the Lords and Ladies lived, when they weren't ripping their fake faces off. The shelters were, as she'd already proved, nothing but traps.

There was one building left that might offer her sanctuary: the dome-roofed circular structure. If it was some sort of church, then at least no one would attack her there, surely? It might be better than that, too. She could make a break for it, come nightfall. Even without magic to disguise her, she was good at sneaking.

The pirates would have to leave empty-handed once they'd flushed Crows out, and by the time the White City had reorganised itself, she'd be long gone, back into a place where magic worked. No Dalip, no Mama with her, but finding a place where a castle might grow wasn't going to be difficult, not with all those maps. Down would provide. Wouldn't it? The Red Queen would start on her own, but she wouldn't stay that way for long.

She spent a second relocking the door behind her, and flinging the key wide and high so that no one would find it amongst the stones, then set off as fast as she could, arms windmilling to try and keep her balance, ignoring the taluses clawing at the soles of her feet.

She knew she was clutching at straws: here, where there was no magic, no sudden unexpected luck would fall in her favour. Despite that, she was still the sort of girl who'd leave herself open to one last let-down, just so she could tease herself with the thought that she was a worthless fuck-up who destroyed everything good in her life.

Dalip was just over the rise, telling his captain that she'd lied to them all, and the maps were right there. They'd be swarming back any moment to find her and force her to hand them over. Or run her through and prise them from her cold, dead hand.

She darted left, into the gap between the high walls of two opposing compounds, and stopped at the corner, opposite the round building. She had to cross the open space between the two, yet she could hear the pirates' horn sound to signal yet another change in direction. She hung on to the wall, back pressed to the sharp stones, head tilted back towards the slit of sky. She was overlooked by the windows of the next compound down, and she thought she could see a flicker of movement behind one of them.

How long before the robed creatures regrouped and came after her as well? What if they decided to use force themselves, rather than rely on their servants? They'd outnumber the pirates then, and they certainly hadn't revealed more than a fraction of what they were capable of.

She swallowed hard, and ran to the side of the domed building, flattening herself against it as if her red dress might disappear when turned sideways. She crept carefully around half of it, and there was no door.

The other half was exposed – no sheltering walls to hide her. The pirates had headed back towards her stone shelter. She could move another quarter of the circumference around.

Still no door.

If she stepped out any further, she'd be seen. It'd take them a little while to spot her, and a little longer to reach her. There was nothing for it but to show herself and hope.

She was almost back to where she'd started when the cry went up. Which would have still given her time, if there had actually been a door for her to open and bar behind her. There was nothing. The circular wall was as blank as the roof. No door, not even the hint of a door. No way in, no refuge.

That, it appeared, was the end of that idea.

She was out of viable options. Time to just pick something

and do it. So she ran down to the road, turned left and along to the sharp bend, where the track met the ridiculous stepping stones and wound up the side of the valley. The noise of rushing and clattering told her that the pirates were behind her, and she didn't need to look back to check.

She skipped off the road, her skirts flying. The Lords and Ladies were all watching her now, openly from their first-floor windows, every one of them seemingly crowded with faces. Could she use them? Dare she?

'What are you waiting for? Come and get me!'

The slope speeded her up. She drew level with the building by the river as the door was just opening. Her path flattened, and the chasm the river rumbled through was right in front of her, the thin pillars of stone looking increasingly dangerous as she closed on them.

She couldn't hesitate. She pushed off from the edge, hit the first square on, took the second one safely, and very nearly missed the third completely. Stumbling was out of the question. It was a long way down, and she was carrying the wealth of Down in one hand.

'That's quite far enough, young lady.' It was Simeon.

She stopped, halfway across. The pillar she was on was wide enough for both feet, but not much more than that. She looked at the far shore: three more pillars to go. She could manage those. If she reached the bottom of the stairs, she could climb up to the top of the cliff, and back into the magic.

Tempting, but no. She shuffled around to confront the pirate band. Dagger in one hand, maps in the other, she held her arms out either side.

'Anyone starts to cross, I jump. Got it?'

The captain lowered his loaded arbalest, the pointed bolt now aimed at the surging river far below her feet rather than at her heart. The whole crowd of pirates was gathering behind him. Some found themselves on the brink of the gorge, and pushed back, even as others were pressing forward to see what was happening. The captain leaned forward and looked askance at the drop, and the narrowness of the stepping stones.

'We appear to be at somewhat of an impasse.'

'If I knew what one was, okay. That.'

The captain leaned into the man next to him and muttered a brief instruction. The man disappeared into the crowd behind, to be replaced by Dalip.

'Mary. What are you doing?'

'I am trying,' she said, 'to do my best.'

'You could come back over here and we could try together.'

'Right now, standing on this stupidly thin piece of rock is the best I can do. Also, you're surrounded.'

They were not quite surrounded, but it sounded dramatic. The figures in robes lurked at the back, their servants in front. The men had swords and clubs. They stood between the road and the river, blocking it and sending the pirate chosen for special duties by his captain back towards his own group.

'Mary,' said Dalip, 'please be reasonable ...'

'I am being fucking reasonable. These maps don't belong to you, and they don't belong to them either. None of you made the fucking things – everybody who drew one, except me, was killed by the geomancers to protect their precious knowledge. I'm the only person here who can say any part of this is theirs. So, on behalf of all those poor fuckers who can't speak because they're dead, I claim the right to say what happens to them.'

'Brave words, madam,' said the captain, 'possibly even true ones. However, I find that possession is nine-tenths of the law: once your property becomes mine, your rights over said chattel become moot.'

'And if that means what I think it means, come and get it. Dare you.'

'Very well. Never let it be said that I abrogated my

responsibilities.' He passed the crossbow to the nearest sailor, and drew his cutlass.

'If you take one step I'll throw myself in the river, and the maps are coming with me.'

'I'm going to call your bluff. I think you'd rather I had them than lose them to the water. Did the dead labour in vain? We shall see.'

He started to size up his first jump when Dalip put his arm across the captain's chest.

'I'll go.'

'Captain's privilege, Singh. Mine the risk, mine the reward.'

'She'll jump.'

'She won't.'

'I bloody will.'

'Stand back, Singh. I believe I have the advantage here.'

But before he could leap to the first stepping stone, a murmuring from behind him distracted him. Exasperated, he turned, and found himself face to mask with a red-robed figure.

'You will not risk the maps.'

The captain lazily raised his sword, contemplated the edge, and pressed the point into the angle between carefully sculpted jaw and cloth-wrapped neck. The figure raised its head slightly to accommodate the intrusion, but made no attempt to back away.

'You will not risk the maps,' it repeated. 'We can fight, or we can talk.'

'Fight,' said a pirate, and other voices immediately agreed.

'Aye, we came to fight, not parley.'

'Loot their houses, and head for the sea.'

'Fight them. Ain't so many that we can't take 'em.'

'So say my crew,' said the captain. He added a little more pressure. The point grated against something hard. 'You do bleed, don't you? Are you men or monsters beneath your disguises?'

'We are monsters far worse than anything Down can imagine.'

Mary seriously considered running away. No one was looking

at her. It wasn't as if the Lords and Ladies of the White City would let the pirates chase after her: neither were the pirates going to stand back and allow the robed figures to pass. This was what she wanted. This was why she'd lied. She, and only she, should determine the fate of the maps. Not these robed clowns. Nor this motley crew. She looked up at the cliff and judged her next jump.

There would be a bloodbath, though, and the survivors would hunt her down to her dying day. Worse still, Dalip would be in the middle of it all, and if he survived, he'd turn against her. That ... would be difficult. She wanted a friend. She wanted him as a friend.

She had the power to decide, one way or the other. She gritted her teeth and turned back around.

'What the fuck is wrong with you people? Seriously, just talk to each other. We might even learn something useful. You in the robe? What makes the maps so important?'

The figure slowly reached up and curled a hand around the cutlass blade. Their grip was such that the sword sank into the narrow bridge of flesh between fingers and thumb, and pink liquid started to run towards the hilt. The captain tried to resist, but the point inexorably moved away from the figure's exposed throat.

With one last little shove, the captain staggered back, red-faced, and was caught by Dalip before he pitched over the edge of the ravine.

'The maps represent our work. Sooner or later, we knew they would all come to us. We had expected them one by one, or a few at a time. Not, as has apparently happened, all at once.'

'So ... what? The geomancers are working for you?'

'As a tree works for a gardener. The tree neither knows nor cares about the fate of its fruit, whether it is eaten by birds, falls to the ground to rot, or is harvested by the owner. So are those you call geomancers to us. They bear the fruit. We harvest it.'

The robed figure turned to address her directly. 'That is our harvest. It belongs to us.'

'But,' she said, 'you know what bastards they all are.'

'We planted the seeds in the minds of the first geomancers: do this and you will control Down, we said. They went forth and the seed grew until it became a tree, a tree that would multiply and cover the face of Down. Now, the harvest is gathered in. You hold it in your hand.'

She felt sick. She swallowed against the bile rising in her throat.

'So what do you want them for?'

'You would not understand.'

'Are you calling me stupid?'

The figure's impassive white mask tilted with its head. 'Let me rephrase. You may have some degree of agency, but you are not in full command of the facts. This leads you to behave in a sub-optimal way.'

'You're still calling me stupid, right?'

'If you understood, you would hand the maps to me without hesitation. You would know you had no alternative.'

There was now a little semicircular space around the figure. The pirates had backed off slightly, wary of this strange creature which ignored gaping wounds in its hand and was far stronger than any normal man. Dalip stepped into that gap and walked slowly around it.

'Why don't you make us understand, then? Go on. They say out there, that if we get enough maps together, we can control the portals, and maybe go back home. Is that right?'

'The truth is beyond your comprehension. Any of you. I cannot explain it simply enough, and your minds are too weak to grasp the complexity of the answer.'

'Try. Or is your own understanding flawed? Do you really know what's going on, or has Down changed the rules for you?'

'You ignorant savage. You dare argue with me?'

'You're the reason Down's been corrupted. You created the geomancers. You're the reason I had to fight for my life in a pit. So yes, I dare. I dare a whole lot more than just argue. Your influence – your contamination – over Down has to end.' He raised his machete, ready to strike.

'Dalip, don't. Don't take it on. Swords won't hurt it.'

'Is that so?' He carried on circling the figure, and the figure kept turning to face him.

'They gave me this dagger to make me feel safer. Work it out.'

The white mask fixed Mary with its impenetrable stare.

'Enough. Give me the maps and you may go.'

With a tremendous and sudden charge, Dalip rammed the figure from behind. It almost wasn't enough, and it was almost too much. It spent what seemed like an age tipped over too far for recovery and yet still not falling. Dalip was dragged back at the last moment by the captain or he would have preceded the fluttering robes into the white-flecked river below.

Mary watched it fall, all the way down, until it splashed down and the water covered it. She thought it would emerge a moment later, spluttering and coughing, but that time stretched and eventually snapped. It wasn't going to resurface.

'Fuck, Dalip. What have you done?'

The servants of the White City took a belated step forward, and the pirates formed a line to face them. Neither side was certain of what to do next.

'They'll never tell us what we need to know now.'

'They never were. Because if we knew, we'd stop them.'

She was running out of steam. 'Stop them from doing what?'

'I don't know! But given the way they're going about it, I don't think I'm going to like the result, and neither are you. We simply don't count in whatever it is that they have planned. We're never going to make them care – you heard it – so we have to work this out by ourselves, for ourselves. This is where it happens, though,' said Dalip. 'Nowhere else. This is where it gets done.'

Mary looked at where she was, balanced on a pillar of rock high above a fast-flowing river, both hands full.

Simeon peered down into the river, where there was still no sign of the robed figure. 'I may have been hasty, good lady. You have my word, as a captain, that if you were to return to us, the maps will remain your property, to do with as you see fit. All I ask in return is no more lies. It seems they are altogether more dangerous and more deadly here than in the rest of Down.'

'Okay,' she said, and nodded. 'You are a pirate captain, though, right?'

'As I informed young Singh here, we're the good kind of pirates. My word is my bond. Besides,' he added, 'I think you'll find throwing your lot in with us is slightly more appealing, now we know they're not human. Remain where you are, while we chase them off the streets again. We'll consider our options after that. Singh? See that no one gets past you.'

He retrieved his hat, set it on his head, and moved through the pirates until he was at the front. He kept walking, and they followed with a shout. The crew met the servants with the ringing of metal and the cracking of skulls. And still the Lords of the White City declined to act, even as they saw their men get cut down, one by one, by the far more accomplished pirates.

'Dalip? Dalip, what are they? You know, don't you?'

He was watching the second rout of the White City that day, but he dragged his attention back to Mary.

'I think – and it's only a guess, but I'm reasonably sure – that they're from the future.'

'Our future?'

'A long time in our future. They look at us and they see savages.' He snorted.

'You killed one of them.'

'I don't think they die that easily.' He shook his head. 'Not savages. I don't know: bees. We do all the work, we live and we scavenge and we die, then they take all the honey.'

She sighed, and let her arms fall by her side. 'That … didn't go as I expected.'

'I think we just have to get used to the surprises.'

22

Did he regret it? Had he given in to anger, and hate? Or had he been trying to dispense some small measure of justice in a world caught up in an age of darkness? Did his motives even matter, when the end result was one less monster?

Any doubt he'd had that the robed figure wasn't human had been dispelled the instant he'd charged it. He'd hit it with everything he had, and it had been like striking a brick wall. If it hadn't been so close to the edge, it would never have fallen. He alone wasn't surprised that it hadn't come up again. It might have had the form of a man, but what lay beneath the cloth and skin was far removed from flesh and blood.

He held out his hand and reached out over the chasm towards Mary. She sheathed her dagger, and jumped deftly from pillar to pillar, catching his fingers over the final gap and landing safely on the bank.

'What now?' she asked.

He looked around. The fight had moved on, up the road, where the tail end of the servants, those who were bravest and had fought longest, were finally scattering, running from locked door to locked door and finding no safety. They'd been abandoned by their masters and mistresses, and the pirates were in no mood for clemency. There were bodies lying on the hard-packed dirt, and between the plants in the fields. The bloodstains looked like evening shadows in the noonday light.

'We do what we came here to do. Try to put all the maps together.' Dalip wanted to get away from the scene of carnage, and eyed up the pale walls of the structure closest to the river. 'What's in this building here?'

'It's – it's the only place apart from the stone hut thing I've been in. It's a big house, square, open yard in the middle of it.'

'Anyone live there?'

'I don't know if anybody lives anywhere, as such. It was where I was told to go, and someone gave me the third degree in there. I thought she was like us, right up until she peeled her face off halfway through our chat and thought I'd be cool with it. It's not a mansion, just a lot of empty rooms.'

'I could really do with knowing where Crows has gone. I don't trust him when I can't see him.' Dalip steered Mary towards the building, and stood outside, staring up at the narrow windows. He wouldn't be able to get through them, but if there was a courtyard he could climb over the roof and drop down inside. The stones in the wall were tightly packed, but there were gaps between them.

On the off chance, and just so he could say he'd tried, he nudged the door with his foot. It moved a fraction. He pushed it harder, and it swung inwards, banging against the jamb. Inside it was gloomy and bare, a corridor with rough limed walls, and doors all the way down.

'Why don't we wait for backup,' he said. 'There's no point in getting ambushed.'

She seemed to accept that and sat with her back to the wall. The big canvas bag she carried went seamlessly on to her lap.

'The maps are in there, aren't they?'

'One lie at a time is enough for me.' She opened the top of the bag and hauled out a brass tin. 'This came with the boat. Our boat. What should have been our boat.'

He took it from her and turned it over, before propping his machete up and easing the lid off. It looked like a compass, but with only one direction – west – marked on it. The disc swung aimlessly about, then slowly settled down. He checked the position of the sun, which was past midday and behind one cliff, but illuminating the upper scree slopes and the wall of rock on the other. That was west, and that was where the W pointed.

'It didn't work when I used it,' she said.

'Seems to be working now.' He bent down to show her.

'When I say "didn't work" I mean the direction was wrong, but it led me here anyway.'

'That's definitely west, over there.' He walked a little way away, sighted down the cardinal, then walked back and did it again. He frowned. 'Simeon would hang me from the yardarm if anything happened to you, or the maps.'

'Do you want me to come with you?'

'If that's okay.'

Dalip slid his machete through the hole in his waistband, and carried the compass over the field boundary. The needle swung about, and pointed in a subtly different direction than before. He watched it carefully as he walked, aware of Mary stalking behind him, trying to see what he was seeing.

He wasn't mistaken. The disc was gradually turning, tracking not some distant pole, but something very close by. When he judged that the W was no longer pointing west, but mostly north, he stopped and sighted along it again.

'That dome: what is that?'

'I know it hasn't got a door.' She looked at her feet. 'I tried to hide from you in there.'

'That's okay.'

'It was stupid.'

'It's fine.' He squinted at the brass tin, but there was no writing on it. The only clue was the single letter on the compass card. 'You found this on the boat?'

'It was in a locker. There was sailcloth and needles and thread, enough to repair stuff if it went wrong. Down's generous like that. You could have sailed it just great.'

'W is for White City, not west. That building is where this compass points: no matter where you are on Down, you can always find your way here. It's like a homing beacon.'

'No shit. How does it do that without magic?'

'Because,' he started, but he didn't know how to finish. How could a boat that had grown out of a sand dune hold a compass that still worked as surely as a satnav inside a magicless area? 'I don't know. Maybe there's something really magnetic in there.'

Even as he said it, he didn't believe it. If it was that magnetic, every piece of iron for a mile around would be stuck to the building. There was something else at work. Something he thought he ought to be able to explain, but couldn't.

'Whatever is in there, it's so important to Down you need to be able to find it half a world away. So at some point, we need to get in there and find out what it is.' He put the lid back on the device, and handed it to Mary. 'It's yours. You should keep it. I … Bell's machines: did Down make those too?'

'That's what I'm thinking. Which is seriously fucking mad.'

The horn was sounding again and the pirates were assembling at the junction. They came down the road to find Dalip and Mary by the open front door.

'That's most of their human lackeys seen to, by God. But whatever those things are, they won't face us like men. The dastards used their slaves as shields, to get back inside their bunkers without engaging with good, honest steel. Door to door it'll have to be.' Simeon spat on the ground and looked up at the building. 'So what's this place?'

'It's big enough for our needs, and a decent enough barracks for those not on duty.'

'Right,' said Simeon. 'Search the place, room by room. Break things if you have to. Look for trapdoors, secret passages. Let's have no surprises.'

Two dozen pirates piled through the doorway, and their voices could be heard, shouting as they banged about, checking every last space.

Elena didn't join them, and she had Sebastian behind her. Dalip saw, and stepped between them and Mary. He held Sebastian's gaze for longer than was normally necessary and inclined his head slightly.

'This isn't your fight,' he said.

'Are you sure?'

Here they were, squaring up to each other like fighting cocks. Considering everything else that had gone on, the situation was verging on the ridiculous, if only they hadn't both been armed.

'Mary had nothing to do with Luiza's death,' said Dalip, loudly enough so that everyone present could hear.

Then Mary pushed past him. 'You can't believe I did. Elena?'

'You went with Crows,' she said.

'I stole the maps back.' She shook the bag of them at her. 'Look. Here they are.'

'You have no honour,' said Elena.

'I have plenty of honour.' Mary threw a cloth bag down at her feet. Worn metal coins spilled out across the dirt.

'What, what are these?'

'My honour. They give them to you, and a weapon, at the ferry. It's all a con, though. Like one of those fairs where all the stalls are fixed, but you never realise until all your money's gone.'

'But you worked with Crows, yes?'

'No. I pretended to work with Crows.'

'You wanted the maps for yourself. You tried to run off with them when we got here. You cannot be trusted in anything.' Elena pushed Sebastian forward, towards Mary, presumably assuming that he'd go for her. Dalip could tell he was beginning to see that the situation previously presented to him as clear-cut was anything but.

'Mary was only doing what she thought was right. The maps don't belong to us,' said Dalip. 'Or rather, they belong to everyone: it doesn't really matter who owns them. What matters is what we do with them. Crows is working for the White City, whatever that means. He was going to give them, or sell them, to the Lords and Ladies in return for who knows what. We do know that once they had them, that'd be the last we ever saw of them. We have Mary to thank for saving them from Crows. Not so we can sell them ourselves, but so we can use them.'

'If I may,' said Simeon. He ambled lazily across in front of them, and then back again. 'It is abundantly clear that Mary would make an admirable pirate lady. She is a liar and a thief, and probably not averse to a bit of the claret, but also she's brave to boot, and loyal to her crew. Her quick-thinking salvaged a tragic situation and wrested control from our enemy. She is to be commended.'

He leaned his sword over his shoulder and dared anyone to gainsay him.

Elena stepped back, her lips thin and her face white. Then she turned and walked away. Sebastian swiped at the ground with his blade and made to follow her.

'Sebastian,' said Simeon. 'Sometimes dipping your wick makes a man lose his head. If you get my meaning.'

Sebastian worked his jaw, said nothing, and trotted to catch up with Elena. Simeon turned to Mary.

'Don't find yourself alone with either of them. I have a premonition of woe regarding that pair.'

'I didn't go with Crows because I ... Oh, what's the point?'

'The maps were the point. I would have done the same: I have, however, learnt through long and bitter experience that the dead stay dead, and that a man can only mourn so many times before he becomes inured. Singh, I charge you with the most solemn duty of keeping Mary alive.' He pushed his hat up. 'Can you manage that?'

'Aye aye, Captain.'

'We'll make a sailor of you yet.'

One of the crew emerged from the building, giving the all-clear, and Simeon ushered Mary and Dalip inside. They followed the corridor to the courtyard.

'What do you need?' Simeon asked them.

'Somewhere big enough to lay out all the maps, arrange them, and make sense of it all. It'll need light, but no draughts.' Dalip looked around at the square, trying to judge the sizes of the rooms that might lie behind them.

'Take whatever room you want. I'll post a guard and lookouts. Then we can start kicking down doors and hauling these dastards out, one by one.' He reached into his jacket and pulled out the plastic egg, handing it to Dalip. 'You might need this.'

When he'd gone, Mary leaned in. 'What is it?'

'Something I took from the Wolfman, along with his boots.' He gave it to her, and she turned it over in her hand. 'It's a light. A little portable light.'

'How does it work?'

'I have no idea. I think it's from the future too.' He took it back and popped it into a pocket. 'Let's have a look around and pick somewhere.'

'We'll need Mama if we're going to piece all these bits together.' She glanced down the long corridor to the outside. 'I know Elena's pissed about Luiza dying, but how can she think I had anything to do with it?'

'Because if something terrible happens, you find someone to blame.'

'Blame the Wolfman. Blame Crows. Don't blame me.'

Dalip shrugged. 'You flew away. You didn't come back. That looks a lot like guilt.'

She was quiet for a while, and Dalip studied the square of sky.

'What did you think?'

'I thought you were dead. That you and Crows had fought over the maps and you'd lost. Otherwise, you would've come back.'

He remembered what it had been like, sitting there, staring out to sea. It was only a few days ago, and he'd wondered if he'd ever get used to the hollow feeling inside. It turned out that he wouldn't. And then on seeing her again – her stabbing him was forgotten – there was no sudden filling up again: simply confusion. How could she be alive when he'd so entirely believed her dead?

'This isn't making a start, is it?' he said. 'Let's find some stairs.'

He was pointed to a rough wooden ladder that led up into a series of bare, dusty rooms that didn't look like they'd been used for years. Their footprints, especially those from Mary's bare feet, left a clear trail when they ventured beyond the search party's tracks.

The windows were narrow, mere slits that hardly let in any light, and more like those in medieval castles than anything else. Dalip put his eye to one, and saw a section of the road and a couple of buildings. Nothing moved outside.

'This is as good a place as any. We can even block up the windows with bits of cloth if we have to.'

'It's a bit, well: dark.' She stalked around the corner room. The doorways – no doors – were adjacent to each other against the innermost wall.

'Why don't we see if this works?' He put the egg in the middle of the floor, which was apparently on a slope, because the egg rolled over and he had to stop it. He frowned, then asked: 'Give me the compass a minute.'

He wrestled it from its tin and placed it on the boards, waiting for the glass face to stop swinging before he set the egg carefully down on its dimpled end, and it settled.

'So we just wait for it to realise it needs to work?'

'Pretty much. It hasn't got an on switch. It's got no switches at all.' He stepped back and examined the room. Yes: it would be big enough, and being on the first floor, away from any of the four ladders, meant there'd be no through traffic. They could even insist on it and have guards warning people away. Or they could have a little viewing gallery so that anyone who wanted to could see their progress. That would be far better. If they had no secrets, there'd be no conspiracy theories brewing downstairs.

Their original plan had been to copy the maps on to a single sheet of paper or parchment, which they were going to buy, or somehow trade for, at the White City. That didn't look like it was going to happen now. It wasn't that sort of city, and he hadn't seen a single scrap of paper. It was, however, still a good plan.

Mary had finally put the maps down, and was looking through the windows one by one.

'Where did the boat end up?' he asked.

'This creepy bay, really tall cliffs, and a ladder cut out of the rock. It was insane. And the beach was covered with old, rotting boats, just sitting there, falling apart.'

'The Bay of Bones,' he said. 'We didn't land there. There's a much easier way here, starting further along the coast.' He almost told her about the other White City, the one buried under the forest. Something stopped him. 'We could use the sail. To draw on. We can spread it out over the floor and once we've positioned a part of the map, we can draw it on the sail underneath. That would work.'

'I pushed the boat back out into the sea, to try and make Crows think I'd legged it. I suppose someone could go and check, see if it's still bobbing around in the bay. But in the morning: it's a bit of a walk and you don't want to be doing that climb up or down at night.'

'Probably right. No point in taking stupid risks, is there?'

She laughed, and suddenly there was no need for him to feel awkward around her any more. They'd seamlessly picked up their friendship where they'd left off. Everything was all right between them again.

'What will you do if we work out a way of going home?' he asked.

'I don't know.' She looked round from the window. 'Let's worry about that later.'

The egg began to glow, a pale moon in the dark.

23

There'd been some supplies in the building, presumably kept to feed travellers: those had been quickly exhausted by the sheer number of hungry pirates. It wasn't Mary's problem, though. It had been made quite clear that she and Dalip were to concern themselves with the maps and nothing else.

She didn't know what to make of that: it wasn't like she had any secret knowledge that would help in either ordering the individual fragments, or making sense of the whole.

Dalip knew more about Down stuff than she did. Mama was better at jigsaws. All she was, was a better thief than Crows.

First thing in the morning, Simeon had hand-picked two small groups, who would leave the valley together, then separate. One was to head back to the pirate ship and collect Mama, the other was to scale the cliffs at the Bay of Bones and retake Mary's boat. The captain had shown more excitement over the possibility of new sailcloth than the use it was to be put, but she understood why, and gave him the compass to help the second group navigate their way back to the White City.

The city itself was quiet, but not calm. Tension seethed behind every barred door. She didn't quite understand how the pirates had taken the place so easily: they'd killed several of the Lords and Ladies' servants, but there were still more. Simeon's crew were more prepared to use violence, which counted for a lot in her experience – one scary fucker could intimidate a whole street – but the figure in the robe yesterday had been able to grab a sword and force it down. And just how many bosses there were was a mystery.

They had to be planning something. This was their manor, and they'd try and take it back, no matter what. All the more reason for them to start soon, and finish sooner.

The egg had burned bright all night. It was still alight in the morning, and showed no sign of going out. They had almost too much light.

Dalip suggested putting the egg higher, near the ceiling. There was nothing to hang it with, or on, but he said he'd come up with something. Mary used the time to start the laborious task of laying all the maps out on the floor. If they were folded, she would carefully open them out. If they were crumpled, she would press her palm on them and try to iron out some of the creases.

There were so many of them. Each one a journey, sometimes short, sometimes long, from portal to castle, where, inevitably, the journey would end. She'd laid out ten, so she left a gap, and started on the next batch. She was up to nineteen when she heard the shot.

She stiffened and sat up. The echo of it came and went, came and went, then faded away.

Dalip barrelled into the room. 'What was that?'

'Someone's got the gun.'

'The gun? What gun?'

'The ferryman had one.'

'He has a gun?'

'Didn't you see it? Over the fireplace?'

'I have no idea what you're talking about.'

'Didn't you see the ferryman when you crossed the river? He's in the hut just behind it.'

'We swam the river and sneaked past. What sort of pirates knock on the door and ask to come in?'

'The sort that just got shot at. Fuck. I forgot. Otherwise I would have told you.' She got up and peered through one of the window slits. 'Can't see anything.'

'Just when you think it can't get any worse. I need to find the captain: what sort of gun was it?'

'How the fuck should I know?'

'Was it long, short, modern, old?'

'I don't know!' She threw her hands in the air. 'Long. Like you'd find in a war film.'

'Some sort of rifle, then.' He turned and disappeared again.

She'd forgotten about the gun: with everything else that was going on, it had just been one of those perfectly normal things. Monsters, pirates, doorless buildings, crappy little towns pretending they're cities.

So when Simeon appeared with Dalip, she shouted out: 'I didn't know you hadn't seen it. It's not my fault.'

'Mary,' said Simeon, 'not everything is your fault.'

'Isn't it?'

'We are now, however, trapped in the valley. We are also one man down, which sorely grieves me. I've sent remnants of that party across the river and up to the top, to see if they can find an alternative route down. Barring that, we wait till nightfall's dark embrace and ambush the shooter. It loses us a day, and it brings my crew discomfort. Maintaining discipline on these fellows just became a great deal more difficult, so I implore you to redouble your efforts.' He looked at what little had been done so far. 'Time is not our friend, shipmates: it is our enemy.'

He left, leaving Dalip and Mary staring at the maps.

'Right,' she said. She picked up a handful of paper and shoved it at Dalip. 'Without Mama, we're going to have to go even faster. You sort these out. I really hope something comes up, because otherwise, we're screwed.'

'It's only one rifle.'

'So? One bloke with a rifle and box of bullets, waiting for anyone coming down that path, could hold off a fucking army.'

'He has to sleep sometime.'

'Does he? If he's one of those face-peeling things, he probably doesn't need to eat, sleep, shit or breathe.' She waved his objections away. 'Come on. Get on with it.'

She turned her back on him and deliberately concentrated on her work, arranging the maps in groups of ten, going back for more when she was done. He was doing the same, following her lead, and by the time they had finished, the floor was half-covered.

They met in the space in the middle, the egg on the floor throwing strange shadows up at their faces.

'How many've you got?'

Dalip looked behind him. 'Eighty-seven.'

'One hundred and twenty-four. That's ...'

'Two hundred and eleven. Any way you look at it, it's a lot of maps.'

'So what do we do now? Apart from wait for the next shot?'

'We had two maps together beforehand. At the beach.'

'And then?'

'Mama might not be here, but we can still use her method.' He turned slowly, taking in all the maps, stroking at his beard. 'We find everything with a coast, and try to line them up.'

They toured their respective collections, gleaned the maps that clearly had a coastline drawn on, and reconvened.

'We know,' he said, handing her his maps, 'the coast goes roughly east-west. Make a line right here on the floor. Just lay them out, and I'll be right back.'

'Where are you going?' She held the papers against her to stop them spilling.

He wouldn't say, just skipped away and out.

She'd just finished laying them in a row when Dalip returned with Simeon.

'I cannot be the wet nurse to this enterprise,' he was saying. 'Do you know how much there is to being a pirate captain?'

'Unless there's anyone else in your crew who knows exactly where they are by the shape of the coastline, then you're the only person who can help. We,' and he pointed at himself and Mary, 'can stare at these until the sun goes out. But if you can do what you say, this is going to take you ten minutes.'

Simeon tutted and looked at all the scraps of paper. 'Ten minutes?'

'Not those.' Mary laid her hand on the nearest strip of coast. 'Just these.'

She passed up the map, and he took it reluctantly, inspecting it almost sideways, as if to give himself an excuse for not resolving the lines and marks.

'This,' he began, 'is not straightforward. There are inlets and promontories, bays and islands. The shape and nature of the land is complicated.'

'We know,' she said. 'But we have no idea what we're doing here. Dalip's right: if you want this finished, we need someone who can at least give us a start.'

'The reason,' said Simeon, 'I keep all this knowledge in my head is so the geomancers can never take advantage of it. A drawn map of it all? By God, I hadn't thought about the implications of this.'

She stood before him. She didn't know what else to do. It didn't seem right to bat her eyelids or wheedle. Her pitch had to stand on its own two feet or fall under its own weight. 'This is the way we break the geomancers, or not. If it doesn't work, we can have a big bonfire of it all.'

The decision appeared to almost break him. He shuddered and squirmed, turning away and turning back. In the end, he said, 'Very well.' He got down on his hands and knees, and silently started to order the fragments to make a seamless whole.

Not quite seamless. As he worked, he pushed pieces of paper

this way and that, creating gaps where there was missing coast-line, and overlapping some where there was continuity. When he'd done that, he turned whole sections to represent the actual geography of Down.

It was, Mary guessed, the first time this had ever happened, and she was a witness to it.

While Simeon was still working, she looked for her own map, and finally spotted it, right at the centre of what was emerging: a block of land thrust out into the sea. To the east and west, the land retreated – to the east, a long, finger-like bay, studded with islands, to the west, the open ocean.

'Is this what it looks like?'

'I suppose it does,' said Simeon. He stepped back and raised a sceptical eyebrow. 'From the sea, you're presented with a line, cliffs or hills or dunes or estuaries, and you make sense of it that way. You know what's before you, and what's to port and starboard, where the safe havens are and where the dangerous coasts lie.'

'This is where we started,' she said, and she pointed. 'Here. We walked inland along the river to about here. Crows' castle is over here. Bell's, up here, between the two mountains.'

'We found you, Singh, just here.'

'There's a portal on this island. Opens up during the plague.'

'And I started over here.' Simeon dabbed his finger down on the far side of the landmass. 'My lodgings were in Guildford Street.'

Dalip squeezed in between them. 'We were in Down Street. That's only a couple of miles away.'

'And yet here that is a distance of some hundred miles.'

'If you controlled the portals, you could cover that in half an hour. You'd not even have to break into a run.'

'Such is the power offered by this prize.' He gave the maps one last look. 'You've plenty more work ahead, so I'll take my leave. When we can source the materials to aid you, I'll send them along. My first priority is to deal with that damnable rifleman.'

He left them, with Mary squinting at the outline, trying to see a pattern.

'I don't get it.'

'I don't think we're meant to yet.' Dalip looked at the unsorted maps. 'We have to try and make a record of what we have so far, even if it's rough.'

'We've got no paper, no cloth, no pens and no pencils.'

'There's a pen and ink back on the ship.'

'Everything we need is back on your ship or mine.' She pressed her lips together. 'This is stupid. There's one rifle in the whole of Down and it's pointing at us. We have to be able to do something about that. I mean, we've done plenty of stupid shit already.'

'You can't turn into a giant bird,' he said. 'We'll have to think of something else.'

'All we need is a fucking pencil and paper. How hard can that be? Anywhere else and we'd nip round the shops. Here, we have to make it our fucking selves.' Her gaze fell on the bag she'd made for the maps. 'Open that up. Cut the thread until it goes flat.' It was her turn to say: 'I'll be right back.'

She climbed down the nearest ladder, not particularly caring if anyone was at the bottom. She ran out into the courtyard, where some of the pirates lazed and played dice. It had gone dark again, and she hadn't even noticed. The sky was a deep, dark blue, while the square yard was lit with lanterns. It looked, for a moment, like one of those classical paintings they'd shown her to try and interest her in something, anything, other than getting into trouble. The light was warm, illuminating the crew's faces and casting soaring shadows against the pale stone walls.

And she stood in the middle of it, a girl in a red dress.

It wasn't what she was here for. She oriented herself, and headed for the place where she'd eaten her bowl of food, and the woman had pulled her face away.

When she found it, she saw that the fireplace, far from being cold, was blazing away, flickering bright flames from the pile of wood that was burning.

To the half-dozen people present she said: 'What did you do with the ashes?'

They hadn't done anything with the ashes. They'd just knocked them to one side, and built a new fire. She could feel the heat on her face and arms as she approached and crouched down. The logs crackled and spat, and the pops they made startled her, making her jerk back, much to everyone's amusement.

She wasn't with them, even though Simeon had extended some sort of protection over her. With the fire in her face, she was intensely aware that she was blind behind her. She ignored the feeling, got out her dagger, and started gingerly fishing around in the white ash. She'd scrape around for as long as she could, then pull her hand back to cool off.

She had retrieved a few small pieces of charcoal, and was in the middle of recovering the mother lode, a piece the length of her finger, when she realised the laughing had stopped and apart from the spitting fire, the room had grown quiet.

'Whatever you think I've done, you're wrong,' she said. She didn't turn around.

'She is dead,' said Elena.

'I know. I was there. If I could've stopped it, I would.'

'You made a deal with Crows.'

'No, I didn't.'

'You betrayed him like you betrayed Luiza.'

'I lied to him because I didn't want him to get away with it. I never lied to you. I've never lied to you.' That was probably a lie, too, but she had her fingers on the precious stick. She dragged it back and let it lie on the hearthstone. She was sweating, and not just because of the heat.

'You are being protected because of the maps you stole. The maps Luiza died over.'

Mary straightened up, dagger in hand.

'Elena, have you done something we're all going to regret?'

Elena, white and pinch-faced, said nothing.

'Those maps are your ticket out of here. What kind of fucking idiot would destroy that, just to get back at me, over something I haven't even done?'

Still nothing.

'Where's Sebastian?'

The other people in the room had silently travelled from being neutral observers to being actively interested in the outcome of the confrontation playing out in front of them. One of them scraped a chair as he rose, and headed out into the night. Another quickly followed. The rest moved to block the doorway.

'If anything's happened to Dalip, I'll run you through myself,' she said. She was trembling. But there was nothing she could do.

24

It hadn't taken him long. Once he'd loosened all the cords and opened the cloak out, there wasn't much left to do. He'd work a seam loose to the point where he could nick the thread with the edge of his machete, and gradually pull the pieces apart, stopping every so often to cut the thread again. He was left with the long back panel and the sides, which eventually lay flat on the floor like a flayed white skin.

When he heard footsteps, he thought it was her. He looked up, and saw that it wasn't.

Perhaps, if he hadn't already had his machete in his hand, it would have ended very quickly and very differently.

The sword came down towards his head. He raised his own arm and just about deflected the blow down to his left. His hand went numb with the shock of impact and he knew he wouldn't be able to block again, so he threw himself at his attacker.

Dalip's head caught him square in the ribs, lifting him off his feet and spilling him backwards into an unforgiving wall. Dazed, they fell together, and Dalip clamped his good hand around Sebastian's wrist.

From then on, it was down to two factors: brute strength and who was willing to fight dirtiest. They were evenly matched on the first. Dalip was hopelessly outclassed on the second. He endured the punches, gouges, kicks, and bites, and simply hung on, making sure that whatever happened, Sebastian couldn't use his sword.

He was aware that maps were getting crushed and muddled as they struggled. If he'd have had the time, he would have suggested they take their disagreement to a different room. But, however worried he was about redoing the work, he was more worried about keeping his guts inside his skin.

He managed to spread his legs wide, brace himself against the floorboards, and tuck his head tight up under Sebastian's chin. He stretched, forcing the other man's neck into an unnatural angle, and gradually he felt the attacks lessen and the defensive twisting and prising increase.

Then Sebastian was abruptly limp underneath Dalip. At first, he thought it might be a ruse, some trick to get him to give up the slight advantage he'd gained. Then, that it was something he'd done, but couldn't figure out what.

'S'over.'

'Dawson?'

Dalip shook Sebastian's pinned hand and rattled the sword free, then levered himself up on his hands and knees. A fat, short dagger, much like Dawson himself, protruded from Sebastian's right eye.

'He's bleeding on the maps,' was Dalip's instinctive response. He pushed the nearest pieces of paper away, but there was one under Sebastian's head. He shoved the body over and freed it, plucking it away with a drop of crimson clinging to one edge.

'All right?' asked Dawson, almost conversationally.

Dalip checked himself. He didn't feel as bad as when he'd gone three rounds with Bell, so he thought he was definitely going to live. Scratched, bruised and sore, yes, but his orange overall had saved him from the worst of the damage.

'Yes. I'll – I'll be fine.'

There was another man behind Dawson. Together they lifted Sebastian's body up, paused as Dalip checked for any scrap of paper that might have got stuck, then carried it away.

He allowed himself a moment's rest, before gathering together the spilled maps and storing them safely away from the blood. He picked up his machete, and Sebastian's sabre. His heavier weapon didn't look to have suffered, but the sword was bent out of true. No wonder his hand still hurt.

Lighter footsteps hurried closer. 'Are you …?'

He was still holding both swords when he turned towards her. 'I'm mostly okay. And the maps are, too. A couple of them are a bit foxed, but I don't think we disturbed any of the ones Simeon laid out.'

'You killed …'

'Dawson intervened. I wasn't losing, but I wasn't winning either. How did he know to come and rescue me?'

Mary held out her hands and showed him the charcoal. 'I was getting this. Elena started talking, and she just let it slip, in a room full of people.'

'Whatever happened, I'm grateful. Grateful I didn't die, at least.'

'And you saved the maps.' She pressed a sooty hand against his breastbone, leaving a dark smudge after the momentary contact. 'Fuck. That was close.'

'Just when you think you've made progress, something like this knocks you back.' He threw Sebastian's sword into a corner. 'What's going to happen to her?'

'Elena? I don't know. Depends, doesn't it?' Mary bent down and straightened some of the maps. 'If you want, one of us can go and stick her with a shiv.'

'What? No!'

'Or we can let Captain Simeon handle it. I mean, that's what used to happen at the homes I was in.'

'You let a pirate deal with any fights?'

She shrugged. 'That would probably have worked out better.'

'We can't just leave her to ...' And now it was his turn. Simeon was going to do whatever it was he usually did, and no special pleading on his part was going to change that. Sebastian was dead, Dawson had killed him, and that was that part over. The captain might consider it to be the end of the matter. He might want to – banish? maroon? – her. He might want to tie her to the mast and give her a lick of the cat-o'-nine-tails. Or something equally piratical. Expediency was going to win out over mercy: keeping the crew working together was going to be the most important consideration, not any pleas for clemency.

'Can't leave her to what?'

'Maybe we have to leave her after all.'

'She tried to have what's-his-face kill you and destroy the maps, so that no one would mind when he came for me. That's seriously fucked up, and I don't know where she's going to go after that.' Mary spread the sailcloth cloak out on the ground, and laid the charcoal on the floor next to it. Her tongue went between her teeth as she concentrated. 'At least the rest of the crew seem to be on our side.'

Dalip squatted down next to her, still breathing heavily. 'Can you do this? Can you still do this, after everything that just happened?'

'Art was about the only thing I was ever better at than the other kids. I graffitied a few walls in my time, and stuff like that. I'm not fucking Leonardo, but I can draw what's in front of me.'

'That's not what I meant,' he said.

She took a deep breath and picked up the burnt stick. 'I don't have a choice. Pull the cloth. Not so tight it wrinkles, but it mustn't move.'

He shuffled around so he could do that without impeding her movement.

'This isn't what I thought I'd be doing this morning,' he said.

'Me neither.' She started the line on her left, slowly,

deliberately, moving to her right in one continuous movement. The coast of Down – a small part of the vastness of a different world – appeared.

Sometimes she would stop and squint at the maps that Simeon had laid out, the end of the charcoal stick hovering over the unfinished line. Sometimes she would tut and scowl at the marks she'd just made. But she never went back. She drew the massive thrust of land projecting southwards, that contained the promontory they had first arrived on, the estuary where they'd first caught fish and encountered Crows and the Wolfman. Then back out into uncharted territory. The deep intrusion of water, that had to be a hundred miles long, twenty wide. And another block of land, its sea-face heading north-north-west, before being broken by another long inlet, and the end of Simeon's knowledge.

She went back along the line, marking in the portals and the castles. Some were on the coast, like theirs. Many were not and, by making the dots inland, she pushed back the boundary of unknown territory. There didn't seem to be a pattern to it, at least for now, but Dalip was hopeful. All the other maps would go north of the coastline. Some would be duplicates, some would be impossible to place because they didn't relate to any other part of the map. Either they had all the information they needed, or not enough. There was still room for educated guesses to fill that gap.

'How does it look?' she asked.

'Like an actual map.' It did too. It looked like a real map, with names, and a history.

'That's a start, I suppose.' Her voice was slightly huffy.

'I didn't mean it like that,' said Dalip. 'I meant it looks like a place that exists.'

'You shouldn't act all surprised by that. It does exist. Otherwise it wouldn't hurt so much.'

'I should know all about that. But I still struggle. Here, not so much. It feels like it's real here. Out there, it's … the magic. I still baulk at accepting it.'

'Even when you know it's changed you?' She looked up from the map for a moment.

'And where magic doesn't work, I change back. I realised when I went for the hooded … thing down by the river. I should have just knocked him off his feet. It was like hitting the side of a truck. I kept on going, and I gave it everything I had, and it almost wasn't enough. I discovered I've lost whatever it is I'd gained, and I never felt more human.'

'Then the fight between you and Sebastian …?'

'Was just me against him. Away from the White City, I could probably have disarmed him and let him live. Here, it was all I could do to get him to the ground and keep him there. And he died not because I was strong, but because I was weak. I needed Dawson to help me. I needed help.' He picked up the egg and held it cool in his hand. 'I have to face facts. I don't want to be a hero. I don't want to be a warrior. I'm not my grandfather. I'm a better person when I'm weak and vulnerable and scared.' He blew out a stream of air, and changed the subject. 'This would still be much better hanging from the ceiling, like a light bulb.'

Mary punched his arm. 'You do all right.'

'You concentrate on the maps. I'll be back with something. At least, now we should be able to move around the building without worrying about getting stabbed.'

He left her with the egg, marking the coastline maps with consecutive numbers, copying those same numbers on to the cloth to show where the information had come from. It was meticulous: something he'd never thought of her as being.

After wandering from room to room, he eventually sourced a small piece of netting and a sharp tack that would work as a nail. On his way back to what he was already thinking of as the map room, he passed by an open window into the courtyard.

There was a trial going on.

He stopped, then got the best view he could without showing himself. Simeon was centre stage, seated at a table that had been dragged out and placed at one end. The pirate crew were arranged around the sides and the back of the yard, and Elena was on her own, in the middle. She wore a veneer of defiance which, considering Sebastian's body had been dumped at her feet, was commendable.

If it had been Luiza, she would have spat in Simeon's eye and damned him to do his worst. It wasn't Luiza.

Simeon looked almost as resigned to his fate as his prisoner did. He plucked his hat from his head, placed it on the table, and turned it a few times, before looking up.

'Elena. Did I warn you? Did I warn you both?'

She nodded stiffly.

'Yet I've lost a perfectly decent sailor and a good crewman because you infected him with your particularly pestilential desire for revenge. And the charge for that is singularly unfounded. We're pirates, if you hadn't noticed. Lying and cheating and stealing and yes, killing, is our stock in trade – just so long as you remember that once you are taken on as crew, you do not indulge yourself in that behaviour with your fellows.' He slapped the table top hard, and the noise cracked the hush in the courtyard. 'That is the iron rule. You do not foul your own bed.'

There were murmurings of assent from the assembly, even from those who previously had to be dragged apart for fighting.

'You were in no doubt of this. I told you to drop your silly grudge. Now a man, who I could ill afford to lose, is dead, and you've placed this whole expedition in jeopardy.'

There was no question which way he was leaning. Everyone could see it. Even Dalip.

'If we were at sea, I'd put you ashore and give your fate no more thought. Circumstances are currently different, so we must arrive at a different solution. Before I give you your sentence, do you have anything to say in your defence?'

She didn't. She stood, mute, surrounded by her accusers,

knowing that she was guilty and there was no justice except this rough kind.

Simeon picked up his hat, inspected the brim for a moment, then positioned it deliberately on his head.

'It is my duty to see that your contagion doesn't spread throughout the crew. You are banished from our company forthwith. Where you go or what you do is no longer any concern of ours, save that you might cause further mischief. With that, and despite that it might be more expedient to allow that damned rifleman to waste a shot on you, you are commanded to cross the river, climb the cliffs and disappear. If we see you again, any one of us, your life is forfeit.'

Dawson stepped forward, took her arm, and started to turn her around. Dalip rushed to the window. 'Wait.'

Simeon pushed his chair back and took off his hat again.

'Do you have any criticism of the court, Singh, or my right to preside over it?'

That there was even a court at all had been a surprise. 'No.'

'Do you have any criticism of the sentence?'

Given the alternatives, he didn't. 'No.'

'Down is a harsh land, with harsh rules. Perhaps if you'd remembered that earlier, Crows wouldn't still be around to make his merry tricks.'

Dalip had voted for Crows to stay with them. Luiza had not. He'd been wrong, she'd been right, and there was a direct line between that decision and where they were now.

'Nothing else, Singh?'

Full of regret, he could only say: 'No, Captain. Nothing.'

He slunk back to the shadows, and Dawson led her away and out of sight.

Dalip went back to the map room, and busied himself with the light, not trusting himself to say anything. Mary was working on the first batch of inland maps. She'd already made one match, which she'd placed, numbered and drawn on to the cloth.

The ceiling was just too far away for him to reach. Although he only needed something to stand on, even that simple act of temporary failure was enough to make him well up. He wiped his face with his sleeve, and told himself to get it together. He'd behaved honourably. Mary had done nothing wrong, and what had started as the disaster of Luiza's death had ended in the tragedy of Sebastian's.

And still he felt responsible for it all. If he'd been wiser, or more assertive, then none of the decisions he'd had a hand in would have piled up into the train wreck of fatal consequences it had become.

A tear fell on to a map at his feet, soaking into the paper. The dark halo expanded across its surface and threatened the drawn lines.

'Careful,' said Mary, and looked up. 'Fuck, Dalip. You all right?'

'They've sent Elena away,' he said.

'Not a lot we could've done about that.' She stood up under his arms, brushing them aside. 'You're not to blame.'

'Thing is, I think I am. And I can't change that.'

She reached up and used her thumb to rub away the line of moisture on his left cheek. He turned his head aside, and she dragged it back.

'I've lived my whole life fucking it up,' she said. 'I still am. But here's the secret: everybody's doing it. Fucking it up, getting over it, maybe learning from it, maybe not. We've got a job to do, possibly the most important job ever, and it'd be really fucking it up if we didn't give that everything, right now.'

'How? How can you ...?'

'Bitter experience. We're not superheroes. We can't do it all. This,' she said, pointing at the floor, 'this we can do. So let's get on with it.'

He nodded in acquiescence, and went to find a box to stand on.

25

She stopped when she became too tired to keep her eyes open. He, driven by a force greater than exhaustion, wanted to carry on and she hadn't the energy to stop him.

At some point, Simeon poked his head around the door frame to see how they were getting on, and at another, Dawson appeared with two bowls of boiled vegetables and little puffy grains.

She'd asked: 'What are the green bits?'

Dawson had replied: 'Seaweed, I suppose.'

She'd eaten it all, every last scrap, and despite the urgings of her stomach, made sure that Dalip ate his too. It had tasted slightly salty, and of very little else. It could have been utterly bland, and she'd have still wolfed it down.

And when she slept, she slept hard and deep, exhausted both physically and mentally. She'd turned her back on the bright light now fixed in the middle of the room, and closed her eyes. When she opened them again, Dalip was slumped on the floor. Still kneeling, but with his forehead resting on the boards, his hands invisible in his lap.

She was about to wake him, because sleeping like that? He was going to be so stiff, she'd need an actual iron to straighten him out again. Then she noticed the position of the maps around him, and she pulled back.

To his right, there was a small stack of paper and parchment, some dozen fragments he either couldn't place or hadn't quite got around to. The rest of the maps were placed in a way that suggested order, not chaos.

She stepped between them, her bare feet falling softly, taking it all in. The scale – it was the scale that had defeated her, how one map of the same physical length could represent a journey of ten miles or a hundred. Dalip had broken that code. This line here was a part of that line there. He'd marked them all on the cloth, too: not the features on the map, but rather sketched outlines of the coverage of the map. Little rectangular boxes, with tiny numbers, were scattered over the sailcloth like ghosts.

The charcoal was half gone already, and the fragment increasingly difficult to hold. She gripped it as tightly as she dared between her finger and thumb, and started to transfer what was on the maps into their marked areas.

What had been obscure before started to become clear. Rivers now flowed from the distant mountains to the sea, jagged through the highlands and sinuous on the plains. Broad lakes nestled in the lows, and everywhere there was a portal, she drew a little doorframe, two uprights and a crosspiece. Villages became pointy-roofed houses, and castles, tall stone towers like chess pieces.

Down took shape, was given form, and became whole. Some of the detail she omitted, because it wouldn't show on the map. If she couldn't imagine seeing it, flying over the land and looking down, it didn't go on.

As she worked next to the sleeping Dalip, making lines and symbols on the cloth, she realised that she was fulfilling her destiny. She was a Beast. A geomancer. She was revealing the position of the portals across the face of Down. Her breathing became ragged. The portals were joined to other portals by lines of power – no more than three, Crows had said. Or had it been Bell? Villages lay along the lines, castles where they crossed.

She could draw those lines. She could actually draw them. She could fill in the areas of the map for which they had no information. Geography didn't matter. What was important was the lines, and that she could predict hidden portals, unknown castle-seeds, and boat-birthing points.

She was, momentarily, the most powerful person on Down. She could roll up the map, leave the building on some excuse, and run. Once out of range of the White City, she could fly anywhere, raise a fortress, gather an army and go forth to conquer. The Red Queen needed soldiers, and she'd recruit them from the slave quarters of every geomancer she overthrew.

It wouldn't even mean stealing anything. All she'd be taking was a copy, just like they said they would when they were bargaining with Crows in the forest. The originals would stay right there, with Dalip.

If she stayed, then she couldn't keep the map. Simeon's pirates were stronger than she was. They could do whatever they wanted with it.

'My lady?'

She gasped and turned around. Simeon stood in the doorway, and she couldn't help but blush. A wave of guilty heat washed over her and left her nervous and blinking. If he could read her mind, she'd be in real trouble.

'Captain.'

'Did I startle you?'

'I … yes. And he's asleep, so keep it down.'

'Then we will repair to an adjacent room.' His gaze rested on the sailcloth. 'Bring that with you.'

'It's not finished,' she said, starting to blush all over again. 'And I don't want to smudge it. Everything's going to rub off if we fuck around with it.'

'Then carry it carefully,' he said.

She put down the charcoal and picked up her former cloak along one edge, bringing it with her. Simeon stepped through to the next room, and she joined him. He opened the shuttered windows overlooking the courtyard, and weak light filtered in. It had become morning, and she hadn't noticed.

'Show me,' he said.

She laid the cloth down carefully, straightening the edges and tugging out the wrinkles. No one but her had seen it, and she felt she was betraying a confidence by not sharing it with Dalip first.

Simeon's face set in a mask of concentration. He said nothing for a long while, only shifting his stance slightly as he examined different portions of the map. He made little motions with the tip of his finger, as if he were tracing his own imaginary lines over the top of what Mary had drawn.

Eventually, he stepped back and walked the length of the dusty room and back.

'Is this what you make of it?' he asked.

'It's the best we can do, given what we've got. What d'you think? Is it, I don't know, right?'

'The coastline is what I know best. That, I think, we can agree is done with some fair degree of accuracy. There are some islands offshore we can append, though I don't know what the import of them will be.'

'One of them has a portal. And the plague. There are skulls along the beach as a warning.'

'I know it. Here-ish.' He pointed to a blank portion of cloth. 'A portal, you say?'

'Opens up in the middle of the Black Death. Almost everyone who comes through is dying. They burn the bodies so that they don't infect the rest of Down.'

'Never had the nerve to go ashore, and calculated there were fairer, altogether less doom-laden isles to visit.' He made a little bow. 'Yet you did. I take it you have no symptoms?'

'Where I come from, we know what caused the plague – fleas. I didn't get close to anyone. I flew in, and out.'

'I had heard rumours about your abilities. You're a Beast?'

'Yes.'

'Can you also do other magics?'

'Yes.'

'You should realise that you would normally be our enemy.'

'I know. Geomancers don't have a great rep, what with all the kidnapping, slaving and killing. But I figured a geomancer doesn't have to do any of that. It's tempting. Fuck knows that's true. To have all that power to make people do what you want. Especially for someone like me who never had shit. There's nothing I should want more.'

'And yet?'

'That's not going to change anything, is it? It's not sticking it to the Man if I become part of that gang. So let's find out what happens when we smash the system. It might turn out to be more broken than before, but it can hardly be worse, can it?'

'In other words, a geomancer is defined by the madness they embrace. And you alone reject that delusion of control?'

Mary jutted her chin. 'You either believe me or you don't. I'm still here.'

''Tis strange,' said Simeon. 'I'm the captain of a vessel named the *Ship of Fools*, and though fools we were for ever entering this benighted land, it is not often we are still taken for fools.'

He raised his eyebrows at her and she felt his forensic gaze uncover her guilt, even though she'd not done anything wrong. Yet. Could she resist the thoughts she was having? She'd had the maps to herself, so it wasn't just the lack of opportunity. Perhaps she really was going to see this through to the bitter end.

'I won't let you down.'

'You don't get to be in charge of a band of pirates by taking anyone at their word, my good woman. Which leaves us caught between the Scylla of blind naivety and the Charybdis of unwarranted suspicion. Steering a course between those two monsters is not an easy task.'

'But I don't want to let people down. I don't want to let Dalip or Mama down: if there's any chance of getting them back home, I don't want to fuck it up for them.'

'Which is commendable. That does not, however, preclude you from rash actions that might harm my domain. If this has not been impressed on you already, allow me to be the first: this is the greatest treasure on Down, and must be treated as such. All men will desire it. All men will kill to possess it.'

'I'd figured that out.'

'Very perspicacious of you.'

'There is a way around it, though.'

'Oh?'

'We make copies of it. As many as possible. Give them to whoever wants one.'

Simeon was momentarily taken aback. 'Audacious.'

'We promised Crows he could have all the maps as soon as we'd copied them.' She held up her hand. 'I know, I know. But he was horrified by the idea of even one copy. So fuck him. Let's make lots.'

'Your plan has merit, though it's not without its own dangers. I'll ponder the matter for a while. However, we must return to the present. For as surely as we have bottled up the Lords of the White City in their palaces, so are we also confined, and this valley is as much a gaol for the gaolers as it is for the gaoled.' He took off his hat and ran his hand through his thinning hair. 'I can no more order a half-dozen men to their deaths than I can a single one. I understand you had sight of this weapon?'

'If you're asking about how many bullets it has or its range or anything like that, I don't know – children's homes were rough, but not that rough. But just going on what it looked like, it was a rifle a soldier would take to war, maybe fifty, a hundred years ago.'

'Or two hundred years hence. You understand my reluctance to confront the threat head-on. The defile is narrow, and as easily defended as Leonides' Thermopylae. Alas, it now only takes one Spartan with a futuristic powder gun where previously it would have taken three hundred with pikes. Can this map solve any of our current travails, or offer us guidance as to our next move?'

Mary looked down at the map. How could it possibly help? 'I don't know. I just don't. Don't make any of your decisions in the hope that something will come up. It might, but ...'

'No, that's wise counsel. We have what we came for. Scouts have been sent to the valley head, and up the steps to the plateau: the moment we have a way back to the ship, we leave.' He laid his hat back on, and rubbed the side of his nose. 'You have that long until we depart, and I'm afraid I must insist on the maps accompanying us, even if you choose to stay here.'

She was in no position to argue.

'It's both my duty and my honour to protect the lives that serve under me. Be forewarned that those who Down has touched with the gift of magic cannot sign on as crew. We have no truck with that, being too deeply scarred by our early encounters with geomancers. Otherwise, I wish you well and, after today, hope we hail each other as fellows, not foes. I must be about my business.'

He bowed again, lower and deeper, and left her staring blindly across the courtyard at the wall opposite.

Shortly, or in a few hours, however long it took the scouts to return, she was going to lose the maps for ever. And Dalip. And Mama. She'd already lost Elena to exile, Luiza to the Wolfman, Stanislav to the storm, Grace to ... whatever had taken her. Of course, Dalip and Mama could choose to stay with her, rather than Simeon, but she couldn't even contemplate them having to make that decision, let alone its outcome.

She could force Dalip's hand, by revealing that he, too, had been changed by Down. He'd have to leave the ship as well. But would he join her?

243

What should she do?

Running wasn't an option – well, it was, but without the maps. No one was going to stop just her leaving. Simeon might even welcome it. And Dalip would be left with the obvious solution, which was going back to the ship, and Mama.

But the White City was where everyone needed to be. Her, him, the maps. This was somehow what Down wanted, and it might never happen again.

She carefully picked up the sailcloth again, and carried it back to the space in front of Dalip. She laid it out and teased it until it was flat, then shook him gently awake.

He came to with a start, desperately trying to work out where he was and what he was supposed to be doing.

'It's morning,' she told him, 'and we have a problem.'

He massaged his face and worked his jaw. He glanced at the cloth, and looked again, harder.

'You finished it,' he said.

'Most of it, yes. That's not the problem.'

'But, you finished it.'

'Dalip. You have to concentrate. Simeon, the rest of the pirates, and all the maps are leaving here, soon.'

'What about the gun?'

'He thinks there's a way out over the top. I don't know if he's right, but there probably is. The point is, you can go with them, but I can't.'

'Why not?'

'Because I can do magic. Now, listen. You have to work out how these portals join together, where the lines cross, and what the fuck it all means before we have to pack this shit up. After that, it'll be too late to do whatever it is we're supposed to do with them. Do you understand?'

'I … yes.'

'Good.' She took one last look around the room. 'Don't fuck up.'

'Wait. Where're you going?'

'I'm going to try and buy you some more time.' She aimed her finger at him. 'Stay. Work. Do what you do best.'

She ran for the nearest ladder, climbed down it quickly, then adjusted her dress and fluffed out her hair. If she was going to do this, then she had to not just act calm, but be calm.

She walked towards the front door. There was a guard posted in the corridor, lolling against the wall. He received a beatific smile. It didn't open the door, but it got her close to it.

'I'm not letting anyone out,' he said.

'That's fine,' she said. 'I don't want to go out, just to stand in the doorway and get some fresh air.'

A look of doubt crossed the man's face.

'Stand in the yard,' he said.

'I said fresh. None of those fuckers has used soap in years.' She gave him another smile. 'Remember soap?'

'I can't open this door. Captain's orders.'

'Okay. Can't blame a girl for trying.' She turned away, then turned back. 'Although,' she added, and slammed her hand hard against the man's chin. His head went back and hit the wall behind him with an audible tock.

He staggered and started to fold. She could have caught him and helped him to the floor, but she was too busy wrestling with the lock. It was stiff, but she managed it. Then all she had to do was turn the huge door knob, which took both hands and even then she could barely manage it with palms already slick with sweat.

Before she bolted, she checked behind her. The guard had fallen awkwardly, and was groggily flailing around, trying to right himself again. He'd have done better shouting an alarm, but it'd only take a moment before he worked that out for himself.

She was outside, running up the slope to the road. Still no pursuit, but no reason to let up, either. Her feet kicked up the dust, and if anyone was looking, she'd be easy to spot. On the road now, arms and legs pumping, dress rising around her thighs. She was between the compounds now, high walls rising on both sides of her. She slowed down and picked a door more or less at random. It happened to be the third on the left: it could have been any of them.

'Open this fucking door. We need to deal right now, or you'll lose the maps for ever.'

Worryingly, the door opened almost immediately, to reveal a drab man and, behind him, a white-masked figure in scarlet. She stepped through, and the door was closed at her back.

'Right,' she gasped. 'No pissing around. We tell each other the truth, or we both go home empty-handed.'

The man at the door deferred to his master.

The mask dipped. 'The truth? Are you certain you're ready for that?'

'Yes.'

'Very well, then. Follow me.'

26

He heard shouting. He was still befuddled by both sleep and Mary's words. He dragged his hands across his face and sat back on his haunches. What was he going to do?

Apparently, the first thing was be interrogated by the captain.

'Singh. Answer me plainly. Has she taken anything physical with her?'

Dalip looked around him. It appeared everything was still almost exactly where he'd left it. He had the maps, the sailcloth, even the charcoal, though much reduced.

'No. I ...'

'And before she left—'

'She's gone? Gone where?'

'She blackjacked the fellow I posted on the door and fled, last seen heading for the buildings north of here.'

'Not back towards the entrance, or up the cliff?'

'I can only conclude that she has gone over to the Lords of the White City. And even if she's not made off with any actual booty, she knows what she knows. What did she tell you before she ran?'

'Only,' he said, and shrugged helplessly, 'only that I had to work on the map. Work out what it all means. Is it true we're leaving?'

'Yes. And sooner now, if we can.'

'And that Mary can't come with us?'

'Those are the rules of the ship. They're older than my tenure, and if I broke them, I'd have a mutiny on my hands. Sometimes, Singh, it is that simple.' Simeon nudged his hat higher. 'By rights, I should sequester all of this and determine your part in this endeavour before letting you anywhere near the maps again.'

'But I'm as close as anyone ever has been to cracking this.' If Simeon took the maps away now, whatever Mary was doing would be wasted. 'Let me keep working. It'll take moments to collect it all together – just say the word and I'll be ready to move out.'

'You'll come with us?'

'Yes. Of course.'

'Are you sure your loyalties don't lie elsewhere?'

'No. I mean, yes. I'm sure.'

What he'd told Simeon wasn't a lie, in as far as it went. He was acting in the crew's best interests – and the interests of everyone on Down. He had to stay with the maps, wherever they went. Mary knew that. Of course she knew that.

'If you two have hatched any kind of plot,' he began, then stopped himself.

'If there's a plot, I don't know what it is.'

'I find two betrayals in one day a little hard to stomach. The person who makes that three will suffer my wrath.' The captain narrowed his eyes. 'Whoever that might be.'

'I understand,' said Dalip. He did. If he was to make the most of whatever time he might have, he had to start now. 'I'll just … crack on, shall I?'

'No one realises how hard this job is,' said Simeon, and stalked off, leaving Dalip with no doubt that if he put so much as a toe in the wrong place, he'd be in mortal danger.

He bent low over the cloth map, looking at the dots and lines

Mary had made. 'No pressure, then,' he told himself. 'None whatsoever.'

What did he have to remember? Lines went from portal to portal. No more than three portals in one line. Villages lay on the lines. Castles lay where lines crossed.

Was there enough information to arrive at a unique solution, or was he going to find multiple ways of joining the portals together, any one of which was as likely as the next? Could he, in fact, predict the pattern before he started?

If he was going to design a system from scratch, he'd want it to be simple and elegant. Something involving geometry. Triangles or hexagons. That was a possibility. The alternative was a hideous spider web of criss-crossing lines that made no sense.

He had stubs of charcoal, but he knew there'd be more rubbing out than actual lines. Something impermanent, then. He narrowed his eyes and thought about that, until he laid sight on the unpicked threads that had held Mary's bag together. He collected the longer sections, and placed them on the floor next to him.

He held up the first thread, and laid it down from the Down Street portal, through the village they'd found, and up to Bell's castle. But he could keep going: the line went just west of north, and through two more portals. That filled the complement of three portals. Another line crossed the coast where they'd waited for the boat to be built. If that lined up with the portal on the island that Mary had drawn in, then that would cross the first at Bell's. But the two portals to the north-east didn't make it a triplet.

The two to the east lined up exactly with Down Street. Down Street was already part of a different three. So if a portal could be a member of two different triplets, the number of possible matches had at least doubled. He could eliminate some of those by looking at the positions of villages. In fact, it wasn't the portals he needed to be looking at at all. If there were dozens of ways to join them together in threes, he needed to ignore them until the very last moment. It was the villages and castles that revealed where the lines of power flowed and crossed.

He took away the second line. His confidence was high for the first: there was a direct path between the portal, the village and the castle. But there were two castles some twenty or so miles apart. Two crossing points on two separate lines: linking them also fitted the two north-east portals, but not the one on the island. If that was the case, then the island portal was on an entirely different line.

He could live with that.

Then he made the connection that when a village was close to a portal, it was likely that they were part of the same line. Villages in the middle of nowhere were more difficult to associate with a portal, and easier to fit to a castle.

Lines danced in front of his eyes. He could almost see it, yet every time he laid down what he thought was the correct track, he'd see that there was a better choice if only he used those markers rather than these. On adjusting it to lie along the new direction, there was an even better way.

No matter how many lines he laid down, no matter how often he changed them, nothing would come. There was no elegant solution waiting to jump out of the map and show itself. It was, in and of itself, the single most frustrating problem Dalip had ever tried to solve. He was so, so close, yet so, so far.

In the end, he staggered to his feet and rested his head against the far wall, beating it gently but firmly against the stonework. He couldn't do it. It was defeating him, and would continue to do so. There was no one he could ask for help. No teachers, no professors, no colleagues, no draughtsmen. This was his task alone, and he was failing.

He turned around and hunched down, back against the wall, staring half at the map, half into the middle distance. He rubbed at his face with his fists, and took a deep breath.

So he couldn't find a solution. There could be three reasons for that.

Firstly, that he was too stupid to find it. That was always his first thought. He didn't claim to be a genius, and he'd always had to work hard to understand the things he'd been taught. But if he had all the information, then he was just a dot-to-dot away from revealing the picture. And it wasn't happening.

Secondly, that he didn't have all the information. He had a map made up of nearly two hundred other maps that he and Mary had cobbled together on a piece of cloth with some rough charcoal. He knew he didn't have all the information. There were map fragments he couldn't place, and there was also the physical limit of the cloth itself. The land it represented stretched far beyond its now-ragged seams, and there might be other continents, all with their own portals and castles.

What he did have was enough, he was certain of that. If there was a repeating pattern, then it would be repeated in the area he had.

Which left him with the third option: that the problem had no solution.

He'd often been given maths problems that had no solutions. Most of the time because proving the problem had no solutions was in and of itself the answer, and a test of his skill. And occasionally, there was no solution because there the question was wrong.

He went back to the map and looked at it with a different eye.

He started to look for things that were wrong, not things that were right, and the obvious – he struggled with how obvious it was – anomaly was the area around the White City itself. No lines crossed it. There were no villages, and no castles. The region that was void, dead to magic. He had always thought so, even calling it Down's blind spot. But what if it wasn't anything natural to Down? What if it wasn't so much a blind spot as an open wound? The body would continue to function the best it could, even though it was injured, and possibly sick, infected.

What did he know? That the White City had been over by the coast, that it had been vast and grand, and then it had fallen. If it had been a castle, he wouldn't have been surprised, because that's what happened to castles when not enough people lived in them. It couldn't, however, have been a castle, because there were no lines of power crossing at that point.

If the lines were taken away, the city would fall. The line would only fail if the portals ... died.

Like the Down Street one had.

If other portals had failed before it, then the pattern had been broken before he'd arrived in Down, it would continue to break until each and every portal closed its doors. And in fact, the map was already wrong. Down Street was gone. Bell's castle would have fallen anyway. Had she known it was failing? Was that why she'd been willing to throw her slaves' lives away on one last mad scheme before the stonework started to crumble to nothing?

That explained why there was no pattern.

What it didn't explain was why there were no lines going through the White City area, as if there was some force explicitly stopping them from doing so. It wasn't just chance: the White City was legendary for its non-magicalness. It had been stable for decades, even hundreds of years.

So that was the answer. Down was not only broken, one portal at a time, it was also altered artificially.

Or.

Down was breaking one portal at a time because it was being altered artificially.

This world was linked to London through the portals. His London was in ruins. The portal had closed. What if the portal hadn't closed because of the disaster, but had caused it? That would mean every time a portal closed, a London died. And if the whole network was unstable, it was going to keep unravelling until there was nothing left. Every London, throughout time, gone.

He couldn't begin to understand how that worked. It was a preposterous conclusion, almost as preposterous as the existence of Down itself.

It would, however, explain why they survived. As the connection was severed, they were reeled in. Everything else was destroyed, except the tiny bit of London that was attached to Down that they, by sheer chance, happened to be standing in.

The odds that he was right with any of his speculation were extraordinarily slight. Yet it was the only over-arching explanation that covered all of the facts. He was either close enough to correct to make no difference, or he was fantastically wrong, and probably suffering from the same madness that afflicted the geomancers.

What it did mean was, there was something here, very close, that had both caused the initial problem, and was still causing it.

He had cramp. He couldn't remember the last time he'd had something to eat or drink. He sat with his legs out in front of him, groping for his toes with his fingers, and tried to stretch the pain away.

It was dark outside again. He'd worked the whole day. How could he have concentrated for so long without anyone coming to find him, or seeing how far he'd got? Or even to tell him to pack up and go because the scouting party had found a way down the cliff?

It was quiet, too. Before, there had always been some sort of noise drifting in from the courtyard – voices or the clatter of cooking pots – but now, with that absent, he found it strangely, ominously quiet.

He reached out and picked up his machete, making sure it didn't scrape across the floor. His boots had tough, flexible soles – he could walk quietly in them. What he couldn't do was account for every last creak the floorboards would make. Hands and knees would be better.

He set off towards the nearest ladder at what felt like a glacial rate, testing each move, holding his breath uselessly. Out of the map room, across the next. He could see the hole in the distance, but the ladder had been pulled up through and now lay next to it. He looked behind him, in front of him, and crawled nervously closer.

There was someone else there, propped up against the far wall. Dalip peered into the shadows, and saw it was the steersman, who raised his finger to his lips in a mime. He pointed downwards.

Dalip crept around the hole and up to the man. There was only so much they were going to be able to communicate through gestures. He put his mouth close to the man's ear and whispered.

'What happened?'

He turned his head, and the man whispered back. It made for a laborious, halting conversation, but it was all they had.

'They came. All of them. Simeon went out to parley.'

'Was Mary with them?'

'The girl? No. They talked for a long time. He left with them.'

'Why?'

The steersman shrugged, and Dalip remained baffled.

'Where's everyone else?'

'They're dead.'

Dalip jerked his head away. He stared at the steersman, then crawled over to the hole in the floor. He peered through.

There was a body in full view. It was just lying there, as if asleep, but there was no rise and fall of the chest, no languorous shift in position. A pair of feet showed through a doorway. Dalip crawled back.

'Then why are we whispering?'

'I heard something moving down there.'

'How did it happen?'

'They just fell over. No panic. No time to panic.'

'Why are you up here?'

'Simeon told me to keep an eye on you. Make sure you didn't go anywhere.'

'You pulled the ladder up.'

'I didn't know what else to do.'

'The other ladders?'

The steersman blinked and shook his head.

'When did this happen?'

'Some time after the eclipse started.'

Eclipse. That was why it was dark. Not because it was night.

'How long ago was that?'

'A while. It's finally starting to get light again.'

It was. It had turned from dark to grey beyond the slit windows already.

'They're going to come back, right?'

The steersman nodded.

'Wait here,' said Dalip.

He didn't crawl. He ran. He ran to the map room, kicked the paper into meaningless drifts and seized the cloth map in both hands, shaking the loose threads off it and on to the floor. The charcoal itself proved remarkably resistant: it smudged, but the outline was still visible. He spat at it and beat it and tore at it, and only stopped when he noticed the robed figure watching him.

He snatched up his machete from where he'd dropped it.

'You can't have this,' he said, holding the cloth behind him. 'This is not yours.'

'You believe you know better than us?'

'I'm not the one who's just committed mass murder.'

'You tried to destroy this unit. Getting rid of dangerous pests is not murder, simply eradication.'

Dalip raised his sword. This was the one he'd pushed into the river. It had, apparently, just walked out again, upstream or downstream, and back into the city. Perhaps he just needed to try harder.

It was like chopping at wood. It stood passively while he swung and swung and swung, at the same point on its neck, and it grew clear that he wasn't damaging it at all.

He dropped his shoulder and charged it. It rocked back on its heels, but without the precipice behind it, it simply put one foot back and steadied itself.

Dalip retreated, panting.

'Show me the map.'

'No.'

'You cannot defeat me,' it said. 'You cannot kill what cannot die.'

'You're probably right.'

'Show me the map.'

'No. There is an alternative to fighting you, though.'

'Surrendering.'

'Running.'

27

She didn't know if she was a prisoner or not.

The idea of her having the upper hand over these … things was fleeting. She was simply stretching things out, trying to play the Lords off against the pirates, to give Dalip the time he needed. She was certain that if anyone could make sense of the map, it was him – not just because he was smart, but because, despite all his protestations, he seemed to understand Down.

There was nothing to say she couldn't just get up and leave, not even when she caught a glimpse of Simeon through the open door. He wasn't being frogmarched as such, but the robed figures guiding him were standing very close.

Despite their agreement to swap truths, those had been few and far between. Yes, they were from her future, in as much as she was as removed from them as she was from the Norman conquest, the Vikings and stuff like that. People from a thousand years hence turned out to be complete shits, rather than enlightened, peaceable and generous. There wasn't much she could do about it, and she'd seen enough films to know that fucking around with time would end in tears, no matter how earnestly it was meant.

Down was their creation. That wouldn't surprise Dalip: she

guessed he'd already been thinking along those lines. They'd made it because they could, because thirty-first-century Earth was crowded with poor people and the rich deserved something better. When she'd suggested they build rockets and go to other planets, the response had been a long silence. Maybe they'd tried that and it hadn't worked. Maybe they'd tried that and it had just turned out to be too far, too costly, and impossible to control. Or maybe it was too much like hard work, when the alternative – cracking the wall between one reality and another and living it up in Down's vast and pristine emptiness – was easier, and they could keep out riff-raff like her.

And inevitably, it all started to go wrong. Down – so named because of some hand-wavy energy level thing, and not the disused Tube station – wasn't what they anticipated. It gave them a world that was superficially the same while being built on a structure that worked to utterly different rules.

Their playground changed. People – uninvited people – started to turn up. What could only ever be described as magic started to infect both the new arrivals and the existing guests. The gatekeepers had abandoned their city by the sea, and then abandoned Down altogether: but they'd left intelligent machines to watch over everything and record their findings. It was useful, interesting even, to see what would happen.

The maps, and it always came down to the maps, were part of the monitoring process. The maps, the Lords insisted, belonged to them. Down was their experiment. She, and everyone else, were lab rats.

That made her feel just great, and screwed down her resolve to beat them somehow.

In return she told them about the fire, about the portal closing behind them and vanishing into the rock as if it had never existed. They listened intently. They asked questions about who had been in the group, and what had happened to them. They were particularly interested in Grace, but Mary couldn't tell them much because she'd hardly known the woman.

And all the while, she was using up time, trying to goad them into acting against the pirates, to keep Dalip and the maps together for as long as possible. When they brought Simeon in, she thought she'd done it – they weren't going to go anywhere without their captain, so the longer he was here and not there, the better.

Now she was alone in a room. The robed figures had drifted away, one by one, until the last one had got up and left mid-sentence. No explanation had been offered, because why would the scientist explain anything to his specimen? Where was Simeon? What were they offering him? Or were they threatening him? Why couldn't they just take what they wanted? They still had servants to do the hard work. They didn't even need to get their hands dirty.

She stood up from her chair and put her eye to the window slit. Outside, it was gloomy – she couldn't work out why it was so dark when it should have been mid-morning. She squinted hard, making out the outlines of a dusty strip of land enclosed by the ubiquitous high wall. She could probably climb it if she had to, but if she had access to the front door, why bother?

There was nothing in the room apart from the chair she'd sat in. The robed figures had all stood, and one of the things that had been niggling at her expressed itself whole: where were the human comforts? These places were just a series of empty, dusty chambers. Apart from the place where she'd eaten which, she presumed, was part of the White City act, none of these buildings seemed much use at all.

These things weren't human and had no human needs or wants. They were simply robots that reported back to their controllers. Their controllers who lived, not down, but up.

How were they talking to each other, if not through a two-way portal that was right here, in this valley?

She hadn't seen one, which meant they were hiding it. It

could be anywhere, but the place she'd want to look first was the big round building with no doors or windows. Of course, having no obvious way in presented its own problems, but that had never stopped her before. She'd been in all sorts of places she shouldn't have.

Mary went to the door and checked the corridor. Two men stood either side of the doorway. Both looked at her.

'Take me to the captain,' she said. Not 'where's the captain?' or 'I'd like to see the captain'. If her status was ambiguous, she was going to make the most of that. The more powerful the decision maker, the more capricious their decisions, so who cared if two of their lab rats were in the same cage or in different cages?

She wasn't going to be able to bounce these two like she had the pirate. They'd left her with her dagger, which was more than a little strange, but even if she stuck the blade in one of them, the other would take her head off with the sword he carried.

The men, used to obeying orders, didn't quite know what to do. They looked at each other over her head, then shrugged. If no one had said they couldn't, then they decided perhaps they could.

One of them led her, the other followed behind, and ushered her into another room. The similarity with hers was startling: the single chair, the slit windows, the single lantern. Simeon was pacing the room, up and down, the knuckle of his right hand between his teeth. When he saw her, he stopped.

'What have you told them?'

'What have you told them?' she retorted. 'You shouldn't even be here.'

'They made a compelling offer. To which, I believe I will reluctantly agree.'

'What offer?'

He put one foot up on the chair and rested his elbow on his knee.

'They want the maps, naturally. More to the point, they want the map that you've made.'

'You told them about that? You fucking idiot!' She stepped forward and kicked the chair away, causing Simeon to stumble forward. He was suddenly furious and raised his hand, ready to swipe it backwards across her face.

'You black witch!'

'Hit me and I'll stick you.' Her dagger was in her hand.

The servants at the door seemed content to watch and not interfere.

Simeon lowered his hand, slowly, and walked away. 'Whatever circumstances brought the maps here, the Lords of the White City have a claim on them.'

'You've changed your tune, mate.'

'He who pays the piper, calls the tune.'

'They're paying you?'

'Handsomely. Do you know how difficult it is to find manufactured goods in Down?'

'Dalip told me you wanted to stick it to the geomancers.'

'They're giving me guns.' He kicked the fallen chair aside, clearing the centre of the room. 'With guns, no geomancer on Down will ever trouble us again. That's the use to which I put the maps. You forget that they're like coin here, and I've spent them wisely.'

'Don't you want to go home?' Mary circled him. 'Don't you want to go back to London? What about your crew? You haven't bothered asking them, have you?'

'There is no way back. After all these years, I have to accept there's no means of returning to the London of any age.'

She waited until she could look him squarely in the eye. 'What if I told you that there's a working portal, right here in the White City, and it goes both ways? Would that change your mind?'

'Oh. You are mistaken. There is no portal here: portals require magic.'

'You realise that those fuckers you've cut a deal with aren't even human? They're ... things that people made years in the future and they're getting their orders from the other side of a portal. Which has to be here, somewhere. Because where else would it be?' She clenched her fists and stamped her feet. 'We were so close! And at the last minute, the last second, you shaft us to get your hands on a couple of antique shooters. Well, fuck you very much. You could have gone home, and now you can't.'

She stopped and turned. She had an audience. The two servants who'd served as her escort were now in the doorway, and behind them, there were the shadows of others.

'What? Where I come from you pay to see a fucking show.'

'Is it true?' one of them blurted. 'Is it true?'

'That you can go home? Shit, I don't know. I don't know when you come from or anything. But I do know that Captain Crapper here has just blown the best chance you'll get this side of forever.' With her back to Simeon, she went straight to the point. 'The round building: how do I get inside?'

'You don't. No one does.'

'That's just bollocks. There has to be a way in, because otherwise what's the point of it being there? I'm guessing a tunnel from one of the nearby buildings – where you're not allowed to go, but they are. Anything like that?'

'There are so many rules, what we can do, where we can go—'

'Then you're just slaves and you need to get out.'

Simeon snorted behind her. 'My crew are better than these whipped curs.'

'Then do something for them,' she said, 'rather than doing something for yourself. Did they show you the guns before you told them about the map?'

He hesitated. 'Yes.'

'They are never going to give them to you, you know that? They are never going to give you anything that might let you hurt them.' She waved her dagger in his face. 'I mean, they gave me this. They insisted I take it. When I asked about the rifle over the fireplace, it was "you can't have that". Which do you think they trust me with? This, or that?'

'What would you have me do, woman? My crew are my concern, and we are already overdue at the ship. I've had enough of this: I'm going to take what I can and get back to the sea.'

'Go on then. Do it. I'll clean up this mess.' She addressed the servants. 'Anything. Anything you can tell me would be good right now. I can't keep making it up as I go along.'

They couldn't even look at each other, let alone her.

'Fine. Just open the front door. I'll take it from there.' She rounded on Simeon. 'And you, you spineless prick, should be right next to me, fighting to save Down from these mentalists.'

'Save Down? Down is a foetid rat-hole of anarchy and greed.'

'Yes, and it could be so much more than that. But it needs us to do something for it.'

'What, pray tell, might that be?'

She held her arms up. 'I haven't got a fucking clue. But at least I'm willing to try.'

She turned back to the servants, and pushed as many as she could back down the corridor. She knew the way out – she just needed their confused permission to let her leave.

As she bundled them forward, she could see one or two falter and try to argue, as they realised this wasn't quite right. She started shouting at them to keep them going, disorientate them for long enough, and above all stop them from talking to each other.

She was there: an entrance hall, big enough for a party all on its own, and the locked door right in front of her. She elbowed her way through, and started on the heavy bolts top and bottom. The first one was straightforward. The second one wasn't, until she put her shoulder to the door to release the strain.

Then the lock. Her hand was on the heavy key when she heard an imperious voice commanding her to halt.

She was as used to disobeying as the servants were to obeying. She hauled on it, and it started to turn.

'Somebody stop her.' The tone was exasperated and ancient, as if all the weariness of a century's boredom had fallen at her feet. Hands came towards her, and she was forced to defend herself with quick, sharp jabs.

The robed figure strode towards her, knocking the men out of the way, left and right.

'As useful as you have been, you are becoming a nuisance now.'

'Knowing that makes me happy, you freak.'

It reached up. She deliberately stuck her dagger in its forearm. It paid no attention whatsoever to her actions and its fingers tried to circle her throat.

She ducked down and darted to one side, into the waiting arms of a man, who tried to grapple her squirming, stabbing, biting form. He reeled away, but she was set on by another two, who overwhelmed her and pinned her to the boards.

'Get your fucking hands off me,' she bellowed, but they gripped her even tighter. She could kick the figure as it approached, but that had about as much effect as sticking it with the pointy end.

It raised its cloth-bound foot, and stood on her chest, right on her breastbone.

How much did the thing weigh? It had barely started leaning in, and it felt like an elephant was settling on her. She tried to breathe, and couldn't do more than sip air. The pressure increased, and even that mercy was gone.

She stared up at the mask staring blankly down. Those holding her arms weren't looking at her. This was it, then. A stupid way to die, crushed like a cockroach by some machine that wasn't going to be made for another thousand years. She was going. Her vision was closing down, like she was falling into a black well, and at the top, that mask.

Something wet splashed across her face, and in the next instance, the incredible pressure was gone. It was going to be agony to breathe in, but she did it anyway, and nearly passed out all over again.

When she moved, it hurt. When she groped for her dagger, which was just out of reach, it hurt more. When her hand jerked away from the severed arm that lay discarded next to it, that hurt the most.

Simeon was on top of the pile of shiny coloured robes. Banging its head against the angle between the wall and the floor, stamping down with all his might. While holding off those servants still upright with his sword.

'You fucking hero,' she gasped.

'If you're going, go.' He grunted with the effort of keeping the thing down, pounding it every time it tried to rise.

She was almost sick when she staggered to her feet. If something in her was broken, then it would stay broken. Either it would eventually kill her, or it wouldn't. The whole room seemed to spin, and she couldn't make it stop, but at least she could head for the door, lean on it and get her hands to the lock again.

'Hurry.'

The key turned. There was movement behind her in the corridor. A line of brightly coloured robes was heading their way. She pulled at the door with numb fingers, and cool air puffed in as it opened.

'Come with me,' she gasped.

'Not happening.' The thing had caught his ankle.

She watched as it snapped his bone like a twig, and Simeon lurched, caught himself on the wall, and started his inexorable slide downwards.

'Don't think badly of me,' he said, and she was gone.

28

Dalip had run, climbed out on to the window ledge, and hauled himself on to the rough tiles using only the strength in his arms. If he was weaker than before, then panic had helped him overcome that, briefly. Now he was on the roof – on the actual roof, skittering over the stone tiles – and wondering what he should do next. The map was screwed up and shoved down his front. He was pregnant with the secret of Down, and he had no idea how he was going to give birth to it.

He didn't think he was going to be followed. The robed creatures didn't appear to be that quick or particularly agile, no matter how resilient to physical damage they were. He scrambled to the apex and crouched down low, looking out over the valley for a sign from God. The moon was vast overhead, grinding past with an almost audible rumble, the shadow it cast blotting out the detail of the land and leaving it a half-tone of grey. The sky at the edges was deep blue, silent, starless.

Then he saw her. She was running, just like he had, her ridiculous red dress as obvious as a neon light. He'd asked for a sign and, as unlikely as the answer was, he couldn't ignore it.

He moved the map around so that it didn't bulge at his front, and threw his machete over the edge to the ground first. It took a disconcertingly long time for it to clatter. The front door would have been easier, but he had no guarantee that whatever had killed the pirates wasn't hanging around in the air, waiting to kill him too.

He lay down, lowered his legs, and dabbed at the stonework until he had the most tentative of toeholds. Going up was so much easier. He climbed as quickly as he dared, and at the half-way point, just jumped. He landed like a sack of flour, dusty and crumpled, lying there for a moment and just wishing it would all stop.

That moment passed. The self-pity would have to wait. He snatched up his machete again, and picked himself off the floor.

He crossed her path at the junction, and she skidded to a halt in front of him, gasping for air.

'Fuck,' she said. 'Where are we going?'

'I haven't really thought that far ahead.'

She doubled over, and spat on the ground. 'Well, think of something fast.'

He looked behind her. She was being chased in slow motion, and when he turned around to check his own path, so was he.

'We can't hurt them at all.'

'Tell me about it.'

'Right.' He made a decision that might well kill them both. 'This way.'

He caught her arm and pulled her in the direction of the valley entrance. She growled at him, but started to run again, her bare feet eating up the distance. So much so that she started to overtake him.

'What about the shooter?'

'What about them?'

'I don't want to get shot.'

'Neither do I.'

'So?'

The buildings had finished – just the small stone huts to pass, then it was into the narrow gorge: sheer cliff on one side, a drop straight down into the river on the other. Somewhere beyond that was someone with a rifle, someone who was possibly already warned of their approach.

The valley narrowed, and the sound of fast-moving water grumbled around them.

Dalip slowed. He could still see the flapping robes of their pursuers.

'Further in,' he said, and at the most precipitous point, he lost sight of them. Ahead, the rock wall curved before it opened out again. They were, for a brief instant, unseen.

He called her back and dragged her to the very edge of the path.

'What are doing?'

'Jumping.'

'What is it with you and cliffs?'

He gave her a tight smile, rocked back on one foot, and leapt, arms and legs milling.

If he thought it was a long way down from the roof, this felt even further. The fall went on and on, until the very last second when the white-streaked black river rushed up at him and tried to pour itself into his lungs. All those warnings about leaping into unknown water, full of hazards and hidden shallows, flooded back too, and suddenly it was all about whether or not he could get his head back to the surface without getting trapped by currents or crippled by rocks.

The river was strong, and deep in its channel. Yes, there were sharp stones and turbulence, but they were below him. He kicked hard, and broke into the air.

Mary was still on the path, watching him get swept away. He raised his arm to beckon her urgently in, but that movement submerged his head again. By the time he resurfaced, she was gone, or out of sight, or something.

The river carried him along, an irresistible force, uncompromising and dense. He trod water the best he could in his saturated overalls, and waited for the drop. It was only a small waterfall, but he needed to be ready.

The rock walls started to pull back. Beyond was the forest, and before that, the lip of the falls. He stretched himself out and he was flung over the edge. There was a moment of dizzying flight, then into the broken, churning plunge pool. He swam down as he knew he should but had never done, then up into the slowly turning eddies of the post-fall river.

He turned on to his back. A flash of sodden crimson shot over the falls, and he swam over to her.

'You fucking idiot,' she hissed.

'Shush.'

She allowed herself to be towed into the slack water. He let her go when it was shallow enough just to sit in, and pulled out the sailcloth from his overall. The water had done what scrubbing at it hadn't, and washed most of the information away.

He reached down by his feet for some fist-sized rocks, which he wrapped into the cloth, then pressed it down into the water. A stream of bubbles popped the surface as it sank. For that moment, only he knew Down's secret. He had to share it, and he had to share it with her.

He moved closer, until their heads were touching.

'I know we're still sitting in a river, but you have to listen to this, in case it goes even more wrong in the next few minutes. Down is broken, and something in the White City has broken it. Because of that, portals keep ripping away from Londons, destroying both the portal and the London in the process. If we can stop that happening, we might fix Down so we can use the portals to travel both ways. It doesn't matter if you believe me, or even understand me: that's what the map says. If it was me, I'd try the circular building first. Okay?'

He pushed himself away and saw her nod, and shiver, but the nodding was what he needed.

He now had to work out how to sneak up on something that was impossible to kill, get a rifle away from it, and then try to kill it. Possibly in that order, but he was open to suggestions.

Mary mouthed the word 'fuck', mimed stabbing something, and held up her empty hands. She'd lost her dagger. As a weapon against the Lords of the White City, it was pretty useless, but something was always better than nothing.

He dragged out his machete and held it out to her, handle first.

She frowned and shook her head.

He made the 'take it or else' face, the one his mother used on him when he was refusing another helping at dinner. She took it.

He picked up two more rocks from the riverbed, one in each fist. It didn't matter that they were sharp. It mattered that they were heavy enough to cause damage, and dense enough that they weren't going to shatter. He jerked his head at the riverbank, and he crept out, keeping low. She did the same, but with more muted cursing.

The path was just above them, rising on its way into the valley. He glanced up at the sky. The eclipse was almost finished: the disc was brightening at the edges, and the sky fluttered with pearlescent rays. There was enough light now to see that someone had built a barricade across the path, just at the gorge mouth. There was a figure crouched his side of it, and he could make out the shape of a barrel pointing into the air.

He pointed to the path, pointed at Mary. He touched his chest and held his hand down and to the left. She scraped her hair away from her face, adjusted her dress, and moved with cat-like grace on to and along the path, stalking her prey.

He advanced more slowly, picking his way through the shrubby undergrowth, watching where his feet fell, turning and bending to avoid branches.

The figure at the hastily constructed barricade – made from

fallen branches and slabs of stone – didn't move so much as a twitch, and the closer Dalip got, the stranger it looked. There were no brightly coloured robes: instead, the whole body was covered head to foot in black. The rifle wasn't trained on the narrow path ahead, but up at the sky. The shape of it made it looked crumpled, not alert.

It looked asleep.

Crows. It was Crows. It wasn't one of the Lords at all. Dalip had just assumed that it would either be the ferryman or one of the others on guard, unblinking in their watch. Instead, it was Crows who'd got the rifle from the ferryman. He'd shot and killed one of the pirates, bottling them all up in the valley, still blindly refusing to let the maps – and the reward he expected – go.

Dalip motioned for Mary to slow down. He moved quicker, not worrying about little noises like scratches against his clothing or the rustle of leaves. He climbed the last of the bank, and stood behind Crows' prone form. He bent down, put one of the rocks on the ground, then held the other one high.

Mary put her hand under his arm to stop him from smashing Crows' skull open. He looked at her: surely this was necessary, surely this was justice for Luiza. Striking now was the safest course for anyone who'd ever had the misfortune to cross Crows' path, before he could open his mouth, tell his lies and weaken Dalip's resolve.

And hadn't he vowed to do this? Hadn't he sworn that he'd kill Crows? Even if it meant killing him while he slept. Didn't Dalip have the right, the duty, the responsibility, to see that it was done, on behalf of Crows' victims, past, present and future?

It wasn't how he imagined it would happen. Yet here he was, and he should really get on with it.

Mary still held his arm. She shook her head, very slowly, very slightly, her gaze not leaving his. She wasn't going to fight him, but neither was she going to let him do this. If he killed Crows, their friendship would be over. If he didn't, he'd blame her later when Crows would inevitably be Crows.

'Just … stand back,' he said. 'You don't even have to watch.'

'No. You can't. Take the gun.'

'When he's dead.'

Crows stirred, and suddenly started, as if he knew he shouldn't have been dozing. His hands flapped like birds' wings as he tried to sit up and control the rifle simultaneously. Dalip reached out and closed his fist around the rifle's midsection, tearing it away from Crows' tenuous grasp. He tossed the rock he was carrying aside and brought the stock to his shoulder.

The safety was off – he checked – and the bolt already home. He looked through the sights at Crows' panicked eyes.

'Shit. Dalip,' said Mary.

'Army cadets. Turns out it was good for something other than being shouted at for an hour a week.'

Crows backed up, pressing himself as far as he could into the barricade. He cringed before Dalip, turning his head up and away so that he wouldn't have to look at the rifle's muzzle.

Mary kicked his feet. 'You … you … bastard.'

'They made me,' he said quickly. 'They made me. I swear this to be true.'

Dalip's finger curled through the trigger guard. Mary couldn't stop him now. Only he could stop himself.

'You could have said no,' she said. She stopped kicking and swiped at him with the flat of the machete. 'Or you could have said yes and lied, like you usually do.'

One shot, anywhere in the chest. At that short range, even Dalip couldn't miss.

'Do you know what you've done?'

'What I had to. Nothing more.'

Dalip could feel the curve of the cold steel trigger. A slight squeeze, and he could end this futile interrogation.

Crows glanced at him, saw him tightening his grip, and shrieked: 'Mercy! I beg for mercy.'

But as he shied away, covering his face with his hands, his gaze briefly crossed the space behind them.

Dalip turned, fired, worked the bolt to extract the still-smoking cartridge, and fired again.

The ferryman staggered. His clothing had puffed twice – two palpable hits – and he pressed the tip of his finger against one of the holes, feeling its size and shape. He looked up at Dalip, who dragged the bolt back, pushed it forward again.

There was no blood. Each bullet should have been enough on its own. Third time lucky.

He sighted carefully, aimed for the centre of mass, felt the kick against his shoulder, ejected the spent shell.

Now the ferryman's expression changed from one of morbid curiosity to one of neutral indifference. He slipped to one knee, then toppled over on to his back, his leg caught under him at an unnatural angle. He lay still, and didn't move again.

Dalip chambered another round, and spun around. Crows had gone. He'd leapt the barricade, and was running as fast as he could towards the White City, his black robes flapping around him.

Deep breath, exhale, aim.

The tiny hole of the backsight lined up with the notch of the foresight. Dalip turned his body fractionally, raised his arms slightly. Crows was merging with the shadows inside the gorge, but he was still just about visible.

The sun exploded out from behind the rolling moon, and he fired blind.

He blinked away the tears. The gorge was a black slit, and he had no idea if he'd hit or missed. Slowly, he lowered the rifle, clenched his jaw and balled his fists. He didn't trust himself to say or do anything.

He'd had him. He'd had him in his sights once, twice, three

times. Crows had still got away. He couldn't blame Mary. It was his own fault. So much for the value of solemn vows.

'I'm sorry. I'm sorry,' she said.

He could hear her move behind him. He stared at the ground, then back into the gorge.

'They're all dead, you know,' he said.

'Who?'

'The crew. Some sort of gas, or biological thing. Wiped out the entire ground floor. Just me and the steersman left, and I don't know about him.'

'Simeon ... I don't think he's ... He saved me. In the end. I ... sorry.'

'Damn,' said Dalip. 'Damn them all.'

'Is he supposed to go so stiff, so quickly?'

When he looked, she was poking the body of the ferryman with the end of the machete.

'If he was human, no. But, I don't know, maybe that's what happens.'

He bent down beside its head, and laid the back of his hand against the cheek. It was cold. He checked the eyes, which were open and sightless.

'Give me the machete,' he said. He moved the safety over to lock the bolt action, and they swapped weapons.

He tore the cloth apart, and revealed an almost featureless torso, made from some thick rubbery material that most definitely wasn't skin. He tried chopping his way through, but it was impossible. The stuff absorbed all the energy, and the edge of the blade wasn't sharp enough to slice it. The three holes made by the bullets formed a wide triangle, one high up on the left, one halfway down on the right, the last, in the middle, where the belly button should have been. He tried to enlarge that hole by pushing the point of the machete into it. It stretched, but it didn't tear.

He stopped and sat back on his haunches.

'There's probably something better in the hut,' she said. 'Do you want me to go and look?'

'If we're going anywhere, we'd better go together.' He looked up at her. 'Don't you think?'

29

Mary opened the door, Dalip trained the rifle on every corner of the room. It looked as she remembered it, a chaotic mess of clothes, weapons, containers and artefacts, but the meaning of it had changed. It was a stage set, the first act of deception in a long line of set pieces and misdirections that were as deliberately designed as a theme-park ride.

He declared it safe, and she went in, still cautious, poking around, lifting sheets and opening lids.

The sheer variety of items was astonishing, like a charity shop, full of discards. Most of it, she could recognise, but the purpose and use of some of the things was lost on her.

'We need more bullets.'

She nodded, and looked up at the hangers over the fireplace where the rifle had sat. Any spare rounds might be close by, so she picked her way towards the cold hearth. She could have spent hours sifting and sorting carefully, but she wasn't that sort of girl. She picked up boxes and baskets, tipped the contents out in a space on the floor, and raked her hand through the pile to spread them out. It took a second or two to confirm there were no bullets, before she swept the space clear again and emptied the next box.

'You've done this before,' said Dalip.

'So? You've got things you're good at, I've got mine.'

There was a pretty brooch in this one, a cluster of deep red faceted stones set in a dirty gilt setting. She pinned it to her bodice, and carried on searching.

Dalip poked at a few things, before slumping into the ferryman's chair.

'I should have ...'

'Well, I don't think so.'

'Really?'

'No. You were going to kill a man while he was asleep. You think that'd make you feel good?'

'It's not about me. It would have been justice. Doing it while he slept would have been more than he deserved.'

'What, you wanted to watch him piss himself before you pulled the trigger?'

'I just wanted him to realise what he'd done.'

'He knows what he's done. He doesn't give a shit about that or anything else. We know that.'

'You stopped me.'

'Since when were you the sort of bloke to kill someone in their sleep? You think your grandfather would've done that?'

'I know he did. He told me he slit the throats of three Japanese soldiers one night when he crept into their camp.'

'That was war.'

'And this isn't?'

'You're not your grandfather, though, are you?'

'No. No, I'm not.' He looked bitter and disappointed, and she kicked herself for trying some stupid easy comparison with a man Dalip had a hugely complicated relationship with.

'Look. So he did that. And yes, I stopped you from mashing Crows' head with your big rock. But I didn't stop you from shooting him. That was you.'

'I know. That's why I'm angry. Not with you. With me.'

277

'Talk to me about the map,' she said. She was running out of nearby boxes and baskets to upturn, but there were still one or two left.

'There's no pattern. There never was. And that's the problem. Whatever they've got in the White City is distorting the natural order, forcing it out of shape so hard the portals are snapping away from London, one by one. Every time that happens, new lines of power are made, but they're not stable.'

She contemplated that piece of information. 'Are you sure? I think there's a portal here that goes all the way to the future. These things in robes have to be getting their orders from somewhere.'

She watched him carefully. He didn't dismiss her idea out of hand. He raised his gaze, resting his head against the barrel of the rifle he held between his knees, and his frown deepened. 'Both of us can't be right.'

'Whatever it is, it's in the round building, right?'

He nodded. 'If we can get in.'

'I asked. No one knows.'

'More like no one's telling. We're going to have to find it ourselves.'

'Just you and me? Against all of them? It took how many shots just to bring one of them down?'

'Three,' he said. He turned the rifle across his knees and unclipped the magazine. He used his thumb to flick out the brass bullets, one by one, into the palm of his hand. 'Five left.'

'Is this a good time to tell you they have more guns? They offered them to Simeon in exchange for the maps.'

He fed the bullets back into the magazine and locked it back into place. 'This just gets worse. We know where to go, but can't get anywhere near it. And we're not going to find any more ammunition, are we? You have what you carry through the portal. No planning, no supplies. You come as you are, or not at all.'

He looked down to his left, and rummaged through the pile

of things there. He came across the bags of honours. 'What are these?'

'They're like fairground tokens. You spend them in the city, but you don't get anything real for them. They give them to you so you think you're in control, but they're cheating you the whole time. You think there are monsters and men, and it turns out some of the men are really monsters. You think that some of the others are people looking for answers, like you, but they're not. And while you're asking questions, they're getting all the answers and telling you nothing. It's like a big experiment for them, and we're the things getting poked.'

'The city, down by the bay,' he said. 'It's huge. It ... used to be huge.'

'That fits. They came here to get away from poor people. People like me.'

'The portal – the original one – is there, somewhere in the forest.'

'They told me that all the other portals just opened up. Magic started happening. They couldn't control it, so they all went home.'

'Not all of them.'

Mary shook her head. 'No, all of them. They left these things behind to see what happened next.'

Dalip got to his feet slowly. 'So they built an anti-magic weapon, to protect their, whatever you want to call them, observers. They turned it on, and pfft. They broke their own portal.'

'So why not just turn it off again?'

'Too late. The energy released in breaking the portal destroyed their London. There was nothing left to connect to.'

'Fuck. But doesn't that mean ...?'

'Yes. Yes, it does.'

'I'm so sorry.' Her hand went to her mouth. What else was she going to say? His entire family had been wiped out. So had Mama's. Everyone she'd ever known was gone too, but that was less of a personal loss for her, because she didn't have anyone. Regret, yes. Grief, no.

'But what are they doing now? What do they think they're doing now? Do they even know what happened to their own London, or was it a case of "we've lost contact" and an assumption that the people back home will be busy trying to reopen the portal?'

'I told them,' she said through her fingers. 'I told them what happened to us. They wanted to know everything.'

'I'm sure they did. We were, what? Lucky to be where we were?'

'We're only guessing, right? We don't know any of this for certain.'

'I don't really feel like asking them. They're only going to lie to us.'

'Makes you wonder what Crows told them.' She hugged herself. 'What the fuck are we going to do, Dalip? Can we do anything at all?'

He sat forward in the chair, and hunched over the rifle. 'If it is an anti-magic shield generator thing, we have to turn it off, because if every time a portal snaps off our world, and a London dies, we have to stop that. Afterwards? If Down can settle on a pattern after that, with at least two Londons gone, and maybe more, then, I don't know: it's more likely that we can hold on to what's left than bring back what's already lost.'

'Down is a time machine, right? Doesn't that mean we can fix this?'

'Do I look like Doctor Who?'

She tiptoed through the debris she'd spilled across the floor. 'You could be, if they'd cast some Sikh bloke instead of what's-his-face.'

She stood at the arm of the chair, at his sagging, curved back, and laid her hand gently between his shoulder blades. She felt the tremors and the quakes and the shudders of his grief. She'd never felt so strongly about anyone to elicit this strength of emotion. People she'd known had died, often through their own stupid fault. She'd watched their relatives in the crematorium chapel, or by the graveside, and she'd wondered what that could feel like.

She might know one day, but today was not that day. She was patient, though, and waited for him to become calm. She needed him focused, because otherwise they couldn't come up with a plan.

After a while, he sniffed and snuffled, and for the want of anything else, he blew his nose on a piece of cloth and wiped his face with a different part of it, before wadding it up and throwing it into a corner.

'There's a lot of them,' he said, 'and two of us.'

'One of us can be the diversion, and one of us does the sneaking.'

'That division of labour neatly matches our well-defined roles.'

'I can be the diversion. I mean, I'm wearing this dress. That should be diverting enough, right?'

'I'm going to break the habit of, well, the past few weeks, and change out of being orange. The night's going to be pitch-black, isn't it? We've just had an eclipse, so the moon won't rise at all.' He put the rifle aside, and started sorting through the drifts of spare tops and bottoms. 'Have you thought about what you're going to do?'

'Fuck, no. You're going to have to teach me how to fire that thing, though. You can't sneak with it, and it's too useful to leave behind.'

She saw him hesitate, then carry on.

'We can't practise actually firing. We only have five bullets left.'

'Then you'll have to teach me properly.' She started her own search, looking for another sword or dagger she could handle. 'I know I try to come over all gangsta and shit at times, but I think

I've held a gun once, and even then I reckon it was fake.'

'If you hit something, it's a bonus. All I need is for you to keep them looking the other way.'

The light from the open door suddenly occluded. Dalip snatched up the rifle and Mary raised the machete. There was a moment when it could have all gone horribly wrong, where no one recognised each other, and might have acted without thinking.

'Dawson,' said Dalip.

The man lowered his sword. Behind him, two other pirates were watching the path.

'All right,' he said. 'What y'doing here?'

'Where the fuck did he come from?' Her heartbeat was still hard and urgent against her ribs, and she turned on Dalip. 'I thought you said they were all dead.'

'Who's all dead?'

'Pretty much everybody,' said Dalip. 'I'd forgotten Simeon had sent people over the top to try and find another way out. I take it you found one?'

'Aye. Why's everyone dead?'

'Because the bastards in the robes decided we were screwing with their experiment.' Mary let her sword arm dangle. 'Can you go up the same way you came down?'

'Everyone?'

'The steersman might be okay. He was when I left him.' Dalip pointed the rifle at the floor. 'Simeon ...'

'It wasn't looking good,' said Mary. 'I don't know. He was fighting them off so I could run.'

Dawson turned his back on them and stared outside.

'Bloody mess,' he said. 'Who had the gun?'

'Crows.'

'Did you kill him?'

Dalip kicked the chair and looked sour, leaving Mary to answer.

'He got away. We got the ferryman, though. He was one of …
them. Some sort of robot.'

Dawson didn't know the word, didn't know what it meant, and
she couldn't explain it other than with a shrug.

'Back to the ship, then,' he said, 'if we've enough crew.'

'We're staying,' said Mary. 'We've got to make it right, somehow.'

Dawson's scrunched-up face raised a single sceptical eyebrow.
'Tell him, Dalip.'

'We have a chance to maybe change everything. We'll only
know once we're inside that round building, back in the valley.'

'What's in it?'

'We don't know. Whatever it is, it might be breaking the portals between London and here. It might mean we get to go home
again, if there's a home left for us to go back to. It might mean
nothing of the sort.'

She took over. 'They don't want this to happen, so we get to
fuck them over whatever the result.'

Dawson scratched the back of his neck. 'You asking for help?'

'Yes,' she said.

'Ship's mine for the taking. Pick up more crew. Job's done.'

'You're going to run out of crew,' said Dalip. 'And after a while,
there aren't going to be any more people coming through, because
there'll be nowhere for them to come through from. Those already
here will grow old, die, and that'll be that. Down, wherever it is,
will just carry on without us. And probably be better for it.'

'I'll show you the way around the cliffs if you want. You
youngsters don't know what you have to lose.' Dawson sucked at
his uneven teeth. 'It's different for us.'

She'd never heard it put like that before. 'If I get to be as old
as you then, well: it'll be a fucking miracle. Just remember us to
Mama, right?'

Dawson nodded, and went out to report to the others in his
group.

'Is that the best we're going to get?' she asked.

'We can't insist people throw themselves at danger, just so we can have an easier ride.'

'Why the fuck not? We're doing it for them.'

'No we're not. We're doing it for people we don't know, in the hope that they carry on living entirely oblivious of the disaster that's waiting for them in twenty-twelve. This isn't the pictures, Mary. What's done is done: right now we're just trying to stop Down from wiping out every single London ever.'

'What if we can fix everything? There's got to be a way of fixing this, right? Maybe whatever's in that building will tell us the answer.'

Dalip looked pityingly at her, even though she knew it meant his family. He moved a lever on the side of the rifle and handed the weapon to her. 'Take it. We'll go through the basics in a minute. At least with a rifle, it's difficult to shoot yourself with it.'

She took it from him. It was heavy, the combination of smooth dark wood and dull grey metal. There were clips, front and back, for a carry strap, but the strap itself had long gone. She kept her hand clear of the trigger.

'Remember they might have guns too,' she said.

'If they're shooting at you, then you're doing your job properly. If they're shooting at me, then I can't get into the round building.'

'And if they hit me,' she countered, 'they'll start looking for you.'

'I'm teaching you how to fire a rifle, not dodge bullets.' He jerked his head at the door. 'Out. I'm getting changed.'

She pulled the door to behind her and sat on the doorstep, rifle across her knees. For the first time in ages, she wanted a cigarette.

30

Dalip was now more likely to be mistaken for a comic-book ninja than someone escaping from Guantanamo Bay. He'd found a pair of loose black trousers and a dark blue shirt – both were slightly too large for him, but he'd tied them up the best he could so they didn't flap or catch.

She'd suggested a mask, like a superhero, or a highwayman. He'd said that the last thing he needed was something that would make him see less well, and besides, he was instantly recognisable being the only man on Down wearing a patka. If there'd been a piece of cloth of sufficient length in the ferryman's hut, he would have fashioned himself a turban.

He had found a comb, a long-handled wooden one with dagger-like teeth, and a bracelet. It might not have been steel, but silver. He put it on under his shirt anyway, and the comb he dug into his hair under the patka. He would, most likely, die trying to break back into the White City. At least he would die a Sikh.

He'd given Mary ten minutes with the rifle, telling her about the safety, about working the bolt, about bringing the stock right up hard against her right shoulder before she pulled the trigger. He warned her that it was going to be the loudest, most startling noise she'd ever heard up close, but no matter what, she had to be ready for that.

She had five bullets. That meant he didn't need to explain about reloading the magazine, or adjusting for windage or range. Just how to look through the sights, squeeze, and not break anything.

Then Dawson had led her off, away from the hut, up into the woods in the lengthening shadow of the plateau, while the other two pirates headed downstream to the ship. He was alone, and if he was honest, he preferred it that way.

In the hour before the sun set, he went through all his doubts and fears, deliberately visiting each one.

His family's almost certain death; the irrevocable destruction of his home; the near certainty of failure of his forthcoming task; his unworthiness before both man and God: it, in the final analysis, didn't change anything.

The secret of Down had been revealed to him, and it didn't matter whether that was by accident or design. He had vowed to do his duty to friend and stranger alike. If the faith of his ancestors was only so many stories, then he'd still struggle and die as if they were true. And if they were true, perhaps he'd reached his apotheosis and would merge back into the divine, as a drop of water joins the vast ocean.

He was calm, preternaturally so. Whatever happened next was the will of God.

It grew cold in the shadow, and he started to walk up and down to keep his muscles warm. The sky darkened and streaks of cloud high above him turned orange, then pink. It was almost time. The gorge was already in darkness, and soon the valley beyond would follow.

He swung the machete a few times to limber up his arm, and he walked to Crows' barricade. One last look at the deep blue sky and glowing clouds told him what he knew already. He climbed carefully over the stones and branches blocking the path, and strode out the short distance to the start of the gorge proper.

He swapped the machete from right to left, and trailed his fingers over the rock. They would be his guide through. He took one deep breath, and started forward.

He kept his elbow bent and his fingertips dragging. As long as he didn't lose contact, he wasn't in danger of wandering close to the edge. Having passed that way once in the light, and once in the dark, it didn't hold any terrors. He knew how far it was, and where it turned.

When he'd gone about half the distance, he stopped, and listened. The water thundered below, and he expected that the noise would block out everything else. But the gorge was an echo chamber, amplifying all sounds, not just natural ones. Could he hear some speech mixed in with the sonorous river? He thought he might.

Slowly, then. He was still in utter darkness, while the valley was fractionally lighter. If there were guards posted, then he'd count their silhouettes long before they could see him.

He edged along, and caught sight of the final part of the gorge, the edge of the rock face just before it opened out. He crouched down and listened again.

Definitely voices. He could possibly handle two, if he was swift and merciless, taking one down before they could react and leaving him the other at better than average odds. Three, he wasn't so sure about. It would only take one of them to shout a warning, and the chase would be on.

He needed to check. He stayed pressed up against the cliff wall and stepped silently until he could see the end of the gorge completely. There were three blank shadows standing there. They weren't even watching the path, but each other, and at least one of them had his back completely to the gorge.

He'd have to get past them somehow. Perhaps he could take three of them on: kill the first one with a single blow, then attack one of the others while they were both reeling.

The shot, when it came, cracked the still air with shocking clarity. The men on guard jerked and cringed as if they'd been hit themselves. As the echo built and died away, he could hear a distant shout, thin but distinct.

'Come on then, you fuckers.'

Four bullets left.

The guards talked to each other in low, urgent voices, and then one of them ran off down the path.

As a plan, it wasn't subtle. It was, however, inexplicably working.

Dalip gave it a few seconds. Neither of the guards were looking in his direction now, but instead staring and pointing across the valley at the top of the steep steps, presumably where Mary stood in full view.

He moved the machete into his right hand, and crept-ran, balancing on the balls of his feet, until he was right behind the two men.

Was he strong enough, mentally, to do this? After Crows this afternoon?

Dalip raised the blade high, and brought it down diagonally, cutting into the neck of the right-most guard. The edge ground to a halt against a vertebrae, but it didn't really need to go any further. He jerked the machete clear, pulling it out backwards while raising his foot to kick the man clear.

The only sounds had been the solid, meaty chop and a phlegmy cough. The guard's colleague hadn't even noticed, his attention fixed on the opposite side of the valley.

Dalip brought his arm up again, and as the body fell away, he had an unimpeded swing. The second guard had barely started to turn before the machete caught him just above the ear. The force of the blow alone would have rendered the man unconscious. That it stoved the side of his head in meant he wouldn't be waking up.

He tipped both men into the river, easy enough with the river's edge only a pace away. He could just about hear the splashes, but only because he was listening out for them.

That had been ... not easy, but necessary. He'd killed two men because they'd allied themselves to evil, even if they weren't evil themselves. The alternative – making himself known, and trying to explain what he wanted to do – would have seen him dragged down, disarmed, and brought him before the Lords of the White City. He knew how that would end.

So there he was. The soldier-saint. The champion of Down.

Time to move on. The small cube-shaped shelters were the next obvious staging point. The path was woefully exposed, but the drifts of loose, pale talus were also a problem. He'd be heard crossing it, even if he couldn't be seen.

Only one thing to do: run, and hope that Mary could keep them distracted. He sprinted the distance to the shelters, then dodged through them to the last in line.

He could see faint lights down near the river. Lanterns would ruin their night sight, which was good for him. Good for Mary, too, because rather than firing blind, she'd have something to aim – inexpertly – at.

He waited, and waited, and just when he thought she wasn't going to do it, she did.

Several of the lanterns went out instantly, and others were simply dropped. Shouting and confusion followed, and one of the cries was sustained and insistent. She might even have hit someone, but it was more likely that they'd fallen and injured themselves as they ran for cover.

Three bullets.

Mary shouted again: 'You're a bunch of tossers!'

Confident she wasn't going to run out of swear words any time soon, he looked at his route ahead. The road ran between the fields and buildings, down to the river turning. Not that way. If he plotted a course above but parallel to it, he'd arrive behind one of the compound walls, and in sight of his target.

There was no easy way to do it. He just had to negotiate an almost featureless surface and hope he didn't trip. The slope from right to left was uneven and severe, and the shards of rock slid over each other all too readily.

The wall was a black slab. He turned and pressed his back against it, and tried to control his ragged breathing. It wasn't the speed or the distance, it was his nerves. He listened over the sound of his beating heart, trying to work out what was happening around him.

The rocks stopped moving shortly after he did. The river was a distant hiss. Raised voices cut through intermittently – orders given, questions raised – and other noises of movement, some of which were coming from right behind him, on the other side of the wall. A door opening? A bucket being filled? Something wooden hitting something else wooden, but beyond that it was pointless to speculate.

He crept away, testing each step carefully, heading for the narrow gap between the uphill and downhill compounds. Beyond that was the deeper shadow of the circular building with no doors or windows.

Dalip's world was now variations of shades of black. His dark-adapted eyes could pick out some of the differences, but he could barely see his own hands in front of his face. Much more use was the slight changes in sound and pressure. He could almost feel the size and shape of the structures around him.

Another shot broke across the valley. There was no immediate reaction that he could make out, but he was blind as to what was happening down by the river, and whether anyone had dared cross the stepping stones to the steps up.

No shout of defiance followed, either. She was feeling the strain as much as he was.

Two bullets.

He moved between one building and the next, and there it was, just ahead. She'd already told him that it was useless to look for a way in, because there wasn't one: he wasn't going to waste time and court discovery by checking for himself, but there had to be an entrance somewhere. His best guess was that the round building was the oldest in the valley, and that year-on-year erosion had buried the door under the ever-encroaching slippage of broken rock.

He wasn't going to start digging, because he assumed someone had already done that. All he needed to find was the start of that hole. It would be disguised. It wouldn't be heavily guarded. It might be made so secure with future technology that he didn't stand a hope of breaking in.

Opposite the curve of the outside wall was a long, low building, bent around in a sympathetic arc. It could easily be mistaken for a series of workshops or garages, except for the absence of doors. Thin slit windows punctuated the line of the wall, but it was ferociously dark inside and peeking in revealed nothing.

When he reached its far end, and around the corner, he found it. A door, locked somehow, and as he ran his hand over it, he couldn't feel a keyhole. Yet from its proximity to the round building, it seemed the most likely candidate. When he pressed against the wood, there was no give at all. This was no ordinary entrance. He'd have to find an alternative way of getting in.

Another shot. Muted this time, echoing over the valley but started away from the edge. She'd been forced back on to the plateau.

One bullet left.

Once she'd used that, the rifle became an empty threat. It could keep people at bay in case it was still loaded, but it would only take one brave or foolhardy person to call her bluff and it'd be over.

He pushed at the door again, just to make sure, and felt its cool indifference to his urgency.

The roofs of all these buildings were constructed in the same way, with thin, flat leaves of overlapping stone. It should be possible to lever some out of the way to make a hole. If he could climb up in the dark, and if he could dismantle the tiles without being spotted – and after that, if he didn't break something important in the fall – then he could finally see what was so carefully hidden.

Mary was risking everything. So should he. He sheathed the machete and ducked back around the wall so he was as hidden from view as possible. His fingers ran over the wall, probing for handholds, and when he found two, he tried to find somewhere for his foot.

But he couldn't see what he was doing, and every moment outside meant more chance of him being discovered. Every move was tentative and painfully long to execute, and he had no idea, face pressed to the rough stonework, how far up he'd gone or how far he had left to go. It wasn't as high as Bell's tower, and if he slipped here, he wouldn't die. He'd just have to pick himself up, bruised and battered, and try again, and hope.

He reached up, felt the overhang of the eaves, and clutched at it with a vice-like grip. This was when he was most likely to tumble backwards. He moved his other hand from its secure hold and slapped it on to the smooth, dusty roof tile. If the pitch on it had been any greater, then it would have been pointless even to try. He pushed down: his feet drifted clear of the wall, and he was now suspended awkwardly over the drop.

He didn't want to dislodge himself with any sudden movement. He gradually brought one leg up and got it over the lip. He was spreadeagled, one foot dangling, one just about maintaining its grip. He moved his hand higher, feeling for anything that might improve his stability.

Then he let go of the eaves, and he didn't immediately slide off.

He was up. Destroying part of the roof was going to be inherently noisy. There was nothing he could do about that. Better it was done quickly.

He eased out the machete, and using his fingertips to guide him, he squeezed it gratingly between two tiles just shy of the ridge. He lifted it a little way, then used his hands to heave it out. The other tiles around it clattered back into position, and he rested the loose one against his knees, letting gravity pin it.

Once one tile had gone, the next one was more straight-forward to access. The clinking and rattling of stone increased as he worked, levering out tiles and stacking them next to him. As soon as he moved, they'd all fall off, sliding along the roof and off on to the ground.

A gunshot, distant, lonely. The last one. If she had any sense, she'd now run, as far and as fast as her legs could carry her. She might still get away. And if she escaped the anti-magic area, she'd be uncatchable, so long as she didn't come back for him. It was something that he'd tried to make her promise, and she'd deflected him each time. She was smart and devious, traits which cut both ways.

He returned his attention to his own predicament. If the ground was the same distance down inside the building as out, then he'd only have a short drop. If there were automatic alarm systems attached to robotic guns, he'd not land alive. Keeping the tiles propped up against his knees, he leaned forward and looked into the hole he'd made.

He could see precisely nothing. No hint of any features, just perfect darkness.

And then, since he'd just thought of it, he slipped the bangle off his wrist, held it over the hole and dropped it. The tiniest of tinny rings came back almost immediately, and there was no roar of gunfire or silent glowing lasing.

There was prudence, and there was prevarication, and he was in danger of slipping from one to the other. He manoeuvred himself above the hole, letting the loose tiles slide away when he had to get his feet through.

They scraped away down the slope of the roof. The first one

flew off the eaves and, a moment later, thudded to the ground. All the others, some dozen or so, pitched after it and clacked and dinked on top of each other, snapping and shifting the growing pile of broken stone until the last one dropped and shattered.

Immediately, a questioning voice called out, was answered, and another shouted for a light.

Dalip bent his knees and let go.

The impact was hard and it hurt, jarring everything from his heels to his jaw. He landed on his side, and lay in the dust while he collected his wits and wriggled his toes to make sure nothing was broken. He was in one piece. He rolled on his hands and knees, took a second to sweep the floor for his bangle, then a second more when he couldn't find it at the first attempt.

He slipped it on and stood up. He staggered, dizzy and disorientated, and for a moment he thought he was being gassed, just like the pirates. But it was just the absence of any reference points, and it was difficult to tell which way was up: when he found the wall and leaned against it, the feeling subsided. He became aware of a tiny red light in the distance. Because it was so dark, he couldn't tell how far away it was – it seemed to float in mid-air, his eyes skittering off it into the surrounding void.

The light blinked at him, and he walked slowly towards it. He noticed that he was on a slope, and was going uphill. The dot resolved into a circle of red enclosing a white bar. The display it was on was dirty, encrusted with an age of accumulated dust. Dalip wetted his thumb and ran it across the little screen.

It now gave enough light to show the immediate surroundings. He was the other side of the door he'd failed to open, and he was looking at an electronic lock of some kind. A cable – a power cable – ran away from it, along the wall, where it was suspended in successive bows down its length.

Would it fail open, or fail locked? If it unlocked itself, he was in the same position as he was with the power on. They could open it, and he couldn't. He twisted a length of the cable in his hand and jerked it, once, twice, and it came loose. The light diminished, then winked out. He half-expected the sound of opening bolts, but it died quietly. If it had remained locked and they now had to break in, he'd bought himself some time.

Then with his back to the door and his feet pointing down the slope, he started walking. He ignored the noise of increasingly urgent hammering behind him. He knew he was close to his goal, because ahead of him was a cold, blue glow, a disorientating fog in his vision.

He almost walked into the wall in front of him, and as he groped around, one of the objects he touched moved slightly. He felt it, and it was big and flat and cold and hard. He pushed it again, and it behaved just like a self-closing door would. The gap next to it seemed to indicate that it had once been a pair of doors, but was now just one.

Beyond it was a space, tall and wide and profoundly deep. He could hear a single tone, low and constant. The blue shine was everywhere, coming from everything: it made him feel sick and blind simultaneously.

He ran his fingers along the edge of the door, and moved around it, his feet scuffing on the floor, searching for obstacles.

There was a click, and the lights came on, all at once. He let out an involuntary gasp, and he covered his eyes. He had to wipe away the tears and squint through his fingers before he could see even vague shapes.

The walls were white, the ceiling too far away in the brightness to discern, the floor covered with a smooth linoleum-type surface that reflected everything. There was a raised area dead centre, a series of circular steps topped by a flat dais, and behind it, other … things: short hexagonal columns with control panels on the sides, and cables snaking away from them. It was as bright, clean, and clinical as a laboratory.

He heard the door at the far end of the corridor finally give, heard the shouts and the running feet. If he was going to do any breaking of his own, he was going to have to hurry. He started across the sterile expanse of the floor, leapt the first step of the platform, and realised that there was a round pit in the middle of it. In that pit was a ball made of darkness and blue sparks in continuous motion.

If the ceiling lights had been bright, the electric bolts tearing along the surface of the sphere left after-images so sharp they hurt. He was dazzled, confused, entranced. This had to be it. This was his target, and he couldn't even look directly at it.

When he was dragged down and landed hard against the bottom step, he could barely tell what had happened. But by concentrating between the flashes burned into his retina, he saw a man grappling with his legs. He kicked out, knocked him back, and swung wildly with his machete, missing but forcing his attacker further back.

He was hit from the side, and he staggered. The glint of metal shone through as it was raised high above him, seemingly near the lights far up in the ceiling, but that gave him time to roll aside and drag his own weapon through the air. He felt resistance, and that man fell away, only to be replaced by another.

Fighting by instinct alone, Dalip used the impression of his opponent's form to guide him, as to where to block, where to move. Then there were two, and it wasn't double vision. He retreated and parried, advanced and thrust, swinging his blade twice as fast to compensate. One of them slipped, and he drove into the space where he expected the man to be. Strike, withdraw, block and counter-blow. Even though he couldn't properly see, he recognised the other man's desperation. But his partner intervened, stepping between them.

Dalip ducked down as the air above him cleaved, then rose with his own cutting blow, angling right to left as he rose. That man faded away, revealing the other. They both swung, and the arcs of their swords met in the middle. The heavier machete snapped the lighter blade in two, and the remnants spun away, glittering.

Dalip's return blow struck home. The second man tried to rise, failed, and called out.

Then it was just Crows left, pushed forward into the bright ring by a white-faced Lord. Crows' dark edges were jagged, ill defined, and no matter how Dalip blinked, he couldn't bring him into focus. But since that was how he saw Crows anyway, he knew it was him.

'So, Dalip Singh, it comes to this. God moves in unexpected ways.'

Dalip backed up until his heels touched the edge of the circular step. 'You won't fight me. You're too much of a coward.'

'And yet here I am.'

Yes, here he was, playing for time, tricking Dalip into long speeches and macho posturing, knowing that reinforcements were on their way, who at that very moment were bundling through the door and down the corridor, ready to overwhelm their self-declared enemy with sheer numbers.

It had to be now, or not at all.

Dalip turned, threw himself up the steps and raised his machete with both hands. He couldn't see what he was striking, but he knew it didn't matter. If he hit anything, it would be over.

He brought his arms down, felt an electric jolt in them as the blade connected, and suddenly he was cold and empty, as if someone had pierced him from back to front and life was draining from him. He felt a prolonged tug, an unzipping of his flank. His machete was wedged tight. It wouldn't move. But the searing light from the device had died, so he let go, and pressed his palms over the rent in his side.

'They gave me this sword,' said Crows, 'and I took it even though I did not expect to ever use it. Their word is – was – wisdom, but it appears we must now move into the future fatherless. Rather, I will. You, unfortunately, will not live to see it.'

Dalip's scarred eyes saw Crows' darkness deepen and grow.

A bloodied sword rattled to the floor, and he was gone. As was the Lord of the White City in the doorway, who watched Dalip impassively for a few moments, before turning and walking away.

31

If she dropped the rifle, and they found it, they'd know that she didn't have it any more. If she kept it, the size and weight of it might mean they'd capture her, rather than losing her. On top of which, she wasn't sure if getting caught would give Dalip more time, or less.

All very different from the every-girl-for-herself, run-like-fuck code she was used to. She needed to keep them on her tail, to tie up as many of their resources as possible, and keep them guessing to the last moment as to how many of her there were.

She could do this, if it wasn't for one problem: she couldn't see where she was going. It wasn't even like when she found her way to the White City, compass in hand. It was so dark, she didn't dare move.

The way up to the plateau had been difficult in the last of the daylight. The way down would be very much simpler, quicker and entirely fatal. If she managed to stay away from the edge, if she could even tell which direction the edge lay, then she could head inland and disappear. Literally disappear, too, but currently no matter how hard she wanted to snap her fingers and see a spark of flame, she could make precisely nothing appear out of thin air.

The rock and scrub near the gorge had given way to a thin, weak forest. She had known which way to go, and which way definitely not to go – had it all mapped out – then night had fallen and made a mockery of her plans.

No one wanted to get shot. That was a given. Her pursuers shielded their lights the best they could as they spread out in a line, to both search for her, and drive her on, assuming that instinct would make her break cover at some point. They didn't seem to realise she was smarter than that, but the ground gave her very few places to hide, even when she could see them.

Everything had to be done by touch and sound. The bobbing row of pale shadows didn't give her much to go on, but moving away from them was the best and only thing she could do. Why did they fight for the Lords? The same reason a geomancer had followers, she supposed: each geomancer was just imitating the things in the robes. The law of the street prevailed. What was it that Crows had said? That the strong did what they wanted, and the weak suffered what they must. That. Hardly a cheery thought.

She couldn't walk forward with both hands in front of her holding the rifle. What was she even thinking? She laid it down on the ground and stepped over it, feeling her way between the sharp, springy branches, making enough noise, she thought, to raise the dead. The lights behind didn't speed up, though. Perhaps she was just imagining that she was being stupidly loud.

The glowing egg would have been useful right now. It would have painted a target on her not even an idiot could miss, but running and being chased would be better than this slow-motion charade. It was going to be better in every sense, leading the men behind her further and further away from the valley.

So now the obvious thing, since she didn't have a light, was to steal one of the searchers'. One of the ones on the end, it didn't matter which, so she chose left, and felt her way in that direction, testing each footstep in turn in case the next sent her plummeting to her death.

Then she crouched low, and waited for them to catch up.

They were widely spaced, the circle of light from each lantern barely overlapping. They'd never find her, she realised. It was a fool's errand, something you'd send the makeweights and the misfits on to make it look like you knew what you were doing. These men weren't fooled, though. Every step they took, lantern held down near the ground, sword, dagger or club ready, reeked of fear and trepidation.

If she'd had enough bullets, she still wouldn't have wasted any on this crowd. Maybe one, to send them scurrying back to the stairs, but no more. They weren't worth her worry.

She scooped up a handful of debris: dust, dried twigs and leaves, a couple of sharp-sided pebbles. She sorted out the stones, and just when she was in danger of being illuminated, she threw one over to the far side of the last man in the line. It clattered, his head snapped round, and he stopped.

'Over there,' he said. 'Right next to you.'

'I can't see nothing.'

She lobbed the other, high and underarm, so that it took an age to fall back to earth.

'There. Five yards ahead.'

She walked out of the gloom, completely blind-siding the man, who was still gesturing and shouting in the direction of a phantom. He only noticed her when she plunged her new little dagger, a broad blade no longer than her finger, into the meaty part of his sword arm.

He dropped both his sword, and the lantern. She already had her hand through the carrying handle, and it fell no further than into her grasp. Then she was off, running before the line, the lantern rattling away like a cow bell. It could hardly be more obvious, yet it was what she'd wanted. She could see where she was going, dimly and sometimes a little too late as she crashed through obstacles she'd have rather avoided, but this was a proper, honest chase, like the old days. Yes, her current pursuers could choose to kill her, but falling through roofs, entangled on razor wire, getting hit by cars … it was an occupational hazard, and it always felt like running for her life anyway.

And though these men outnumbered her ten to one, they weren't really trying. The hired help rarely did. Occasionally she'd encountered some mad fucker who'd decided that going full Terminator on her was an appropriate response to finding someone on enclosed premises, but mostly they'd go for the easy way out: get her off the site, follow her to the end of the street, then stop, honour satisfied.

At the speed they were going, she could keep this up for a little while.

But apparently, her pursuers hadn't read the script.

That was one of the things about Down, then. By walking everywhere, doing manual labour, eating no burgers or drinking fizzy pop: if you weren't dead, you were as fit as fuck. She'd been here a few weeks. The blokes behind her could have been here for years.

She started to fade. Slowly at first, because she couldn't quite believe they were still right on her tail, and that gave her extra impetus to carry on. Then increasingly struggling, even as the candle in her lantern shrank to a guttering stub. If they wanted her alive, they were going to have to carry her back, because her legs and her lungs burned white-hot and acid-etched. If they wanted to kill her, then at least the pain would stop.

The endless miniature forest, with its spindly trees, too narrow to provide cover, too dense to give her a free run, always changing course, thrashing her face and arms with whip-like branches, sapped what was left of her energy. She couldn't continue, she was faltering, running entirely on empty. She'd fold in another few steps, just the other side of that dip, against that thicker trunk. She kept finding reasons to dig deeper, keep on going, another yard, another two. She cycled between determination and despair.

Then her legs went. Not tripped up or misstepped, but properly failed like they were suddenly boneless. She sank to the ground like she was wading into quicksand, and she couldn't get up again.

She'd done what she'd intended. She'd provided a distraction. She'd given it everything.

The other lights converged on her solitary one, forming a ring around her that precluded further flight. She was gasping for air, lathered in sweat, quite unable to stand, and still they were reluctant to approach her in case she had something else up her sleeve.

Like this.

She wearily raised a hand over her head, pressed her middle finger to her thumb, and clicked.

A bright yellow flame sprang up, plain for all to see.

The circle stopped contracting, and started expanding, losing its form and breaking apart, the ordered constellation of lights sliding into chaotic motion.

That was all it took, one trivial display of power, to send them all into retreat. If they'd not seen magic at all, or for a long time, they were probably wondering what else she could do.

Currently, not much, and she hadn't even known she could do that. She was too exhausted to fly, or to batter them with sticks and rocks, or even wreathe the area in fog and make her escape. What she could do was take herself out of the picture. She smeared the air with darkness, painting a barrier between her and the dwindling lights, and cut herself off completely in a cocoon of night while she recovered.

The question was, had she managed to run far and fast enough to leave the anti-magic zone, or had Dalip done what he thought he was setting out to do? She hadn't felt Down's influence return any more than she'd felt it leave, yet if she tried she could taste it on the wind. There was, she supposed, only one way to find out, and that was to head back to the White City, clicking her fingers as she went, and seeing how far she got.

Not just yet, though. She stretched out on the ground and stared at the top of her dark shelter, feeling her body sag into every hollow under her, as if she was made of wax. When she was done with all this, she was going to take a holiday. In a different world, a lifetime ago, she'd seen an advert: a lithe, tanned woman was running through the surf on a white-sand beach, while a warm blue sea beckoned her further in. So – that. That's what she would do. She would camp, and swim, and build fires every night, and catch and cook her own food, and she'd be alone. No Mama fretting to go home, no Dalip worrying about tides, no Crows whispering his poison in her ear. No Luiza, or Stanislav, or Grace. No Elena.

She was up here, somewhere. Maybe there was a chance for forgiving and forgetting, because Elena didn't seem the sort of woman who'd last long on her own. If Simeon had died – died giving her long enough to escape – then Dawson would be wearing the captain's hat now, and it'd be up to him if she could rejoin the ship. Otherwise, Down was big enough that they'd never run into each other again, as long as any of them would live.

One thing was absolutely certain: no matter what happened next, whether the portals were open to traffic both ways, whether her London was still intact, she wasn't going back. She was not exactly enjoying it, but she was appreciating the novelty of being able to speak and act and have people pay attention to her, take her seriously, even fear her. She belonged in Down.

If that was the case, of course, she needed to make sure that it was going to survive. Time to go.

She hauled her aching self off the ground, brushed herself down, and wiped away the darkness. She sheathed her little dagger at her side and picked up the lantern, now barely lit, and realised that she had no idea in which direction to go.

The compass would have been useful, but she didn't have it. If she could change to bird form, fly up, look for lights, fix the direction and land, that would also be acceptable. But if she blundered into the anti-magic zone, she'd fall to her death. So, not that.

If she simply started walking to see where she ended up, then she'd waste time, which she didn't have, and energy, which she didn't have either.

There was an alternative, but could she, should she? It wasn't like anyone was going to stop her from trying.

She settled the lantern at her feet and took its thin, feeble flame. She gathered it up, breathed life into it, cradled it and brought it to a radiant perfection. Then she launched it upwards. It burned its way high into the night sky, and exploded like a second sun. The flash of light was soundless, but the shadows fled before it all the same.

In the moment between first ignition and last dying ember, the landscape was laid bare. Not only the plateau, but everything. The coast, the sea, the forests, even the distant hills glimmered with reflected glory. The Lords of the White City would know she was coming now, coming for them, and that was good because, like their servants, she wanted them to be afraid of her.

She scooped up the lantern, and set off, the clicking of her fingers a beat in common time. Each spark was a fresh revelation, and each step back towards the valley territory regained. She realised as she walked just how far she'd managed to run, even in the dark. There was no sign of her erstwhile pursuers, which was just as well, because she was both weary and pissed off.

She launched two more air-burst rockets, just to keep her on the right path, and she found herself back at the valley's edge, looking out over the drop-off at the buildings below. She still had magic, this close to the city. So Dalip had succeeded, one way or another. She needed to see whether he'd survived the encounter, but was also wary. Just because she'd run out of bullets didn't mean the guns they'd offered Simeon were useless.

Even presenting them with a target could encourage them to

take potshots at her. She lifted up the lantern, the candle no more than a piece of string floating in a puddle of wax, and puffed it out.

There was movement down below, lights skittering in and out of view, inside buildings and behind walls. She could hear voices, but not what they said. The tone, however, was unmistakable: panic.

As she watched, she realised that one of the buildings was flickering, becoming more solid even as the orange glow visible in the windows started to break out through the roof. Puffs of flame spiralled into the sky from between the tiles until it became a mosaic of fire. The sound of the roof trusses snapping was a series of sharp retorts, and the resultant rush of air into the space below made the conflagration roar.

Burning timbers were thrown clear by the collapse, but they didn't appear responsible for the spread of the flames. The servants had gone on the rampage. Too numerous to stop, too fleet to catch, they went from compound to compound, pillaging and setting fires, taking everything they could carry and destroying everything else.

The Lords could no longer protect them, feed them, and no longer needed them for their games in trapping travellers and extracting information from them. If Dalip's calculations were correct, then all the portals, the lines of power, the places where villages and castles grew, had all just changed. Across the face of Down, geomancers would realise that their own manors had become unremarkable plots of land, and that their castles would inexorably sink back into the ground. Good luck to them trying to hold their little empires together.

She decided that no one was looking for her, or at her. It was time to descend into the valley and see what she could find. She remembered what it was like to change, and in doing so, changed. She perched on the precipice, the fires below reflecting in her black, glassy eyes. She leaned forward, and dropped down, spreading her wings as she drifted silently over the burning buildings, feeling the hot air rise and buoy her up.

She flew the length of the valley, banked and turned. About the only building that wasn't on fire was the round one. Which was something, she supposed. She flapped and settled on the scree slope behind it, and changed back with a shiver.

It was chaos. Everything that could burn was burning. She supposed, with a twinge, that the maps would also be only so much ash by now, but they had at least served their purpose. She watched the flames a little longer, then started down towards the road. Away from the main buildings, there was no one, though by firelight she could see people in ones and twos, their arms laden with looted gear, heading out of the valley towards the gorge.

The heat grew, and became fierce, but it was cooler inside the long, low building with the broken-down door. The floor angled downwards, and just a little way in, there was a hole in the roof. She looked up through it and at the drifts of orange-tinged smoke that drifted by.

She clicked her fingers to raise a light, and slowly made her way in. The walls were made of the same rough stonework as everything else, but there was a cable tacked to the wall down the left-hand side. It was something so familiar, and yet so very out of place.

At the end, the tunnel – she had to be underground by now – turned a sharp left into a doorway, where only one door of a pair was left hanging. She held up her hand and tried to illuminate the dark space beyond.

'Dalip?'

'Just step in. The lights will come on on their own. Cover your eyes.'

She extinguished her flame, and eased around the door. The room, vast and cold, was flooded with light.

'Fuck. That's bright.'

'You forget, don't you?'

Most of the lights seemed to be high up, so she held her hand to her forehead to give her some shade.

Dalip was sitting on a raised circular plinth in the centre of the floor. It took her a moment to recognise him, dressed in black and not orange, and a moment longer to realise that there were one, two, three bodies on the ground in front of him.

'Shit. You all right?'

Then she noticed the way he was sitting, slightly forward, slightly to one side, his left hand held across his body and buried deep in his flank.

'I've felt better,' he said. He screwed his face up, and tried a smile. He failed.

'Let me see.' She ran forward a few steps, and he waved her back.

'I don't think you can help.' His eyes were closed, his skin sweaty, his breath deliberate.

'Fuck off. I'm having a look.' She knelt down in front of him and tried to move his hand. All of the cloth there was glistening. If hadn't been black, it would have been red.

'I'm serious. I think I'm holding my guts in.' He grunted. 'It ... was worth it. The more complicated the mechanism, the less you have to break to stop it working.'

'Lie down on the floor, or something.' She saw for the first time that the whole expanse of the floor was smooth, slightly rubbery, like a hospital ward. 'I don't know what to do!'

'Don't do anything. It's fine. It's fine that you don't do anything.' He slid from sitting to lying, and he tried to lift his legs up on to the plinth. When he couldn't, she did it for him and gently set them down.

There was a thick, sticky pool of blood now smeared across the whiteness of the plinth.

'I need to find someone. You need ... someone.'

'Stay. Stay with me.'

'Dalip. Dalip, no.'

He opened his eyes. They were milky white, and she gasped.

'What the fuck happened?'

'Crows happened. But it doesn't matter, not now. Tell me what's going on outside. You can use your magic, right?'

'Yes, yes. It's all fixed. The city's on fire. The people are stealing everything and burning the rest down. It's a proper riot out there.'

'Never been in a riot.'

'You had parents to stop you joining in.' She looked around at the room, the bodies, the exotic machinery. 'You did it, then.'

'Yes. Take a look behind me.' He rolled his head towards the centre of the plinth.

There was a lip, then a hole. In the middle of the hole was an intricately woven ball of metal strands, the size of a beach ball. It was now distorted, and Dalip's machete was still sticking out of it, wedged between the severed wires.

'That was it?'

'That was it. I don't think they've got a spare. At least.' He stopped, grimaced, and continued. 'They gave up at that point. The experiment is over.'

Blood was dribbling over the edge of the plinth, a moving red line, straight and awful.

'I need to go and get help,' she said. 'That's not good.'

'I won't be here when you get back.'

'Where're you going?'

'I don't know. I can, hope, I suppose.'

'You're not going to die.'

'I don't think I've got much choice.'

His eyelids fluttered.

'You have to hold on.'

He sighed.

'It's fine. I have been holding on. I was waiting for you. Now I can go.'

309

His hand dropped, and she pressed her own in its place, feeling the warm, slippery ooze of blood coat her fingers.

'You're not going to die. You're not going to die, you hear me?'

He didn't hear her.

32

Waking up ought to have hurt less than it did. He didn't know where he was or how he'd got there, only that he shouldn't be able to contemplate either of those questions.

'Well now,' said Mama, 'don't you look like something the cat dragged in?'

He tried to speak, coughed, winced, and gave up. The square of cloth suspended over him from poles, like a four-poster bed, flapped in the cool breeze, and the hammock he was lying in swayed gently.

'You're not right yet, so don't you go tiring yourself out.'

He blinked, and felt the grittiness of his sleep-filled eyes. The canopy rattled above again. He could see. That in itself was a miracle.

'Wind's picking up,' Mama observed. 'Maybe a storm coming over. It'll have to find someone else to take. It wouldn't dare have you.'

He could smell the brine, and hear the waves build and fall on the beach. If he looked to his left, he could see Mama, round and solid, sitting on a sea-chest, holding the little board-backed diary they'd found together. Beyond her was the bay: a curve of sand, a flash of surf, a hint of the forest beyond. To his right were the ragged cliffs carved out of cream-coloured blocks. Somewhere down by his feet should be a long boat, but he couldn't raise his head that far. He couldn't raise his head at all.

'What happened?' he asked.

He knew what should have happened. He'd wedged his bloodied machete into the glowing ball of energy embedded in the plinth. And then ... then Crows had cut him open and left him to die. He'd realised how badly he'd been hurt, and that holding the edges of the wound together was only going to do so much. He'd been bleeding, inside and out, and it would only stop when he ran out of blood.

After the Lord of the White City had left, no one else had come until Mary turned up, and by then he'd been long past help.

'Why am I alive?'

Mama folded the book shut and laid it down next to her on the sea-chest.

'There's no easy answer to that,' she said. 'Not that I'm saying you should have died just so I don't have to give a reason. The short way of saying it is that she fixed you up. The long way is, well: more complicated.'

'Mary? But I was ...'

'Cut stem to stern down to the giblets? There was that.'

'So what did she do?' Mary had arrived with nothing, not even the most rudimentary of first-aid equipment, let alone anything that would have saved his life.

'Be easier to show you,' said Mama. 'Shame I haven't got a mirror.'

His hands were across his chest. He worked out that his fingers would move, even his wrists, but there was no strength in them. All the same, he had to know. 'What did she do?'

'She fixed you up that only way she could.' Mama clasped her big hands together. 'If she can explain it, she's learnt to do it since she tried explaining it to me.'

313

'Magic? She used magic?'

'She did. She did it well enough that you're still here and you and me are talking about the hows and the whys of it.' She shrugged and her hands drifted apart, gesturing to the sea. 'The whys are simple enough. She wasn't ready to let you go.'

'She wasn't ready to let me go?'

'We can spend all of today you just repeating me. I don't mind. I've got nothing to hurry for, and neither have you, but if you wanted to make it easier, you could just believe me.' Mama leaned forward and pressed her hand on his forehead. 'There's no fever. If anything, you're colder than you ought to be. We'll get a fire going later, see if that makes any difference.'

'I was ... dying,' he said. 'I'd made my peace with God. I was ready.'

'Listen to yourself! How old are you?'

'Nineteen. Maybe twenty. I don't know any more.'

'Let me tell you something. Boys your age know nothing about anything. They don't know when to be scared, when to run, when to back down or when to shut up. Give it a few years and you might have something worth saying.' Mama huffed. 'Peace with God indeed. You need a life of service and knowing you're on the right path for that.'

Dalip found he didn't have the energy to argue.

'Am I going to get better?'

'Mercy, considering the state you were in when we brought you here, you are better. You can open your eyes, you can breathe, you can talk. And don't you be ungrateful, either. No one likes a failed martyr.'

'Martyr?'

'You're alive, and you'll just have to get used to it. And try not to throw yourself into the mouth of the nearest lion next time.'

'There were no lions.'

'Don't get fresh with me. That was a metaphor.' She huffed again. 'You hungry?'

'I don't know. I don't think so.'

She frowned. 'You should be hungry. I've got some clear broth I made for you.'

'Maybe later.'

'You should have some. See if you can take it.'

'Later.'

If anything was going to make him better quickly, it was the thought of being nursed back to health by Mama. She meant well, but it was going to drive him to distraction. He was already twitching.

'Actually, I do want something. I want to see what's happened to me.'

'You're not up to that yet.' Mama stood up and stood over him. 'Promise me you're not going to try and look any time soon.'

'Okay, I want to look even more now.' He took a deep breath and moved his hands to the sides of the hammock. He tried to lever himself to a sitting position, failed, and slipped down even further towards the knotted end by his feet.

'I'm not helping,' said Mama. 'I sewed you up, and I see it every time I look at you. I just don't think you're strong enough right now.'

He was so frustrated. He wriggled uselessly until he was almost completely cocooned in the hammock, and was in a worse position than before.

'You want some of that soup now?' she asked him.

'No. Thank you.'

She sat back down and opened the board-covered book, peering at the page held almost at arm's length. Her lips moved with the archaic syllables, and eventually he stopped struggling and watched her.

'I thought you couldn't read it.'

'I had help: a man called Edmund who's on the boat. He's from the fifteenth century, you know. Anyhow, once you get your eye in, it's not so bad.' She ostentatiously turned to the next page. 'It's very interesting. Especially where it talks about the Lady Grace of Almond Eyes.'

'It does what?' He couldn't sit up, but his whole body started.

'Oh, you think you know everything there is to Down, then it comes up with another dirty little secret. Turns out half the crew have met Grace at some point or other.'

'How? We've been here for, what?'

'A couple of months. Might be three by now. Grace has been here for years. Decades. Maybe even longer.'

'But she came through with us.'

'She did. Doesn't mean she hasn't been here before. Repeatedly.'

'Then how? That would mean—'

'She has a way of travelling back through the portals. And always had.'

'But then—'

'She was no waif we picked up. She was using the portal to get out of danger. She knew what was coming.'

'All this time, we've been wondering what happened to her. And she ... that's ...' He didn't what else to say. 'What's she doing here?'

'She's crossing Down, going from one door to the next. Going back and forward through time, I suppose. Safe to say, if we stay here long enough, we'll get to ask her ourselves.' She closed the book again, her point made. 'We could have gone home. She was there, with us, at the portal. She could have done whatever it is she does, and we'd all be home now. Stanislav and Luiza would still be with us. You wouldn't have suffered the way you have. Mary wouldn't be out looking for Elena right now. Simeon wouldn't have been dragged into this fight of ours, and we would never have met Bell or Crows.'

'Crows,' said Dalip. 'I could have killed him, twice over. Instead, he killed me.'

'Oh hush. Mary told me what happened, but he'll have

escaped the valley, you can count on that. He's slipperier than the Devil himself. But Grace: she could have kept us away from all those people. And even if she couldn't, then, have sent us home through a portal, there are others. We could have gone to the next one along and used that. Instead, she just abandoned us. What sort of person does that?'

'She does. Over and over again, apparently.'

A shadow flicked over the canopy. His gaze followed the movement and saw a giant falcon skim the sand.

'Mary's back,' said Mama.

'So where's Grace now?' He was wondering out loud, but she took it as a question.

'Who knows? We don't. We don't even know if she's working with, or against, the White City. There's no one left to ask.'

'There's the ferryman.'

'You shot him, remember?'

'I might be able to repair him. If I ever get out of this hammock.'

'Good luck with that. Good luck with both, because I don't think you've the faintest idea where to start mending some robot from the future. What you've got to do is rest, Dalip, and take it easy.'

Mary was walking across the beach towards them, the breeze driving her red dress against the shape of her legs. She looked thoughtful, determined, in control, and when she ducked under the edge of the canopy, she smiled at him.

'You're awake.'

'Yes,' he said. 'We need to talk.'

'How're you feeling?'

'Like I need to talk to you. About what you did to me.'

She stopped smiling and stared at her sand-speckled feet. Mama rose from the sea-chest and slipped the book under its wooden lid.

'Why don't I give you youngsters some space?' she said, and went to stand, trouser legs rolled up, in the washing waves.

Mary sat down in Mama's place and wouldn't look at him.

'Mama won't tell me,' he said, 'but I need to know.'

'You were dying.'

'I know. I'd accepted that. I'd done my duty: I'd fought bravely, and won through. It was always likely. It's not like I wanted to die. I'm not a martyr, whatever Mama says. This, though, is unexpected. How did you keep me alive?'

'It was all I had to work with.' She bit at her lip. 'Light and dark. That's all there was. I didn't know what I was doing, only that I had to do something.'

'She won't show me, or tell me anything about it. Is it that awful?'

'No,' she said, then equivocated. 'It is a bit weird, though.'

He waited for her to explain, but she just knotted her fingers together in various permutations and looked uncomfortable.

'Tell me.'

'I ... I just tried to stop the bleeding. It was all running out of you, and I couldn't hold it in. I threw stuff at it and hoped.' Her face grew pinched. 'It worked.'

'Tell me,' he said, almost howling with frustration. 'Just ... tell me.'

'Mama doesn't think that's a good idea. I ... I don't know. If you promised me you'd never look, then I'd tell you. But you're going to look anyway, so what's the point?' She stood by the hammock and pushed the material down on one side so that she could take hold of his legs and turn him without spilling him on to the ground beneath. He let her guide his body, and realised that he wasn't wearing the same clothes as he had been before. Of course. Not when the other set had been soaked with his own blood.

His bare feet connected with the soft sand, and the sudden change in orientation made him dizzy. He swallowed hard and concentrated on stopping the world, this world, any world, from spinning.

'I think standing's beyond me at the moment.'

'You're just saying that because you haven't done it for a bit.'

'How long?'

'About a week.'

'A ... week?'

'You were pretty beat up. I found Elena, by the way. I think I convinced her to come back.'

'That's good.' He pressed his toes against the sand, feeling its texture and cool dampness as he burrowed them in. 'Assuming you're ready to forgive her.'

'It's okay. If she tries to pull any shit on me, I can take it from there.' She slipped her hand under his shoulders, reaching around his back. 'Ready for this?'

'Not really, but let's do it anyway.'

She counted to three, and lifted him. He hung on to her, draping his mostly useless arms about her neck. They stood like that for a while, her steadying him, him trying to work out which way was up. Every little movement he made sent the horizon tumbling.

It settled, eventually. She didn't let go of him, but let him lean on her than her holding him up.

He gathered up his new, clean shirt, and lifted it up.

His torso was wrapped with bandages, which his dull fingers eventually untied and unwound. He could tell that something wasn't quite right, because he couldn't feel that he'd been cut at all. His mind remembered the strange tug and release of skin and flesh as it was first caught, then sliced apart. Yet his body had no memory of it all.

The bandages dropped away. He couldn't see it all, but he could see enough. There was a puckered wound, where the flesh was gathered together by Mama's neat stitching, that ran all the way from his front, around his flank, to where he couldn't quite see at his back. It looked paler than the surrounding skin, not livid with infection nor black with dried blood. It wasn't terrible to look at, although it was very long. He didn't know how he could have possibly survived: one little nick on his intestines, and he'd have died of septicaemia.

Crows' sword had done far more than that.

He could feel the ridges and knots under his fingertip, but there was no reciprocal sensation on his side. Odd, but not unusual. Then he realised that the skin hadn't started to knit together, and never would. He placed one hand below the cut line, and one above, and gently stretched the wound apart.

There seemed to be a universe nestling in there. Holding the skin taut, he caught glimpses of stars, moving against the black of space. Whole galaxies were turning in the far distance. He stared for some considerable time, before letting go and allowing the wound to press together.

Some other reality had been incorporated into his body, filling the hole where his flank had been breached with its vastness.

'I'm sorry,' she said. 'I didn't know what I was doing.'

'You did this, accidentally?'

'I didn't do it on purpose! I don't even know what it is I did. You were losing blood, I wanted to seal it up. And I did it. It worked. You didn't die.'

'How far inside does this go?' It was difficult to see, from his viewpoint.

'I looked at it – into it – and I couldn't see an end.'

He took his hands away, and let his shirt fall back down. He didn't know whether to be grateful or terrified. He didn't know if what she'd done changed him irrevocably or allowed him to stay the same. He didn't know if it would grow until it consumed him, or if it would dwindle away as he healed, or whether he would simply be like this for ever.

One thing was obvious to him, though. He was now being sustained only by magic.

'You know you've trapped me here, don't you?' He disengaged himself from her arms and took an unsteady step away. 'I can't leave Down. Not ever.'

'What?'

'If I step through a portal, back to London, where magic doesn't work, I'll die.' He took another step. 'All that, all that … effort. I did it because this place is worth saving. Not because I wanted to stay here for ever.'

'It could have been worse.'

'How?'

'You could have died a week ago, Dalip. You could not be here at all.'

There was a shell on the beach. A little one, not much bigger than his thumb. He snapped it in two, held out his forearm, and ran the razor-sharp edge along it, splitting the skin like it was ripe fruit.

She started towards him, waving her hands, trying to stop him. But it was too late. He held up his arm to show her, and a swirl of stars moved behind the ragged gash, the same stars that passed in the dark of his eyes.

'Tell me,' he said: 'what have I become?'